MW00930424

The Whale Has Wings

by David Row

Published by David Row

Copyright 2012 by David Row

Other titles and further information on David Row's books can be found at

http://astrodragon.co.uk/Books.htm

2345, 31st December 1939.

Lit only by glimpses of the moon through the scattered clouds, the warships ploughed through the waves at 20 knots. They comprised the most powerful force the Royal Navy had deployed in the North Sea since the First World War - three aircraft carriers, three battlecruisers, and over twenty escorts.

Most of the ships were quiet, the men at cruising stations watching the dark water, but the carrier decks were alive with men and planes as they prepared for the strike. In the briefing rooms, the pilots were getting their final briefing from the air commanders and the met officers.

"Very well, gentlemen, that's it. No changes from yesterday's briefing, the main targets haven't moved since the last set of photos. The crews have done a great job in getting the planes operational for us, so now it's down to us to show the Germans there isn't anywhere they can hide from the Royal Navy."

He pointed one last time at the details chalked up on the board behind him.

"The first wave will be 42 torpedo-armed Swordfish from the Formidable, Victorious and Courageous, plus 30 Dive bombers. Flight leaders will carry flares to illuminate the harbour. You will launch at 0045, and you should be over the target by 0230. We will launch the follow-up strike at 0130. Another 30 Swordfish, but this time 18 of them will be carrying 500lb bombs, and 18 Cormorants. You should be over the target by 0315"

He paused for a moment "By that time we hope the first wave has the target well lit up." His dry delivery was greeted by a ripple of slightly nervous laughter from the assembled crews.

"Don't delay getting back. We expect to have the last planes onboard by 0445, and we'll be heading back at 0500, so don't be late. Recovery will be by beacon and IFF - remember, don't turn your IFF on until you are on your way home after the attack, we don't know if the Germans can detect it, but let's not take any chances, shall we. Only flight commanders are authorised to use their radios until the attack starts - after which, we expect them to realise we have arrived!"

There were more grins and muffled laughter at that, and the Commander was glad to see his crews in good spirits. Not that he had doubted that, but it was always good to end a briefing on a good note.

"Now, get to your planes and get ready. We've been planning this for a long time, and this is our first chance to hit the German fleet with a heavy blow. Go and make the Fleet Air Arm proud of you!"

The crews filed out - the first waves to man their planes, the rest to wait until the deck was cleared to bring theirs up from the hanger. He wished he was going with them, but flying at sea was a young man's job. Nearly ten years to get here, he thought to himself. A long and difficult path, but one which he hoped would all prove worth it tonight. He knew his crews wouldn't let them down, but the next part would be the worst for him - waiting and hoping nothing had gone wrong, while being unable to do much if it had. He would much rather be facing German flak.

It was the 31st December 1939. What was officially known as Operation Chastise (and very unofficially to the Fleet Air Arm as the Happy Hogmanay Raid) was about to begin.

Chapter 1

1932. The Admiralty, London.

The results of the sometimes heated discussions that had taken the Sea Lords and a number of other senior commanders all day were summed up by Admiral of the Fleet Sir Frederick Field, the First Sea Lord.

"Very well, gentlemen, we are agreed. The development of the new Martin dive-bomber by the Americans renders the conclusions of the RAF completely wrong. It now seems that in the near future, a dive bomber will be able to deliver a 1,000lb bomb at a reasonable range, and presumably a 500lb bomb at longer ranges. We also have reports from observers that the US Navy has allowed to view their exercises, and further information gleaned by our chaps talking to their fliers that with practice dive bombing can be damnably accurate, even against more agile ships, when used in numbers.

While our battleships are still safe of course, everything smaller is now in danger of either serious damage or even sinking, and I feel sure that once this plane is in operation, it will only be a matter of time before similar aircraft are developed by the Japanese or other unfriendly powers. We have nothing to match them, as the RAF assures us that the dive bomber is no threat!

I have had talks, both official and unofficial, with my opposite numbers in the RAF, and I am afraid that they refuse to budge from that conclusion. It seems that no amount of evidence will make them face the facts when it affects their convictions about the strategic bomber concept. Which is a wonderful concept, I am sure, but has little relevance to the Royal Navy.

We also have the likelihood that the torpedo bomber will only get more effective, with heavier torpedoes, as aircraft development continues. As you know, I view the problem of attack by aerial torpedo on the fleet with considerable disquiet.

And the problem just gets worse."

He looked down at the paper on the table in front of him.

"The primary defence of the fleet against air attack [by gunfire] is not justified by data or experience. No realistic firing against aircraft has taken place since the last war and, in my opinion, the value of our own High Angle Control System Mk I is rated too high. In common with others, we are apt to over-rate the capabilities of our own weapons in peacetime.

The words of Rear-Admiral Henderson are quite clear, and I am sure we all agree that as Rear-Admiral (Carriers) he knows what he is talking about. We not only need dive bombers of our own, we need better protection against them - and torpedo bombers as well. That means better fighters, and more of them. AA gunfire is all very well, but we need defence in depth.

So our course is clear. Either we lose ground and take second place to other nation's aircraft and carriers, or we take action to restore the Navy's place."

He looked around the table at the other uniformed figures, and the expression on all the faces left it clear which of the two options was acceptable to them all.

"The problem here is the RAF. We have no control over their opinions or actions, even when we deem them not just mistaken but actively dangerous. We also know that they have little interest in naval air, but just see it as something they have to give lip service to supporting, while spending the bare minimum on it.

Now I am sure there are many individual officers in the RAF who don't share this thinking - indeed, some of them are ex-naval officers, and have been quite helpful in giving us the true, if unofficial, story."

Vice Admiral Forbes nodded as the Admiral looked around for comments.

"While I think we all agree with the conclusions, all that does is to state the situation we are in. We need a way out of it. A balanced fleet needs its own airpower, or we have to control our ships at the mercy of enemy airpower, which will be inconvenient and limit our choice of options when we are within range of it. And we all know the advantage of using our own planes to locate, and then slow, the enemy battle-line so we can close with it - we cannot do that if our planes are being attacked by the enemy. Aircraft are a most important aid in making the full, effective use of our battleships"

There was another general nodding of heads.

"Well, there is a solution to the problem. I won't say it will be easy, but we need to get back control of our own aircraft."

"You do realise that means declaring war on the RAF, don't you? You know how possessive they feel about anything that flies!"

"So? We have as many friends in high places as they do."

Admiral Field raised a hand to pause the varied comments from around the table. "Gentlemen. I think we are agreed in the direction and actions we need to take. I propose that we set out a plan of campaign to recover naval air under our control - in secret. I also wish Admiral Henderson to study what we will need to do as soon as we achieve our objectives. Having a plan ready will show we are not just looking for control for the sake of it, and will help us get backing from some of our political allies."

1933

"Please sit down, Admiral."

Chatfield looked at the permanent undersecretary, who was not looking pleased.

"Chatfield, this public argument has gone on far too long. It has to stop."

Admiral Chatfield looked back, his face impassive.

"It needs to be resolved - not stopped. Our arguments are valid, and as you know we have growing appreciation of them and support in parliament."

"You mean you are getting all the agitators on your side... It's already being referred to as the RN-RAF war of 1933."

"I mean the Navy is weak, dangerously weak in air power, and getting weaker every year. If we don't do something soon, we are going to be a second-rate power."

"I could order you to stop this campaign"

"You could, of course. However I cannot stop members asking questions in the house, and I do have to answer them honestly, you realise. And certainly I cannot stop the newspapers, even if the government can pressure the MP's - which is unlikely, not all of them are on the government benches, and people like Churchill won't be quietened anyway."

He paused for a moment.

"I do agree, this needs to stop. So I have prepared some detailed proposals which I think will solve the matter, defuse the issues in public, and let everything settle down."

Chatfield reached into his briefcase, and put some papers on the table.

"The basic issue is that the Royal Navy simply cannot accept the current level of aviation support provided by the RAF. You've heard all the arguments, probably far more often than you would care to. There is, however, a quite simple solution, which is for the Navy to get back control of the FAA, and fund it ourselves. We realise that there are issues regarding the efficiency of such a plan, and problems with implementing it, but we have had discussions both among ourselves and informally with the RAF and feel we have an adequate solution.

First, the FAA will revert to RN command and control, as it was pre 1918, on 1st April 1933

The FAA will be funded by the navy, and the funds currently spent on it in the RAF will be added to the appropriate navy vote. So this won't involve any extra funding, which I am sure will please the treasury.

The Navy will cooperate with the RAF in funding development of planes and equipment. While we realise the FAA will require carrier planes that have different requirements for those used by the RAF, we understand that many of the expensive developments such as engines, armament and controls can be to a very considerable extent common. Where they are, the RN will fund an appropriate proportion of the development costs. Where the requirements are purely for the RN, we will fund them ourselves.

It will take some years for the FAA to build up a satisfactory pilot base. Until that time, the RAF will continue to lend pilots until we can replace them with RN personnel. RN and RAF pilot training will be in common, except for the final stage of carrier training, as it would be uneconomical to duplicate the training commands, and this will continue to be under RAF control.

This solution covers all the arguments we have been making, and the RAF can now concentrate on its land-based aircraft and heavy bombers. We will of course continue to cooperate fully, and indeed it has been suggested that some committees, like the ones to research future aircraft and needs, be made common ones.

We consider the proposals sensible, and they will stop this infighting which is, we agree, reaching unacceptable proportions.

"The RAF are not going to be happy at losing control of some of their planes, Chatfield."

"With respect, it's the only sensible solution. No-one realised in 1918 that the issue of naval air would end up being so specialised and controversial, this way we cut the Gordian knot of what the RAF has to do to keep us happy.

The undersecretary did not look happy, but this did, as the Admiral said, cut the knot.

"Very well, Chatfield, I feel compelled to agree with you. Unless the RAF can come up with some very compelling reasons why not to, I intend to present this to the Prime Minister as a solution. If I do, I expect the navy to stop this mutual war at once. Is that clearly understood?

Admiral Chatfield nodded, hiding his smile. "Of course."

Chapter 2

May 1933

The Defence Requirements Committee report laid out the problems with the FAA and the carrier force in blunt language.

First, the two other powers operating fleet carriers both had two large, capable ships modified from WW1 battlecruisers. Of the experimental carriers the Royal Navy operated, only two of them, Courageous and Glorious, were considered anything more than experimental (the Furious was considered useful in limited circumstances), and both Japan and the USA had plans to build new, purpose built carriers in their next annual building programs, which would leave the RN even more at a disadvantage. The aims of Germany and Italy were unclear, and in the case of Germany they had of course no sizeable navy, but future threats needed to be considered.

The conclusion was simple; at least one new design carrier, the building of which had been proposed - and put back - since 1925, must be set in motion as soon as possible. The shipbuilding capacity was more than adequate; indeed the construction of such a ship would help alleviate the terrible unemployment in the North of England. A carrier, it was pointed out, was considerably cheaper than a battleship, and not subject to supply bottlenecks like its main guns.

Second, if a new carrier (and ideally more than one carrier) was to be built, it would need suitable planes. It was clear from looking at the ongoing designs and requirements for the RAF that a new generation of carrier planes based on the all-metal monoplane design would be needed. Granted, that would be expensive, but their development would take four years to maturity, so a specification should be offered to the usual aircraft manufacturers for some suitable designs.

Getting additional funds for aircraft development and carriers would not of course be easy, but it was pointed out that the threat in the Far East was only getting greater with each year, and the aims of Germany were looking worrying in the long term. Also, Britain had ample tonnage available under the London treaty, so it would hardly be warmongering to build a carrier or two to replace the old and obsolete conversions.

Discussions with the treasury took time, but the Admiralty was quite adamant about their needs (neglecting to mention that they also wanted to get the carriers underway before they needed more money for new battleships). In the end, they didn't get all they wanted. One carrier was approved for the 1934 program, and new fighter, dive bomber and TBD models were authorised for development. To reduce costs, engines and all other equipment (where possible) was to be either existing or commonly developed by the RAF. The Admiralty had hoped for two carriers, to at least match the Americans, but one was better than nothing.

There had been considerable argument over exactly what the new carrier would look like, and in the hope of getting approval the Admiralty had, after many, many meetings, decided on a design. It didn't please everyone, but at least no-one hated it enough to resign over it.

Since the maximum displacement allowed under the treaty was 27,000t, the DNC had been told to look at a number of proposals in the 25,000t range, to allow some additions if necessary and to keep the displacement to a level that the government would be pressing for in the next naval armament talks. The politicians were still hoping that a general naval (and indeed overall) international disarmament program was possible, although privately the navy disagreed. The big arguments had been over the armour scheme and the hanger size and arrangements. There had been a suggestion of copying the Americans with an open hangar, but the conditions that RN carriers would usually be operating under were different from those faced by the USN. In the end it was decided that the advantages of a closed hanger, with its ease of protection against gas, easy blackout and warmth in winter conditions outweighed a few more aircraft and a cooler condition in the tropics.

The armour had caused a lot more argument, added to which was the fact that armour production was currently quite limited, and while expansion of the plant was being arranged, there wasn't an infinite amount of armour to play with. It was first of all agreed that deck armour of some sort was necessary; the carrier would certainly be used in the North Sea and Mediterranean, where land based air would be found, and the carrier needed to survive direct attack. This was considered less likely in the Pacific, where the distances involved meant only naval air was likely to be encountered, but it wouldn't hurt to have it. In the end it came down to three main choices

A heavily armoured deck to keep out 500lb bombs.

An un-armoured deck, with a protected hangar deck.

A flight deck thick enough to initiate a bombs fuse, plus a protected hangar deck sufficiently thick to protect from 1,000lb bombs.

It was pointed out that while on paper the flight deck armour looked promising, it would involve a lot of weight high up, and probably limit the hangar height from the 16' currently under consideration for the new planes. While stopping 500lb bombs would be good initially, bombers were steadily increasing in performance, and once the 1,000lb bomb was a threat the heavy armour would be rendered useless.

Finally, it was decided to compromise and go for the initiating flight deck and a fully armoured hanger deck to protect the magazines and machinery spaces. To reduce the weight, the side armour was reduced to 2" from the 4.5" necessary to defeat heavy shells, as it was felt that the whole point of a carrier was NOT to get close to enemy heavy ships in the first place! However protection sufficient to stop splinter damage and aircraft cannon fire was considered essential. A flight deck an inch thick would be laid down - this would also handle the planes currently being designed, as well as future planes which would certainly be heavier, and a 4 1/2" thick hanger deck protecting the machinery and the magazines. Since this effectively 'wrote off' the hanger in the case of bombing, it was decided to fit a horizontal armour plate (with opening door to transfer aircraft if necessary) so that a single bomb hit would only take out half of any aircraft stored below. Since the structure above the hanger deck was (relatively) light, it was expected this would make repairs in case of a successful attack take less time.

DNC reported that on 25,000t with the suggested armour scheme he could provide space for about 45 aircraft in a single hanger, depending on the type. This was looked on unfavourably, particularly compared to foreign carriers current or building, and in fact Courageous already carried 48 (admittedly slightly smaller) planes. DNC offered to carry another 20 aircraft as a deck park, but the feeling was that while a deck park was fine in the Pacific, it made less sense in the North Atlantic in winter, as well as leaving more aircraft out in the open and vulnerable to attack. It also caused aircraft to deteriorate faster, and the Treasury was already complaining at the cost of the carrier. Again a compromise was reached with what was called the 1 1/2 hanger carrier - a full length upper hanger, 16' high, and a half length lower hanger, again 16' high. This would carry 64 aircraft, comparing much more closely to foreign designs, and the rest of the space at the lower level would allow the necessary crew quarters and to allow some maintenance to be undertaken on long deployments. And if for some reason it became necessary to carry more aircraft, the deck park was still an option.

To reach the necessary speed of over 30kt, it was felt a 4-shaft ship was necessary, on about 148,000hp.While trunking the exhaust gases for 4 shafts required more weight than for three, the arrangement was actually a bit simpler, as the design displacement and hangar size allowed more flexibility in the disposition of the necessary trunking. The Torpedo Defence System would have a depth of about 15' given the hull width necessary to carry the weight of the armour, slightly more than had been originally intended, but this also allowed more oil to be carried inside it.

Finally, the ship would carry 8 twin 4.7" guns for high altitude defence, and 6 octuple 2pdr pompoms for close defence. It had originally been hoped that the 5.1" gun currently under development would prove suitable, but it had been found that the shell was simply too heavy for use at sea without power assistance (in fact the 4.7" gun proposed wasn't developed, and the ship completed with 8 twin 4.5" AA guns) While conversations with the Americans had consolidated the internal opinions that the air group was the most efficient defence, no defences were perfect and defence in depth would give far more security. Hence the heavy AA and the armour, in view of the need to operate in the Mediterranean and the eastern parts of the North Sea. While these arrangements in fact reduced the size of the air group, it was felt that overall it gave the best chance of the carrier surviving air attack. There were concerns and discussions about surface attack, but it was pointed out that even in the worst case of surface attack during bad weather, the carrier could run away from anything big enough to damage it (and in that bad weather, even destroyers were unlikely to be able to catch it)

The design displacement was 24,800t (although the complete ship would actually come in at over 25,000t)

The Ark Royal would be laid down on 1st June 1934 for commissioning in July of 1937.

Of course, both the new carrier and the existing ones would need aircraft. Under the RAF's control, supply of aircraft had been kept to a minimum, indeed there was a serious shortage of aircraft. While the international scene was darkening, it was not felt there was a serious chance of a major war within five years, so the decision was taken to go with a larger purchase of new aircraft rather than more of already obsolete types. This was a calculated risk, but one it was felt worth taking to get better aircraft.

The RN had for many years been proud of the quality of its ships and weapons - not always deservedly so. It was felt that the 'armament' of a carrier should be equally capable, bearing in mind the Royal Navy's unique commitment to arriving anywhere in the world at any time on short notice.

Admiral Henderson chaired a committee that reviewed both the likely existing opposition (particularly with carrier based planes in mind), with an aim to specifying development and purchasing of planes, and also looking at the requirements for the next generation to follow them. It was decided that while it was useful to minimise the number of type of planes to be supported with a carriers limited maintenance facilities, three different types of planes would be needed. These would be a fighter, a dive bomber (which would also have a reconnaissance role), and a torpedo bomber (TBR) that would also be able to level bomb. This plane also would be used for reconnaissance, and would serve as both a shore and sea based anti-submarine aircraft.

The fighter would have a single pilot, the dive bomber a crew of two and the TBR plane a crew of three. It was reluctantly decided that a common engine wasn't practical at present, although it was seen as a very useful development for the future. It was expected that a radio suitable for single-person operation to allow the fighter to find its carrier would be bought or more likely licensed from America, where there was considerable experience of operating single-crew fighters.

The TBR requirement it was pointed out could be filled by the private venture Swordfish, which would be available in service from 1935. Concerns were raised over its rather old-fashioned design, but its performance was similar to other planes in service with other navies, and it was expected that a more powerful version of the engine would give some improvements in performance. The conclusion was to go for an initial production order, while looking at a better plane as a replacement in a few years time. While the Swordfish would have a less powerful engine than that intended for use in the other two aircraft, it was felt that such an aircraft was the most likely one to find use outside of the highest threat areas, and so a later TBR aircraft could replace the Swordfish and allow it to be deployed to lower threat areas.

As no dive bomber was available, a specification was put out to tender. The two selections for development were the Blackburn Skua and a navalised version of the Hawker Henley being designed for the RAF. The Admiralty were a bit concerned by the non-radial engine of the Henley, but at present there wasn't a radial equivalent. This lack was noted for further action, and Hawker were asked to look at the possibility of replacing the Merlin with a radial engine if this could be done with minimal performance loss.

The Henley was expected to fly in late 1936, and be available to the FAA in 1937. The Skua was also expected to fly in 1936, with delivery in early 1937. The FAA would have preferred earlier development and delivery times, but Hawker in particular was busy with RAF orders.

Finally, the difficult choices were over the type of fighter. Previously the RAF had argued that two men were needed to operate any homing beacon and navigate the plane at sea. The USN, on the other hand, seemed to have no big problems doing this with one man (although they did have a superior radio system), and it was obvious that a one man fighter would have a better performance that a two man plane. There was considerable argument that the 'best' performance wasn't necessary, in that land based planes wouldn't have fighter protection, but in the end this lost out to the fact that if they did indeed have modern land based fighters in attendance then things would go poorly for the RN planes, and just because the RAF couldn't do something that didn't mean the RN couldn't. Especially since the USN demonstratably could. Suggestions that the choice was made partially to put one in the eye of the RAF were studiously denied. There was still the problem of the workload on a single man for navigation on long raids (escorting the carriers own strike), but it was hoped progress could be made on this during the development of the plane. If the problem proved too difficult, the single-pilot fighter would be retained for fleet defence and either a version of the dive-bomber converted to fighter use, or a second crewman added to the fighter.

Since this would be the first specialised fighter for the FAA, the aircraft under development for foreign navies were investigated to allow a specification to be written to exceed them. Aircraft from Japan, Germany, Italy and the USA were considered; while the USA was not considered to be an enemy, the fact that they were one of the only three navies to run carriers did make them useful for comparison. The committee was quite surprised, when the reports came back, that the initial response of the British aircraft industry was that they could do considerably better, even without any development of new systems and engines. It was pointed out that the planes due in service with the USN and IJN in the timeframe were the Grumman F3F, a biplane fighter with a reasonable performance by biplane standards, but weak armament and protection, and the IJN planes would be the Mitsubishi A5M, a monoplane fighter with a higher speed (although still only around 235kt) and again a weak armament. It was therefore suggested that they requirement should try and meet the one currently being looked at for the RAF, which was a monoplane of at least 300kt speed with a heavy armament of 8 .303 guns or an equivalent. A number of British manufacturers claimed they could come close to this even with the current radial engines, and if a higher powered engine could be developed then they could exceed this.

Consideration was given to pressing for development of a more powerful engine, and as a result some discussions were held with the Bristol company, the main supplier of radial aircraft engines in the country. There was some surprise at the Admiralty that the company didn't see any need for more powerful engines than those in their current inventory, since the FAA could clearly see advantages in an engine in the 1200-1500hp range for a fighter and for a better dive bomber and TBR aircraft. Informal discussions with Roy Fedden at Bristol led to the interesting possibility of developing what he was calling the Hercules engine with a version available for test flights in 1935. This would allow it to be used for a fighter developed for acceptance in late 1936, which was the FAA's preferred timescale. Such an engine could also be used to drive a dive bomber capable of delivering a 1,000lb bomb (or a 500lb bomb at longer ranges). This was a weight of bomb that would allow the FAA to sink or seriously damage any ship short of a battleship, and indeed only modern battleships would be safe against it. Fedden also pointed out (without wanting to be quoted, of course), that considerable pressure might have to be applied to the Bristol board to persuade them to develop the engine. The Admiralty, fresh from its victory over the RAF, so no reason why they couldn't persuade an engine company to do as requested - especially if they were funding the engine. As a result a contract to get the Hercules available for flight testing in mid-1935 was placed with Bristol (the initial contacts had been resisted by the Bristol board - well known for its reluctance to try what they saw as unnecessary advances - however after the Admiralty had leant hard on the Bristol board of directors, mentioning getting the engine developed by Napier, or even in the USA, they had been persuaded), and the proposed performance made available to the aircraft companies.

A pair of fighter designs was chosen for development, the Gloster G.38 and the Bristol type 153. Both were specified to fly in early 1936 so as to be in production at the beginning of 1937 in time for operational use before the new carrier completed. The initial designs had been for lightweight land based planes, but the naval requirements meant they would have to be heavier and more robust. The power of the Hercules engine would compensate for that. The armament posed problems, as there was still ongoing argument in both the RN and the RAF as to the best choice of weapon. It was found that the RAF was going for 8 .303 machine guns. While this was considered a good armament, there were issues as to the size and destructive power of the bullet against bombers. In the end it was decided to develop two prototype aircraft with different wings, one carrying eight .303 as the RAF designs, and one with four .5 inch as an alternative. A final decision could then be made later when the expected opposition could be better evaluated. The chosen aircraft was expected to show a performance of over 300kt, and allow a heavy armament as well as the longer range required by a naval aircraft.

The future after these planes was considered to be a longer term issue, especially as it was known that land-based air was currently in the throes of defining a new generation of higher-performance aircraft. It was complicated by the fact that the preferred engine type for naval planes was the radial engine, whereas the RAF seemed to be looking to a new generation of high performance inline engines produced by Rolls-Royce, although this hadn't been definitely decided yet. It was decided to form a committee to look into the future needs of the FAA in terms of equipment and planes, which would liaise with its equivalent in the RAF. While the relationship between the FAA and the RAF was rather strained at a high level, the lower ranking members actually doing most of the work got along much better, as long as everything could be kept off the record. Something the British officers were quite skilled at, fortunately.

Chapter 3

1934

By the beginning of 1934, the Royal Navy had made considerable progress of the planning for the new-look FAA.

The first and most important business was the laying down of the Ark Royal. The new, purpose built carrier had been waited for so long that in some quarters it was almost mythical. Longer term actions were mainly to do with the support and infrastructure of the FAA, which were seen as quite inadequate in view of the expansion in both size and capability expected in the next few years.

What was needed to be done was fairly obvious, although there was, as expected, some dragging of feet among the battleship Admirals. However the new independence and coming equipment gained for the FAA had given those closely concerned with it a sense of optimism that managed to at least find ways around the more restrictive practices being proposed.

The most necessary requirement was for more pilots and observers, and in particular senior pilots. In the past, a small number of naval pilots had been supplemented by RAF pilots, but this was not going to last for long. Accordingly, arrangements were made to allow a considerable expansion of the RN pilot training program. Since the increased importance of naval aviation that was coming made it clear more prominence would need to be given to more senior air-aware staff, it was also felt that a better career path for pilots would be necessary. Unfortunately many of the officers who would have made admirable senior officers of this type were now serving in the RAF, having left the RN in 1918; however while it would take time, the process could at least be started. A number of the more flexible senior officers had expressed interest in learning much more about naval aviation and the detailed possibilities it offered, and arrangements were made to develop and include an air staff officer role into the staff of the senior admirals.

There was also a considerable exchange of information at lower levels with the USN. While the senior officers in the USN often had issues with the RN, it had been found that aviators liked to talk shop, and getting a few drinks into a US pilot on a hospitality visit was a very good way of comparing tactics and training. As a result some things that the RAF had apparently found 'too difficult', such as over-water navigation and large fast strikes were put back onto the training syllabus.

While the new aircraft were looked forward to with considerable anticipation, they wouldn't be ready for some years, so the main aims of the FAA were

17

deemed to be training to increase the pool of skilled pilots (and supporting engineering staff and crews), and examining and testing concepts and tactics that would be possible once the new planes arrived. They would also look at the defensive problem posed by aircraft with the capabilities of those being designed - after all, once the RN deployed planes like those, foreign powers were certain to try and match or exceed them, and it was unclear that the current defensive measure for the fleet could cope with them.

On the construction side, the current effort was finishing the design of the Ark Royal so as not to delay her start. It was still hoped to persuade the treasury that the continuing building of carriers by the Americans and the Japanese meant that more should be ordered, but in the meantime initial development work shifted to the concept of the Trade Protection carrier, or light carrier as it came to be known.

There were of course issues with the allowed displacement under the London Naval treaty. This allowed the RN 135,000 tons of carriers. The existing carriers could be discarded at any time (they were deemed to be experimental), but they still couldn't build all they wanted to. This was a continuing problem due to the global commitments of the navy. The current design was hoped to come in at around 24,000 tons. Building 5 of these would allow one additional, smaller carrier in the range 12,000 tons - 15, 000 tons, or building 4 would allow 3 smaller carriers (once the existing ones had been scrapped). The current proposal was for a minimum of 4 fleet carriers; this allowed one to be deployed in each main area (Home, Med and the Far East), while allowing for one to be unavailable due to maintenance and refit. If a fifth fleet was built, this allowed a second to be sent to whichever area was under the most threat. The final smaller carrier would normally be used for training, but it would also be available either for deployment or to relieve a fleet carrier in a lower threat area. It was hoped that something more suitable could be arranged when the talks came up for renewal.

The idea of a smaller carrier for use on the trade routes and to cover commerce raiders had been considered for many years, but with not enough aircraft coming from the RAF to fill the existing carriers, it had always fallen victim to ships considered to be needed more urgently. There wasn't, after all, much point to a trade protection carrier without planes.

Such a vessel would be ideal for supporting a hunting group looking for a commerce raider, as its aircraft could cover a far greater area than the cruisers usually assigned to that task. It would also be an ideal support for high value convoys in dangerous waters, and suited to task force support which did not merit the use of a fleet carrier. It was intended such a ship would be of similar cost to a cruiser, and as such could be risked in areas when a fleet carrier would be considered too valuable.

Given that the displacement of the fleet carrier was around 25,000 tons, the first studies of the CVL were around half this. As the vessel was expected to be used and risked as a cruiser, it was important that cost be kept to a minimum, and corners could be cut in a way that wasn't considered sensible for the fleet carrier. The capacity was to be around 25 planes. A number of studies and proposals were investigated, and these slowly consolidated around a proposed ship.

This would displace about 12,500 tons, and carry 25 aircraft, with space allowed for reasonable maintenance work (as hunting groups in particular were often away from base support for long periods). This would fit in with the displacement limits, and some hope was entertained that small carriers in the 10,000 - 12,000 ton range might be exclude in future (as they had been until the London treaty in 1930), in which case this ship would serve as a model for a slightly smaller ship. Considerable agonising had been done of the fitting of a TDS, as it was felt that the usage of such a ship was such that a torpedo from a submarine would be one of the most likely threats. However it was extremely difficult to fit a useful TDS into such a small vessel. A solution was proposed that basically solved the problem by going around it; instead of a TDS, the ship would be well subdivided, and drums would be installed into spaces to provide buoyancy in case of underwater damage. Such a system was planned to be fitted to liners marked down as auxiliary cruisers. To aid the ships survival, the engine and boiler rooms would be split so one torpedo wouldn't take out both.

In order to keep the displacement down, as well as the cost, it was decided that the ship would only have minimal armour; sufficient for splinter protection except over the magazines where a box would be fitted. It was not expected that a CVL would be used in an area of high air threat - that was, after all, what fleet carriers were for - except in an emergency, and like cruisers performance and capability were more important than protection.

To reduce costs and manning requirements, the ship would not carry a heavy AA armament; instead it would carry 3 octuple 2pdr systems for self defence. Since the ship would have to work with cruisers and the fleet, a modified cruiser propulsion plant was proposed that would give a speed of about 28 - 29kt.

The Admiralty was still worried about the carriers existing or planned by the USA and Japan. The USA had two very large converted carriers, one new carrier (Ranger) coming into service this year and two more new designs starting in 1934. All of these carried more planes than Ark Royal would (although the FAA were somewhat disbelieving of the number of operational planes as opposed to just planes carried). The Japanese again had two huge conversions, one smaller new carrier and another being laid down this year. To counter this, the RN only really had two smaller conversions, and one new carrier being laid down shortly. They wanted more new build, and after considerable negotiations with the Treasury, they got funding for the new 'trade protection/training' ship and a repeat Ark Royal in the next years building program

This year also led to some progress in the development of the new aircraft.

First, there was a surprise when another aircraft company offered a proposal for the new dive bomber, Martin-Baker. The company had not been one of the ones 'approved' by the unofficial Air Ministry tender system, and so they had approached the Admiralty directly with a design. They also pointed out that Hawker were very busy, and even starting later they could supply a prototype for testing just as fast as Blackburn. The Admiralty was interested (they were looking at the advantages of building up a number of aircraft companies skilled in producing naval aircraft, as it was realised that only the largest companies would be in a position to build any type of aircraft), and so agreed that they would fund one development aircraft.

Secondly, the rather technically complex issue of what type of 0.5" gun should be fitted to the fighter (and to the dive bomber, which would carry two in the wings). The USN was intending to use the Browning 0.50 M2, but the FAA was not terribly impressed with its performance. The 0.5" Vickers was another contender (and had the advantage of being a British gun), although again the performance wasn't exemplary. In the end it was decided that the initial fit would be the Vickers 0.5" (the FAA were still worried that the .303 favoured by the RAF wouldn't be enough to shoot planes down on the way in, which, as their airfields had a greater tendency to sink than those of the RAF, was rather important to them). Research did continue for a better solution, coordinating with similar RAF work.

There were worries from some of the aircraft manufacturers about the availability of the untried Hercules engine (the Bristol board were still not that keen on it, although the Admiralty was determined to keep pressure on the development), particularly Gloster. They suggested, since they were contracted to produce two prototypes (one with each type of wing armament), that they could use the Bristol Perseus engine for one of the planes, in case the Hercules had problems. Of course it would produce much less power, but it was the same diameter and the plane could be weighted to allow the new engine to just be a replacement, so no time would be lost. The Admiralty agreed to this, as it would produce the first prototype in the shortest possible time, and even if the Hercules was delayed, would allow testing to continue without delay.

A somewhat ironic situation arose when the RAF sent out a requirement for a radial-powered fighter for use in hot climates and from rough airfields. The RN did have a certain amount of pleasure in pointing out that a de-navalised version of their proposed fighter would in fact be ideal for this, since a plane designed for the harsh treatment of carrier landings would be very suitable for short unprepared strips. While the irony of a naval aircraft being supplied for the RAF wasn't lost on the RAF either, in the end it actually went some way to restoring the relationship after the internecine warfare of the previous year. The RAF agreed to partially fund the Navy's plane (in the end, they RN funded the plane and the RAF paid for much of the equipment development), and it was agreed that once flight trials had completed the RAF would select one of the planes for their use. The removal of the naval-only items would them allow either higher performance, better armament of more protection, whichever was felt more important at the time. If the two services selected the same plane, the initial deliveries would be to the RN, then a joint production line could built it in the two required versions.

Chapter 4

1935

At the start of 1935, most interest in the RN aviation community was centred on the design of a follow-on improved fleet carrier, and the waiting for the planes in development to fly at the end of the year, hopefully with the new Hercules engine. So far, progress was very promising, although Blackburn's dive bomber was progressing more slowly that was liked, and Hawkers workload was threatening to slow down the Henley.

The good news was that the Fairy Swordfish TBR was finished, and deliveries were starting. While it didn't have the performance the FAA was looking for from the other new aircraft, it was considerably better than their current planes, and was looking to be a good, reliable carrier plane. A specification was therefore sent out for its replacement at the beginning of the year, this time for a monoplane built around the Hercules. It was expected that a much higher performance aircraft would be available in around 3-4 years.

In order to utilise the higher performance of the proposed new plane, it was decided to look into the possibility of improving the current airborne torpedo. Currently the Swordfish couldn't carry a much heavier weapon, or drop it any faster than the current design allowed, but there were obvious advantages for survivability in a faster and higher drop speed, and at the same time, the overall performance would be looked at.

However world affairs soon turned the attention of the planning staff to a number of different topics that would prove to be eventually very significant.

The first of these occurred at the beginning of March, when a letter was received from Air Marshal Dowding concerning a recent trial to detect an aircraft by means of radio beams. As a result of this, some urgent conversations were held first with Dowding, then with the boffin concerned, Watson-Watt. The results, and the possibilities, astounded the FAA and the navy - this was what they had been looking for as a way of implementing a successful fleet defence. The FAA in particular felt that if this system could be successfully developed, it would solve many of the still-intractable problems they had been wrestling with. They hadn't really managed a good solution to the problem of enemy raid interception; basically the enemy arrived too close too soon, especially in bad weather. One of the reasons they had specified a new fighter with a high speed was to help with a faster interception, but exercises had already shown that this wasn't going to solve the problem. RDF would both solve the problem of weather, and give sufficient range to allow the bombers to be intercepted before they could get in range. As a bonus, the still tricky problem of getting single-seat fighters back would be fixed by tracking and controlling them back, allowing them to intercept even further out. On escort missions, the pilot would only have to get back to the general area of the carrier, making the task much easier. The FAA recommended that RDF should be given the highest priority for technical development (rather unnecessarily as the RAF was looking equally hard at the possibilities). A section was set up at the navy's signal school to evaluate the results of the RAF development, to proceed in parallel with a system for the navy, and to design new operational tactics offered by the new system.

In retrospect, this discovery was well-timed.

On the 16th March Adolf Hitler denounced the disarmament clause of the Versailles treaty, and that the German army would be expanded to 36 divisions. While the announcement of a bigger army didn't worry the navy directly, the announcement of the Luftwaffe certainly did. The air threat to the RN in the North Sea and eastern coastal waters had just gone from a minor nuisance to a potentially major threat.

As a result, a major review was undertaken with some urgency as to the state of the fleets air defences, both with and without air support. This was split into three areas - fighter cover, HA air defence gunfire, and close in gunfire.

Fighter support was considered inadequate at present, due to the very limited number and performance of the planes. Given the steps already taken, it was felt little more could be done on improving this until the new aircraft were in service, although there were big issues as to numbers and control of them. Number of aircraft would be a function of the numbers and availability of carriers, and a number of exercises were planned to work on the most efficient number to use. As to control, it was already known that it was inadequate and subject to the weather, although it was pointed out that poor weather would help ships hide as well as make it difficult to spot an air raid. Even more hope was placed in the RDF experiments.

The position of HA gunfire was felt to be in a better state. A steady and significant improvement in capability was already in progress, and when completed was felt adequate to break up the mass high level formations that were the only real threat to ships. While it was recognised that only limited numbers would actually be shot down, the main effect would be to stop them actually hitting anything.

The biggest issue was with the close range defences. While the multiple pompom was considered a good weapon, it had been a long while in development, and supply was still inadequate. The problems had been brought into greater clarity by the exercises over the last couple of years, with the increases emphasis on dive bombing. Before these, it had been felt that the system was adequate, but a number of issues had been shown up in the additional exercises. Due to the existing shortage, and the problems associated with speeding up production that were already being encountered, a decision was made to look at a program of improvements that would have the minimal impact on production while improving the capability of the system, with particular attention to the four and eight barrel versions. A report was requested, with recommendations and input from the firms involved, within six months

In order to try and keep the German naval build-up under some sort of limitation, the Anglo-German naval agreement was signed on the 18th June. This limited Germany to 35% of Britain's surface tonnage, 45% of submarine tonnage. While seeming to give Germany the opportunities to build a considerable fleet, The Admiralty were quite happy with it for two main reasons; first, they thought that allowing Germany to build up prestigious capital units would stop them building the 'freak fleet' of fast cruisers and submarines that was their biggest worry, and second that while Germany could in theory build up a carrier force, it had taken them, the USA and Japan well over 10 years to work out many of the problems, so any early German carriers would have to go through a similar time-wasting learning curve.

While this was going on, the arguments over next years' carrier construction program went on. The government understood that Germany could easily build up into a major threat, and that this meant that they could no longer ignore the need for increased defence spending. While they didn't see the German army as a threat at the moment, the Luftwaffe was clearly able to attack Britain, if not immediately then in the near future. British air defences had to be improved, and work on strengthening the RAF was speeded up. The land-based air defences were also planned for major improvements, although delays in the 3.7" AA gun meant this would take time before it could become implemented.

The Navy argued that the air threat extended to them as well, and since it was not certain that the RAF would be available except in cases like the coastal waters off the UK, the obvious way of increasing the defences of the fleet was to build more carriers. In addition, the carriers based at Scapa could also help defend the base (and if necessary Scotland), thus freeing up RAF fighters for other use. While the government agreed that this was logical in principle, there were issues over the cost and the tonnage availability under the London treaty. The navy did point out that at the moment there were ample large building slips available (while they were reserving five for the battleships they hoped to start in 1937, they still had ample capability to build carriers).

At the same time, the DCN continued to finish its design for the next carrier. This was to be an improved Ark Royal class, slightly heavier but with better facilities and somewhat better protection; studies since the design of the Ark Royal had made Admiral Chatfield concerned that the level of protection of the ships should be improved. They would also have a heavier close in AA armament of eight octuple 2pdrs.The other obvious difference was the length of the stern round-down. In the first two ships, this had been quite large, as aerodynamic studies showed this improved the airflow over the deck for landings. However it also reduced the space available for spotting aircraft prior to a strike. This hadn't been considered important before, as the RAF had insisted that only small strikes were possible. After taking to the Americans, and after some experiments, this was shown to be completely false. As a result, the round-down, while not eliminated completely, was shortened considerably, allowing another 100' of deck spotting area. The ships were also slightly longer, making them a little faster. This made it more difficult to dock, but the advantages of a longer ship (with a correspondingly bigger flight deck and upper hanger) were considered worth it by the FAA. In fact, the new ships would carry 68 planes rather than the 64 of the original class. This was actually exaggerated to 85 (the Ark Royal had been stated publically to hold 80; not exactly untrue as this was quite feasible with a deck park) in order to hide the amount of armour used for protection of the lower spaces in the ship. A number of studies had looked again at the concept of putting the armour on the flight deck rather than the lower hanger, but the FAA had pointed out that in the event of heavy attacks the carrier would still be put out of action as a carrier, and that the damage, while probably less severe, would be more difficult to repair as in order to achieve any sort of feasible weight the armour would have to be worked structurally. The extra weight so high up in the ship would mean the ship would be single hanger only, and that some of the space would be further reduced by facilities originally lower in the ship having to be at flight deck level - indeed, the internal capacity of the ship would be halved. Showing their calculations and based on exercises, they were able to prove that with the new fighters they would be getting (and with the assumption that at least a prototype version of RDF would be available in a few years), the average damage taken to the carrier (and to the ships in company) would be less with more fighters than with heavier armour.

The arguments were still ongoing when international relations again took a step closer to war.

In October, Italy, with intentions of being a great power in the Mediterranean and in Northern Africa, invaded Abyssinia (Ethiopia). The British Mediterranean fleet was put on alert; however the only diplomatic steps taken were that the League of Nations imposed economic sanctions against Italy. This was actually a relief to the Navy, as the air defence of the fleet was seen as inadequate against Italian air power, and there was concern that while victory against Italy at sea was highly probable, this would involve losses that would take time to recover from, and in view of the steady deterioration of the international situation this might not be possible.

In view of the area to monitor, and its remoteness, it was decided to use air power, in particular carriers, to enforce the League of Nations sanctions. The navy was actually very happy with this, as while it did impose wear and tear on the ships and crews involved, the experience gained in intense carrier operations in near-war conditions turned out to be invaluable. As the first pilots from the enlarged training scheme were now available, the patrols were also used to give them more intense training.

The patrol of course only strengthened the navy's case for more carriers, and the treasury finally released more money for the 1936 vote as the year ended. It was looking more and more as if the new treaty would allow (at worst) more carrier tonnage, and given the worst case possibility of using new carriers to replace the inefficient older ships, the 1936 estimates would include two more fleet carriers to the improved Ark Royal design - HMS Formidable and HMS Victorious.

It was noted that although enhancements in the supply or armour plate had been made, and that more increases were planned, the need to reserve capability for the battleships planned for 1937 meant that there was going to be a shortfall. Accordingly, a foreign supplier of armour was looked for. This caused considerable difficulty - at one point Germany was asked to bid - but in the end 20,000 tons of armour would be supplied by the Czechs.

Chapter 5

1936

In January, the Air Ministry had organised a series of trials between various calibres of aircraft weapons, basically .303", .5" and 20mm cannon. These tests showed the .303" calibre would be an inadequate weapon for future air combat and that the .5" calibre wasn't much better (and weighed more). The best solution was the 20mm cannon. The results of these tests were passed on to the Navy.

At the end of January, the government announced an expansion of the shadow factory program for aircraft production (these were intended as factories to be activated in time of war). The navy was promised that some of this effort would be allocated to them.

The international situation was however getting worse with increasing speed during the year.

On the 7th March, Hitler denounced the Rhineland provisions in the Treaty of Versailles and the Locarno treaty, and German troops marched in to occupy the Rhineland. This was seen, in the navy at least, as a sign that Germany would only be increasing its naval and anti-shipping capability in the near future, and that the proposed fleet levels and makeup would need to be accelerated. Unfortunately, while the government agreed that there was a need for more defence spending, the Treasury was still insisting that this had to be moderate and not disrupt normal commerce. While the Admiralty did make the point that at the present moment the shipyards were still not fully utilised, there were bottlenecks (both current and approaching) in a number of areas such as guns, armour and Fire Control systems which would limit the number of hulls that could be sensibly laid down. While there were plans in place to improve this situation, it wasn't going to change overnight.

In addition, the main area of concern to the government was air defence - while it was appreciated that the naval threat was growing, the Royal Navy was still the most powerful in the world. The navy realised that this priority wasn't going to change immediately, but that it would be possible to get some improvements that were connected to the worries about air attack. A Shadow Factory system was being set up for the RAF, and it was pointed out that this would not only be important for the navy, but that in extremis navy planes would also be available to defend British airspace. Secondly, that improvements in the fleets light AA equipment, which they had been looking at for some time, could be developed partly with the (official) aim of improving land based defences. The government had already promised a portion of the effort would be for the navy, but the Admiralty retained certain suspicions of the RAF.

In May, the Air Ministry issued specifications for new cannon armed aircraft. Demonstrations of the Hispano 404 cannon had convinced them that this was currently the best gun available. The Navy (who had been invited to the demonstrations as observers) were in agreement, and it was agreed that the 20mm would be developed to fit both RAF and FAA planes. Since this would be an identical fit in RAF and FAA aircraft, and the bulk of the aircraft would belong to the RAF, the Air Ministry was given full control of the project.

Studies had been ongoing for some time of the problem of close defence. This was intended to stop torpedo bombers and dive bombers - the HA systems were seen as adequate against high level bombing, as it wasn't actually necessary to shoot them down (although that was ideal), but to disrupt the attack so as to render it ineffective. However torpedo planes had far more opportunities to evade while attacking (and indeed the RN's own exercises had shown how effective they could be), and the speed of a dive bombing attack meant that the HA system just wasn't capable of stopping it - the system simply wasn't able to cope with the rate of change of the gun aiming required to intercept a diving plane.

These facts had been addressed some 10 years ago with the development of the multiple pom-pom system. However it was 10 years old (although thanks to the treasury there had been considerable delay in getting it into production), and as the latest trials and input from the FAA showed, it could use considerable improvement. However, resources were limited. There were also two foreign weapons available, the Swiss Oerlikon 20mm and the Swedish Bofors 40mm. The Bofors in particular was of interest as it was a much more modern system and had the range and stopping power the fleet needed. 20mm was seen as really too short ranged (although it was at least better than the 0.5" multiple machine guns currently in use) to be an ideal defence.

The report recommended two main actions. The first was the use of the 40mm Bofors gun in single and double mountings for lighter ships or merchant ships, where heavy mounts and director control were inappropriate or unavailable. Because the gun used clips rather than a belt feed, they were much lighter (and without director control were felt not to need the long firing time of the belt-fed pom-pom). Since it was expected that these mounts would be used without a director, a heavy proportion of tracer was specified for them. It was noted that efforts needed to be made to speed up the manufacture of the guns in the UK, as the demand was seen to be high for both the land and sea based system. The navy would also consult with the army, who needed the single mounts for their own air defence.

The second action was to improve the 4 and 8 barrel pom-pom. Given the shortage of these, any improvements must cause minimal disruption to production for maximum benefit (refit would of course be ideal), and not add to the production time. Three main points were chosen for improvement. First, Remote Power Control was recommended for all 8 barrel, and if possible 4 barrel, systems, allowing training of the guns under direct control from the gun director. This had been recommended before, but the cost had made the treasury decline to fund it. This would also add weight, so new construction and larger ships would be the intended first recipients. Second were improvements in the belt feed, which was felt to be rather too fragile and temperamental. Any improvements or changes should be straightforward to retrofit. The third change was to the guns themselves and the ammunition. Tests seemed to show a considerable advantage to the Bofors over the pom-pom. The gun was longer, and the shells thus had a better range, improving the chances of shooting down at attacker. While the explosive charge was a little lighter, this wasn't thought important as a direct hit from a contact-fused 40mm would bring down any torpedo plane or dive bomber currently anticipated. It was therefore suggested that new and existing mounts should be modified to take replacement barrels as per the Bofors (this would be connected to the improvements in the belt feet mechanism), thus giving a notably better performance with the desired minimum changes. Finally some reports from the manufacturer and relevant engineering consultants indicated that the mechanics of the mount could be improved (and the mount itself lightened) by application of current manufacturing methods. Since this would entail changing the production line (which was not practical), it was recommended that some prototypes would be made, and all the improvements rolled into a new version for which new production would be set up (thus helping address the current shortage). The existing production line would then either be modified to produce the new mounts, or used to provide the older ones for air defence of land based targets (for which the deficiencies were not such an issue)

The treasury was not happy at the preference for the 40mm, as they pointed out that there were huge stocks of 2pdr shells available in storage. The navy didn't object on principle to using these, but considered that the value of ships mandated the best possible weapons for them, and that the older 2pdrs would be adequate for shore based defence. They pointed to their tests showing that the current mount would not be adequate against dive bombers, and that a ship cost a lot more than ammunition. New ammunition for the ships allowed the existing stocks to be allocated to home defence (the navy was well aware that AA defence of the UK was a very high priority), so strengthening it.

As the existing Naval treaty limitations were now seen as the bare minimum force level, it was expected that at least Courageous and Glorious would be retained for some time (and one of the other old carriers as a training carrier, at least for the next few years). It was pointed out that while this was good, the original assumption was that the new ships would be replacements, and therefore would use the escort vessels assigned to the older ships. If the Royal Navy were to be deploying more carriers, more escorts would be needed.

There was an additional problem regarding the endurance of destroyers. An aircraft carrier had a large fuel load as it was expected that its normal operations would involve more (and higher speed) steaming while launching and landing aircraft into the wind. While escorting destroyers could refuel from their carrier, this took time and was not currently a well-practised procedure. So ideally, destroyers designed to escort carriers should have a longer range. Secondly, there was the issue of numbers. The ideal the Admiralty was now aiming for (though it didn't expect to get there before around 1944) was the 8+8 fleet and light carriers. Assuming a reasonable escort of 4 destroyers per carrier, this meant 8 flotillas of destroyers! While the staff appreciated that carriers were important, allocating them over a third of the current destroyer strength as escorts was certainly not possible. The solution was to assume that half the carriers (on average) would be with the fleet or fleet units, and hence would share their escorts (they would still need a dedicated ship as plane guard to rescue crews who crash-landed) so 5 additional flotillas of destroyers would actually serve. This was thought possible to achieve in the 8 year period under discussion.

The destroyer building program for this year was quite high, but current plans had only one flotilla of the J/K class building over the next two years. It was therefore decided to build 2 additional flotillas, one each year, then take a closer look at the problem. By now, the naval designers were heavily loaded; they were looking at a new generation of capital ships and cruisers, and there was not much effort available to design new destroyers. A compromise of a modified Tribal class destroyer was designed. One of the twin 4.7" guns was removed to save weight for a heavier close in AA suite (it was assumed a destroyer acting as a carriers guard would draw unwelcome attention from enemy planes). Four twin 4" guns was considered to give a better AA performance, but this was rejected due to concerns as to the suitability for low elevation fire, and the ability to protect the carrier from enemy light units was considered more important. Removing two 4.7's allowed the ships to carry an octuple pom-pom in its place, and two quad pom-poms forward, making them very heavily protected. This was also to allow them to engage dive bombers (and, if rather suicidally, torpedo bombers) attacking the carrier. The navy was quite confident that the seamanship of its destroyer captains was up to the close manoeuvring required, even if some of the carrier captains were a little nervous at the idea. They would also, of course, be able to act as close in AA escorts for other ships, depending on the circumstances. While the general policy was to carry defensive armament on the ships under attack, there were bound to be times when this ability to reinforce defences would be useful. The ships beam was widened, and the internal fuel tanks made somewhat larger (as a result of losing the 4.7" magazine); in addition, the machinery was slightly modified to give better economy at the expense of a small loss of speed. The net result was a ship with 50% more range than a Tribal, at the expense of a couple of knots of speed. Given the high speed of the Tribal class, and the fact that the main purpose was escort, this was deemed acceptable, although it was noted that later ships should have more powerful machinery.

In June, the situation in Europe took another turn for the worse, one which again involved the navy. The Spanish Civil War broke out, and the Navy was tasked to undertake neutrality protection patrols. Both Hitler and Mussolini sent aid to Franco, and both the RAF and the FAA watched the introduction of modern types of German and Italian planes with interest and considerable concern.

In September, negotiations on licensing the Hispano cannon designs began. With prompting from the Navy (and an allocation of some funding to help), the Air Ministry gave funding to some British arms companies to test and evaluate the design in detail, and to start looking at what would be needed to change the specifications to Imperial measurements

After seeing the way in which Italy and Germany were cooperating in Spain, it came as no surprise that in late October an official Rome-Berlin Axis was announced. It did however worry the navy; up until now Italy had been seen, if not as an ally, then at least as a neutral. Now Italy moved to the status of a potential opponent, which meant more ships and resources had to be allocated to the Mediterranean. Despite the recent increases in spending on the navy, due to the time taken to build ships these resources would not be available for some years

At the beginning of the year the FAA were looking forward to the first results of the new aircraft development program. As had been half expected, there had been some small delay in getting a flight-certified version of the Hercules in the middle of 1935, and in fact, the first one received its certification in November of that year. As intended, Gloster had flown the first of their two prototypes with the Bristol Perseus engine, and even with the considerably lower power available, the Admiralty was most impressed with the reports on the plane. When the Hercules version flew in March 36, they fully expected to get a plane as good as any current land based fighter. The Bristol plane was expected to fly in April, as they were waiting for a Hercules engine.

The progress of the dive bomber prototypes was causing a little more concern. Hawkers were very busy with the development of the Hurricane fighter, and as a result the Henley development had been slowed. As this had been rather a fall-back design, they weren't too concerned, but the Blackburn aircraft was only coming along slowly - indeed, the Martin-Baker machine, which has been started later, had almost caught up and was expected to finish its trials earlier. At the moment, both aircraft were expected to begin trials in May-June.

A requirement had been sent out late in 1935 for the Swordfish replacement. While the FAA was happier than they originally expected with the general performance of the Swordfish, its slow speed and lack of any protection was worrying. Accordingly (and bearing in mind the flights of the American Douglas Devastator) a monoplane TBR aircraft using the Hercules was specified. With this engine, it was hoped to get a speed of around 200kt, while carrying either an 18" torpedo or 2,000lb of bombs. Fairy, Bolton-Paul and Vickers had put in proposals, and a decision to fund the two most promising would be made before February.

While they had been waiting for the new single-crew fighter, the FAA had 'borrowed' a few modified Gladiator fighters for trials. The big problem, of course, was how to get a plane back to a carrier with a single pilot. In fact, they had two problems; first, the retrieval of a CAP patrol, and second the recovery of strike escort fighters. The Americans had showed that this was possible, if difficult, using a better design of beacon and radio, aided by better navigational training, but it was still very worrying - the current beacon and radio system was only really usable by one man up to 10 miles away.

The Admiralty had originally approached the Pye Corporation with a view to them developing the US system under license. After examining it and its performance, they came back and announced that they could make one, better and cheaper, and it wouldn't need any license fee. The FAA thought about this, and decided to let them try. The need wouldn't be urgent until the new planes were operational, and they could always buy American if needed. In fact, Pye were as good as their word; they delivered a prototype early in the year that was indeed lighter and had better performance (in fact, a more developed version was later licensed back to the USN!). This still hadn't really solved the problem, but a range of 15 miles was a start. In peacetime, they could pull in planes using direction finding, but this wasn't thought practical in wartime as it was, well, rather obvious. At the moment, the FAA were carrying on training while keeping a close and increasingly interested eye on radar, which on paper looked like solving the problem for them.

At the London Naval conference, the Admiralty had set out its minimum requirements for the talks; a displacement limit of 25,000t per carrier (although if really pressed they would go to 24,000t, any lower didn't give the capacity and protection they thought acceptable), and either a high total displacement or (as in the Washington treaty), no limit on numbers on smaller carriers -10,000t as a bare minimum, 12,000t if at all possible.

Discussions with the USN showed that the Americans wanted to press for 20,000t as the carrier maximum, as this was the size they thought suitable for their new carriers. It was pointed out by DNC that the USN only had to design the ships for one area of use and one opponent, and that they were prepared to accept carriers relatively unprotected to get the number of planes they wanted on a 20,000t ship. The extra 4,000 - 5,000t of the British carriers was mainly protective, as these ships would have to operate in the North Sea and the Med, and also that the poor weather in the Atlantic made it desirable to house the normal complement of aircraft under cover in the hangers rather than on deck; if Ark Royal was to use a deck park, DNC was confident she could operate 100 planes, even more than the US carriers.

It came as a surprise to the Admiralty when they were given the final agreement for the new naval treaty, in that they got everything they wanted and more. It was rumoured that some members of the FAA staff took a day to sober up after reading the proposal. There would no longer be any limitations on the total displacement of aircraft carriers, and the maximum for a carrier would be 24,000t (while this was slightly less than the Formidable, it was expected to be no huge issue getting a few hundred tons off her weight (in the event, by the time she completed, going over the weight limits was being ignored).

As a result of the ending of overall displacement limits, the RN and the FAA undertook a complete reappraisal of their options. It would now be possible to fill their needs without being bound by treaty, although there would still be the treasuries financial constraints.

After considerable deliberations, the future needs committee came up with the following requirements.

First, fleet carriers would be needed to work with and cover the most likely deployments. These were Home Fleet (covering Germany), the Mediterranean (covering the Italians), and in the Far East (covering Japan)

The German threat was seen mainly as heavy ships attacking convoys. They had three pocket battleships and some heavy cruisers, which could be engaged by RN cruisers and heavy ships, and two (with two more building) fast battleships, which could only be stopped by the RN battleline. The expected counter to these ships was twofold; first, hunting groups to be deployed early in the war to hunt existing raiders (it was assumed that the longer range units would have been sent out in advance of a declaration of war), and a strong Home Fleet to bottle up the ships in German ports. While the navy was confident they could destroy the German battleships if they could catch them, they needed some way of both finding them and slowing them down - the new ships were expected to be considerably faster than the Royal Navies older battleships. It was considered that a force of three carriers with the Home fleet would be needed (as one might be undergoing repairs or refit, and the Germans could come out at any time). While these would ideally be fleet carriers, it would be practical to have one be a light carrier, as in this situation they were unlikely to be encountering the Luftwaffe. The number of carriers needed by the hunting groups was, again ideally, around six, to have one with each group. This was felt unlikely to be achieved (in the short term), so this was set at three, which would be deployed in the areas most difficult for land-based air support.

In the Mediterranean, it was considered that the western end was reasonably secure due to probable French support from land-based air, although a carrier would be based at Gibraltar as part of a hunting group. The eastern Mediterranean had more area to cover, and would be working in range of the Italian air force, so a fleet carrier was considered essential.

The Far East was a more difficult area to evaluate. It was felt that the land-based air threat would normally be minimal due to the ranges involved, and for operations close to land our own air cover would be close to hand. The problem was evaluating how many carriers of the IJN would be needed to be neutralised. In the end, the ideal cover was thought to be two fleet carriers and two light carriers, the light carriers allowing air support for lighter striking forces than the main fleet.

This made a total of five fleet carriers and five light carriers, plus another fleet and light carrier to allow for refits. This of course made no allowance for reserves, losses and the need to reinforce a high threat situation - it was thought that in the event of war in the Far East, five fleet carriers would be needed, plus three at home, which implied 10 fleet carriers alone (allowing for those temporarily out of service). After considerable discussion as to the operational uses of a protected fleet carrier against a lighter, smaller carrier, the total needed was set at 8 fleet carriers and 8 light carriers.

There was also the issue of convoy protection. The RN had been steadily working out how to run and protect convoys. Air cover was seen as useful for three main purposes; locating a surface raider so the convoy could evade, or protection could be reinforced, covering the convoy against air attack and driving off search aircraft looking for the convoy, and conducting A/S sweeps in front of and around the convoy.

 The direct air threat was seen as minimal in the Atlantic, as current planes simply didn't have the range to get there from Germany (although in a WW1 type situation (with Luftwaffe bases further west), and with the constant improvement of aircraft, this might change, at least in the eastern Atlantic), and coastal convoys would be covered by the RAF where necessary. The Mediterranean was more complex, but unlike the Atlantic, convoys would be minimal and directly escorted, so the fleet units would probably be sufficient. In the Far East it was felt the air threat was small due to the distances involved, at least as far as convoys were concerned - they could be routed to avoid enemy air bases.

Surface raiders were seen as a threat in all oceans except the Mediterranean, but because of the sheer number of convoys at sea, support would only be practical for high value convoys.

The submarine threat was again likely anywhere (although most likely in the Atlantic and the Mediterranean), but this wasn't currently seen as the main threat (they were more worried by the surface raider threat), although it was acknowledged that air cover would significantly reduce the threat of submarine attack.

The problem was availability; the existing analysis already required far more carriers than were available (and more than the treasury was likely to fund), and the demand could be quite high. What was needed was a very cheap ship that could carry the minimum number of planes needed. The current CVL's were costing about £1.8M (as opposed to about £4 for a fleet carrier), and they would like if possible to get the price down to around £1M. DNC was asked to provide some layouts and costings for a ship with the following capabilities; it would be in the 10-12kt size (it was felt anything smaller wouldn't be suitable for use in the Atlantic), no armour, minimal self defence, carrying a squadron of 12 TBR + 4 fighters, with space for an addition 4TBR and 2 fighters to cover damage. Maintenance support would be minimal (damaged planes would be offloaded and replacements put on). Speed would be ideally 24kt (which would actually allow them to support the older battleships), and also be useful when being used as a plane transport, but 20-21kt was seen as adequate, especially if this reduced the cost. Manpower requirements should be kept to a minimum.

The Admiralty (and Admiral Chatfield in particular), was still very worried about what they saw as the lack of armour on the CVL class. They had agreed, reluctantly, that HMS Colossus would build to a light, only partially armoured design, because the carrier was seen in part to be used for training. However they worried about its lack of protection. The large fleet carriers were seen as being adequately protected, if somewhat light on side armour, and a number of studies were done on the possibility of a small protected carrier (carrying the 25 planes of the Colossus class). These showed that the penalties of armour were very expensive, both in terms of weight and in terms of aircraft carried. A carrier with deck armour and a Torpedo Defence System built for a similar purpose would come in at around 17,500t, and be slower and carry less aircraft, although it would have heavy AA guns. More worrying was the cost; Ark Royal was costed at £3.8M, and Colossus at £1.8M, giving them a similar cost per plane carried, but the small armoured carrier would cost £2.8M. This was not seen as efficient compared to the Ark Royal class. The obvious answer was to build more fleet carriers (even if it was necessary to lower operating costs by reducing the number of aircraft carried. A study was authorised to see what was possible for a budget of £1M (an interesting divergence as usually the Admiralty asked what was possible for a certain tonnage).

While technically it wasn't allowed to exceed the old treaty until January 1937, the Admiralty pointed out that by designating them as replacements for the older carriers it would be allowed (just) to lay down two more of the Colossus class. In fact, the Navy had no intention of letting go of the Glorious and Courageous at least, but they needed to get busy if they were to have any hope of meeting their needs in carriers. Accordingly, it was agree to lay down two more ships in the autumn, a supplementary budget having been approved. The Navy's arguments had been directly aided by the start of the Spanish Civil War, and the need to conduct neutrality patrols, a task for which the CVL were ideally suited, and that the Courageous and Glorious were already committed to them.

The ordering of the new carriers could of course not be concealed (especially since the Anglo-German Naval treaty required the RN to inform the Germans of their plans), and it was no real surprise (given, in any case, how deeply Admiralty intelligence was into the Germans building programs) when they learnt that Germany was laying down their first carrier in October 1936 (although they were interested to note it had been advanced a few months from its initial timescale). The design of the carrier they found poor by their standards; it didn't seem to be armoured to anything like the extent of the RN fleet carriers (although it was nearly as big), and carried a heavy surface armament. It was estimated to be able to carry around 45-50 planes, assuming these would be similar size to current FAA planes, and the estimate was that this would probably be split evenly between fighter, dive bomber and torpedo bombers. The FAA started to consider which planes they would be; it was not clear whether the Germans would develop new planes purely for carrier use, or modify existing ones.

In view of this development, an analysis of the other major naval powers was undertaken. The French, while aware of the improvements of British naval airpower, considered that at present their scope of commitments was covered by land based planes. They were considering a modern replacement for their aged aircraft carrier, but at present they had other projects with a higher priority for funding.

The USA had its own needs and a plan for meeting them. They had two large and very useful conversions, the Lexington and Saratoga, plus their first modern carrier the Ranger in operation. They had two more improved modern ships, Yorktown and Enterprise, well under construction, and another one, Wasp, would be laid down in April. That would give them six modern and powerful ships, each of which carried 80+ planes, which would give them a fleet carrier strength greater than that currently under construction for the Royal Navy.

The Japanese were, as usual, keeping very quiet about exactly what they were up to, especially since they had announced their withdrawal from the naval treaties. It was known that they were extensively rebuilding Akagi, Kaga having already finished her reconstruction, in addition to the modern if small Ryujo. The larger Soryu, similar in size to the new American carriers, was expected to complete next year, and a sister ship the Hiryu was to lay down sometime this year. That would give them a similar strength to the Royal Navy.

The plans of the German navy had already been analysed; and some conclusions about the likely use of their first carriers discussed. While it would be possible to use one or two carriers to accompany a large scale raid by two or more fast capital ships into the Atlantic was possible, it was seen unlikely as any discovery would mean interception by superior RN forces, and the carriers would be isolated and would run out of planes. A much more likely scenario was the use of a carrier force to cover the escape into the North Atlantic of one or more raiders; this would allow the carriers to retreat once the aim had been accomplished, thus preserving the valuable ships. A third possibility was to cover operations in the southern part of the North Sea out of effective range of land based air.

Finally, the Italian navy did not seem to have an aim of developing a carrier arm, probably due to the relatively easy availability of land based planes to support their operations in the Med. It was noted, however, that there seemed to be plans to improve the anti-ship capability of the Regia Aeronautica.

The Admiralty used the points of the Japanese and American construction to press hard for an expanded construction program of their own; in particular, they wanted two more Formidable class ships to order in early 1937 to give them rough parity in modern carriers. The treasury was sympathetic, but was being difficult in actually making the funding available.

Chapter 6

1937

On the 1st of January the Royal Navy's new battleship, HMS King George V, was laid down, the first ship to be built after the naval treaties exclusions on new building expired. Considerable discussion had gone on over the design of the ship (especially before the conclusion of the naval talks), with respect to gun calibre (14" or 15"), and the amount of armour. The naval staff preferred a ship armed with 3x3 15" guns, but Admiral Chatfied was unhappy about the thickness of armour possible with this design. There were also issues as to whether the USA would go down to 14". It was then pointed out that this ship (intended to be deployed primarily in European waters), didn't need its own aircraft; it would normally be working either with a fleet or light carrier, and in any case the 2-3 planes it could carry were not going to be much use. As a result of eliminating the aircraft, the armour belt could be made shorter, thus thicker for the same weight, and the staff settled on the 9x15" design, which the USA was agreeable to. KGV was expected to commission in the middle of 1940.

The Gloster Goshawk fighter started to enter service in March. The RN had initially ordered 300, although there were issues with the mass-production of the Hercules which were being looked at. Gloster expected to be able to deliver up to 20 a month once production was established. It had been found necessary to reduce the priority of the biplane Gloster Gladiator to achieve this, but in any case, this aircraft was seen as obsolescent (intended to leave service as soon as the Hurricane and Spitfire were available in quantity). While the problems with mass production were worrying, the initial need was to get the plane carrier-rated and for the pilots to build up experience.

The FAA's second new monoplane, the Martin-Baker Cormorant dive bomber, started to be delivered in April. Again, the Hercules engines were in short supply. The initial order was for 300 planes.

The Swordfish orders, including delivered aircraft, were now 700 (to be delivered up to mid-1939). The progress and capabilities of its replacement would determine if any additional orders would be placed. The Swordfish had impressed by its ability to land on small carriers in all sorts of weather conditions. The Admiralty wished to keep the production going ahead strongly, as while it was seen as inadequate as a Torpedo bomber against modern opposition; it was beginning to look like the ideal aircraft for the anti-submarine and search role operating off the smaller carriers. This would also allow its replacement to be concentrated on the fleet carriers.

While these orders were seen as quite large, the FAA pointed out that allowing for normal use and attrition this will give only about 400 planes in service (not enough for all the projected or building carriers). It also would not allow for the use of FAA squadrons based on shore in areas not well covered by Coastal Command (i.e. outside of the United Kingdom). While obsolescent aircraft could be used to some extent in secondary theatres, this was not considered a sensible option where a modern threat is likely to be encountered.

Since HMS Ark Royal, the first of the new carriers, was not expected to be commissioned until July (and is expected, as first of class, to be on trials and working up until December), the initial squadrons will operate off HMS Courageous and HMS Glorious to allow the fleet to get experience with them.

Contracts for development of a new TBR prototype have been given to Fairy, Blackburn (on strict instructions it will be ready on time), and Boulton-Paul. This will be a bigger and faster aircraft than the Swordfish, although it is hoped better design of the folding wings will allow it to be fitted in a similar space in the hangar.

The Hercules engine continues its development, the big problem being not so much the engine as the difficulty of getting the sleeve valves it uses produced in the sort of numbers that will be needed in wartime. While this is addressed, engines are being produced as fast as possible. While not a major issue yet, it is seen as a considerable problem in wartime when the number of engines needed rises far above peacetime levels of production. Bristol Aviation is asked to treat a solution to the problem as urgent, and funding is assigned to help with the issue.

The FAA continues discussions with Roy Fedden (despite the sleeve valve issues, they are pleased with the Hercules) on the next generation of engines - naval aircraft are large, heavy, and always require a big engine, and Fedden had informed them that the new generation of engines won't grow in power as much as in the past, he expects the Hercules to top out at around 1600hp. The FAA therefore contracts with Bristol for studies on what is being called the Centaurus engine, with Rolls Royce for an advanced descendent of the Merlin called the Griffon, and with Fairy for a version of their P.24 engine. Given their relatively small range of aircraft types compared to the RAF, they only expect to order one, but will pass on the data to the RAF to see if any of them are of use, they know the RAF is looking at engines in this power class for its bombers - they have put in a starting power of 1,800hp. The Navy is looking at availability in around 2 years to match up with new fighter and dive bomber specifications (and possibly a TBR re-engining), as they are looking at a new set of specifications for planes to be available for squadron service in 1941-2 (having seen what the Air Ministry is expecting during this period, and on the assumption that rival powers will be updating an improving their aircraft during this time period.)

Glorious and Courageous in particular have been heavily worked in the last few years, in both normal usage and the crises off Africa and Spain. Both need a refit. A full rebuild is examined and found uneconomical (it would cost almost as much as building a new CVL), and would take too long (2 1/2 years). Accordingly they are planned for a major refit lasting 3-6 months as soon as the new Ark Royal is available; this will involve making the flight deck a full length and covering in more of the lower deck (this will allow them to carry 48 planes as before, but the new, larger planes), a refit to the engines (basically to do as much refurbishment as they can in the time available), and general improvements and repairs. It is hoped to get the material ready in advance so as to reduce the time of the refit, as they are aware the situation in Europe is steadily deteriorating.

As a result of the larger number of planes to be carried on the new carriers, the FAA reviews its squadron size. It was seen as important to not break up squadrons where possible, but the old 12-plane ones looked rather inefficient. After some studies, they decided to go for 18 as the new size (it's thought that an 18 plane torpedo or dive bomber attack is about the optimal for a single strike), while retaining a 'small' 12-plane squadron where these are too large for the desired aircraft mix.

Ark Royal would have a squadron of fighters, dive bombers and TBR (54 planes), plus a 12 plane squadron of TBR, for a total of 66 planes. This is a few more than designed, but they can just fit them in and in any case expect a few on deck at any time for operations (the 18 plane TBR squadron will be the strike squadron, the 12-plane one will handle reconnaissance and A/S work). Half the fighters are allocated to defence, the other half to escort, although if no fighter opposition is expected they will all be retained for fleet defence.

In April, a problem was encountered with the 20mm Hispano cannon. The Air Ministry had been evaluating it in Hurricanes and Spitfires, and an unforeseen issue had arisen. The original gun was mounted upright, fed by a 60-round drum. In order to fit in the thin wings of the new fighters, it had to be mounted on its side, and it didn't seem to like the position. The 60-round magazine was also seen as insufficient, and a belt-fed system was thought to be necessary. The Air Ministry, pushed somewhat by the FAA representative, who was eager to see the gun available to the navy, passed this information on to Marc Birkigt at

Hispano-Suiza for investigation. As the drawings for the gun were already being examined for translation to imperial measurements, it was suggested that they could also look at possible solutions and collaborate with Hispano. The firm was rather reluctant to allow this as the gun had not yet been licensed, and the Air Ministry was not pressing the issue hard. However barbed comments along the line of' if you won't license it we will, and then we MAY let you have some' from the Navy got them to release the money (which had already been allocated by the Treasury) rather more quickly.

Ark Royal, the first purpose-built aircraft carrier for the Royal Navy, commissioned in July. The carrier was earmarked for an immediate series of trials and exercises, with the squadrons embarking with the new Goshawk and Cormorant as soon as they were considered operational.

Only days after this, an incident at the Marco Polo Bridge in China developed into a full scale war between Japan and China. This caused mixed feelings in the Navy - on the one hand, it would probably require more strength to be sent to the area to act as a deterrent. On the other, if the Japanese were spending their resources on a land war, that left them less money to expand their fleet, which was already worryingly powerful.

As a result of increasing war tensions, especially in Germany and Japan, the Royal Navy carrier building was speeded up. Two more fleet carriers were laid down in April to the 'Formidable' design, and two further light fleet carriers would be laid down in May. There was insufficient armour making capacity in the UK to allow the armouring of the new ships (the production capability had been heavily run down during the 1920's, and although it is being increased this takes time). Accordingly, an additional 8,000t or armour was ordered from abroad (bringing the total up to 20,000t)

For some years, the British Government had been trying to get Australia to buy a modern capital ship to strengthen its (admittedly weak) defences, but Australia had always found the idea too expensive. Consideration had been given to 'gifting' them a ship built around the 4 spare 15" turrets still held in stock from WW1, but even this way it would still cost around £5.5M

Given the new light carrier design, a different suggestion was made - why not buy a light carrier, plus its airgroup, and a few escorts? This would cost half of what a battleship would cost (the running costs were only slightly smaller, but they didn't stress that point). The function of the RAN was, after all, not to fight the Japanese fleet. It was to supplement RN forces, and provide a reasonable basis for showing Australia was doing enough to justify RN reinforcement. If the Japanese attacked and RN forces were not in place, their job was to buy time for a fleet to arrive from UK waters. A carrier would actually do a better job in many respects than a battleship; it could cover a much greater area with its planes, and discommode light forces over a greater area. If a second was purchased, these and their escorts could cover 2-3 places at once, while only costing the same as a battleship, while together they would be a formidable striking force against anything not supported by its own carriers.

Secondly, such a purchase would solve the problem of the RAAF, who had no modern fighters. The Gloster Goshawk would be very suitable to the land based role - it could fly off unprepared or primitive strips, it was tough (built to handle carrier landings), fast and capable of outperforming anything in the area, sea or land based. Licenses could be arranged for the aircraft and engine, and the Australians could start to supply their own aircraft in a couple of years (by the time the carrier could be delivered). The naval version would equip their carrier.

Australia was quite interested in the idea. It still couldn't afford a battleship, but the new war in China made it clear that they couldn't just keep on ignoring Japan, and getting the bonus of a modern fighter, built in Australia made it a very interesting idea to them. It was also a good deal for the UK (who were involved in arranging generous licensing terms), as they were running out of shipbuilding ways (or more accurately the manpower to build ships as fast as required), and orders in hand were already at the limits of the British aircraft industry. The new China-Japan war was the final argument, and a deal was made that a light carrier would be built in the UK for Australia (the indigenous shipbuilding capacity couldn't handle so large a ship), being laid down in September 1937 for delivery in November 1939. A production line for the Goshawk and the Hercules engine would be set up in Australia (although some equipment would, at least initially, have to come from the UK). Two carrier escort destroyers would be built in the UK and two in Australia (with the assumption that further escorts would all be built in Australia). Australian pilots would be trained as part of the FAA, to gain experience ready for the delivery of the carrier.

The other big development as far as the FAA (and indeed the rest of the Navy) was concerned was radar. This had now been under development for 2 years, and the results had been very promising. There was an initial parallel development program with the RAF, but this only progressed slowly (which was of increasing worry to the FAA, as they saw it as essential to efficient operation of their new planes and carriers), and it was decided to bring the programs under the overall coordination of Watson-Watt, and as a result a prototype version of the Type 79 air warning radar was successfully demonstrated in the middle of the year. HMS Glorious was due to go in for her refit and modernisation in September, expected out in January 1938, and she would be fitted with the first model for full evaluation. HMS Rodney and HMS Sheffield would also be fitted at about the same time for an evaluation of its use with a surface force.

Planning was also started for the refit of HMS Courageous. It was expected to allow for the installation of a radar system during the refit. Taking the two old carriers out of service for refits was inconvenient - it had originally been intended to wait until the new light carrier was fully in service, and they refit the ships one at a time, but the increasingly worsening international situation meant some risks had to be taken.

Of equal interest was the demonstration in August of a prototype ASV radar developed by Eddie Bowen. This showed it could be possible to fit a radar capable of detecting surface ships on an aircraft, which if it worked would expend the capability of the FAA to detect ships in poor weather and night immeasurably. While it was currently fitted on an Anson, it was felt that if it worked it could be carried by the Swordfish. If necessary the FAA was prepared to dedicate a Swordfish to the role, as the effect on the capacity of the FAA to conduct night strikes (still a closely held secret) would be huge.

Good news in October was that the Hispano 404 was fully licensed for production in the UK. The version had been modified from the original version, with a stronger spring mechanism to allow it to work properly sideways, and a belt feed to allow a larger ammunition supply and to fit properly into the thin wings of the new fighters. The FAA was allocated a proportion of them. During the modification period they had been experimenting with a wing containing two cannon plus two .5", and one with 4 cannon (the original RAF experiments indicated that 4 cannon was the best solution). While both are suitable for use, due to the initial shortages of cannon, the intent is to produce the first 150 planes with four 0.5", the next 150 with two cannon and two 0.5", and then to move to four cannon for follow-on orders.

During the year, Naval Intelligence had been keeping a close eye on the developments in naval aviation in rival countries.

In Germany, they had noted an increase in priority in the building of the Graf Zeppelin; this seems to have been achieved at the expense of the Tirpitz. Oddly, they do not seem to have been able to detect any developments in torpedo planes, or dedicated naval aircraft. Their current assumption is that Germany will navalise a fighter, most likely the Me109, and probably a variant of the Ju-87 as dive-bomber, but they are concerned that they haven't detected a

44

modern torpedo plane. The Intelligence staffs are instructed to concentrate their efforts on finding it.

Japan is of course rather busy in China. It was much more difficult to get details on Japanese construction, but indications are that the demands of the war have if anything slowed naval construction. The Navy was keeping an interested eye on the use of Japanese carriers to support land operations.

The Japanese have a new torpedo bomber undergoing flight testing, the Nakajima B5 'Kate'. It is assumed that the testing will be accelerated to allow it to be combat tested in China. There is limited intelligence on this plane, but it is thought to be fast and long ranged. They are also thought to have a new dive bomber under development, but as yet little is known about the plane. Naval Intelligence recommends placing observers and intelligence specialists in China, as this seems to be the best place to actually observe the new aircraft in use.

France was now considering a replacement for the aged Bearn, and looking with interest at the Royal Navy's light carriers, which they see as more cost-effective for them than a fleet carrier. Negotiations are in hand for one to be built in British yards, with a possible second ship to be built in France. The main problem for the RN is that there is now very little available space left in the shipyards for the long slips required by a carrier. The Admiralty was considering the diplomatic advantages of delaying one of their own carriers to allow a French purchase to be laid down.

Italy was heavily involved in Spain, and as a result seems to be rather neglecting its naval aviation, although the traditional naval building program continues. Development seems to be on prototype aircraft, and it is assumed that the demands of Spain on the small Italian aircraft industry will continue to limit any major deployment of aircraft. The Italians have debued a new dive bomber, the Breda Ba.65, in the Spanish Civil war, and its performance is seen as good, although its range is thought to be limited

In America, the issue was, as usual, politics not resources. A new carrier, the USS Hornet, was to be laid down in September 1937, and it was thought the bringing forward of this ship was due to the RN building program. Or maybe the China-Japan war. Or maybe for some other non-understandable American reason; the Admiralty often has difficulty working out the logic of the US building program.

The Americans have a new torpedo bomber entering service, the Douglas TBD Devastator. This has considerably better performance than the Swordfish, and one of the aims of the new torpedo bomber design is to comfortably improve on the Devastator. They also have a new fighter, the Brewster F2A Buffalo, due to fly late in the year. This comes as no surprise as the performance of their current biplane fighter is well below that of the Goshawk, an initial data suggests the new plane will have a similar performance (although it isn't expected into service until 1939)

Chapter 7

1938.

The level of tension in the international scene ramped up yet again as Germany announces a peaceful union with Austria, absorbing the country into the third Reich in March. It's not clear to observers why a peaceful democratic union requires quite so many German troops.

The increased tension plays a part in the crisis in Czechoslovakia in May, when the country almost goes on a war footing as a result of what they think is an impending German attack. While this proves to be a false alarm, one of the effects is to move British war preparations along more rapidly, as the country is at this point nowhere near ready for war.

The tension also had effects on the allocation of British defence spending; it was deemed that the major threat was from the air, and the RAF was going to get priority in resources. This was obviously bitterly resented by the other two services. The Navy's shipbuilding wasn't terribly affected, as this, and much of the equipment for the ships, was specialised and not able to do anything for the RAF anyway, although there were difficulties with some of the general engineering firms used. The FAA, however, considered it likely to have much greater impact on their planned air program. A certain amount of discussion went on behind closed doors, as a result of which the navy kept its priority for airplanes along with that of the RAF, but agreed to use its fighters to cover its own bases, and land-based attack squadrons would also be available to Coastal Command. To some extent this was already the case, the FAA and Coastal Command (which included quite a few ex-navy senior officers), already had quite a good relationship, and in any case it had been pointed out that the RAF's airframe requirements were limited to some extent by engines the Navy didn't use. It also pointed out that the Goshawk was as good a fighter as the Hurricane in everything but rate of climb, and it would be foolish to disrupt or stop its production line to produce more Hurricanes, especially as it was looking likely the Merlin could not be produced in sufficient numbers yet. The political issue of planes needed by the carrier under construction for the RAN was also used to bolster the FAA case.

The Navy was obviously concerned with the flow of planes needed for the carriers coming into commission in 1939; the pilot training program had been arranged with the assumption the planes would be available, and it would be embarrassing to have the carriers sitting there without their aircraft. In case, production for the FAA was only about 10% of what was being produced for the

RAF. The FAA was looking forward to a considerable expansion of planes at sea in 1939 as the new carriers commissioned.

The situation on Radar was somewhat confused. The FAA had been pushing the need for a radar able to detect planes at long range, and also something which could have a shorter range but which would allow them to control their planes, ideally in a manner similar to that of the RAF command system. While this had impressed them, it obviously wouldn't fit on a ship, and something simpler and less capable, but which was at least ship-sized, was needed.

An improved model of the type 79 radar, the 279, was available by the middle of the year and was on order for fitting to a range on ships. The most vital were seen as the Carriers, Battleships and some of the cruisers. The model gave a good detection range, but couldn't do much more than detect a group of aircraft. This was deemed acceptable for the carriers, as it would allow much better management of the Combat Air Patrol.

More useful was the type 286. This was developed from the early AI radar work, and used a lot of the technology developed for the Army's Coastal Defence (CD) radar. This was accurate enough to allow the ship to vector aircraft onto an enemy raid. It was scheduled to go into production (the initial run of sets were hand-assembled) towards the end of 1938, and a set would be fitted to the carriers in addition to the 279 set. This did require additional masts on some of the carriers, and it was intended to add radar, some additional facilities for the first, primitive Operations room and some upgrades to AA, etc, in a two month period, rotating the carriers through the shipyard. The set was also intended for use on the cruisers being modified for AA use, as it seemed logical that they should be able to control (or at least advise) FAA or RAF aircraft. The 286 would later be fitted to many ships down to the destroyer size. The fitting of these radars also required the replacement of the early model radio beacons fitted to the Ark Royal and the Illustrious; it was not compatible with a radar fit.

Considerable thought had been given as to what to lay down in the way of fleet carriers in 1938. While the FAA was happy to get as many as it could get its greedy little hands on, the number of available slips had been reduced by five due to the KGV class battleship program. Also, the RN would be accepting two fleet and three light carriers in 1939, and even with laying up some of the older ships, this was a lot to absorb - especially if the growing war meant the older ships would continue in service.

It was therefore decided to lay down just one new fleet carrier, HMS Bulwark, in April for completion in 1941.

The light carriers were rather easier; they could fit in slips suitable for cruisers, and while there was a shortage of cruisers, the building program was limited by supplies of guns and fire control equipment as well as armour. Space could be found for three more light fleets, and it was pointed out that this would basically meet the Navies 8+8 requirement by 1941, some three years earlier than originally intended.

In addition, a carrier maintenance ship, HMS Unicorn, would be laid down in February to complete in Aug 1940. She would be built to a modified Colossus design, not able to operate aircraft and with half the engine capacity, allowing her space for the facilities to support up to three fleet carriers on an extended deployment. She was expected to be deployed to either the Mediterranean or more likely the Far East, and so her light AA armament was increased over the normal Colossus-class fit.

Finally, a second flotilla of escort destroyers was to be laid down. It was not expected to produce more for at least a year, as the available berths were reserved for two flotillas of conventional destroyers.

The Royal Navy had long expected to need additional carriers in war, to allow for the availability of aircraft in many locations, and to allow for war losses. They had intended to supplement the existing fleet from two sources; first the building of very simple carriers (not suitable for use in intensive operations, but suitable for use in relatively peaceful areas, allowing the more capable ships to be used on more dangerous operations, and the conversion of some merchant vessels into auxiliary carriers. The concept of the very simple, low capacity, carrier had been under consideration for quite a few years. By this point, the concept was fairly stable. The ship would be at least 12,000t not (anything smaller was thought to be able to have a flight deck big enough for Atlantic operations). It would be built to merchant standards (to save time and money), and with the same torpedo 'protection' planned for the merchant ships marked for conversion to Auxiliary cruisers. Hanger and maintenance facilities would be minimal, as would AA - there would be no heavy AA, and the ship would be fitted for (but not with) sponsons for 4 quad 40mm guns. 20mm guns would be fitted as available. It was expected that these ships would be used to protect convoys either out of range of enemy aircraft (such as the Atlantic), or in regions where we had control of the air. The sponsons were intended to take AA guns if it was found necessary to deploy the ship outside of these areas, but it would save money to only do this where necessary. The ship would carry 12 TBR planes (for reconnaissance and AS duties), and 4 fighters (to eliminate patrol planes trying to find the ship and its convoy). Speed required was around

21-22 kt, ample for a merchant convoy, and just fast enough for the slow battleships. No armour would be fitted, and maintenance facilities would be minimal.

The problem of the propulsion plants had been an issue; the dockyards and turbine manufacturers were busy with the large workload of new ships, and these carriers would not have a high priority. This had been solved some years previously, however. During the mid-30's the RN had scrapped a large number of R & S class destroyers from WW1. While a few had been retained, they were considered simply too small and fragile for conversion to anything useful. However they had 27,000hp of turbines. As the ships were scrapped, the propulsion machinery, particularly the turbines, had been put aside in storage. It had been estimated that with some work for new parts and boilers, and refurbishment, around 30 of these sets would be available for a relatively small cost and, more important, a small drain on manufacturing resources. By using this machinery, it was expected the cost of the ship would be under £1m, a bargain for a carrier. A single ship (HMS Audacity) was ordered in April 1938, with an expected completion of October 1939.

In addition, plans were drawn up for the conversion of six liners to auxiliary carriers. There was some opposition to this, as the number of available liners was smaller than expected, and they were seen as needed for auxiliary cruisers armed with 6" guns. It was pointed out that while these would be useful, it would actually be more effective (at least for those engaged in blockading choke points in places like the Atlantic, if six carriers supplemented the 40-odd cruisers. As a result, ships were earmarked and plans drawn up ready for use in wartime. It was expected that conversion would take around six months per ship.

In September, the RN's second new fleet carrier, HMS Illustrious, commissioned. There had been minor changes to the design, which had delayed the completion of the ship slightly - the new Mk2 pom-pom was fitted instead of the older version in Ark Royal, and provision had been made for the fitting of radar and an Operations room. It was hoped to fit the radar in the short refit after her trials.

The arrival of the new ship was overshadowed by what will later be called the Munich crisis. The navy was put on full alert, indeed it was considered an informal war warning, as Germany placed demands on Czechoslovakia that came close to surrender to Germany. It was only averted at the last moment by the signing of the Munich Agreement, allowing Germany to annex the Sudetenland portion of Czechoslovakia. It was signed by British Prime Minister Neville Chamberlain, French Premier Édouard Daladier, Italian leader Benito Mussolini, and Adolf Hitler. Prime Minister Neville Chamberlain says "This is the second time that there has come back from Germany to Downing Street peace with honour. I believe it is peace for our time."

Many in the navy, and increasingly in the country, see it as peace for a few months more before the inevitable happens. The FAA is looking worriedly at the large batch of carriers due to complete in the next year. Orders for planes are increased, although limitations of manpower on the aircraft production lines means they won't be delivered for some time, but the navy is keen to build up reserves - due to the nature of its operations, it has a lower ratio of its planes actually available in service. The navy was also keeping a worried eye on Japan, as a significant commitment to the Far East will be almost impossible if the country is at war with Germany.

Progress on new engines for a new generation of FAA planes was progressing. The Centaurus was tested in February 1938, and it was flight qualified in August. The Bristol Taurus engine was put on hold, as the Hercules engine seemed more suitable for the range of planes it was intended for, and the Hercules was in full production and was undergoing improvements. Stopping development of the unreliable Taurus allowed scarce engineering expertise to be transferred to the Hercules and Centaurus projects.

The sleeve valve production problem was finally solved by the use of specialised machines, and the Hercules went into mass production. This will still take some time to ramp up to satisfactory levels, as there is now a serious shortage of skilled manpower. While this was anticipated, the amount required has been far higher than expected, and the RAF's Merlin engine still has the highest priority for production.

The Rolls-Royce Griffon had been tested in late 1937, and is flight qualified in March 1938. Additional resources had been found by deciding that there would now not be any use for the originally propose Exe engine, originally considered for a FAA specification - it had been superseded by the Hercules. This is useful as Rolls Royce is heavily committed to Merlin development)

The Fairy P.24 was tested in March 38, flying in October. This engine is seen rather as a backup in case one of the others fails, although the nature of the 'dual' engine is of interest as a safety feature for patrol planes. While it is a promising engine, at the moment there are simply not the resources to consider engineering it and building it in full production.

Contracts for development of a new TBR prototype (based on a specification in 1936 that has changed a few times) had been given to Fairy, Blackburn (on *strict* instructions it will be ready on time.), and Boulton-Paul. One condition was that each company would produce 2 prototypes, one using the Centaurus, one with a different engine. The FAA prefers a radial, but there is always the chance of a problem in development.

The Fairy Spearfish flies with a Griffon engine in March and the second prototype with a Centaurus in September. The planes performance is very promising, although the size and weight of the aircraft is rather intimidating to aircrew who grew up flying the older planes. In fact, it is obvious that the current catapults will not be suitable for the plane when loaded, and a new design capable of handling much heavier aircraft is put into development. It is thought possible that as a result of this the plane might have problems flying off the Ark Royal and the Illustrious (it is already considered too heavy for the Courageous and Glorious)

The Blackburn Blackadder flies with a Centaurus in October (Blackburn is late again), and won't fly with the P.24 until 1939. The FAA is increasingly unhappy with Blackburn who seem incapable of keeping to any sort of delivery timetable.

The Boulton-Paul SeaLance flies with a Griffon in May and a Centaurus in October. While it does not have the speed or carrying capacity of the Spearfish, it is a lighter aircraft and so is more suitable for the older carriers.

Trials of the SeaLance and the Spearfish look very promising, although there are issues with both the new engines (and the issue of cooling the radial engine has only got worse with the increase in power - the Centaurus shows a disturbing tendency to melt on occasion).

A new fighter is wanted now that the new high-power engines are available. A specification was issued in 1937, and Hawker, Gloster and Martin-Baker are selected for prototypes (while Martin-Baker didn't win the fighter contract, the FAA were impressed with many of the features on the aircraft), and now Hawker have the Hurricane well into production they have some interesting concept aircraft. It is hoped that the prototypes will fly towards the end of 1939.

* * *

France laid down its first modern carrier, the Joffre, in October. It is not expected to be available until 1942 - French shipyards are not nearly as efficient as the British ones. Help was offered with the design, but the French have decided to design the ship themselves.

In the USA, the USS Wasp is launched in April. The new carrier fighter, the Brewster Buffalo, is undergoing testing and is expected to enter service next year. The FAA is not terribly impressed, as they consider the Goshawk to have better performance and armament, while the Buffalo isn't even in service yet.

More promising is the Grumman Wildcat, but this isn't expected to be in service until 1940. Even so, the FAA considers the Goshawk to be marginally superior, and expect further improvements to increase this superiority.

In Germany, their first aircraft carrier, the Graf Zeppelin, was launched in September. It is expected to be completed sometime in early 1940, but the FAA considers it will take a considerable period before it becomes operational due to the lack of experience in Germany with carriers. Surprisingly there is still no indication of a carrier-borne torpedo plane in development. Intelligence confirms that a 'navalised' version of the Me109 fighter and Ju87 dive bomber are under development, and Naval Intelligence redoubles its efforts to find the 'missing' torpedo plane.

A second carrier, the Peter Strasser, is laid down as soon as the slipway is available. It is clear that Germany fully intends to develop a naval air arm

Japan lays down the Zuikaku in May. The Japanese are using naval aircraft in China, and as a result some more details are emerging about them, although these are incomplete and often contradictory. The main current fighter, the A5M 'Claude', seems to be a very lightweight plane, probably very agile, but considered under-armed with 2 7.7mm machine guns, and its low weight suggests a fragile plane.

The B5 'Kate' torpedo bomber is being used in a bombing role. It again seems quite light, and from reports its performance is better than that of a Swordfish (but inferior to the replacements now under development)

The Aichi D1A 'Susie' is a biplane, and the performance of this dive bomber is considered unexceptional at best by current standards. There are rumours of a prototype replacement undergoing trials (given the codename 'Val'), but there is no evidence of its use in China

Chapter 8

1939

The Royal Naval Volunteer Reserve Air Branch, which was to supply a great proportion of the naval pilots and observers who fought at sea from 1939 to 1945, had been formed in the Spring of 1938 as it was realised that even with the considerable expansion of the FAA numbers, both to form new squadrons and to reduce the RAF contingent, there would be a shortfall to man the new carriers coming into service this year. As a result of the increasing international tension, this branch was (nominally, at the moment) increased in size to allow for a war reserve of personnel to be built up.

At the end of 1937, the RAF had agreed that Coastal Command aircraft would be dedicated to that role, and would not be considered part of the RAF available for other actions. The Navy was less pleased to find that by the 1st April less than 2/3 of the calculated numbers would be available, and that this included what they considered obsolete type like the Anson.

They had already had issues with the RAF concerning Coastal Command, with some of the weapons supplied to it. The anti-submarine aircraft had a light bomb which was intended to be used to attack surface U-boats. The FAA considered this very sensible, and arranged to get a number to see what would be needed to fit them to a Swordfish (as they were expecting to supplement Coastal Command with these, especially outside of the UK). They were less than thrilled when tests in late 1938 showed that the bomb not only was useless, but also was rather better at 'shooting down' the attacking aircraft than sinking the submarine. Fortunately no crew were killed in the trials, although one very experience FAA pilot was recorded as saying 'if the RAF's bombs were as effective against the enemy as they are against us, there wouldn't be a submarine threat"

The result of this debacle, which the RAF seemed to have little interest in investigating, prompted the navy to set up a group under a Cdr. Blackett, first to investigate and solve the problem of attacking a surfaced U-boat from the air, and second to work out ways to make sure this sort of fiasco didn't occur again. This was to lead, in late 1939, to the formation of the Navy's first Operational Research department

On the 1st February, after the completion of the trials program, the decision is made to produce a number of prototypes of the Fairy Spearfish (with the Griffon engine). The navy would still prefer a radial engine, but the high-power Centaurus is seen to be not quite ready yet, and while the Griffon is both less powerful and an inline engine, the performance improvement over the

Swordfish is impressive. They give Bolton-Paul advance notification that IF the planes trials conclude satisfactorily they will place an order for the Griffon powered SeaLance. They expect to be in a position early next year to choose the plane for carrier operations (and the loser will still be very useful as a land-based TBR plane)

On the 14th of February, the German press announced the launch of the battleship Bismarck. The navy expects her to be in service some time towards the end of 1940. Her sister ship, the Tirpitz, isn't launched until late June - she has been somewhat delayed due to the increased building priority given to the Graf Zeppelin, which is fitting out and expected to be starting her trials in the spring of 1940.

In March, the international situation starts to deteriorate with increasing speed.

On the 21st of March, Hitler reiterates his demands against Poland for the return of Danzig and the "Polish Corridor" to the Reich.

On the 22nd, Poland again refuses German demands for the return of Danzig and the "Polish Corridor."

The next day, German troops occupy the city of Memel, which is situated on the border of East Prussia and Lithuania. Poland warns Germany that any similar attempt to seize Danzig would mean war. Poland partially mobilizes its armed forces.

The situation in the British government is tense, with the arguments of the appeasement faction now being openly derided. On the 27th, at a Foreign Policy Committee meeting of the British Cabinet, the Ministers decide to side with Poland, rather than try for a multi-nation agreement involving the Soviet Union. Poland again rejects German demands that Danzig be ceded to Germany.

At the end of the month, France and Britain declare that they will stand by Poland. British Prime Minister Neville Chamberlain announces in an address to the House of Commons British support of Polish independence.

On the 1st of April, almost ironically, Franco declares the end of the civil war in Spain. All this means to Britain and France is that the Italian and German forces there will all be back home and ready for action again very soon

As a result of the annexation of Czechoslovakia and the renunciation by Hitler of the Anglo-German naval treaty, as well as the actions involving Poland, the government secretly approves the Audacious carrier design, despite the fact it considerably exceeds the nominal displacement under the 1935 treaty. Naval law experts have pointed out that in any case it can always be declared as a battleship if need be.

The Audacious class is a design that DCN has been looking at for a couple of years as a successor to the Formidable class. It has been recognised that this class has pretty much reached what is possible under the 25,000t limit, and that any improvements will be minor. As carrier aircraft are only getting bigger, it is obvious that a bigger ship is needed.

The Audacious would displace 30,500t (in fact, after some changes due to early war experience, she would come in at around 32,000t). Engine power would be increased to match the speed of the earlier fleet carriers, and additional fuel would be carried. The air group was initially estimated at 66 planes (carried in hangers), but it was now expected that a deck park would be used more often to allow 72 (these would be the new, larger aircraft currently in development). Petrol supply and accommodation would be based around this number. To allow for further aircraft growth, the ship was designed to operate planes up to 25,000lb in takeoff weight. The hanger height remained at the 18' in the Formidable class (higher hangers were felt to add too much height to the ship, and increasing plane size meant reverting to the 16' hangers in the Ark Royal was too restricting.

 The deck armour remained unchanged at 1" (this was still sufficient to support the heavier planes), but the hanger deck was increased to 5 1/2", thought sufficient to keep out 1,000lm SAP bombs. Subdivision was tight, and the hanger was subdivided by armour doors into 2 sections as in the earlier ships. As a result of the wider beam required, the opportunity was taken to improve the TDS to handle a 1,000lb torpedo warhead.

This would be the first carrier with operation room facilities and radar designed in, and space was allocated to allow for future increases in the size these would require, as this carrier was expected to be the command ship for a number of aircraft carriers when used in the strike role. The AA armament stayed at 8 twin 4.5" guns, but the light AA was increased from 8 octuple 40mm by an additional 4 quad 40mm, giving her 80 40mm guns. Additional 20mm guns would in fact be fitted during the war

Not only did the navy have to keep one eye constantly on Germany during the year, it was also a very busy time for the FAA as the plans laid over the last few years reached a peak. No less than five carriers of different types were to be completed during the year, and the training of the aircrews and men to support them was putting a great strain on the existing ships, bearing in mind all the other demands for training and preparing for war. The original intention had been to spread out the completion over the year, to allow for easier inclusion into the fleet, but the obvious war now approaching made it imperative to get them available for action as soon as possible.

First to complete was HMS Venerable in Jan 1939, followed by HMS Formidable in May.

Working up these two ships engaged the FAA to the full, and in fact although the light carrier HMS Mars was completed in mid-June, she only went to sea with a single squadron to work-up, as the remaining available squadrons were earmarked for HMS Victorious , which completed in July.

HMS Glory had been deliberately delayed in order to accelerate the completion of HMAS Melbourne by the end of August, and in fact, she completed and sailed for the West Indies with workmen and equipment still on board on August 21st - it was intended to get her clear of Europe and off to work up in a quieter area. As soon as she had done so, she would sail to Australia to match up with her airgroup, the planes for which had been shipped out some weeks ago. In order to give them the maximum flexibility of use of the light carrier, the RAN had purchased 150 planes (split evenly between fighters, dive bombers and TBR) to allow them to support three squadrons. The Australian production line for the Goshawk wasn't ready yet, neither was the engine plant, but it was hoped they would both be ready before the end of the year. In the meantime, the RAAF would be training up pilots on some of the spare naval fighters, as it seemed unlikely that the UK would be able to produce the complete order.

As a result of this HMS Glory would not complete until November, but in any case the planes and pilots would not be available until the end of the year.

On the 19th August, intelligence reports indicated that up to 14 U-boats had left Germany to take up patrol stations in the North Atlantic. The Navy treats this as a war warning. Worse is to come

On the 23rd, Germany and the USSR sign a non-aggression pact in Moscow. A severe blow to the hopes of Britain and France, and Poland's death-knell, since one of the clauses agreed a split of the country between Germany and the USSR. It also gave Russia a free hand in the Baltic States and Bessarabia. Hitler now gives orders for the invasion of Poland to begin on the 26th August 1939. Another German pocket-battleship, this time the Deutschland, sails through the North Sea, without the British noticing.

Intelligence suggests that Germany will invade Poland at any moment. On the last day in August the Royal navy is put on full alert. Army and navy mobilization is commenced, censorship of all communications to and from the British Isles is imposed, the Stock Exchange is closed, and civil airplanes are banned from flying over half of Britain

On September 3rd, Britain declares war on Germany. Winston Churchill is appointed First Lord of the Admiralty.

Chapter 9

1939 - War

One of the uses that carriers (in particular the light carriers) had been intended for was to hunt and suppress submarines. There had been considerable discussion about the best way to do this, between the school of defending the convoys (and letting the submarines come to them), and that of hunting the submarines down, particularly those near to the UK, before they can actually sink any merchantmen and when the hunting group have complete freedom of action.

The Navy had allocated Colossus, Vengeance, Argus and Hermes, with attendant destroyers, as four hunting groups to find and destroy any submarines found in coastal waters. This was considered especially important during the early part of the war, as many ships were not yet sailing in convoy. As well, the idea of hunting and sinking the enemy submarines at sea appealed to the new aggressive First Lord. Consideration had been given to using some of the fleet carriers as well, but the shortage of escorts meant that initially only four groups could be formed.

The policy was to be found to have unintended consequences, due partly to the fact that Germany had penetrated the RN codes, and had a reasonable idea of where the hunting groups were.

On 14th September an attack was made on HMS Vengeance west of the Hebrides by U.39. One torpedo missed, the other hit the carrier but did not explode (it was suggested later that this was due to a faulty magnetic exploder). The carrier was accompanied by three destroyers, and as a result the U.39 was attacked and sunk with all hands.

On the 16th September the carrier Argus was spotted in the Western Approaches by U.29, who had been alerted some days earlier that the carrier was working in the area. The U.29 fired four torpedoes, two of which hit the old ship which sank in 20 minutes, taking over 300 of her crew with her (the underwater protection of the old WW1 ship was no-where near as good as that of a modern warship). Attacks by the destroyers were unsuccessful.

It was pointed out that in a few days we had lost one carrier and almost lost a second. As a result, the policy of hunting submarines in this way was terminated, and plans were made to have the light carriers provide close escort for convoys where they would have the protection of a greater number of escorts, and, somewhat brutally, be in the middle of the convoy protected by the bulk of the merchant ships. In the harsh logic of war, a merchant ship was far more expendable than a carrier was.

While he understood the logic of the decision, Churchill was not happy with what he saw as a Royal Navy too busy with defensive actions to take the fight to the enemy. While the main fleet simply couldn't see any way to tempt the German ships out into range of their guns, the FAA did have a plan they had been working on for some years. Operation Chastise was presented to Churchill.

The day after, a memo arrived on the First Sea Lords desk. "Chastise. Expedite immediately"

North Sea

On the 25th September news was received at the Admiralty that the submarine Spearfish had been badly damaged off the Horn reef and as a result was unable to dive. Admiral Forbes ordered the 2nd Cruiser squadron and 6 destroyers to proceed and extricate her. The battle cruisers and the 18th Cruiser squadron, with the carrier HMS Illustrious in company, sailed as a covering force.

On the 26th the damaged submarine was met by the cruisers and destroyers and safely escorted to Rosyth. Meanwhile German flying boats had started to attempt to shadow the covering force. The force had been operating under radio and radar silence until the first shadower was spotted, thereafter the Illustrious's radar was in use. It was found difficult with this early model to get an accurate reading on a single aircraft, but it proved good enough to guide one of the carriers CAP of Goshawk fighters into visual range. A number of the flying boats seemed to have been assigned to find and track the force, two of which were shot down. Although radar could show the presence of a single plane, it was difficult for the fighters to close with them as they continually took cover in cloud.

During the afternoon, a single bomber, believed to be an He111, attempted a glide bomb attack on the Illustrious. The primitive operations room had been concentrating on the shadowing floatplanes, and as a result had missed this single plane. It was spotted visually as it moved into attack, and received the undivided attention of 72 40mm cannon from Illustrious and her two escort destroyers. The plane was shot down, but not before dropping its bomb, which missed the carrier by some fifty yards. The Illustrious's captain reported later the dedication with which the plane carried out its attack in the face of such heavy AA fire. Later analysis of this action led to the interesting comment that the fire from the twin mounts on the destroyers (which were using tracer as these mounts did not have a director) seemed to cause move evasion by the bomber than the much heavier fire from the carrier which only used minimal tracer.

What was identified as a full squadron then attacked in similar glide bomb attacks over the course of the next hour or so. This time, indication was given by radar, and four of these planes were shot down either approaching or after their attacks by the CAP. No more planes were shot down by the close range AA, although a number of planes were damaged. What was noticeable and worrying for the force was the ineffective nature of the 4" and 4.5" AA fire, although it had been warned pre-war that this would only be effective against horizontal bombers (presumably attacking in formation). Although there were a number of near misses, no ships were hit by any of the bombs.

Admiral Forbes later stated in his despatch that 'the control personnel were obviously unprepared for such high performance dive-bombing', and as a result a review was to take place on how to better control and coordinate the close range AA defences of the fleet. It had also been noted that considerable improvements needed to be made to the control and direction of the carriers defensive aircraft - fortunately the Germans had attacked in singletons, minimising the inexperience of the organisation.

The next series of carrier operations took place after the 5th October, when it was confirmed that Germany did indeed have commerce raiders at sea - this had been anticipated, but not confirmed until then. It was suspected that at least one of their pocket battleships was somewhere at sea, probably in either the North or South Atlantic where the bulk of unescorted merchant ships were.

This had been allowed for in pre-war planning - indeed, this was one of the reasons for building the light carriers in the first place. A number of them were therefore allocated to the hunting groups (in particular, those felt least likely to have good land based air cover.

Venerable was detached from Home Fleet to the South Atlantic as part of raider hunting group G, with the cruisers Cumberland and Exeter (later Ajax and Achilles as well)

Courageous was detached from Home Fleet to the West Indies as part of raider hunting group N with the French ship Strasbourg.

Glorious was detached from Home Fleet to the Cape of Good Hope as part of raider hunting group H with the cruisers Shropshire and Sussex

Ark Royal was detached from Gibraltar and was based on Pernambuco as part of a raider hunting group K with the battlecruiser Renown

Eagle (which had already been in the Far East) was based at Ceylon as part of Raider hunting group I, with the cruisers Cornwall and Dorsetshire.

As per the pre-war plans, each carrier was accompanied by two of the carrier escort destroyers, to protect her and to help in close search and identification of a suspected raider. Given the nature of the threat, the light carriers carried an airgroup of 12 TBR and 12 DB, all of which could be used for reconnaissance, and three fighters. Given the time of year and the deployment areas, the FAA considered the use of a small deck park quite acceptable.

The rest of the carrier force was held with the Home Fleet; partly as a reserve for deployment as needed, and partly because they had the least experienced aircrew (the more experienced, with the exception of those of the Illustrious, having been sent with the deployed carriers). They were as far as possible conducting exercises, particularly the aircrew, for Operation Chastise (while this operation had been developed over the last two years and trials and exercises conducted, many of the pilots allocated were not familiar with the techniques that would be required). It was expected that Colossus, Vengeance and Hermes at least would be allocated to convoy escort duties once the system was in full operation (the Admiralty was also looking ahead to the protection of high value Canadian troop convoys which would be sailing soon and would require a heavy escort).

On the 9th of October, aircraft from the Ark Royal, which was on passage to Freetown with her two escort destroyers, sighted a stopped ship to the west of the Cape Verde Islands. She claimed to be the American S.S. *Delmar*. (It was later ascertained that the *Delmar* was in New Orleans on that date). Vice-Admiral Wells (Vice-Admiral, Aircraft Carriers) decided not to close and investigate himself, but instead sent one of his destroyers to inspect the ship. It was just as well he did, as the 'American' ship turned out to be the armed German supply ship the Altmark. As the destroyer closed and demanded that the ship allowed an officer about to inspect her and her papers, the ship fired on it with one of its 6" guns. Fortunately for the destroyer, a merchant ship with some guns added is rarely an efficient gun platform; although she took a few hits from the Altmark's light AA guns while taking evasive action and firing back. The Altmark was basically only a tanker, and the destroyer's 4.7" guns soon had her in flames. The action was of course reported to the Ark Royal, which was a prudent 10 miles behind the destroyer. The action ended when the destroyer put two 21" torpedoes into the ship (armed merchant ships didn't have turrets, so it was often easy to fire on them from a point to which their guns could not be made to bear). The Altmark quickly sank, leaving the British to rescue some 80 survivors.

This was to prove of considerable inconvenience to the Graf Spee, as the Altmark was her tanker. The Altmark had sent out a message during the action, which, while it was not received by the Graf Spee at the time, was relayed to her later. As a result, arrangements had to be made for her to use the tanker originally intended for the pocket battleship Deutschland (which by this time was already on her way back to Germany). This change meant that the Graf Spee was only able to intercept one British Ship, the Doric Star, before she decided to change her hunting ground from the African coast to South America.

In the early hours of October 14th, the battleship Royal Oak was torpedoed while at anchor in Scapa Flow by the U.47 captained by Lieutenant Prien. As a result, the fleet left Scapa to its alternate anchorage at Loch Ewe. The anchorage's defences had been run down over the inter-war years, and although modernisation was underway, it was not yet complete. Ironically, blockships needed to close the approach Prien took would have been in place in a few weeks.

Three days later, the submarine raid was followed by an air raid by two squadrons of Ju88's. This was rather a disaster for the Luftwaffe for two reasons. The first was, of course, that the fleet wasn't there, rendering the exercise rather pointless. Second was that while the fleet had left, two squadrons of Goshawk fighters, part of the fleet FAA contingent whose job was to protect the base, were still there while it was decided where to move them to (the final temporary anchorage for the fleet was still under discussion, and while Loch Ewe was a good anchorage, it had no facilities for aircraft).

The Navy had been experimenting for some time with a version of the RAF's fighter control system. While they thought it did a fine job for the RAF, their requirements were rather different. First, they had little need to track raids all over the place - the only ones that concerned them were the ones heading for them. Second of course was that whatever they designed had to fit into a ship, one not designed for it. The system was operational at Scapa - indeed, Scapa was used as a test and trial system, where they didn't have to actually shoehorn the equipment into a ship, and so allowed much easier testing and development. It picked up the incoming raid on radar at 70 miles.

The FAA fighters were not, at that time, on such a high alert as was to become common for RAF fighter squadrons later in the war. Up until now, only an occasional reconnaissance plane had come their way, and these were usually at too high an altitude to be easily intercepted (the Goshawk was, like the bulk of navy fighters at this time, optimised for performance under 20,000feet, as aircraft flying higher had little chance of actually hitting a ship at sea).

The duty squadron had three fighters on 10 minutes warning, the rest of the squadron being on the field but not at their aircraft. When such a large raid was detected, the three ready planes were got up as fast as possible, while there was a frantic scramble to get the other 15 ready. The Ju88 was a very fast plane, unfortunately for them not as fast as the Goshawk. The defenders had about 15 minutes to get up to the Ju88's, and the ready planes managed this. The rest of the squadron was still getting airborne as the raiders arrived, but fortunately they were attacking the (empty) moorings, not the airfield. The attacking planes did do some damage; they dive bombed the old training ship HMS Iron Duke, damaging her and causing her to be beached, and did some minor damage to the base itself. They accomplished this for the loss of one aircraft to the AA defences. However once the Goshawks arrived it was a different matter. The FAA planes were armed with two 20mm cannon and two 0.5" guns, and the Ju88 was not a heavily protected plane. The initial attackers attacked with complete surprise, and although the later aircraft had to chase the Ju88's as they made their escape, the result was five aircraft shot down for no loss to the defenders (it was later found that three more planes had crashed on the way home, either due to accumulated damage or to running out of fuel due to damaged tanks, and one more had ditched in Norway!).

The FAA was quite pleased with the results, although it did show up some significant deficiencies in the detection and control system, and the amount of warning actually give, As a result improvements were put in hand, with some advice from the RAF, which led to a considerable improvement. It was noted that if the Luftwaffe had attacked the airfield as well, or had had better intelligence, the result would not have been nearly as favourable.

Battle of the River Plate - 10th December 1939

The allied hunting groups seeking the German raiders varied considerably. The heaviest forces - those including a fleet carrier or battlecruiser - had been sent to patrol the areas though the most likely hunting grounds for the raiders. The movement of the Graf Spee from the coast of Africa to off the coast of South America had moved her away from some of the most powerful hunting groups. It was ironically the loss of her tanker to the Ark Royal's escorts that had caused this.

Covering the South American coast, which included the important food shipments from countries such as Argentina, was Force G under Commodore Harwood. The initial force had been the heavy cruisers HMS Cumberland and HMS Exeter, but this was considered too light a force to deal with one of the large pocket battleships, and had been reinforced with the light cruisers HMS Ajax and HMNZS Achilles, with the light carrier HMS Venerable to give the force air cover and reconnaissance capabilities.

Commodore Harwood had considered the likely areas a raider would go to if it wanted to interdict the merchant ships. He considered the most likely area to be close to the exit to the River Plate, which would give it the target of the regular shipping. The only problem was the size of the area - the mouth of the 'river' at sea was the best part of 100 miles across. Nevertheless, it was the best place to hunt a raider, and while he realised it might take a sinking or two to allow him to close, there was nothing else to do but to make his best guess as where to start. As luck would have it, the first contact with the Graf Spee was before it had managed to sink any ships in this area.

The Graf Spee was first spotted by one of HMS Venerable's patrolling Swordfish to the north west of the British force at 1000 hours on the 10th December. The weather was very good, and the plane caused considerable consternation on the German vessel. The plane had already reported the ship as a warship, and a large and suspicious one - the two triple heavy turrets made it extremely likely this was a pocket battleship. On hearing of the sighting, Commodore Harwood ordered his force to close her in order to make a definite identification.

The Graf Spee had no real indication of where the plane had come from. It was most likely from a carrier, but there was also the possibility it was based on land, as it was just about close enough. The initial thought, that this was a spotting plane from a cruiser, was discarded once it was seen the plane had wheels, not floats. Unfortunately for the Germans, the British cruiser force was fairly close, and in any case had a considerable speed advantage. For a short time, the ship tried to bluff off the patrol planes increasingly pointed questions by signal lamp, but when smoke was detected to the south east this was given up, the ship cleared to action stations and turned north at full speed. Since the British cruisers had a speed advantage of some seven knots, escape was going to prove difficult.

As per standing instructions, the Venerable allowed the cruisers to draw ahead, while she spotted eight swordfish with torpedoes on deck (the other four of her swordfish were on patrol). As the Graf Spee turned away, the other patrol planes were called back, to help keep an eye on her. Such suspicious behaviour from a ship looking awfully like a pocket battleship really only had one likely cause. The initial identification of the British ships was in error; the Graf Spee thought she was being closed by a light cruiser and two destroyers (the Venerable being too far away to be spotted at this time). This led her to believe that this was the carriers (by now the idea that it was a land based plane had been discarded) escort ships, and while it was going to be very difficult to evade the carriers planes on such a glorious day, if she could destroy or at least heavily damage her escorts, the carrier might withdraw for long enough for them to make their escape that night. It was most likely a British light carrier, in which case it was known not to carry a large number of planes, and the German commander had a good expectation that he could evade or absorb their attacks without much serious damage. At this time no ship at sea had been sunk, or even seriously damaged, from the air.

Sadly for Captain Langsdorf, as the British ships drew closer it was seen that they were in fact cruisers. By now the actions of the Graf Spee, and her lack of response to questions, had decided it for Commodore Harwood - this was an enemy pocket battleship. Final confirmation was when the ship opened fire on the Swordfish (it was later ascertained that this was to prevent it spotting for the cruiser force's gunfire). Harwood had made allowance for this sort of encounter in his preparations. Since the Graf Spee outranged the cruisers, and with heavier guns, there was no point in closing with her when the weather was good and he had a carrier full of full of planes following him. So instead of closing, the cruisers moved to keep the range at around 25,000 yards. Given the good weather conditions and the availability of at least four TBR planes, there was no worry about losing their quarry.

The first attack from the Venerable was by eight Swordfish using torpedoes at 1230. Since the target was on her own, they attacked in a hammer and anvil attack of four planes in each section. AA fire from the Graf Spee was heavy, and fairly accurate; one swordfish was shot down, and two others damaged. However this left seven torpedoes heading towards the ship. While the pocket battleships were never going to win any prizes as the most agile of ships,

Captain Langsdorf managed to avoid six of them. The seventh hit the ship forward, causing shock damage and a considerable hole - while termed 'battleships', the class was only an oversized heavy cruiser, with correspondingly poor torpedo protection. Although the fighting power of the ship was not directly affected, she took on a list and slowed considerably as hundreds of tons of water flooded into her. The Swordfish returned to the carrier, being recovered while the ship carried on preparation for its second strike. Harwood viewed the attack with satisfaction; whatever happened now, that torpedo hit would likely doom the Graf Spee to eventual destruction, as even if she still proved too much for his cruisers to handle, they would be able to trail her while heavy forces were brought to bear. For the moment, however, he was perfectly happy to stand and cheer on the FAA as they made her an easier target for his ships. The Graf Spee had fired an occasional salvo at him before the attack, but at the range he was shadowing her there was really no chance of a hit - all the giant splashes of water did was raise ironic cheers from the crew.

The Venerable's crew had been busy breaking all records for the time taken to arm a dozen Cormorant dive bombers with 1,000lb SAP bombs. In order to save time (and as the risk of any air attack on them was negligible to non-existent), they had armed and fuelled the planes in the hanger to leave the deck free to recover the Swordfish. As soon as this had been done, and the planes struck below, the Cormorants were brought up and arranged for a strike. This would happen only 60 minutes after the torpedo attack on the Graf Spee.

Meanwhile the Graf Spee had brought the damage mainly under control; the airborne torpedo didn't carry enough explosive to do serious underwater damage except by a lucky hit, and although the ships speed was now down to 20kt, and there was still a 4 degree list, she was still capable of fighting. It all depended on how many planes that damn carrier had, and how effective they were.

The crew watched with morbid fascination as the Cormorants neared. At first, they expected this to be a level bombing attack, and Langsdorf was quietly optimistic that a dozen planes wouldn't be enough for a successful one. This belief was rudely broken as the first three planes dropped into a ridiculously steep plunge aimed straight at them. The AA fire of German ships was no better against dive bombers than that of the Royal Navy, and the light AA of the ship was quite limited - indeed, with eight 37mm and 4 20mm guns, she carried less close AA than one of the Venerable's escorting destroyers.

The Cormorants stooped in four groups of three at 1400. The AA fire did damage a couple of them, more by luck than judgement, but that had no effect on their attack.

The first group of three managed a complete miss and two near missed that showered the ship with water and splinters. Before the crew had time to do more than breathe a sigh of relief, the second wave was heading down. This time, they were more successful. One bomb landed in the water close enough to cause shock damage to some of her machinery. The second bomb was a miss, but the third sliced straight through the 2" deck armour and exploded enthusiastically on its first (and last) encounter with a German diesel in the forward engine room, causing the entire propulsion system to shut down due to the shock. With the ship slowing rapidly, the last six planes had an easier target. Even so, there was only one more hit, although a number of the others were close enough to cause more splinter damage. The final bomb, however, landed straight on top of the aft triple turret. While this boasted 4" of armour plate, the effect of the 1,000lb bomb was to completely wreck it, jamming it on its turret ring and killing the crew by blast and shock

All the planes made it back to the carrier, although two were too damaged for another strike, and one had to ditch next to one of the escorts. Fortunately, both of the crew survived.

The cruisers followed the ship like hopeful vultures, as the Venerable informed Harwood that they would be able to launch another six Swordfish in 30-40 minutes. The Graf Spee's engineers had managed to get some of her propulsion working, however she was obviously going nowhere at 11 knots. Harwood decided to wait and let the planes get in one more strike. He had the afternoon left, and even if this strike was unsuccessful he could afford a second dive-bomber attack before committing his cruisers. The more the Graf Spee was damaged, the less damage he would take in sinking her. The second Swordfish strike took off some 40 minutes later, and was in range of the Graf Spee not many minutes later at about 1515. As there were only six of them, and the ship was moving slowly, they went for a simultaneous attack on either quarter. The flight attacking on the port side missed although one torpedo came very close, but the attack from starboard hit her twice. One torpedo hit forward, causing damage and letting in yet more water; the other hit amidships, and the shock effect stopped the remaining diesels even as the water started to flood into the engine compartment

Harwood saw the explosions and the obvious sudden slowing of his target, and grabbed the opportunity. The three cruisers bore in on the Graf Spee at full power, the Exeter opening fire first, the Ajax and Achilles closing into effective range of their 6" guns. They had a window of opportunity as the Graf Spee was temporarily paralysed by the bomb damage, and by the time the men on its bridge had realised of their attack, the cruisers had already closed the range and were straddling the ship.

Despite this, the Graf Spee fought back as hard as she could, but the shock from the air attacks had damaged her rather delicate radar fire control and as a result, the fore turret and the 5.9" guns were having to be worked in local control. While they did manage a number of hits on the British ships - Exeter was hit by one 11" shells and two 5.9" which did considerable damage, and the light cruisers received a number of 5.9" hits, the damage from a growing number of 8" and 6" shells turned the superstructure of the Graf Spee into ruin. With only the forward turret operational and with the 5.9" guns only having limited arcs of fire, the agile light cruisers made the most of the vulnerable stern aspect of the ship, closing the range to where even their lighter 6" shells could cause serious damage. The growing list of the Graf Spee didn't help, slowing her rate of fire considerably. Finally the Exeter hit the forward turret; while it was heavily armoured, the concussion put it and the crew out of action for a time. With the ship now nothing more than a listing, wallowing target, only two 5.9" guns on the port side of the ship, Harwood indicated to the Achilles to close and finish her with torpedoes. The cruiser fired two 21" torpedoes into the Graf Spee's starboard side, and the larger warheads were the final blow to the ship. Within minutes, the crew could be seen jumping off as the list rapidly reaches an unrecoverable angle, and less than 10 minutes later the ship capsized and sank.

There was later a certain amount of criticism of Harwood for attacking before using the final dive-bomber strike, but as he pointed out it was starting to get hazy, and while a night action was quite acceptable, it was far better to attack the Graf Spee while she was temporarily incapacitated by the torpedo hits, and he still had a final strike available that day - in any case, it would not have been ready for 3-40 minutes. If his ships had taken heavy damage, he would have withdrawn and used the final Cormorant strike before closing again.

As it was the Admiralty, the British public and the First Lord were most pleased with the result. One of Germany's heavy pocket battleships had been sunk with minimal damage to the British ships, and many in the Admiralty were very satisfied that the concepts of the FAA and the light carrier had been so well vindicated. While there was still a strong battleship lobby in the Admiralty, even they acknowledged the usefulness of the carriers now. The battle was dubbed by the press the Battle of the River Plate, something that made the Admirals sigh as they were well over two hundred miles away from the Plate itself; however the name stuck.

The result of the battle was also to provide the final argument for Operation Chastise, which was scheduled for the end of December (the plan ideally needed a 3/4 or better moon, and some of the carriers spread across the world needed to be brought back home.

Chapter 10

Operation Chastise

One of the first demands made by Churchill in his new post as First Lord was to see the Navy's offensive plans against Germany. He was, perhaps unsurprisingly, unhappy with the very limited options. It was pointed out that in fact, the very weakness of the German navy made it difficult to attack them, and in the case of the dispersed raiders and submarines, the problem was in finding them at all. The rest of the German fleet was sitting happy and snug in harbour, only coming out for occasional operations and slipping back home straight after.

However, there was one operation that could cause very considerable damage to the German fleet while avoiding the minefields and coastal defences set up to protect the warships. This was a plan which the FAA had developed and been training for for some years, Operation Chastise. In fact, this plan had two versions, one for use against Germany (Operation Chastise), the other against Italy (Operation Judgement), since the basic premise was the same in both cases. A heavy attack at night, by carrier planes, on the enemy fleet while it thought itself safe in harbour.

The FAA had been training, practising and planning such an attack for over three years, in fact as soon as the availability of the Swordfish made it practical. The original problem had been how to use aerial torpedoes in a shallow harbour - when dropped, a torpedo normally dived to around 50-60 feet before coming back to its attack depth. The issue had been solved (something the USN was later to regret) by special attachments to the torpedoes which stopped them diving too deep and bottoming out, and when the Cormorant dive-bomber became available it was added into the plan. At first, it had been intended to use it as a level bomber, but when the plan was finalised in September, some details of the possible targets made the planners revert to their dive-bombing role. Dive-bombing at night was of course risky (it was all too possible to dive the plane straight into the water), but an automatic pull-out mechanism was fitted to the planes, and given the circumstances the risk was deemed acceptable. Technical estimates gave the pilot a better chance of surviving than during a daytime attack with the port's AA defences alert.

The Royal Navy had practiced carrier groups of two ships since 1930, and even three carriers at times (although until recently lack of numbers had made getting three carriers together for training very difficult). They were quite confident they could coordinate a three-carrier strike, especially since it would be a night attack and there would be time to arrange the attack carefully. It was realised that setting up such a large attack, at night with the threat of U-boats to consider, was not a small task, however it was likely they would only get one chance to surprise the enemy, and it was necessary to take a few risks to make this a decisive blow. A simultaneous strike on two targets had been considered, but there were problems with hitting both at once (navigational issues alone meant that one would be alerted), and it was decided that a decisive strike against one target would be more practical. There were also issues with coordinating the number of carriers for a two-target strike, this would mean five fleet carriers, and no-one had tried using that many together before .

The actual timing was mainly set by the availability of the carriers and the moon. In order to aid in the attack, a 3/4 or better moon was considered necessary, and a waning moon best (since its late rising would help hide the attack force before launching). The final date was set after the destruction of the Graf Spee, which allowed some of the carriers dispersed for hunting to be recalled, thus allowing the striking force to finalise its intensive training. It also allowed for carriers with the home fleet in case of damage or loss of part of the striking force. The force was to consist of a heavy surface force as well as the carrier group, in order to protect the carriers in case of detection on the way to the target, and to help them get home again. The date was set for the 31st December, with an additional hope that the defenders might be more surprised by an attack on this date.

Command of the force was given to Rear-Admiral Lyster, flying his flag in HMS Illustrious; not only was he an expert in carrier operations, but the original plan (against the Italians), had been designed and perfected under him. Finally, the Home Fleet would be out in the northern part of the North Sea, apparently in a sweep of the area. Partly in the hope that if it was spotted it would distract the enemy, and second as a backup in case something went very wrong with the operation.

The attack force was expected to come under enemy air attack, at least on the morning after the raid. It therefore included two AA cruisers, as well as the eight carrier escort destroyers of the 8th Destroyer Flotilla. Since the attack would take place at night, and no effective German fighter opposition was expected, the carrier fighters were retained for use against the expected attack - it was expected that they would have to fight their way clear on the day following the attack.

It had originally been hoped that the attack could be combined with a follow-up raid by the RAF (one navy navigator was heard to say that surely even the RAF couldn't fail to find a target after the FAA had left it burning...), but after two earlier raids by Wellington bombers, with heavy losses, the RAF declared that a daylight raid was too dangerous. They were persuaded to do reconnaissance flights by the new stripped-down version of the Spitfire for three weeks before the raid. This was to determine exactly what there was to target, and hopefully get the Germans lulled into ignoring the regular recon flights.

Fleet Order of Battle for Operation Chastise

1st Carrier group; HMS Formidable, HMS Illustrious, HMS Courageous.

Total airgroups 78 Swordfish TBR, 48 Cormorant Divebombers, 48 Goshawk Fighters

1st Battlecruiser squadron; HMS Hood, HMS Renown, HMS Repulse.

18th Cruiser Squadron; HMS Curlew, HMS Coventry, HMS Aurora, HMS Edinburgh, HMS Sheffield.

6th and 8th Destroyer flotillas (16 ships)

The attack would be in the form of two separate strikes, as it was not possible to get all the aircraft off in one go. This also avoided some of the problems of having a very large number of aircraft trying first to form up in the dark, and then attack. The plan was for the second strike to arrive shortly after the first one had finished its attack

The first strike would consist of 18 Swordfish (Formidable) 12 Cormorants (Formidable) 12 Swordfish (Illustrious) 18 Cormorants (Victorious) 12 Swordfish (Courageous)

A total of 42 Swordfish and 30 Cormorants, plus six Swordfish carrying flares to illuminate the targets.

The second strike would be 12 Swordfish (Formidable) 6 Cormorants (Formidable) 18 Swordfish (Illustrious) 12 Cormorants (Courageous)

A total of 30 Swordfish and 18 Cormorants, plus four Swordfish carrying flares

Home Fleet covering force (in the northern part of the North Sea);

2nd carrier group; HMS Colossus, HMS Vengeance

2nd Battle Squadron; HMS Rodney, HMS Ramillies

12th Cruiser squadron; Effingham, Emerald, Cardiff, Dunedin

7th Destroyer squadron (9 ships)

In addition, six submarines had been sent to cover the waters the attack force would be returning through

Target - Wilhelmshaven

There were actually three parts to the Chastise operation - getting into position to launch the strikes, the strikes themselves, and getting safely away afterwards.

In order to get into striking range of Wilhelmshaven, about 150 miles, it was considered best to approach from the north. This avoided coming in from the west over the Frisian Islands off the coast, as the planners did not know if there were any warning systems set up on them. Coming in from the north in theory meant going in through a declared British minefield, but this was by no means complete, and they had carefully left a wide area mine-free to come in through.

The biggest problem was avoiding detecting during the approach. Weather conditions were normally favourable at this time of year (i.e. cloudy), and they would be keeping a CAP in the air to, hopefully, shoot down any reconnaissance plane that came close enough to identify just what they were. To aid in this, the cruiser force was split from the main body on the approach down through the North Sea, in a position that would make them spotted first. The idea was then to shoot down the spotting plane, probably after it had identified a few cruisers or destroyers, at the best stopping them sending a sighting report, at the worst miss-identifying them.

There was also the possibility of being detected by a submarine leaving for or returning from a patrol, but again they would have Swordfish in the air, which would hopefully keep any submarines safely down and unable to transmit. The 'run-in' from the North Sea into the area north of Wilhelmshaven would, thanks to the time of year, only have daylight for some eight hours, and as it was likely that any planes would prefer not to land at night, the detection window was quite small. The worst that could happen was that they would have to retreat without attempting the raid.

Getting away after would be the more difficult task. It was expected, if things went to plan, that they would be able to start the withdrawal at around 0500. The first job was to head north/north west in order to get out of range of the short ranged German fighters. Without having to handle these, the defending Goshawks would have a much easier time protecting the fleet from bombers. There was also the submarine threat, but they expected to be sailing at 25kt and this was considered a small risk - a submarine would have to be in an attacking position by pure luck.

As it was, the run-in to the attack position went perfectly. The weather was with them - the day of the 30th and 31st were cloudy, with the cloud breaking up late on the evening of the 31st. Of course, the choice of these dates was quite deliberate, and was intended to reduce the chance of alertness on the part of the defenders. The only worry was that if the cloud continued to break up, they would have clear weather on the first for the enemy planes to spot them, but by then the damage would have been done and they were confident of their ability to fight their way out. The sea state was moderate (although it would have required a full-blown North Sea gale to prevent the FAA from launching once they had got that far!), and once night fell the crews started to prepare the planes for the raid.

Normally it was not practice to keep armed and fuelled planes in the hangers, indeed normal procedure was for the fuel lines to be drained when not actively in use, but in this case the need to get a large number of aircraft off, followed by a second strike, in a very short time had made them decide to take the chance. As it was night and they were in the middle of the fleet, it was considered a more than acceptable risk. In fact some planes had to be armed on the flight deck - in order to manage the attack, a number of Swordfish, picked from other squadrons for the skill of their navigators, were to lead the strikes and then illuminate with flares for the attacks to go in, and there wasn't room for all the planes in the hangers. Everything was prepared by 2200, and all they had to do then was worry and hope noting detected them at the last minute.

At 2330, there was a final briefing for the aircrew, giving them the latest weather data and probable positions of the targets inside the harbour. The first Swordfish would take off at 0045, with the first strike expected to arrive on target at 0230. The raid expected to move down the coast of neutral Denmark, which conveniently had no idea what a blackout was, then cut southwest to hit the port with minimal chance of warning. It also allowed them to fly lower, with less chance of detection. As it was the experimental Freya radar only picked them up when they were close (it was mainly set up to detect aircraft coming from the west, not the north-east, and by the time they had got themselves sorted out the attack had almost arrived. Ironically, the two earlier failed RAF raids helped - the defenders made the assumption that this was another medium-high level raid by Wellingtons, which led to more confusion and an inefficient response. No-one had ever considered a mass night raid by carrier planes possible, let alone likely, as it was well known that the harbour was too shallow for torpedoes, and naval planes couldn't carry the weight of bombs necessary to make an inaccurate high level attack sensible. Indeed while the speed at which the local defences got the 88mm guns into action was impressive under the circumstances, they, and the searchlights, were all looking in the wrong direction. By the time they realised their mistake it was too late.

The job of the first flights of attacking planes was to illuminate the harbour with their flares. Since it was intended to make a short, sharp attack these planes were slightly ahead of the main strike force, which had orders not to attack until the harbour was well illuminated, in order to drop as many flares as possible in a short time. Very soon indeed the harbour, and the planes targets, were well lit by the flares and the gibbous moon. In addition to giving the attackers a clear view of their intended victims, it also hindered the German light AA, who were straining to see what was going on past the brilliant spots of the flares. The port did, of course, have considerable AA, plus searchlights, and the area even had an experimental Freya radar, but the night-time AA defence in 1939 was not what it would come to be in the next few years.

Once the flares were dropping, the following planes fell into their strike formations and determined the best line of approach to their targets. It was helped by the recent photographs from an RAF Spitfire; it seemed that the ships they were looking for were still moored as they had been a couple of days ago.

The first to make their attacks were the torpedo planes. They weren't too worried by the AA (although it was quite heavy - a real 'Brocks benefit' as it was later described), due to the very low altitude of their approach; their main concern being to manage their approach runs to avoid any torpedo nets protecting their target. The first victim was the pocket battleship the Admiral Scheer (sister to the recently despatched Graf Spee). She was the target of 12 Swordfish from HMS Illustrious, lying at anchor fitfully backlit by the parachute flares. Even though a considerable degree of surprise had been attained, her crew had manned her AA guns, although they were obviously having a problem finding the attackers as they bore in at 50 feet.

Given the Sheer's helpless and immobile situation, the flights had split up, six planes attacking from each beam. In theory, she was a helpless sitting duck, but of course the need to avoid the nets, and the rather impressive AA display made it rather more different. The first six planes, attacking from the port side, only achieved mediocre results, one hit out of six. This impacted the vessel about amidships, with a spectacular plume of water, and breached her hull, sending water flooding into the forward engine compartment.

The planes attacking from starboard and led by Lt-Cmdr Edmonde (the raid leader) had more luck (they later insisted it was mere skill). The ships AA had obviously been distracted by the attack from port, and as a result, they were not spotted until the first drops. This time 3 of the aerial torpedoes hit - one forward, and two further astern. All three breached the hull, and the flooding went from worrying to serious. One of the torpedoes also caused the second engine room to flood, and the ship lost power, a situation which hardly helped to reduce the amount of water entering. The Scheer took on an increasingly growing list to one side, while the crew tried frantically to get power restored to work the pumps.

At about the same time, flights of Swordfish had been converging on the three light cruisers in the harbour. The first of these to be attacked was the Emden. As with the Scheer, the 12 planes from HMS Courageous had split up into two groups of six, attacking this time in pairs due to the need to aim for the gaps in the torpedo nets. The attacks from the starboard side were a failure, all six failing to thread the gap in the nets and hit the cruiser. Almost ironically, one of the torpedoes swam past the Emden and impacted with unerring precision on the destroyer Bernd von Amim, which soon started to sink. The attacks from port were more accurate, the gaps in the nest were slightly greater for their angle of approach, and that made all the difference. A total of three Mk XII torpedoes hit her, two slightly forward, one aft. The old, small cruiser had never been designed to handle this amount of damage, and as the water poured in she rapidly took on a list that was to prove fatal. Not long after the attack, her crew abandoned ship as the Emden rolled over onto her port beam and capsized.

Next in line for the loving attention of the FAA was the Koln. Again the Swordfish split their attack, the 12 planes from HMS Formidable managing to get a total of four hits on her, two on each quarter. Since the damage was (albeit accidentally) fairly well distributed the ship didn't develop a fatal list as had the Emden, but the water entering was again too much for her and over the next hour she slowly settled before finally sliding under the water

The final light cruiser in the harbour was the Leipsig. She had been seriously damaged by the submarine HMS Salmon some two weeks earlier, and having been temporarily patched up was presumably waiting for proper repairs (it was in fact found out after the way that she was considered a total constructive loss) and was in fact just there while it was decided how best to strip her for parts!) Attacked by six Swordfish from HMS Formidable, she was hit twice. As she had nothing but a skeleton crew on board, and in fact still had many of her watertight doors open, she sank quickly (later reports indicated the blast of the torpedoes had opened some of the patches over her earlier damage, and she went down in 10 minutes.

While the Swordfish were attracting the attention of the defences (if only by some of the bizarre low-speed acrobatics some of them were doing to keep out of the way of some of the harbour equipment and barrage balloons) , the dive bombers had been circling ready to pounce. As planned, additional flares were put down specifically for them, and in groups of three the Cormorants from the Illustrious stooped on the biggest prize in the harbour - the huge bulk of the battleship Tirpitz, sitting massively in the fitting-out basin.

The planes were carrying 1,000AP bombs. It was not certain how well they would penetrate the ships decks, as only estimates of her protection against bombs had been made. However the FAA had one big advantage - Tirpitz wasn't completed, she was fitting out with no crew aboard, and the Royal Navy knew exactly what a disaster waiting to happen a ship in that condition was. The aircrew had been undergoing intensive training for this particular attack, included some hair-raising practice at night dive-bombing. As a result devices had been fitted which should pull the plane out of its dive at a predetermined point. Even so, it wasn't easy targeting a ship at night, lit only by flares and the moon (which was mainly visible through the broken cloud), even when the target was a big a ship as the Tirpitz. Of the six groups of three that attacked, only four bombs hit the ship, one forward which did little more physical damage than blow her anchor away. The other three hit the main body of the ship, but all three failed to penetrate the main armour deck, although splinters from the bombs did slice deeper into her hull. In addition, one bomb fell close enough in the water to breach her hull, causing water to start to fill one of her engine rooms.

However sinking the Tirpitz by bomb damage wasn't what the attackers had in mind, a ship being fitted out is a firetrap - full of wood, paint, gas tanks, even fuel for some of the equipment, with her watertight doors open (indeed, not fitted in numerous cases to allow the finishing work to be made easier. The white hot splinters from the bombs had already ignited numerous fires inside her, and as the total crew consisted of four night watchmen (who had, with remarkable sense, taken cover as soon as the air-raid sirens went off), at the moment no-one even knew of the damage.

The other 12 Cormorants from HMS Formidable had a different target this time, the Admiral Scheer. Already in serious danger from the torpedo hits, and with no power, the crew didn't even respond to the diving aircraft - indeed, it was possible they didn't even see them in all the confusion. The first three planes missed the target completely, merely drenching her in spectacular plumes of dirty water. The second flight was rather more dramatic. The first two bombs were close, enough to cause shock damage, but nothing more serious. The final bomb was far more spectacular, as 1,000lb of bomb sliced through the ships armour, forward of her bridges, and ended up in the forward 11" magazine. Bombs and magazines don't get on too well, and even as the pilot was recovering from the pull-out after his dive, the entire forward part of the ship seemed to lift itself out of the water in an explosion which lit the entire harbour, and actually fired the huge turret some distance into the air. A Swordfish pilot was later heard to complain about this, as he considered it rather excessive for an ant-aircraft weapon, and surely in breach of the Geneva Convention.

As the first wave of aircraft left, the harbour was already full of damaged and sinking ships, and the burning hulk of the Scheer (at least, before it slid to the bottom of the harbour). Just in time for the second wave to arrive. First to arrive were the 12 Cormorants from the Courageous. They were carrying 1,000 SAP bombs, and their target was the Tirpitz. These bombs weren't intended to penetrate deep into the ship, instead the idea was to cause serious damage to the superstructure (full of equally generous amounts of inflammable material as the hull), and of course to impede any fire-fighting and damage control that was in action after the first attack (in fact, this still hadn't been reported, and in the confusion no-one had as yet taken any action to inspect the ship)

This time they managed four hits, but one of the bombs didn't explode due to a faulty fuse, However the three that did went off most satisfactorily, leaving parts of the ships superstructure ablaze (the more serious fire was deep inside, but this couldn't be seen by the aircrew)

Next in line were the 12 Swordfish from the Formidable. They had been sent as backup if the initial attacks on the cruisers hadn't been successful, but in view of the circumstances, they changed to their backup targets, the six destroyers. One of these was obviously already in serious trouble (it was the one struck by the errant torpedo in the first wave), so their attentions were concentrated on the other five. One received two hits, which caused it to settle and sink (although it was, eventually, salvaged), while a second had its stern seriously damaged, and settled until the stern of the ship was stuck in the harbour mud.

The final strike of the second wave were 18 Swordfish from HMS Illustrious, carrying 500lb bombs. In view of the devastation clearly visible, they ignored the burning and sinking ships, and headed for their main target, the U-boat slips and fitting out area, which they peppered with a total of 54 bombs. Ironically, in what had been seen as the most dangerous attack against the defences, all the AA was so busy concentrating on the planes attacking the ships that not one of the planes was hit. As a result, one U-boat and one under construction were heavily damaged (both were later declared total constructive losses and broken up), and two under construction badly damaged (although both were eventually rebuilt). As well as these, serious damage was done to the fitting out basins and the slips, which would impact the construction facilities of the port for the next six months.

Last plane to leave was that of the raid leader, Lt-Cdr Edmonde, who despite the AA fire had been circling and observing the raid while directing some of the attack waves to their targets. His actions in this and in leading the raid (indeed, due to his staying over the target his plane barely made it back to the carrier) led to his award of the Victoria Cross.

The devastating raid had not been without loss.

Of the first wave, two Swordfish and two Cormorants had been lost to flak. One Swordfish had run into a balloon cable and crashed, and one damaged plane, originally though lost, was later found to have crash-landed in Denmark (much to the astonishment of the Danish farmer whose field it landed in, when three rather battered Navy airmen knocked on his door in the middle of the night). One divebomber was also lost when it failed to pull out of its attack on the Tirpitz and flew into the water

Although smaller, the second waves suffered nearly as badly. Another four Swordfish were victims of the by then thoroughly aroused flak, and one damaged so badly it had to ditch just outside the harbour (the crew survived, although captured). One Cormorant was a flak victim, and a second damaged so badly it ditched - sadly, this time the crew did not survive.

The total losses were eleven Swordfish and five Cormorants, a loss rate of 15%. This was very satisfying, as the loss rate had been predicted at 40% (although the crews hadn't been told that!) Another dozen aircraft were in fact written off after landing due to damage.

Chapter 11

The Run Home

The last of the strike waves landed at 0515, and the fleet immediately turned to the NW and increased speed to 25kt. The idea was first to get out of range of the short-ranged single engine fighters. They knew the longer ranged Me110 would still be able to reach them, but the fewer fighters they had to intercept, the easier it would be to shoot down the bombers they were expecting. Crews were all at action stations, but somewhat relaxed as it was going to be a long day. At 25 knots, if there weren't any problems, they expected to be out of range of any serious attack by the next morning.

The carriers were maintaining a constant CAP of nine planes (three from each carrier), with six more ready on deck. This would hopefully allow up to 27 planes for interception duties, with a further 27 ready in the hangers if needed. So far, the Germans seemed to prefer to attack in squadron or perhaps two-squadron force, so this was thought to be the best solution to defend themselves for the entire day. It was assumed that German efficiency would have worked out the most likely area they would be in (they had no option but to go NW as the escape route to the west was blocked by a German minefield. And a British one).

In fact, the speed with which the Germans could coordinate a concerted attack in response had been overestimated. It wasn't helped, of course, by the fact that it was a naval base that had been attacked, and that the Luftwaffe was needed to find and attack the fleet responsible. It had taken a series of increasingly acerbic telephone calls between the two organisations to get the planes into the air. It wasn't until 1200 that the first reconnaissance plane was spotted by one of the cruisers at the edge of the formation. A Goshawk was vectored in to attack it, but passing the message to the carrier by signal lamp, and then to the plane, took time, and before this happened the plane was transmitting a contact report.

Up until now, the fleet had been operating under radio and radar silence - the whole policy of emission control verses detection ability was in its infancy, and in fact, a perfect solution was never attainable. Radar was still unreliable and not terribly accurate, so the decision had been made not to transmit until the first reconnaissance plane detected them. Given the circumstances, it was felt highly improbable that an attack would be launched until they had been found. Once they were detected, the radars would be used to spot any other enemy planes.

The German plane, having made its report, tried to get away by hiding in the cloud cover, but there was far less cloud than the day before, and it wasn't long before the far faster Goshawk sent it tumbling flaming into the ocean. By this point, the fleet was the best part of 200 miles from land, and rather further from the Luftwaffe airbases. Far enough in fact that they were out of effective range of the Me109 fighters. However the first planes to attack were not escorted by any fighters.

This was a staffel of 12 He115 floatplane torpedo bombers. These had been allocated to support for the Kriegsmarine, and for a floatplane had a very good performance - indeed, considerably better than the Swordfish. Unfortunately for them, the Mk5 torpedo with which they were armed was a very different story - while its warhead was heavy by the standards of aerial torpedoes in 1939 at 440lb of explosive, it only had a speed of 33kt for 2,000m, and had to be dropped at 75kt. Indeed, most if not all of the ships in the fleet could run away from them!

The torpedo planes approached initially at about 5,000feet, presumably in order to locate the fleet. Unfortunately for them, this made them quite detectable by the carriers radar, and as soon as they were detected at some 40 miles at 1400 another nine Goshawks were being attached to the catapults (while the planes could easily achieve takeoff from a run along the deck, using the catapults meant the ships didn't have to break formation to put the wind directly over the deck). By the time the attack had closed to 10 miles 12 Goshawks were on top of them. In the resulting fight, the fighters shot down seven of the He115's for only one loss (a fighter which had to ditch, although the pilot was picked up by one of the destroyers). Of the remaining five, all were in full retreat, one trailing smoke, having dropped their torpedoes to make a faster getaway.

The carriers launched the nine Goshawks still ready on deck, and then recovered the original CAP. These were struck below, and nine more fighters placed on deck, while the second nine were kept airborne. This routine was intended to keep air cover and replacement fighters available all through the day. It was felt that they would be needed again before it got dark, and this proved to be correct. It was never known if the floatplanes had reported the presence of fighters, or the second attack had already been allocated them, but this time a large blip on the radar turned out to be 24 He111 level bombers and 12 Me110 escort fighters. Again the carriers launched their nine ready aircraft (they had brought up another nine, but these had to be warmed up - the radial engines of the time would not perform properly or produce take-off power until they had been warmed up), and the first nine were directed to the raid. When they radioed in the size of it, the rest of the CAP was directed onto it and efforts redoubled to get the next nine fighters in the air (fortunately at this time the Luftwaffe had neither the numbers or the training to conduct a multi-axis attack, as the primitive radar direction on the carriers wasn't up to handling one).

The first group of Goshawks went for the bombers intending to break up their ordered structure. When they did, they were intercepted by the Me110's. The result was a confusing dogfight between the Me110's and the Goshawks. The German aircraft was faster, with a heavier armament, but the Goshawk could both outmanoeuvre it and out-accelerate it. The result was four Goshawks shot down for the loss of six Me110 (plus a number damaged, two of which would not make it home, and one which ended up in Norway).

While this was taking place, the He111 were still boring on into the heart of the fleet. They were intercepted at about 10 miles out by the other nine Goshawks, but kept their formation and kept heading for the ships -in fact, it was very soon clear that they were heading for the carriers. Three of the Heinkels were shot down, for some damage to a Goshawk, but at that point the aircraft were ordered clear so the fleets HA guns could engage them. This was later adjudged to have been an error, but at this time the lack of efficiency of the HA systems was still not appreciated. Despite the orders, and the black puffs spotting the sky, one Goshawk completed its attack to shoot down a fourth plane. The other 20 planes headed for the carriers in an increasingly dense cloud of AA fire.

Given the state of the art at the time, the fire was not that ineffective. The fleet had an impressive number of 4" and 4.5" guns available (and at the angle they made, the destroyers LA 4.7" guns could also be brought into action). Also, the Heinkels held their course with admirable dedication. As a result, three planes were seen to fall, and the formation itself finally broke up into a far looser grouping.

While this was happening, the carriers were making frantic efforts to get the last group of fighters into the air. They managed it, just, but the planes could not engage the bombers until they had reached sufficient height. The rest of the planes were safely in the hangers, unarmed and unfuelled, with the in-hanger fuel systems purged (as per normal practice during an attack), and the ship fully ready for an attack. The Heinkels had by now split into two loose groups, one of ten and one of seven planes. The larger one attacked the Illustrious, the smaller group the Formidable.

While the decision to call off the fighters was already obviously wrong, the groups of planes had been turned from a coherent group able to 'shotgun' a ship, to a far looser grouping that would only get a hit by luck. This was enough to save the Formidable, as her captain dodged through the falling bombs at full power with the sort of agility you don't really expect from 25,000 tons of carrier. The Illustrious was not so lucky.

While she also attempted to dodge the falling bombs, she was hit twice by 250kg weapons dropped from around 15,000 feet. Very luckily, neither penetrated into the hangers. One bomb hit her rear starboard 4.5" mounts, destroying them both. Some of the explosion did vent into the hanger, but the bulk was directed up and out, and the hanger spray systems and fire curtains worked as advertised. Three aircraft were wrecked, but with no fuel or ammunition to turn the fire into a conflagration it was soon well under control. The guns flash protection worked admirably, although the magazines were flooded just in case

The second bomb came very close to missing completely - in fact, it actually went through the flight deck very close to its leading edge, and then dived into the sea near to the bow, leaving a rather impressive hole on the port side of the deck. The impact had initiated the fuse, and as a result the bomb exploded just before hitting the sea, showering the front port side of Illustrious with splinters. While this caused some considerable damage internally, none of this was considered serious (the hit was too far forward to be close to any critical areas).

Once the planes had dropped their bombs, they became the prey for the Goshawks, 16 of whom were concentrating on them. Due to the inexperience of the crews, all but three were on the Heinkels who had bombed Illustrious, as a result of which seven of the ten planes were shot down. Of the other group of seven, only one fell, although two others were seen leaving trailing smoke (one of these planes ditched on the way home, the second just made it to land to crash-land in Germany)

The fleet carried on at 25 knots, the damage to Illustrious being worked on. Although her deck was usable in an emergency, for the time being her fighters were recovered to Formidable; due to the early sunset at this time of year it was not likely there would be any more attacks before dark, and if necessary she could launch fighters. It wasn't certain yet how much damage had been done to her catapults, so as there was no intention of flying off heavily loaded bombers, it was decided not to use them except in an emergency; the Goshawks could easily take off from the deck.

By the next morning, the fleet was well clear of both Germany and Norway, steaming north east to get back home. However there was one more action before they finally made their escape. It was obvious that the Luftwaffe was still searching for them; as the weather today was cloudy, and it would not have been possible to detect a search plane before it reported in, it had been decided to use the radar. They were now too far away for coastal monitoring to be useful, and it seemed unlikely that any plane could pick the emissions up. They did, however, stay under radio silence (all necessary reports had been made yesterday while under attack, since at that point it didn't make any difference). The radar showed an occasional echo which they thought were planes searching for them, but the only close contact came at 1300. This was a single plane, and as they did not detect any signals from it, it was thought they hadn't been spotted. In fact they had, and the planes radio was picked up shortly afterwards, by which time there wasn't much point in sending a fighter after it.

As it seemed likely there was time for an attack before dusk, the carriers sent up a new CAP and landed the old one so as to give the ones airborne maximum endurance. After yesterdays experience, nine fighters were spotted on each carrier, three fully warmed up. At 1600 a large formation (22 planes) was detected approaching from the south at 50 miles. The ready planes were launched, and the rest warmed up to be launched as soon as possible. Meanwhile the CAP gained height, as these planes were at 15,000 feet. It wasn't clear what the planes were until they got visual contact; the formation was coming in fast, and at first it was thought they might have been Me110's, which were thought capable of a fighter-bomber role. When they were seen, they were identified as Ju88's.

The first interception was made at about 15 miles from the carriers, the Goshawks bouncing the enemy from above. This was made easier as they were steadily losing height, and it was assumed that they would try a level bombing at around 10,000 feet to gain accuracy. The Ju88 was a fast plane, as had been found out at Scapa, and as a result it took time to make multiple attacks against it. The earlier actions against the plane had, though, shown it was very vulnerable to the defenders 20mm cannon. The first group of planes shot down four Ju88's in their initial attack, and then turned to close and attack again. After the debacle yesterday, it had been decided that the planes would not be called off until they attack closed to five miles, and at that point the decision was up to the carrier.

Nine more fighters were heading for the formation, and as they were now only 10 miles from the fleet they made a head-on attack, which resulted in three more Ju88's either shot down or turned away with damage. There were still 15 planes heading for the fleet. The original CAP had by now caught up with the fast bombers again, and another two were brought down, two more retreating with obvious damage and trailing smoke. The remaining 11 saw yet another group of fighters heading for them, and at this point obviously decided to pick a target and get home, leaving the carriers alone as being too difficult a target.

Instead, they went for the nearest ship, which was the cruiser Southampton. What they did next surprised the defending fighters - they dropped into a dive-bombing attack. No-one had expected such a large plane to have this capability, and as a result the fighters did not react until they had started their dives. Southampton's close range AA engaged the first group of three planes, while the fighters went for the four that still had not started their dives; due to the confusion, only one of these was shot down, the other dropped their bombs at random into the North Sea and escaped.

The cruiser wasn't as heavily equipped with light AA as desired, but she was firing everything she had. It was noted later that the defence seemed to confirm what had already been suspected (and would also be confirmed by the after-strike reports from the FAA own attacking planes), that the tracer streams seemed to make the attackers react more. The light AA failed to shoot down any of the three attackers, however none of them managed any hits, although the impressively tall waterspouts were close enough to the ship to soak men on the upper deck and bridge.

The second group of three were more successful. One bomb hit right forward, destroying the ships cable locker and some crew quarters - fortunately empty as everyone was at action stations - and starting a fire in her paint locker. The other was far more damaging, the 250kg bomb penetrating the ships armour and impacting in her forward boiler room. The ship slewed to a stop as power was temporarily lost due to shock damage, and a large fire developed around the ships seaplane, probably caused by a shell splinter igniting the fuel.

It was lucky for the Southampton that this was the last attack that day. While the fire would take a considerable time to quell, the one forward was not terribly dangerous, and once the fuel had burnt the one amidships was also brought under control. Power was restored quickly - the aft boilers and generators were undamaged, and while there was flooding due to the bomb, this did not spread further through the ship. As the air threat seemed to have passed, the fleet split into two sections. Two destroyers and the AA cruiser HMS Curlew remained with Southampton to aid her, the rest of the ships continued to head for home. Half an hour after he damage, Southampton signalled she could make 20knots (in fact, she actually worked up to 23, the engineers understandably reluctant to take longer than necessary to get home)

Aftermath of the Raid

The safe arrival of the strike fleet back at Loch Ewe was greeted with relief in the Admiralty. Using such a substantial force in what had been seen as a risky operation, mainly because at this stage of the war the defensive efforts of the Germans could only be estimated (and in particular after the rough handling the two RAF raids had had), had been a constant source of worry. Pictures of the results of the raid, and the complete devastation of the harbour, had made it before the arrival of the fleet - indeed, one of the things taken onto the flagship when it anchored was not only the congratulations of Admiral Frazer, but also a set of photographs to be admired and passed around. The pictures proved particularly popular on HMS Illustrious, since she, as well as HMS Southampton, had been claimed as sunk by the Luftwaffe - a claim that was to be repeated a number of times for Illustrious as the war went on.

The analysis of the raid showed it had been as successful as might have been hoped.

Tirpitz had been on fire internally for an hour before fire crews arrived, and by the time they had managed to restore some sort of control most of the interior of the ship had been burnt out. There was significant blast damage to the superstructure, and splinter damage deep into the ship, plus water damage lower down due to the flooding from the near miss. In some areas the fire had been hot enough to cause some distortion. It would take 2 months to thoroughly survey the ship and determine what needed to be done to repair her, and the rebuilding plus a complete re-fitting-out was estimated to take over 2 years. In fact, while plans were made to repair and refloat her, by the summer it was decided she was a total constructive loss, her guns dismantled for coastal defence and the ship broken up for her steel

The Admiral Sheer, having blown up in the raid, was sunk on her side (the water not being deep enough for her to turn over fully), and a total wreck.

The three cruisers were also complete write-offs, and two destroyers were later found to be also, although a third was finally repaired. There was also damage to some of the U-boats under construction, two being declared unrepairable. Two more probably should have been, but maybe for political reasons they were rebuilt instead. There had also been considerable damage to the U-boat slips and fitting out facilities. The main damage, though, was to the morale of the Germans. Wilhelmshaven had been the second most important navy base, and to have it violated like this made the men mutter about what might happen to other ships in the future. It was bad enough having to face the Royal Navy at sea, but there you had a chance, in port you could be bombed while asleep in your bunk.

In the end, the Kriegsmarine decided that as a point of honour they had to keep using the base, although its defences were built up considerably. Which was rather a waste later in the war, as the only real use for it was to build U-boats

The effects on the Royal Navy and the Fleet Air arm were rather more subtle. The money spent on the new carriers had, they felt, been fully vindicated - while surface ships were very useful, nothing but a carrier force could have done that damage. It was also apparent that ships under air attack without a carrier could be in trouble, and that high value units needed their own air protection. While this had been suspected already, the raid did make it more apparent. As a result, work was started on improving the control of the aircraft (the attacks by the Luftwaffe had shown that the existing system was too primitive and inaccurate). The attacks had also shown that the existing HA defences were inadequate, at least against determined attack. Both these conclusions would be reinforced by the actions later in the year, but it would take years before things were in a satisfactory state. The aim was to develop a doctrine based, where possible, around a force of surface ships with carrier support, but it was realised this would take time and practice. While some of the more fervent carrier supporters did suggest that they could do without battleships altogether, this was never considered a sensible attitude, particularly due to the constant threat of bad weather in the North Sea and Atlantic during the winter. The concept of a balanced fleet was, however, changing to meet the new challenges.

The biggest effect however was the political one. Churchill was most impressed and pleased with the victory. As he said in the House of Commons the day the force returned:

"It has been said that a war between a land power like Germany and a naval power such as ourselves is difficult, as it is a war between an Elephant and a Whale. Well, on New Year Herr Hitler learned that THIS Whale has wings!"

As a result of Churchill's approval, the Admiralty was able to fend off some of the requests from the Air Ministry for greater resources, especially where aircraft were concerned. Not a huge amount, but then the FAA was much smaller than the RAF. This was very helpful as the naval building program was being examined with the need to cut back in some areas - without the raid, the fleet carriers might have been slowed in construction or stopped. Indeed, it was found possible to get some extra manpower and investment in the FAA's new programs, although the RAF build-up still consumed the great majority of the aircraft industry.

Chapter 12

Jan 1940 - HMS Illustrious

As a result of the damage to HMS Illustrious, it was decided to give her a refit at the same time as her repairs. This had been considered for some time, in order to bring her up to the standard of the Formidable class.

The carrier was fitted with a new, more powerful, catapult. While her existing ones were adequate for the current aircraft, the new aircraft being designed were considerably heavier, and since one of her catapults had to be taken out for repair (the bomb that hit the deck had indeed caused some collateral damage to the port catapult), this may as well be done now. The equipment was already available, having been waiting originally to upgrade HMS Ark Royal.

Her arrestor gear was also replaced to take the heavier aircraft (in fact, this meant she would be the first carrier to operate them), as the combination of more weight and a higher landing speed exceeded the safe limits for the current gear. The Navy had been rather shocked at the weight and speed requirements when the initial designs had been proposed, but it had been pointed out to them that restricting the weight and landing speed also severely restricted the performance - if they wanted the best performance, they had to pay the price. Fortunately, the estimates made when the carriers were initially conceived had been adequate for the current generation of aircraft. While the Implacable and the Indefatigable had the new equipment, the earlier four carriers would need a refit before they could operate the new planes.

Her light AA suite was inferior to the Formidable class (48 40mm as against 64), but there were difficulties in fitting an additional 2 octuple units. Instead, two quad 40mm were fitted to bring her up to 56 guns. In addition, 12 20mm were added (basically anywhere they would fit!).

In view of the increasing power requirements of the radar and other systems, a 275kw diesel generator was fitted. Two of these had actually been in the original plans, but in the end more steam powered generators had been used instead. It was considered that they were more efficient than the diesels available at the time, but replacing one of more with more powerful units would have taken too much work and time, while addition of the diesel until was much simpler. It would turn out that even this would be inadequate, and later on in the war she would receive her second diesel.

At the same time, she would receive an improved radar fit. The actions so far had shown that while radar was already useful, it still needed significant improvements before its true potential could be used. The 279 set was replaced with an improved version, and the Type 286 replaced by a new set, the Type 281. She would be the evaluation ship for this new radar set.

Her repairs would take almost three months, and she would rejoin the fleet at the end of March. It was then hoped to bring in HMS Ark Royal for similar improvements, a hope which turned out to be overtaken by events.

As the ship would be in dock for four months, the opportunity was taken to train her squadrons on the new planes just entering service. These were the Goshawk Mk2, the Cormorant Mk2 and the first of the Boulton-Paul SeaLance TBR, the Swordfish replacement.

The arrival of new planes and weapons, Winter 1939-40

Goshawk Mk2

This was basically the original plane with a number of improvements and modifications based on the in-service experience. There was a new version of the Hercules engine, using 100 octane petrol for higher performance, and already giving 1,450hp. This was driving a Rotol variable-pitch propeller; which had been suggested for trial by Bristol (they did, after all, own half of the company). Results had been most satisfying. Other changes involved things like removing the few fabric-covered control surfaces, and small changes to enhance the handling and ease of use of the plane, plus safety features like self-sealing fuel tanks. Bristol were still working on the Hercules, and current intentions were to produce one more version of the Goshawk with a more powerful version before transferring production to the next-generation fighter currently testing. At the moment, the Mk2 seemed capable of taking on and beating the currently expected opposition. The Mk2 was faster than the Mk1 (despite the inevitable addition of some weight), and the new propeller made it more economical. While it was intended to mount four 20mm cannon, the weapon was still in limited supply and as a result the first batch would complete with two 20mm and two 0.5".

After the experience of fighting German Me110 fighters after the Wilhelmshaven raid, the pilots asked if better protection could be put into the plane - a couple of the pilots had been shot down from behind, and one other had had a very lucky escape when the cannon shell destroyed his radio rather than his back. Gloster were uncertain, but some experiments with 'salvaged' armour plate from various RAF aircraft showed that the armoured back made for the Battle would fit (with a bit of modification), and that the weight wasn't an issue as it actually helped to compensate for the heavy Rotol propeller. A modified seat would be fitted to new planes later in the year, but a number of the squadrons fitted them themselves, as and when they could acquire the armour.

How they acquired some of the plates is perhaps best not looked into too closely. The information was passed on to the Air Ministry (who filed it), and more informally to some of the RAF squadrons (who immediately started agitating for the same fitting to their Hurricanes and Spitfires) - as a result of the Goshawk flight tests, the RAF already had orders in to Rotol for the variable pitch propellers. It was also felt very useful that the self-sealing fuel tanks had now been incorporated - a couple of the fighters in earlier actions had landed on their carriers with leaking tanks and not much fuel left, and it was fortunate that the air actions had been close to the carriers.

As part of the increasingly close (if still unofficial and secret) cooperation with the USA, one of the first Mk2 Goshawks had been taken to the US for secret flight comparison with the USN's new fighter, the Grumman Wildcat (F4F-3). On paper, they were very similar aircraft. The Goshawk was somewhat heavier than the Wildcat (the Mk 1 was very similar in weight, but the addition of things like self-sealing fuel tanks, the Rotol propeller, etc, had added a good 500lb to the weight, compensated for though by the more powerful engine). The speeds were similar, although with its extra weight and power the Goshawk dived more quickly, as was the overall performance. The straight line speed of the Goshawk was also greater. The FAA considered the Goshawk to be more manoeuvrable, and in general they were considered comparable aircraft. The big advantage the FAA considered the Goshawk possessed was its much heavier armament - 2x20mm + 2x0.5" as compared to 4x0.5" on the Wildcat, and the RN pointed out to the Americans that they actually considered this to be too light, and that as soon as supplies permitted they were fitting 4x20mm cannons.

Cormorant Mk2

As with the Goshawk, the main changes were the new engine and variable pitch propeller, plus small changes, giving better performance, and the self-sealing tanks and armoured glass put into the new Goshawk. Some testing had been done carrying a 1,600lb AP bomb, which it was hoped would penetrate most battleships, but this was felt to be a little too heavy for the plane. However it was hoped that further engine development would make this bomb a usable and powerful addition to the FAA's armoury.

Bolton-Paul SeaLance Mk 1

The replacement for the Swordfish was now available. Indeed, the aircraft had entered production in 1939, and some planes had been delivered in October. This was the first of the two aircraft being developed, and it used the Rolls-Royce Griffon engine. Production was still limited, as the performance of the Griffon I was still not as good as was desired. However with the country now at war, the navy wanted to get some into operational use for evaluation. The engine was still not giving the power output required (it was currently operating at 1,700hp), but RR were confident that this could be improved significantly in the next 6-12 months. While the Merlin was by far the most important project at RR, the cancellation of the Exe by the Navy had allowed effort on the Griffon as well. The MAP (Ministry of Aircraft Production) had tried to shut down the production of the Griffon on the grounds it was only needed by the FAA, but the Navy pointed to the earlier agreements made when they regained control of the FAA, and that all the other engines they used were also in use by the RAF (even though the Navy had funded the early work on the Hercules), and one engine for them was hardly excessive. Given the success of the FAA so far in the war, and Churchill's consequent support, the Griffon production was not paused.

The other TBR aircraft, the Fairy Spearfish, had finished trials, but was being held until the Centaurus engine was running more reliably (and with a lower propensity to melt bits of itself on occasion). Bristol were confident that these problems could be fixed, especially with the extra resources made available by the cancellation of the Taurus engine, but as a result the RN was reluctant to put the plane into full production. Instead, preliminary work was done on the production facilities to allow the plane to move into full production as soon as the engine was satisfactory, and in the meantime additional work and testing could be done to refine the airframe.

The SeaLance was a big, heavy plane (hence the need to a powerful engine, and the improved facilities for launch and recovery needed), coming in at 9,500lb empty - to put this into perspective, this was close to twice the empty weight of a Swordfish! However its performance was expected to be considerably improved. Even with the Mk I Griffon it was getting a speed of 210kt with its torpedo, and a range of 800m. It was hoped that this would give it a much better chance of survival on attack, especially when using the new Mk XIVA torpedo.

One of the results of the new, higher-performance aircraft coming or soon to come into service was a re-evaluation of the weapons available, and a number of programmes for more advanced torpedoes and bombs to be used by these planes.

The Mk XII was the standard aerial torpedo of the Royal Navy from 1937, and a new torpedo, the Mk XIV, had entered service in late 1938 (both versions were still in service). As a result of the expectations of the new torpedo bomber, it had been pointed out that requiring the plane to slow down to around 100kt to launch its torpedo was just giving the enemy AA a better target. This hadn't really been an issue with the Swordfish, as it couldn't go much faster than that while carrying a torpedo. Considerable research had gone into modifying the Mk XII to be dropped into a shallow harbour, and once that had been completed, they carried on to see if similar modifications would allow a faster and higher dropping speed. As a result, the Mk XIVA had been developed; basically the same as the Mk XIV, it could be dropped from 200 feet at up to 200kt, thanks to break-away control surfaces. Development continued steadily as the SeaLance and Spearfish should be capable of dropping both the Mk XIV and the proposed Mk XV at between 200 - 250kt. A target of dropping at 300kt has been set to the developers, which was a bit ambitious, as even the Spearfish could not carry a torpedo at that speed.

There was also a new torpedo under development, the Mk XV, which would exploit the full capability of the new planes, but this would not be ready for use until early in 1941 at best. It would be heavier, with a larger warhead, and somewhat faster. It was hoped to get a warhead of 545lb into it, which would make it a much more effective weapon against heavy ships. The torpedo would be around 200lb heavier than the Mk XIV, but the warhead is 50% heavier. Research work was progressing on the possibilities of a more powerful explosive (certain compositions showed promise, but need research), as the RN would like to get the aerial torpedo into the damage range of the pre-war 21" torpedo, which would make a huge difference to the effect of torpedo strikes. Current aerial torpedoes damage larger warships - the Mk XV could sink them.

The RN was reasonably happy with the performance of its 500lb and 1,000lb bombs, although use and tests had indicated the fuses were not as reliable as they would like. Indeed, when the fuses were tested at random some 25% failed to work. A temporary solution had been better selection at the factory and careful work on them by the carrier crews (since the FAA cannot drop very large numbers of bombs over a number of nights onto a target as the RAF can, it is far more important that the bombs they do drop work correctly). As with the torpedoes, work was ongoing as to the possibilities of a more efficient explosive - this was of particular interest to the Admiralty due to the relative small number of bombs they drop compared to the RAF. A larger bomb of around 1,600lb was being developed as an AP version for use against heavy ships - this would penetrate the armour of anything other than the latest battleships.

Changes at the Admiralty

On January 6th, Admiral Pound, the First Sea Lord, had what was an apparently innocuous slip on some ice outside the Admiralty building. Due to his damaged hip, this forced him to a hospital bed for some days, as he was unable to walk on that leg. While he was there, however, in an apparently unrelated conversation, his doctor happened to mention to a colleague that 'he wondered if anything was being done to treat the Admirals brain tumour'. While he had known about this for some time, it had not been mentioned to other doctors or the Admiralty.

As a result of this becoming known, Pound was given a thorough medical, where it was shows that he was suffering from some sort of growth on the brain, hence the distortion of his eye that some of his colleagues had already remarked upon. As a result of this, it was decided that it was impossible for him to continue in the role of First Sea Lord, especially with the terrific strains war imposed on that office. It must be admitted that there was a certain amount of internal Admiralty politics at work here. There had been acrimonious discussion about the building program for the next year (a plan, agreed on pre-war, had been implemented in September, but it was in the process of being reviewed so as to set the program for the next year or two, especially important for the larger ships). Pound had been particularly keen, if not almost fanatical, in promoting the battleship program, suggesting that the carrier program be halted or cancelled completely in order to make capacity available. This had not been popular in those sections keep on the FAA, and as the air arm's stock was riding high after Wilhelmshaven, an Admiral with a more balanced view was looked for. The airmen fully recognised that a balanced fleet was still needed - the carrier was essential to this now, but it could not yet defeat an enemy fleet on its own - but were not prepared to accept the abandonment of the carrier for what they felt was a class of ship now in its twilight - especially after the years of fighting and struggle to get the FAA prepared for war.

The problem was who to replace him with. A number of senior officers had had to retire in the last few years due to injury, and indeed Pound had only become First Sea Lord because of the untimely illness and death of his predecessor, Admiral Backhouse. Looking at the number of senior naval officers who had died in the last few years, and with a reluctance to remove what was seen as some of its best fleet commanders whose services would be very much in need, it was decided to appoint Admiral Bruce Fraser from Third Sea Lord to the post, at the same time promoting him to Vice Admiral. He was an officer of proven ability, with experience in both gunnery and having commanded a carrier. He was to hold this post with distinction for the rest of the war.

One of the things the raid had done was to cause revived interest in the Royal Navy carriers abroad, particularly in America and Japan who had their own carriers (and lobbying Admirals!). One of the first things the RN did after the reports of the raid had been broadcast (and in the case of the USN, an 'unofficial' source had disclosed more details than went out on the public newsreels) was to analyse what effect the now-revealed abilities of the Fleet Air Arm would have on foreign navies. The report came to the following conclusions.

France

France was of course concentrating the bulk of its resources on its army and air force, not helped by the state of confusion its over exuberant mobilization has caused (France had called up so many reservists as to cause serious industrial problems, and had had to release some back into civilian life).

The aircraft carrier being constructed (the Joffre) is expected to be available in early 1942. There have been discussions about the British selling them a light carrier, but at present the RN needs all it has for itself, and a new build wouldn't be ready any sooner than the Joffre - in any case, British yards are at full capacity (indeed, overfull capacity).

Germany

Germany's first aircraft carrier (the Graf Zeppelin) was launched in September 1938, and is expected to be ready soon (intelligence estimated in May 1940). There still seems no sign of development of any torpedo plane for the ship, and it is now suspected she will only use fighters and dive bombers, which will seriously limit her effectiveness against capital ships. Current intelligence indicates this will be carrier-conversions of the Me109 fighter and the Ju87 dive bomber. As yet, the navy has inadequate data on their performance. As this will be the Kriegsmarine's first carrier, the RN does not expect it to be actually operational until the spring of 1941. The second carrier, Peter Strasser, is expected to launch around the middle of 1940.

Italy

Italy seemed to have no plans for a carrier; perhaps not surprising in view of the land bases it has available to cover its navy. It has been noted that the country seems to be strengthening its land-based planes used for maritime support, with increasing numbers and a speeded-up development work on successor planes. The FAA have expressed no worries about the current generation of planes, but are less certain about their replacements. It does seem that the Italians, unlike the Germans, do rather seem to like torpedo planes. Of course, at the moment Italy is not an enemy power, but in view of the relationship between Italy and Germany, and the nature of the Italian government, it must be viewed as an unfriendly neutral.

Japan

The carrier Hiryu was commissioned in July of 1939.The Shokaku was launched in June 1939, and is expected to be ready in early 1941. Her sister ship the Zuikaku launched on the 27th November, and is expected in late 1941. Once these ships are completed the IJN will have 6 large fleet carriers available, which is of considerable worry to the RN as they will have to find the ships to match them in the Far East (US involvement, although likely, cannot be counted upon as the Americans are still resisting any formal commitments). As yet, the Japanese do not seem to be laying down anything similar to the British light fleet carriers. It is suspected that, like the American navy, this is due to the lesser protection given to trade routes and the long ranges needed to operate in the Pacific Ocean.

The use of the IJN carrier force to assist operations in China, and the use of some of their squadrons on land, has given more information on the aircraft expected to be used on the carriers.

The A5M 'Claude' is a lightweight plane and agile, but considered under-armed with 2 7.7mm machine guns. It isn't fast by the standards now being applied by the RN (indeed, it is barely faster than the Cormorant dive bomber), and as it has been in service since 1936 the navy is anticipating a replacement appearing soon. It is very difficult of obtain intelligence in Japan, but there are indications that a new Mitsubishi fighter flew in the spring of 1939. Efforts are being made to find out more on this aircraft, as it is suspected that this will be the new IJN fleet fighter

The B5 'Kate' torpedo bomber is now confirmed as the main torpedo plane, and its performance is better than was originally thought; it s speed seems to be around 200kt, which means it isn't that inferior to the SeaLance, although once the engine issues are fixed the SpearFish is expected to comfortably outperform it. It also seems to have a good range, and the FAA and RAF boffins are puzzling how it gets the reported performance on a 1,000hp engine. It is suspected that the reports are exaggerating the planes performance.

The current dive bomber, the Aichi D1A 'Susie' is a biplane, and the performance of this dive bomber is considered unexceptional at best by current standards. However it is known that a replacement has been under development (this was expected by the navy), and intelligence suggests it will be operational some time in 1940. It is known to be a monoplane design, and presumably with much better performance than the Susie, but until the IJN (hopefully) uses it in China little information is available.

USA

The new US carrier, USS Wasp, commissioned on the 18th December 1939. Another carrier, the USS Hornet, was laid down on the 3rd March 1939, and is expected to be ready in the second half of 1941 - the building program has been expedited to speed up her construction, and the Americans seem to be using double construction shifts.

No other carriers of this class have been announced, but unofficial talks between the USN and the RN have revealed that due to the war situation the Americans are working on a new class of carrier. This is broadly similar in capability to the British Audacious class, but as yet they are still working on the design. The UK is (unofficially) keeping the US informed of the results of their wartime experience, and a number of USN officers (sorry, Canadian officers...) have been attached to some British ships.

The new fighter for the USN, the Grumman Wildcat, is expected to be operation in the summer of 1940 (the Americans have been pushing the development after getting performance reports on the Goshawk and the German fighters). The F4F-3 is expected to be broadly similar to the Goshawk in performance, although the FAA considers it under-armed. A new fighter, the F4U Corsair, is being developed by Vought aviation, and is expected to fly in may-June 1940. The RN are interested in this plane, as it uses a similar large engine to their Goshawk replacements, and would like to see how it solves some of the problems they have been experiencing.

The USN has two new dive bombers under development; the Curtiss SB2C Helldiver (expected to fly at the end of 1940), and the Douglas SBD Dauntless, expected to fly in April 1940.These are expected to be broadly comparable to the Cormorant dive bomber.

Work has begun on a successor to the Devastator torpedo bomber, but as yet no development contracts have been placed.

It is of course too soon to see any foreign reaction to the raid itself; France sees no issues, as Germany doesn't have aircraft with the range to attack its Atlantic ports. The Americans have a similar expectation - their continental ports are out of range, and they consider Hawaii also outside range of carrier attacks, although they admit their bases in the Philippine Islands could be at risk. As the Japanese navy does (or will soon have) a carrier force capable of replicating the Fleet Air Arm strike, a committee is being organised to look at strengthening the defences (particularly against night attack) of its potentially vulnerable bases.

Chapter 13

The ships available to the Royal Navy for deployment did not only come from Britain. At the start of the war, the other countries in the Empire had also made their ships available to the Admiralty, in particular Canada, Australia and New Zealand. Both Canada and Australia were engaged in building or obtaining aircraft carriers.

The Canadian Aircraft carriers.

The first of the new very light 'Escort Carrier' design, HMS Audacity, had commissioned in Dec 1939 (slightly delayed from her original schedule due to the huge amount of early wartime conversion work in the shipyards). While she had been finishing, the Admiralty had been talking to the Canadian government and their navy about the best way in which Canada could contribute to the naval war. Canada had decided that, as they had no heavy ships and that the Atlantic was obviously the critical convoy area, that they would concentrate on light escort ships to add to the antisubmarine effort in the North Atlantic. This also fit in well with the abilities of the Canadian shipbuilding industry - it was capable of building merchant ships and simple vessels, but gearing up to build the more complex naval vessels would take considerable time (for example Canada could not manufacture complex items like a ships Gyro-Compass) and the early ships would be slow in completing.

The Admiralty were quite happy with this concept - they already knew they were short of the numbers they wanted for light escorts, and passed on details and plans of the new Corvette class. However based on their early experience in the first months of the war, and their projections, they suggested an alteration, which was to also build a couple of escort carriers. This would allow the Royal Canadian Navy to field a couple of balanced escort forces as well as just building corvettes. The Escort carrier was basically a modified merchant ship, so should be easily in the capabilities of the Canadian shipyards. They would supply the machinery (they had, after all, around 50 sets of turbines just sitting in a warehouse), and all that had to be done was to build the hull. By the time it was complete, there would be Swordfish available that had been replaced by SeaLance for the air complement.

This proved of considerable interest to Canada. It fell in with their existing ideas, yet also showed Canada was capable of more than just producing a few small ships. As a result, four sets of machinery were to be shipped to Canada before Christmas, along with all the necessary plans, and they would lay down the two ships in March of 1940, expecting them to be complete around September of 1941; the Canadian corvettes were expected earlier, but the RN thought it would be possible to allocate Canada two of the converted merchant carriers now being constructed early to allow them to become familiar with the use of a carrier as part of an escort force. The RN had six fast liners being converted into simple carriers; this had originally been expected to take around six months per ship, but the heavy load of merchant conversions at the start of the war, and a few problems, meant that they would not be coming available until June-July 1940, 10-11 months. They would carry 12 Swordfish for reconnaissance and anti-submarine patrol, plus 2 fighters to shoot down any enemy planes trying to locate the convoy. While it was hoped later to fit them with radar, the shortage of sets meant that would not happen for some time. However as yet, the air threat in the Atlantic was seen as negligible, only the Condor having the range to operate there. Operationally however it was hoped that by the time they came into service at least one radar-equipped ship would be available in each convoy.

The Admiralty had also been pressing for more of their own escort carriers, but due to the load on the shipyards (and the need to finish trials of Audacity), these were not planned before the spring of 1940.

The Australian Carriers.

The Australian light carrier HMAS Melbourne had been working up in the West Indies in the autumn of 1939. She then sailed for Australia through the Panama Canal, arriving in Sydney on the 20th December to an impressive reception. Minor defects would be fixed in Australia over the next month. The Australian production line for the Goshawk had been delayed to allow it to start off with the Mk II (although as yet the variable-pitch props and a few other items still had to be shipped out from the UK), but it was expected to get the first planes off the production line in March 1940. Originally plans had only allowed for a small production (around five planes per month, just barely enough for Australia), but as war became more certain, this had been increased until the new production line would be producing 15 planes a month, with the option to increase this to 20. There was also the possibility of selling some production to the Dutch, who had evaluated the Mk I with intense interest, especially since the plane and (hopefully by the end of the year) all its parts would be made in Australia, close to the DEI which was where they intended to use them.

The RAN cruisers and destroyers were already being used in coordination with the Royal Navy, particularly in the Mediterranean, but two carrier escort destroyers were building in Australia, and would be ready to join the carrier by the end of 1940. In the meantime, the RAN concentrated on how to use the carrier in the peculiar conditions of the Pacific, and also in learning how to conduct larger operations with the RN carrier assigned to the Far East (in January 1940 this was HMS Eagle). This was considered especially important for two reasons; Melbourne was the first Australian ship to be equipped with radar, and in the event of anything happening with Japan, the two carriers would be in the forefront of any actions against the IJN. While the Australian government had paid for the ship, its arrival was seen as a large and visible sign that Britain had not forgotten about Australia (and to be honest, the RN could at present spare a light carrier rather more than the cruisers and destroyers it was controlling in exchange)

* * *

One conclusion drawn from Operation Chastise was the importance of radar. While this had long been known in the Navies technical departments, the use of it during the raid, and the difference it had made in the fleet defence (even with the mistakes made) had brought this home to the Admiralty. Without the lessons of the raid, it might well have taken much longer for the need for effective radar and control of it to be realised.

Accordingly, the program of fitting the larger warships with radar would be given a very high priority, as would the ongoing program of improvements to the radar systems themselves.

The 279 set (long range air warning) was being fitted as fast as possible; this set also had some surface detection ability, and it is fitted to all the fleet carriers. Work on fitting the light carriers continues. The set is also being developed for better performance.

The ASV Mk I had been developed by the team working at the Royal Aircraft Establishment at Farnborough (they had moved there at the outbreak of war at the instigation of the FAA, who were desperately waiting for a working version). The Mk I set was a disappointment, but Hanbury Brown, who had been in the field helping Coastal Command get ASV.I working, helped another researcher, Gerald Touch of the Farnsworth company, get started on an improved ASV set. An order was placed for 4,000 ASV.II sets in the winter of 1939, but AI was the production priority, and ASV deliveries were delayed. A small number of sets were handmade to give the FAA enough sets to conduct field trials, and pressure was kept on to get the sets in full production as soon as possible.

Touch's "ASV Mark II" was still not everything that was needed, but was a big step forward. On patrol, beams were shot out in the direction of the wingtips to scan a track 40 kilometres (25 miles) wide. If the radar operator picked up a positive contact off a wingtip, the pilot pivoted the aircraft in that direction, with the radar beams sent forward, using lobe switching to pin down the target. The hope of the FAA was that a radar with these capabilities would greatly aid the ability of its search planes to find the enemy in poor weather and particularly at night. The ability to make night attacks had been partially revealed in the Wilhelmshaven raid, but the fact that the FAA could also attacks ships at sea during the night was still a close secret.

The Type 286 radar (a 1.5m system) was being superseded by a new system, the Type 281 (a 3.5m system). This had been developed following work in South Africa and the ongoing development of radar systems for the army. A prototype set was installed on HMS Illustrious during her refit in early 1940. This system offered considerable range and resolution improvements over the Type 279, and a different version (to be fitted to HMS Sheffield in the late summer) would also have surface search capability.

In order to help control the carriers planes (something which had been found difficult to do properly in the action after Wilhelmshaven), the planes were being fitted with by "IFF Mark II", which had been development for some time. Mark II could respond not only to Chain Home (the RAF land-based radar system) signals, but also to 7 meter (42.9 MHz) signals from the MRU and Type 279, the 1.5 meter (200 MHz) signals of Chain Home Low and Navy sets, and the 3.5 meter (86.7 MHz) signals. Unfortunately, though it worked better than IFF Mark I, Mark II was overly complicated and still required in-flight adjustments which made it unpopular with the pilots, although the inconvenience was better than being shot down accidentally by your own fighters.

The navy had also been working on a 50cm system for fire control; this was being developed in two versions, one for surface fire control and one to help control AA fire. It was expected to have this available for service before the end of 1940.

The success of the raid also caused the Admiralty to review its carrier programme. Before his replacement, Admiral Pound had been keen on reducing the current building program in favour of escorts. After the requirements for these had been filled, he had intended to then build more battleships. His replacement was not so fixed on this, and indeed the First Lord, Winston Churchill, was very keen on the carriers, as they seemed to be the only really effective way of going on the attack, rather than just responding to German threats. It was also pointed out that while indeed escorts were urgently needed, a more flexible escort group, centred around a carrier, was more effective and that continuing the carrier program would in fact lead to less losses to U-boats over the next couple of years. As a result of this, the carrier program would have second priority after the escorts (which in any case used smaller slipways), and the cruiser program would be slowed while the battleships would be halted indefinitely.

The Carrier building program as of 1/1/1940 was as follows :

Fleet Carriers

HMS Implacable (April 1940), HMS Indefatigable (June 1940), HMS Bulwark (July 1941).

It was hoped to keep to this schedule, although it was realised there might be some slippage; it would also depend on the pilot training programme continuing on schedule, although if necessary carriers could come into service with reduced air groups.

HMS Audacious (Jun 42), HMS Irresistible (Aug 42)

The navy would like to order additional Audacious class carriers, but there were issues as to fitting them into the building program. Discussions are ongoing; the FAA wants more carriers at the expense of the Lion class battleships (which have barely been started, and are currently on hold), the surface ship Admirals want the battleships, as they point out the number of carriers building compared to five replacement battleships.

Light Fleet carriers

HMS Ocean (June 1940), HMS Edgar (July 1940), HMS Theseus (Sep 1940).

HMS Unicorn (carrier repair ship) was originally expected in Aug 1940, but due to the pressure of other, more urgent, work, is now not expected until Nov 1940.

The navy wants more light carriers to release the fleet carriers for more offensive roles. The Colossus class has proved very successful, and a modified, larger version has been under design for some time. This will incorporate some improvements, and allow the carriers to continue to operate the same size air group with the newer, larger planes. The arrangements are also being altered in the assumption that (by the time they are complete), deck parks will be much more prevalent, as it is already acknowledged that their main failing is lack of aircraft.

Three ships are authorised to start building in Dec 1939; HMS Magnificent, HMS Terrible and HMS Majestic. They are expected to complete in Feb-April 1942

Escort carriers

The Admiralty wanted additional purpose-built escort carriers to the recently-completed HMS Audacity, to allow the faster, better quipped light carriers to be used more with the fleet, and in the Far East. The building program, while heavily loaded, had sufficient capability to allow 4 more Escort carriers to be started in December 1939, completion expected around May 1941. Fortunately, these ships did not suffer from the equipment bottlenecks already affecting the build of the surface fleet, and the machinery was already available for them.

Converted merchant ships

Pre-war plans had provisionally allocated 5 liners for conversion to escort carriers (Winchester Castle, Warwick Castle, Dunvegan Castle, Dunottor Castle and Reina del Pacifica). These were retained for that purpose, although there was pressure for these to be converted to auxiliary cruisers; however as nearly 40 ships were already allocated to that role it was felt that additional light carriers would be more useful and flexible.

In addition two ships, Athene and Engadine, has been taken up for conversion to aircraft transport ships. When the FAA looked at the proposals, they pointed out that if these ships were also converted to Escort carriers, in addition to that role they could carry nearly as many planes (on the hanger deck and flight deck) as the dedicated transport ships, and would be far more flexible.

As a result, all 7 ships were taken up for conversion; the time to convert varied considerably due to the individual ships, but the first conversion was expected in Oct 1940, with the rest to follow soon after (having the plans ready before the war had helped, but the shipyards were rather busier with early war work than had been anticipated). These ships will be slower than the escort carriers, and are intended to work with the slower convoys, allowing the faster purpose-built ships to be reserved for the fast convoys.

Chapter 14

16th January.

Three British submarines, HMS Seahorse, HMS Undine and HMS Starfish, are lost after penetrating the Heligoland bight. This attempt to keep pressure on the German fleet and its training grounds shows that the area is currently too dangerous for ships, and that any attacks should be made by air. The problem is that Bomber command seems unable to find anything much smaller than a country at night, and if the carrier force is to be kept at a reasonable distance, there is a problem with the range. The problem of attacks will be investigated assuming the new TBR planes are fully in service, with a view to a possible future raid

21st February

The German freighter Nordmark, who had replaced the sunk Altmark as the Graf Spee's supply ship during her brief raiding career in the South Atlantic, is intercepted by British destroyers in Norwegian waters thanks to British intelligence on her movements. The ship was supposed to have been searched by the Norwegians (the transport of captured seamen through a neutral territory being forbidden), but they had apparently been 'missed'. Captain Vian of HMS Cossack boarded the Nordmark, and released the prisoners with subsequent publicity. Both the Norwegian government and the German government protested the boarding of a ship in neutral waters; the British government simply pointed to the released prisoners.

This incident as, however, to strengthen Churchill's hand in his insistence on mining the Norwegian leads, and the operation was planned, to start in April.

16th March

The Germans bombed Scapa Flow again, as the anchorage had now resumed its function as the Home Fleets main base. About 20 Ju88's attacked during daylight.

Unfortunately for the Luftwaffe, in addition to the new AA guns placed at the base since their last raid, there was also a considerable fighter presence. Scapa was currently home to three fleet carriers, as well as having its own two dedicated squadrons of Goshawks, and the radar system had been improved, giving the defence a longer warning period. There were therefore five squadrons of fighters at the attached airbase, although only two were on alert at any time (the squadrons belonging to the carriers were tasked with sharing the defensive duties for training purposes). As it was, 36 fighters were available, 18 of these on short notice and 9 available immediately (5 minutes warning, and the rest on standby).

The attackers were detected on radar some 60 miles away. With more training, and more experience, the warning and control system was working more efficiently now. The 9 ready planes were able to get airborne and to a suitable altitude for interception (the Ju88's apparently intended to attack from about 10,000 feet, either by level bombing or dive bombing) The other 9 aircraft got airborne, but had to attack on the climb as they did not scramble fast enough to gain altitude. Fortunately, this was not as dangerous against unescorted bombers as it would have been against fighters.

This was the first time the Luftwaffe had encountered the Mk II Goshawk, and it was not a pleasant surprise. Six of the attackers were shot down before the fighters broke off to regroup and let the rest of the squadron engage. The approaching fighters attacked from head on, which not only broke up any remaining semblance of a formation among the bombers, but also shot down another three aircraft. As soon as they had passed through the bombers, the original fighters dove down at them again, causing four more to crash into the sea.

With 13 out of their original 20 planes already shot down (and still 5 miles away from the target), the remaining bombers jettisoned their load and ran. Two more were shot down in the process (the Ju88's were a fast bomber, but the Goshawk was faster), and two more were damaged (one of these crashed on the way home)

Of the 15 planes shot down, one managed to crash on land, the crew injured but surviving. Of those that went into the sea, one crew was rescued by a navy trawler, the others were lost - the waters off Scapa are very cold in March.

After this, it would be a long while before the Luftwaffe decided to try another attack on Scapa Flow, the only air activity would be very high altitude reconnaissance flights which the Goshawks lacked the high level performance to intercept

During the period January-March, a number of the light carriers had been tasked to escorting convoys (in particular the high value and fast convoys). Unlike the earlier abortive attempts last September, these had been close escort missions, using their TBR planes to search and if possible attack surfaced U-boats, or keep them down so their low underwater speed made it impossible for them to intercept the convoy before it was out of range.

This had been very successful. It was not certain yet exactly how well the system was working - the bulk of sinkings by U-boat were still of stragglers or ships sailing independently, but only one ship had been sunk in a convoy with air escort (it was thought this was possible a U-boat which had simply been in the right position, by accident, to make an attack), and the method was looking very promising. The main problem was the lack of carriers, and also a lack of escorts which were stopping the escort groups from being able to do much more than protect the convoys - only a handful of U-boats had been sunk.

One carrier, HMS Mars, had been damaged by a mine (thought to be a magnetic mine) close to the UK on the 14th Feb. The mine had caused serious underwater damage, but the navy was very pleased to learn that the ships protective system, designed to work against torpedoes, worked well against mines as well. The ships aft engine room had been flooded, but the two engineering spaces were separated, and the system of sealed drums had limited the flooding. Indeed, she arrives back at port under her own power (though rather lower in the water than usual), and her Captain claimed that if necessary she could have flown off aircraft! The damage was estimated to take about 10 weeks to fix, and the ship was expected to be back in service in early May (in fact due to pressure of other damage repairs she was not actually ready until the end of June).

Chapter 15

The Norway Campaign

The fight for Norway was one of the most confusing and mismanaged campaigns ever fought by the British in recent time.

It didn't help that it was started by the collision of two completely different plans, the British plans to lay minefields to close off the sea routes that iron ore ships were taking to Germany, and if necessary land troops, and the German plans to invade Norway to, among other things, safeguard those same ore supplies, ran head on into each other, and in bad weather at that.

In spite of abandoning plans to help Finland, Britain and France had decided to disrupt Swedish iron ore traffic to Germany by mining Norwegian waters (Operation Wilfred). Plans were also made to land troops in Norway, from south to north, at Stavanger, Bergen, Trondheim and Narvik to forestall any German retaliation (Operation R4). The entire operation was timed for 8th April.

On the 3rd April, the first German troop transports sailed for Norway as part of Operation Weserubung. They were followed on the 7th by naval vessels, some carrying further troops, the others to cover the entire operation. This basically consisted of all the available surface ships in the Kriegsmarine.

However on the 4th April sixteen Allied submarines ordered to the Skagerrak and Kattegat to serve as a screen and advance warning for a German response to Operation Wilfred. On the following day, HMS Renown set out from Scapa with HMS Colossus and 12 destroyers heading for the Vestfjord. As the opposition of heavy units was not expected, Colossus had embarked 12 Dive Bombers and 9 Fighters, plus 8 TBR for reconnaissance and anti-submarine work (it was intended to use the Cormorants in the reconnaissance role to supplement the Swordfish.

German attack Gruppe for the initial Norway landings

Gruppe 1 - 9 destroyers (headed for Narvik)

Gruppe 2 - Hipper + 3 destroyers (headed for Trondheim)

Gruppe 3 - Nurnberg, Konigsberg + support ships (headed for Bergen)

Gruppe 4 - Karlsruhe + support ships (headed for Kristiansand)

Gruppe 5 - Blucher, Lutzow + support ships headed for Oslo)

Gruppe 6 - 4 minesweepers (headed for Egersund)

The Scharnhorst and Gneisenau are with Gruppes 1 and 2 before they separate

7th April

On the 7th April, the weather worsened in the North Sea, causing large areas of thick fog and heavy seas, as well as rain and snow. Renown's force was, as a result, unable to operate the usual aerial reconnaissance. During a heavy snowstorm, one of the escorting destroyers, HMS Glowworm, dropped out of the formation to search for a man who had been swept overboard in the heavy seas. For the Germans, however, the weather was a huge advantage, as it gave them a much better chance not to be spotted by the RN on the way to their targets, and Gruppe 1 and Gruppe 2 set out early on the morning. They were accompanied by the Scharnhorst and Gneisenau who would be their covering force until they separated.

At around 0800 on the 7th, the two groups were spotted by RAF reconnaissance planes 100m off southern Norway. Although this was reported to Renown, this took some time (coordination between Coastal Command and the Fleet was still inefficient) and due to the poor weather and the range, no strike was attempted as the RAF had agreed to attack them (even though they were, apparently, not a city...) Unfortunately as was the norm with RAF attacks on shipping no hits were obtained, and it was not until 1730 (the aircraft were, oddly, operating under radio silence even though their location had been obvious once they attacked) that the forces was reported as being a battlecruiser, two cruisers and ten destroyers. They had also been found 80 miles north of the original position.

As a result of the sighting and movements of the force, Admiral Forbes (C in C Home Fleet) decided that the force was attempting a breakout into the North Atlantic (due to failures and miscommunications in British intelligence, although there was clear indications of an invasion of Norway, he was not informed of this possibility). Units of the Home Fleet sailed from Scapa at 2030 that evening to take up blocking positions, into weather that was still worsening.

That evening, in the middle of appalling weather and snowstorms, the Glowworm encountered two of the destroyers escorting Hipper. She attacked them, and they turned away, leading her onto the Hipper. The destroyer attacked the heavy cruiser with little effect. Although hit herself she managed to ram the cruiser, damaging her side, before being sunk. Unfortunately HMS Glowworm did not get off a complete sighting report.

On the morning of the 8th April, the Polish submarine Orzel sank the clandestine German troopship the Rio de Janeiro off the Norwegian port of Lillesand. In the wreckage of the ship were found uniformed German soldiers and other military supplies. This was reported to the Admiralty, but at the time they were busy with the Glowworm encounter, and still thinking that the Kriegsmarine was planning a breakout. As a result, they did not pass the information along to Forbes.

Norwegian fishing boats and the Norwegian destroyer Odin rescued German soldiers from the ship, and on being questioned revealed that they were being sent to Bergen to 'help protect Norway from the Allies'. This information was passed on to Oslo and the Norwegian Parliament, who ignored it.

At 1400, aerial reconnaissance by Coastal Command informed the Admiralty that they had located a group of German ships west-northwest of Trondheim, heading west. This course was due to the Gruppe 'marking time' until ready to land their troops. However the position and course suggested that the Germans were indeed trying to break out into the Atlantic and the Home Fleet units changed direction to northwest to try and intercept them. While the weather was still very poor, the Illustrious (carrier support for the Home Fleet detachment) flew off a reconnaissance force of 8 Swordfish (although the 18-strong strike squadron was now equipped with the SeaLance TBR, the search and anti-submarine squadron was still flying Swordfish) to try and pinpoint the location of the ships. The strike squadron and the dive-bombing squadron were held until a target had been found.

Until the aircraft had had a chance to locate the German fleet it was decided to hold the cruiser and light forces available in the UK until the disposition of the force could be determined, although to allow them to sail at short notice the troops they had embarked were offloaded. Forbes had HMS Illustrious available immediately, with HMS Colossus close by, and despite the poor weather felt that search planes from these two carriers would be sufficient to allow him to pinpoint the Germans. His air advisor had pointed out that the weather would also limit the visibility from surface ships, and that more ships 'swanning around' would just lead to the possibility of confusion in identification. It was now April, with reasonable hours of daylight, and he hoped to get sighting reports before the evening. If that failed, he had in reserve the 4 SeaLance of his search squadron equipped with the early ASV II radar. The sets were new, and the operators not yet expert, but it offered the chance of finding and shadowing the Germans after nightfall, which meant he could conduct a night attack by air then close to sink them with his battleships in the morning. As soon as the enemy was located, the waiting cruiser force would join up with HMS Formidable. His main problem at the moment was actually finding the Germans with the state of the weather.

The aerial search revealed nothing - possibly because of the bad weather. The main reason was probably that the enemy force had in fact headed for Trondheim rather than keep to their original course. By the evening, Forbes had been getting numerous reports and sightings of German ships south of Norway (ironically perhaps they seemed to be just about everywhere except where his search planes were looking for them...), and as a result started to change his mind as to the possibility that the Germans were planning a breakout into the Atlantic. The Home Fleet turned to head south to the Skaggerak, while HMS Repulse with a cruiser and some destroyers headed north to join Renown. In order to give himself more aircraft, he ordered HMS Formidable to come to two hours notice to steam, and HMS Victorious to stand by to unload the aircraft she was loading to take to the Mediterranean (she was currently loading 24 fighters for Malta, then would replace Ark Royal at Gibraltar so that she could return home for a minor refit). Once he had more information about the enemy, his intention was to move Formidable up with a cruiser force, either for a joint attack with Illustrious or a pincer movement, depending on where he found the enemy. Alternatively, if the Germans seemed to be staying close to Norway, he would send in one or more coastal sweeps of his light forces, supported by airstrikes as soon as conditions improved.

At 2300, just as Forbes was learning of the Orzel's action, Gruppe 5 (the cruisers Blucher, Lutzow, plus support ships) was being confronted by the Norwegian patrol vessel Pol III off the Oslofjord. Raising the alarm, the patrol boat attacked the German force. The German forces continued into the fjord, clearing the outer defensive batteries without damage, and then split off some of their small ships to capture the bypassed forts.

This activity was reported to the Norwegian cabinet in Oslo. The cabinet ordered a mobilization, however for reasons which were not understood at the time (or indeed later), the Defence minister did not point out a secret mobilization would be done by post and take days; he had already refused repeated calls for mobilization from his senior generals.

Further north, Whitworth in HMS Renown was waiting for support and for the weather to ease to launch a new search for the enemy units he was sure were close-by. In view of the weather and very limited visibility, he did not want to leave the carrier unprotected - the mix of bad weather, poor visibility and possible heavy enemy units in the vicinity being the 'worse case' scenario discussed before the war, allowing a carrier to be surprised by a surface force.

His problem was the same as Forbes; actually finding the enemy. He was reluctant to simply run around chasing (possibly misleading) sighting reports, as this could do more harm than good. Once he had a cruiser and some more destroyers, he would detach the carrier with protection and close the Norwegian coast while the carrier planes hopefully located the enemy for him to attack. His decision making was not helped by the rather contradictory information coming from the Admiralty.

Despite the bad weather, his force then encountered two German destroyers (they were part of Gruppe 1 heading for Narvik, separated from the main force due to the terrible weather conditions and having eased further away from the notoriously dangerous Norwegian coast. These made the mistake of running into Renown and her escorting destroyers. The carrier kept her distance with her two escorts while the Renown and her destroyers engaged the German ships. One of them was sunk quickly - 15" shells and destroyers do not make a good combination, while the second was pursued by the British ships. She was soon hit and disabled by one of the British destroyers, and then, surprisingly, surrendered. She was found to be heavily laden with troops (presumably why she had surrendered), but it took some time to establish this and that they had intercepted part of a force landing at Narvik.

9th April

Whitworth hoped that his interception of two of the nine destroyers heading for Narvik would help the defenders. Sadly, this made no difference, as the Norwegian commander surrendered immediately to the German troops without a fight (He was later tried and sentenced for treason). To try and aid the Norwegians, Whitworth detached six of his destroyers with orders to enter the fjord and sink the German destroyers. The weather was easing, and he expected to be able to support them with an air search and strike from Colossus. The other search planes were tasked to locate the heavy ships apparently with the German force (unknown to him, Scharnhorst and Gneisenau were now to seaward of him). HMS Repulse would soon join his force, and once he had located the enemy he intended to attack with the battlecruisers and their supporting destroyers (with, if possible, a disabling air strike from his carrier). The attack on the fjord was planned to go in at 1000 on the 10th - given the poorly charted and rugged nature of the fjord, and the availability of air cover in daylight, a night attack was considered too risky. It would hopefully allow him to locate the German ships sometime during the day; if he found them, then the destroyer force would keep station outside the fjord and keep them bottled up until he could destroy them at odds (he saw no reason to offer the Germans anything like a fair fight if he could avoid it), although the decision on when and how to engage was left up to the destroyers.

Four of the cruisers currently ready in Britain were ordered to Scapa to join up with HMS Formidable. This would give a second force capable of pinning any German units found against the heavy ships of the Home Fleet.

The landing by Gruppe 2 at Trondhiem encountered only minor resistance, the Hipper engaging the defensive batteries while the destroyers steamed past. Only one of the destroyers received minor damage. Once the landings had taken place, the examination started of the Hipper to determine exactly what damage had been done in the ramming so she could be patched up to get back to Germany safely where she could be properly repaired.

The landing by Gruppe 3 at Bergen was subject to more resistance, and the fortifications damaged both the light cruiser Konigsberg and the artillery training ship Bremse. The damage to Konigsberg was serious, and would take some time to repair sufficiently for her to travel safely to Germany (the poor weather lead the Captain to insist on making the ship seaworthy before sailing). The forces landing ships were, however, able to dock without serious opposition and the fortifications surrendered when Luftwaffe units arrived overhead.

Gruppe 4 encountered much stiffer resistance at Kristiansand, the fortifications twice repulsing the landings and damaging the cruiser Karlsruhe, which nearly ran aground as it attempted to evade their fire. However there was confusion among the defenders when the Norwegians received a general order not to fire on French or British units, and the Germans had captured codes from Horten which they also used to deceive and confuse the defenders. This allowed the Germans to reach the harbour and the town was captured by 1100.

The most serious resistance to the landings was encountered by Gruppe 5 in the inner defensive fortifications of the Oslofjord. The heavy cruiser Blucher approached the forts, apparently with the idea that they would be taken by surprise, but instead the ship was fired on when it reached point blank range, finally being sunk by salvo of 40-year old torpedoes from land-based tubes. The light cruiser Lutzow was also damaged, and withdrew 12 miles south to Sonsbukten with the rest of Gruppe 5, where they unloaded their troops. This delayed the arrival of these troops to Oslo by 24 hours, but the city would be captured in less than 12 hours by troops flown into Fomebu airfield.

There was no significant opposition to Gruppe 6 (aided by paratroops) at Stavanger and the objective was captured without loss.

While these landings have been going on, the Royal Navy had belatedly deduced that the German operation was an invasion of Norway rather than at attempt at a breakout. There were currently two main forces at sea; heavy forces of the Home Fleet with HMS Illustrious (currently sailing north around 70 miles west of Bergen), and the battlecruisers with HMS Colossus southwest of Narvik, with 6 destroyers detached to the Narvik fjord.

In view of the use of her planes to support the destroyer attack on Narvik, Colossus was not able to mount a full search with her remaining planes - she only had eight TBR aircraft, and in view of the invasion needed some of these for A/S patrols. She kept three of her nine fighters up in a CAP, as it was considered only a matter of time before the Luftwaffe intervened. Her search planes did not find any German ships in the vicinity (at this point, Scharnhorst and Gneisenau were sailing west, away from the force, and the search planes were looking in the wrong place)

In order to strengthen his airpower, the main concern at the moment being to locate the German forces and protect the surface ships, Forbes ordered HMS Warspite and HMS Formidable, with a cruiser and a destroyer escort, to sail from Scapa to a position about 100m west of Trondheim; they could then either operate independently or reinforce the two forces as needed.

HMS Victorious was ordered to disembark the fighters for Malta, and to re-embark her air group. HMS Glorious, currently undergoing a minor refit, was ordered to be ready for sea in 72 hours; in addition, HMS Venerable, then escorting a convoy close to the UK, was ordered to Scapa, the intention being to reinforce the battlecruiser force to two light carriers, a single light carrier not considered sufficient when both air and submarine attack was probably, which would soon be the case close to Norway.

The cruiser forces currently available in the UK were to prepare to conduct operations under the air cover of the carriers. There was, unfortunately, still a severe shortage of destroyers, and consideration was given to how and when to use Force H as reinforcements.

Coastal command was also asked to help the fleet units search for the rather elusive heavy units in the North. Forbes was confident that they would be found soon enough; with Whitworth off Narvik, and a sizeable part of the Home Fleet off Bergen, at some point they had to come past one or the other of them to try and head back to Germany. While Churchill at the Admiralty was fuming at what he thought was the timidity of Whitworth in not attempting to close the Germans, Frazer had (with considerable patience) pointed out that he was doing what he and Forbes wanted; covering Narvik while waiting for the Germans to emerge from the cover of the weather. They couldn't get home without getting past the Home Fleet, which he thought unlikely as the weather was slowly improving and he had considerable air assets available to spot them, at which point he could engage and destroy them at favourable odds. Indeed, if he gone in search of them then they would not have encountered the Gruppe 1 destroyers, and they might not have known about Narvik.

While the German land forces had up until now been extremely successful in the seizing of key targets, and the naval forces (rather more by luck and bad weather than anything else) had delivered their cargoes, the British now had a clearer idea of where and where the German forces were.

The British had received information as to the action at Bergen from Norwegian radio reports, although they did not realize that the Konigsberg was seriously damaged. While Forbes only had one carrier with him, unlike the battlecruisers this was a full fleet carrier, with an air group of nearly 70 planes available. As the force reported at the port was two large ships plus some supporting vessels, the estimate was that they were two cruisers - it was not thought likely one of the twins would go into Bergen so close to the Home Fleet units. Accordingly, a full stroke of 18 Cormorants was prepared, with 6 Goshawks as escort. Forbes did consider releasing forces for a surface attack, but it was not known if the shore batteries were operational and in German hands. A backup strike with torpedoes was planned in case the dive bombing proved insufficient (or there were more German ships in the fjord than was thought); the Cormorant strike would hopefully provide that information.

The strike gave some concern to the operations officers; this was to be the first strike that was expected to encounter enemy fighters and the first escorted strike in wartime. While it was hoped that the navigation of the fighter pilots, aided by radar and the homing beacons, would bring them all back safely, this was the first time it would be tried in combat, rather than in training. The FAA had made a decision years ago to follow the US practice of single-pilot fighters, and were fervently hoping all the worrying they had done since about not providing a navigator would be proved false. The remaining 12 fighters were reserved for the defence of the fleet; three planes on CAP, three ready on deck with six more planes available.

While the crews had been nervous about the presence of Luftwaffe fighters, in fact the port was undefended, (the Luftwaffe was indeed in Norway in force, but busy in the southern part of the country against the Norwegian resistance). As a result they were able to conduct an undisturbed attack. The first target was the Konigsberg - the crews did not realize she was already heavily damaged, and she was the first target they saw. She was attacked by a total of 12 Cormorants, who achieved two hits. In addition to the earlier damage she had suffered, two 1,000 bomb hits were more than enough to finish off the cruiser, and she sank on an even keel in the harbour.

The remaining six planes targeted the cruiser Nurnberg. Only one bomb hit, although a second was close enough to cause underwater damage by shock and some flooding. The bomb hit the ship forward, destroying one of the turrets and causing considerable damage to the bridge and forward structure, killing many of the bridge crew. Unfortunately, the damage was not great enough to leave the ship in danger of sinking, although it took the crew the rest of the day to handle and temporarily patch the underwater damage and flooding.

The reports of the strike, and the evaluation that a second cruiser was damaged, but not yet sunk, would normally have resulted in a second attack from Illustrious (she had a full TBR squadron available for a torpedo attack, and it was now known that as yet the port had no air defence. But this was cancelled as the fleet suffered the first Luftwaffe attack of the Norwegian campaign, a mixed force of Ju88 and He111 bombers attacking from the south. The CAP was directed onto them, but obviously more than three fighters were needed and the ready flight of three was sent off immediately. This was to show up a weakness in the RN's use of defending fighters; when they were needed to reinforce the CAP they were needed soon, if not immediately, and the current practice of rationing the available fighters was not working well enough. It had originally been designed to cope with reconnaissance flights or small groups of planes, and while the possibility of larger strikes from land bases had been considered, the doctrine hadn't been updated to cope properly with these.

The first three fighters intercepted the bombers well away from the carrier and heavy ships, breaking up the attack of the Ju88's (due to their recently-discovered dive bombing ability, these were now considered priority targets over the Heinkels), shooting down one. A general melee ensued, but the complex situation was not well handled by the still-inexperienced controllers on the carrier, and although the attackers were forced away from the fleet, aided by the arrival of the next three fighters, no more bombers were shot down, although one was damaged (it later crash-landed in Norway). The bombers dropped their bombs vaguely in the area of a couple of the escorting destroyers, before making their escape (giving the bridge crew of HMS Gurkha both a scare and a soaking from a couple of near misses). The fighters were called back from pursuing the bombers as it was not known what other Luftwaffe forces were in the area.

Once the fighters had been brought back (and the original CAP landed on to refuel and rearm), the fleet headed west to give themselves more room and hopefully warning in case of subsequent air attack. The withdrawal did not, in the end, help the Nurnberg; she sailed that night in an attempt to sneak home to Germany, but was intercepted by the submarine HMS Truant (who had been lying patiently in wait all day), torpedoed and sunk.

10th April, Narvik, 1000.

Although the British destroyers still did not know the Narvik garrison had surrendered, their intention was to attack and destroy the German destroyer force (while it was possible that heavy units had accompanied the destroyers into the fjord, this was thought unlikely, as they would be trapped there).

The attack was coordinated with a search mission flown off HMS Colossus; two Swordfish had been flown off to search the fjord and act as spotting planes; four more of her Swordfish were searching for the heavy ships, the other two being used on A/S duties. The carriers 12 Cormorants were readied to carry out a strike at Narvik once the information as to the size and the location of the German destroyers was know; the dive bombers were thought to have a better chance of hits against an agile destroyer.

The two Swordfish spotted six destroyers in the fjord (there were actually seven, but it seems they missed one), and what they assumed were supply ships of some sort, as well as a considerable amount of neutral shipping. The carrier strike was timed to arrive over the fjord just as the destroyer force entered. Weather was poor (there were constant snow flurries), but acceptable, and as there seemed no risk of fighters this far north the dive bombers could take their time.

As the six British destroyers entered the fjord and commenced to sail up it to Narvik, the dive bombers arrived. Since they had enough fuel to permit them to loiter for a time, the examined the fjord themselves, and picked out three German destroyers as targets. The visibility was poor, with snow showers, but the limited sea-room in the fjord meant that the planes could get frequent sight of targets (although not always the same target!). Because of the poor and variable visibility, it was decided to attack the first two ships visible in groups of three planes once the attack order had been given. Soon after the British ships entered, the German destroyers started to head out, it was assumed alerted by spotters near to the fjords entrance. The Cormorants immediately attacked two of the destroyers, in an attempt to sink or disable them and to throw the force into confusion before the British force closed.

Apparently the Germans had not realized that the new planes were actually dive bombers; it was later found that their examination of the fjord had been taken for more reconnaissance, a view confirmed (to them) by the arrival of a British destroyer squadron. As a result, the two attacks were much more successful than

115

anticipated. The first destroyer was hit by one 1,000 bomb and immediately slewed to a halt, on fire. It would sink 15 minutes later. The second was hit by one bomb, amidships, but this was more than sufficient to wreck a destroyer's relatively fragile machinery and bring her to a halt in the middle of the fjord. A second bomb landed close enough in the water to stove her in underwater, and she was seen to be going down by the head.

The attack indeed caused confusion among the remaining five German ships, and as a result the Royal navy force had arrived and was firing on them before they had recovered from the air strike. Two of the large German destroyers were hit before they managed to get a single hit on their attackers. The attack developed into a sort of free-for-all, with destroyers trying to manoeuvre radically in the confined fjord, while shooting at each other and trying for torpedo attacks. Seeing this, the second Cormorant flight decided to make a dummy attack (they had no bombs left), on one of the German destroyers to see if they could help. Ironically, this attack with no bomb load proved at least as damaging as their earlier attack. Not realizing that the planes were unarmed, the destroyer responded by some violent helm actions to evade, which ended abruptly when she ran onto the rocks.

The final result of the action was two German destroyers sunk by the dive bombers, one sunk (or at least a permanent decoration on one side of the fjord) after running aground, one sunk by torpedo attack and the other three disabled and on fire. Three of the Royal Navy destroyers were seriously damaged, one sinking later due to a torpedo hit. The remaining three only received light damage, which left the Royal Navy in command of the fjord. No Cormorants were lost to the AA fire. Once the German destroyers had been defeated, the destroyers also sank or forced to surrender a number of German supply ships, but as they had no troops with them there was nothing they could do about the Germans in the town itself except report the fact.

The decisive defeat of the destroyers was, however, to prove of value in the battle for Narvik. While a number of survivors from the destroyers made it to shore, the bulk of the crews were rescued by the British destroyers. If they had been allowed ashore, it is possible they could have been a considerable help to the 1500 German soldiers already ashore; as it was, they ended up in British PoW camps, and only around 200 were available to help the invaders. Having full control of the fjord, the British force boarded the merchant ships in the port (there were around a dozen, including some British ships), the small number of German soldiers on them being rather intimidated by the sight of the muzzle of a 4.7" gun pointing at them, and a small convoy was assembled higher up the fjord (it would sail for the UK on the following day). At one point in the action, a small force of German soldiers in the port area tried firing on one of the destroyers, but with nothing heavier than a machine gun they were driven away by the ships light AA weapons.

10th April, North Sea/Trondheim, 1200.

The movement west of the Home Fleet units had allowed them to join up with HMS Warspite, HMS Formidable and their escorts. The carrier air groups were at nearly full strength (Illustrious had lost a few planes due to damage and landing accidents), and as a result Forbes was able to put out a comprehensive search pattern to the north of his ships (there were not thought to be any German heavy units to the south, but in any case this area was being covered by squadrons from Coastal Command.

While the search for the mysteriously missing German heavy ships went on, Forbes had ordered a strike on the Hipper, last reported in Trondheim harbour. At 1200 the strike was readied on deck; Two reconnaissance planes (with an escort of two fighters), had been sent off a half hour earlier to check that she was still in the port. She was (apparently the crew were working to repair the damage caused by Glowworm ramming her sufficiently to allow her to return safely to Kiel for more lasting repairs). At 1300 18 SeaLance torpedo planes and 18 Cormorants set off for Trondheim, accompanied by 10 Goshawk fighters (the search planes had not reported any fighters, but the carrier force still had 26 fighters available for fleet defence). In addition, the search planes reported two destroyers (there were actually three)

The weather had improved noticeably since the previous day, and the planes found the fjord and flew up it to the harbour. The reconnaissance planes had been radioing the position of the targets and that there seemed to be no AA except for that of the Hipper and her escorts. As yet, there was no sign of enemy fighters. These had in fact been requested by the Captain of the Hipper, but the situation in southern Norway was still confused, and cooperation between the Kriegsmarine and the Luftwaffe was never good at the best of times.

The torpedo planes attacked first, in heavy AA fire from the Hipper and her three escorting destroyers. While they had been on their way to the fjord, the ships had got underway and were making their way out of the fjord - not, as it turned out, fast enough, and nowhere close to evading the planes watching her from above. Although Trondheim is a fjord, it is a very large fjord and neither the ships nor the attacking planes were particularly constrained in their movements. As usual, the torpedo planes attacked in groups of three. They could clearly see the damage to the cruisers side, though at this time they could only speculate as to what had caused it. The cruiser managed to evade the first six torpedoes, but one of the planes in the third wave got a hit on the forward

117

section of the ship. The next wave missed again, but the last two flights were much more successful, two more torpedoes hitting her, one centre, and one aft. The aft hit seemed to have damaged her steering, as the ship started moving erratically, then slowed, listing to starboard.

The timing of this was poor, as there were still 18 dive bombers circling waiting to attack. The attack itself was, however, disrupted by the late arrival of eight Me110 fighters, which were engaged by the escorting Goshawks. They managed to gain the attention of six of the Me110's, however two evaded the defenders and went for the dive bombers waiting to attack. The torpedo planes, less two which had been shot down by the AA fire (one crashed-landed in the fjord, but sadly the crew did not survive the freezing waters), were in the meantime heading out of the fjord at zero feet and maximum speed.

The first planes were already in their attack, and indeed half of them managed to avoid the attention of the attackers by continuing their dives, a manoeuvre the Me110 couldn't match. As a result of the chaos, only one bomb hit the Hipper (the dive bombers being understandably distracted), which destroyed her B turret but did not appear to cause much more damage. The remaining 9 dive bombers stayed in a group to defend themselves, and the massed firepower did cause the Me110's difficulties. Although they damaged a number of the Cormorants, they only shot down two, and at that point they had to break off due to lack of ammunition. Meanwhile the six planes attacking the Goshawks had shot down two Goshawks and damaged one more for the loss of two of their own. Again, this fight petered out.

Five of the Cormorants had survived the Me110 attack without apparent damage, and despite the fact that they did not know if more defending fighters would arrive, they attacked anyway. One more bomb hit the Hipper, and this time the 1,000lb bomb did much more serious damage, destroying one engine room and causing numerous fires. The Hipper was left listing steeply and burning as the planes made their way back to the carrier. One divebomber was lost - it went straight into the water without trying to pull out, and it was assumed that the pilot had been hit or the controls damaged.

Back at the Illustrious they were very disappointed at the poor results obtained from the strike (it was not realized yet just how inopportune the intervention of the Me110's had been). The search planes had still not identified any heavy units at sea, and so a cruiser and three destroyers were detached to move southeast to block an attempt to escape south by the Hipper, while the Formidable spotted another twelve dive bombers and six fighters. This strike was not ready before the first strike returned, but by using one carrier it was possible to land all the damaged planes on Illustrious so as not to delay any further - given the terrain of the fjord, a night attack was not considered a serious option for just a cruiser. This time the planes would be on the lookout for fighters. The carriers were close enough to Trondheim that the undamaged planes could wait for the strike to clear. Landing planes on a different carrier was not the preferred option for the FAA - keeping the squadrons together was considered very important - but in this case the advantage was obvious. Once the strike had been struck down, the carriers launched of CAP replacement (they now had eight planes in the air), as it was assumed that the Luftwaffe would be searching for them. The hope was to finish the Hipper, then retire west away from the coast and reorganize - there were still hopes of finding at least one of the German battleships at sea, as they hadn't been reported as being involved in any of the coastal actions.

The second strike arrived at Trondheim at about 1600. This time the protecting fighters looked carefully for any enemy air cover, but as none was seen, they signalled to the dive bombers to go in. Although the Hipper's captain had been requesting air cover, it was simply not possible at this time for the Luftwaffe in southern Norway to provide continuous cover. This time, the report of planes over the fjord would result in the Luftwaffe arriving too late.

The air strike had headed first for Trondheim as they were not sure if the Hipper would still be there, of if she would have made it out to sea - while she seemed to have taken heavy damage earlier, this was thought a possibility. However the cruiser was found close to the harbour - the original damage by two 1,000lb bombs and three aerial torpedoes had damaged her severely, and she only had damage control parties on board, the rest of the crew having been evacuated to the town. This was the sort of sitting, undefended target that FAA pilots prayed for. The first six Cormorants got two hits on the ship, both of which exploded spectacularly. So much so that she was seen to be clearly sinking (in fact she sank only 15 minutes later from severe flooding, with no power available for her pumps).

The remaining six planes decided to try their luck on a German destroyer they had spotted. This proved to be a far more difficult target than a cruiser - the ship had room to manoeuvre, and although the bombs killed some fish and probably added to the captains white hairs, no hits were achieved. It would seem that destroyers with room to manoeuvre at speed were more difficult targets than had been anticipated. Nevertheless, the crews were happy with the cruiser, especially as it had been obtained without loss to themselves, and headed back (ironically, six Me110's sent to protect the Hipper arrived just in time to see her finally sink below the freezing waters of the fjord).

Once the strike was recovered, the fleet headed out further from the coast, hoping to avoid any attention from submarines at night - it was assumed that there would be heavy concentrations of U-boats off Norway, and particularly off the ports, and while the TBR planes could keep them down in daytime, they were ineffective at night.

The Captain of the Hipper was later court-martialed for not having tried to escape earlier; apparently he had been advised that British fleet units were in the area, but had decided to fix as much as possible of his damage and then escape that evening under cover of darkness. This might have worked if he had only been facing surface units (or maybe not, the Royal Navy was not known for its timidity in attacking the enemy), but as it was the presence of the carriers had doomed his ship.

10th-11th April, Narvik

The defeat of the German destroyers, and the effective control of the Narvik fjord was greeting with jubilation in the Admiralty. Followed by an immediate push by the First Lord to do something about occupying the town and ejecting the German troops already there. Signals were sent to both Warburton-Lee (in command of the destroyers), and Whitworth (controlling the Battlecruiser force) to ask if they could land enough armed sailors to take the town 'at a rush' as it was suggested in Whitehall. Both of the commanders closer to the scene were unenthusiastic about this, as they had few men available, and were unconvinced of the idea of sending armed sailors against the elite German mountain troops now known to be in Narvik.

However there was a change in the situation on the evening of the 10th. After sinking or neutralizing the German forces in the fjord, the British destroyers had been patrolling and keeping an eye on the town while waiting to see if they would be reinforced or withdrawn the following day. Emergency repairs were also underway on the damaged ships; two of these were too badly damaged to remain on station, and it was intended to retire them as soon as possible; the other ships damage was less serious and they would wait until relieved.

It was while this was in progress that a lookout on one of the destroyers noticed a signal from the shore, some miles seaward of the port itself. Curious, the Captain replied, and found that the signals were being sent by a survivor from one of the Norwegian patrol ships sunk by the Germans when they had entered the fjord. He was in company with a force of about 150 Norwegian reservists, who had escaped from the town when it was surrendered, unfortunately without any arms. They wanted to know what they could do to help when the British landed.

This raised some interesting possibilities in Warburton-Lee, who like most British destroyer captains had the aggressive tendencies of a wolverine with toothache; the main issues he and Whitworth had felt a landing a bad idea was due to the lack of men, the deep snow surrounding the town, and the lack of any information about what the German troops were doing. The addition of 150 local troops with excellent local knowledge and skilled in working in the weather conditions made the idea of landing less outrageous.

A boat went to pick up the Norwegian leaders and brought them back to his destroyer for more talks, while he radioed the battlecruiser force and the Admiralty. His suggestion was fairly simple. He could muster about 150 men (assuming the two badly damaged destroyers were to return to Britain tomorrow, they wouldn't be expected to fight, and so could spare some men). He had enough spare small arms on board to equip the Norwegians. That would give him a force of about 300 men (in fact, it would be closer to 400, as more Norwegians were in fact trickling in as the discussions went on). The heavy ships could supply another 200 (no more, as they still needed to be able to fight), which could be there over the night by destroyer. A force of 500 men obviously couldn't take the town, but they could, with the help of the Norwegians, picket it from the seaward side of the fjord, and keep some of the defenders occupied. If anything went wrong, they could evacuate the men on the destroyers.

This would only make sense if stronger forces were on the way, and quickly, otherwise the Germans would reinforce and he would be forced to withdraw the sailors. Two options were available. There was a force of cruisers in the UK, originally loaded with troops as part of the aborted Operation Wilfred. These had been unloaded, as the cruisers were due to sail with a carrier arriving from convoy duty. However the ships, although empty of troops, had not yet left; they could be reloaded overnight with sufficient troops and equipment for some days, and be at Narvik by the morning of the 12th April. While the port itself was under German control, there were plenty of places on the fjord, known to the locals, where light forces could be landed. From interrogating prisoners (a man just fished out of an icy fjord tended to be easy to question), the Germans themselves had few heavy weapons but for some light AA. He had 12 4.7" guns available if necessary, more when the cruisers arrived.

Secondly, according to one of the Norwegians, there was a Norwegian division moving down from the north under General Fleischer, which would have the best part of 4,000 men, fully equipped, close to the town in a few more days. There were in addition about 200 men currently blocking the railway line from Sweden, who could be moved in to support British troops landed higher up the fjord. This would allow the Anglo-Norwegian forces to surround the town. Given that they would outnumber the defenders by 3:1, it seemed likely that they could either capture Narvik or force its surrender quickly, as it would take a while for German reinforcements to arrive; the men landed at Trondheim were only sufficient to capture the town and there was confused fighting going on in Southern Norway. It was thought unlikely that the Germans could bring up substantial reinforcements from the south in less than a week, which would give time for at least one attack on Narvik.

This suggested plan was received enthusiastically at the Admiralty, or at least by Churchill. Frazer was a bit more sceptical, but agreed on the condition that if the situation deteriorated, the troops and sailors would be withdrawn pending a properly planned assault, and that this decision would be left up to Warburton-Lee and the Army commander.

Accordingly a battalion of troops (around 1,000men) with equipment and minimal supplies were loaded onto two cruisers, which would sail on a high-speed run for Narvik as soon as they were ready. A second battalion was to be embarked on the other two cruisers to follow, and supplies for both forces would be loaded onto a merchant ship; it was hoped to have this ready in 2-3 days, before the supplies with the troops ran out. The Home Fleet had detached a number of cruisers that night to return to refuel, so two of these would escort the supply ship (or ships, if two ships could be available without undue delay).

The plan was thus to have a force of about 1,200 men to the seaward side of the port, and another 1,000 on the landward side, hopefully to be supported by a sizeable Norwegian force attacking from the north. Intelligence placed the German forces at around 1,600 - 1,700 men, so they should be outnumbered about 3:1 if everything went to plan.

10th - 11th April, Home Fleet, North Sea, North-West of Bergen, Norway.

While the Illustrious and the Formidable had been busy dealing with the Hipper, the Scharnhorst and Gneisenau had been finally making their way south. They did not have detailed information on the disposition of the Royal Navy, but based on the actions so far they could make a reasonable guess. There was likely a force of some sort off Narvik - given the destroyer attack in the fjord; this was probably cruisers, maybe a battlecruiser, in support. The main body seemed to be off Trondheim, or maybe between Trondheim and Bergen. As the Luftwaffe had not located them close to the coast, they were presumably standing off. They obviously had at least one carrier, maybe more, with them.

The original intention had been to either head south close to the coast (allowing the Luftwaffe to attack the British if they followed or tried to intercept) or, if the Royal Navy was spotted close in, to slip by to seaward until they could swing back towards the coast again. The presence of a strong carrier force complicated this. Wherever the main fleet was, if it could strike at Bergen and Trondheim, it could strike at them as they slipped along the coast too. Going seaward also had its dangers; with reconnaissance planes from both the fleet and the UK searching the area, they would need luck to escape attention.

Staying where there were wasn't an option either; the British must have planes out searching north and west, sooner or later one of them, or a ship, would spot them and then they would be trapped with the British fleet between them and home and no hope of air support.

As a result, they decided to try and slip past the Home Fleet at night, hoping that by the time they were discovered the Luftwaffe would be covering them, and they could even hope to lure heavy British units south, where they would learn the FAA wasn't the only people who could sink ships from the air. In order to do this, they ideally needed the location of the British fleet fixed, and reconnaissance by the He115 planes allocated to naval cooperation.

The fleet was finally located by an He115 acting in its reconnaissance role at about 1400 on the 10th. This was in fact the second such plane to encounter the fleet, but the first had been shot down by a Goshawk before it could complete a sighting report. Given a rough idea of where the British were, it was seen it would not be possible to slip by them in the dark at this time of year. They therefore decided to do the northern part of their escape under cover of darkness, and trust to the Luftwaffe in the morning. They knew they could outrun anything the British had except maybe their battlecruisers, and at least one of these had been reported as off Narvik, well to the north of them. It was thought unlikely that the Royal Navy would pursue with only one battlecruiser, as this would be heavily outgunned by the German ships.

The location of the British fleet had another advantage, in that they were now preparing for another air strike (unknown to the search plane, it was the second strike on the Hipper), which tended to take their attention away from the surface threat for a while.

The He115 which had located the British force had done more than just reported the location so it could be passed on to the Twins - the location was also passed on to the Luftwaffe. While naval cooperation was supposed to be an important part of the Luftwaffe's role in Norway (considering the strength of the British fleet that the Kriegsmarine was tempting , this cooperation tended to be less organized than opportunistic in the first week of the campaign). Goering's planes were very busy in the south - covering the German army, aiding them to drive the disorganized Norwegian resistance north and out of the way, and flying in more paratroops and their supply.

So when the British fleet was reported, the duty fell on the handful of squadrons who'd normal role was that of naval cooperation. The report hadn't gone into much detail as to the strength of the British force (the pilot, understandably, hadn't flown too close), but he had spotted at least one fighter as he slipped in and out of clouds, so they certainly had a carrier with them. The location was too far away from the bases currently occupied by the Luftwaffe to allow an escort of Me109 fighters, and the Me110's, although they had the necessary range, were busy on tasks thought more important (at least by Goering's commanders) than escorting planes 'for a raid on a few ships' , as it was put.

The result was an unescorted strike by 10 He115 torpedo bombers, and 12 He111 high level bombers. In order to maximize their chances of both damaging the ships and getting out alive in the face of enemy fighters (the Goshawk was already getting a feared reputation among German bomber crews) it was planned to do a single synchronised torpedo and bomb attack, the planes withdrawing as soon as they had released their weapons. Since by the time the fleet had been reported, plotted and the usual issues of who was going to attack them had been worked out, it was too late to launch a strike that day. It was therefore arranged to plan one for dawn, three search planes having been sent out earlier to locate them - as soon as they location was give, the strike would be launched.

Dawn would also be the time the Scharnhorst and Gneisenau were hoping to have slipped past the British on their way south down the coast (they were at that point just south of Trondheim, the British force having stayed well clear of the coast overnight). This hope was misplaced, as the British had moved south closer to Bergen; at the moment, German air attacks seemed at least manageable, and the Admiralty wanted more reconnaissance flights as far south as possible. With two fleet carriers and over 30 fighters, Forbes felt he could take the risk of being in range of the Luftwaffe's longer-ranged planes (as yet, they had no knowledge of the long-range Ju87R Stuka variant)

11th April 0900, North Sea, North-West of Bergen, Norway.

For once, the Luftwaffe search planes had had some unexpected luck. They had to guess at the movements of the Home Fleet units overnight, as they had no night-time search capability. This meant starting the search at dawn where they estimated (well, to be honest guessed) the British would be. For once, they guessed right. The contact report was immediately radioed back to base, which was good for the strike force waiting ready on the runway. Not so good for the search plane, who's attempts to keep contact with the fleet and report fell afoul of a roving Goshawk CAP patrol.

The strike got airborne as soon as the position of the fleet had been reported to the navigators, and by 1000 was closing on the fleet. It consisted of two parts, He115 torpedo planes, and He111 high level bombers (the Luftwaffe command still insisted that all of its Ju87's were busy), along with six Me110's that the Kriegsmarine had managed to get out of a grudging Luftwaffe.

The fleet had nine Goshawks in the air, with another nine ready on deck. They knew that they were in range of German aircraft, and while the reports were still of heavy air activity against Norwegian ground forces in the south, they assumed that at some point someone would decide to do something for revenge against the fleets sinking of German ships.

The strike had managed (more by luck than by judgement, it must be said) to coordinate the low level and high level strike. The radar had picked up the high level bombers, and sent the CAP in that direction as the carriers turned into the wind to send up another nine planes. This had the unfortunate effect on making the controllers, still not terribly experienced at this, concentrate on the He111's and not notice the 10 torpedo planes boring in below them.

As the fighter escort was considered woefully inadequate to defend both forces, it had been decided to protect the high level strike. The carriers radar had given them clear warning, and the Goshawks had climbed above the attack. So that when they dove down into their attack, they managed to shoot down two of the He111's in their first pass. As they turned to re-engage, the Me110's escorting the bombers turned to engage them, and it turned into a dog-fight between the fighters as the bombers kept on towards the fleet. The Goshawk pilots were starting to get used to the Me110 now, and knew that while it was powerfully armed, and fast, it had poor agility and a lack of the acceleration often needed to get out of trouble. As a result, the nine Goshawks were able to shoot down four of the Me110's for the loss of only one plane (the pilot bailed out and was lucky enough to get picked up from the icy North Sea by one of the British destroyers. The other two Me110 turned away at full speed, and after a minute or two the Goshawks realised they couldn't keep up, and turned back to the bombers.

While the duel between the fighters had been going on, the newly-launched fighters had been climbing to intercept the bombers (as a result of which, they still hadn't noticed the torpedo planes). While ideal practice was to gain height on the bombers for an initial diving attack, this wasn't possible if they were to engage them before they could start their attack runs on the fleet. So instead, they attacked head on as they climbed - a dangerous tactic, but a workable one against unescorted bombers.

There were still 10 He111's heading in when the Goshawks attacked, but this was rapidly reduced to five, two of which broke off trailing smoke and headed back to Norway. By now, the final three were inside the fleet's AA zone, and the Goshawks gained height to regroup for a new attack. The air around the remaining three bombers was almost immediately black with the explosions of AA shells, and as they held their course for an attack on HMS Illustrious, one of them was hit, falling into the sea not far from HMS Mohawk. The other two, with impressive bravery, held their attack. Sadly, the chance of a hit on a fast moving carrier with a handful of 250kg bombs was small, and although some of the waterspouts were fairly close, the ship was never in any danger. It was spectacular enough, however, that HMS Illustrious would be claimed as sunk by the Luftwaffe. Again.

While this was happening, 10 torpedo planes had, without being noticed, reached the fleet. At which point they gained the undivided attention of every close in AA weapon that could be brought to bear on them. As soon as they were spotted, the original CAP patrol was ordered to engage them, but despite the advantage of diving from altitude, and getting dangerously close to the fleets AA (two Goshawks were damaged by this, fortunately not critically), only two of the planes were splashed before they could make attack runs. The remaining eight were somewhat split up by the combination of heavy AA and the diving Goshawks, fortunately preventing them from managing a mass attack.

Five of the torpedo planes attacked HMS Formidable, in one group of three and one of two, both from the port quarter. While a carrier was a good choice from the targeting point of view, it was not such a good choice in view of the weight of defensive armament the carrier luxuriated in. HMS Formidable had 32 40mm guns (plus a number of 20mm) than could engage an incoming torpedo run, and her close escort destroyer another 8 40mm. A hailstorm of fire enveloped the first of the attacking planes before it could get into dropping range, and it was quickly brought down. The He115 was a fast, twin-engined torpedo plane, and the delayed in engaging the next bomber did allow it to get into range (although nowhere close to optimal range). Seeing the amount of tracer surrounding them, both planes dropped from around 1,500 yards, before turning. This didn't help them; one was destroyed before it got out of AA range, while the final one succumbed to a vengeful Goshawk. The carrier, turning with a grace that belied her 25,000 tons, evaded both of the torpedoes.

The second two planes had decided to attack the nearest large ship, which was the cruiser HMS Manchester. While a modern ship, she could not manage anything like the mass of close AA firepower the carrier enjoyed. Although her defensive fire was seen to damage one of her attackers, they both dropped their torpedoes from around 1,200 yards. The cruiser evaded one, but unfortunately this moved her into the path of the second, which hit and exploded on her port quarter. Fortunately for the ship, this was an aerial torpedo, not the heavy 21" version used by submarines, and although damaged and taking in water, the strike was not critical. Both the attacking planes made their escape at zero feet.

While the attack was going in, the fleets own search planes had been reporting. Overnight, one of the SeaLance fitted with the very new (experimentally new, it might be more accurate to say) ASV sets had reported a large contact to the north, heading south at speed along the coast. This wasn't enough to identify, but the speed indicated warships, and the carrier's pre-dawn search had allocated two aircraft to examine the suspected route. At 0940 she reported 'two battleships (sic) heading south along the coast'. This was what the fleet had been hoping for, and while the carriers were ordered to prepare a strike against heavy surface units, estimates were being made as to how it would be possible for the fleet's battleships to intercept.

All these preparations were abruptly halted when the air attack was seen on the radar screens. The carriers had only just started their preparations, and as the radar gave them some 15 minutes warning the ordnance loading was halted and the handful of torpedoes sent to the hanger deck sent back to the magazine. As was normal practice, there would be no fuelled or armed planes in the hangers, or fuel in the fuel lines, in case of a bomb hit.

At 1100, the last of the attackers having fled over the horizon, the decision had to be made about how best to attack this new target. The search plane, aided by intermittent cloud that allowed it a certain degree of safety, was reporting that the targets were the Twins, heading south at over 30 knots. The attack had wasted over an hour of time, and the carriers restarted their preparations. The delay had allowed the German ships to get nearly 40 miles further south, and this was a problem. There was not enough time left for the battleships to engage them before they slipped away, and at 30 knots they would never catch them.

The plan was therefore for the carrier planes to attack and slow them down so that they could be caught. The fleet split into two parts; HMS Warspite, the cruisers HMS Sheffield and HMS Glasgow, and four destroyers, would advance as fast as possible (the reconstructed Warspite could make 24 knots (in fact her engineers managed to get her up to 25), while the other ships (less the damaged Manchester), could only make 21 knots.

The need was for speed, and in order to speed up the preparation and launch of the strike, it was decided to use 18 torpedo planes from HMS Illustrious, and 18 dive bombers from HMS Formidable, with an escort of six Goshawks. It was considered likely the battlecruisers would have air support on their run south, but in view of the fact that the fleet had been spotted and attacked once already that day, it was not thought wise to reduce the fleets own fighter defence by too much.

At 1245, 18 torpedo planes and 18 dive bombers set course in the attempt to be the first planes in the war to sink a battleship in open waters.

Chapter 16

1315, the North Sea, over the Scharnhorst and Gneisenau.

The orders given to the strike leader had been simple and quite specific. Make sure that if you can't sink them, slow them down enough for them to be caught up. Concentrate on one ship first, only go for the second if the first looks like sinking - better to be certain of one of the twins than try for both and get nothing.

More carefully than they had been doing before their recent experiences, the pilots scanned the sky for any sight of the Luftwaffe. This time, the Goshawks stayed above the strike, ready to pounce if any German pilot was as unfriendly as to break into the entertainment they had planned for the Twins. First to go into their attack were the SeaLance torpedo planes. Considerably faster than the old Swordfish, their speed allowed them to close to range without exposing themselves to more enemy AA than they had to. As usual, they attacked in two groups of nine, in flights of three planes, targeting the closest battlecruiser, which happened to be the Gneisenau.

For such a large ship, she manoeuvred with considerable skill and managed to avoid all nine of the torpedoes coming at her from the starboard quarter. Unfortunately, against a classic hammer-and-anvil attack that made it more difficult to dodge the attack from the other side and in a few minutes she had been hit by three torpedoes. Two hit forward of her centreline, causing damage and flooding, but nothing that couldn't be handled. The third, though, was much more critical. It hit aft, close to where one of the ships propeller shafts entered the hull, the shock damaging and distorting the shaft, rendering it useless and also damaging one of the other propellers. The ships engineers cut power to that shaft as soon as they could, but it was clear there was no chance of it being used again without a long period in dock.

As the torpedo planes drew away to reform, the dive bombers dove in. Again, they all targeted the Gneisenau. Despite her shaft damage, the ship was still snaking and trying to avoid the falling 1,000lb bombs, something she did quite successfully. Sadly in this case quite wasn't good enough.

The first bomb hit the Gneisenau close to her aircraft, causing considerable damage and starting an aviation fuel fire. The explosion and the fires also caused serious injury and damage to the adjacent AA guns and their crews. The second hit her on her port secondary batteries, wrecking the guns and again causing injuries to the AA crews. The final of the three hits was the most spectacular;

hitting the deck just forward of A turret, the bomb exploded (fortunately without penetrating the 11" magazine) with enough force to raise up the front of the turret and jam it into immobility, as well as leaving a rather impressive hole in the deck.

Two more bombs were close enough to cause splinter damage to the superstructure and any exposed crew, but no severe structural damage. The ship didn't stop, but had slowed drastically as thick clouds of smoke billowed from her deck and superstructure.

The planes departed with minimal losses, one torpedo plane and one diver bomber. It would seem that the Kriegsmarine AA fire wasn't much more effective than that of the Royal Navy. As soon as the attack was completed, the planes headed back to the carriers, although one SeaLance stayed on station to report.

The news that one of the battlecruisers had been seriously damaged and slowed was greeted with jubilation at the fleet. The question now was could they be intercepted by HMS Warspite and her consorts, or would this only be possible with another air strike? There was a certain amount of argument about this; there was also the issue of what would happen if the fleet, its position now known, was attacked while in the middle of spotting a full strike on deck. While losses so far had been thankfully low, the two carriers were now down to 28 fighters between them, and they had to maintain a CAP over the Warspite as well as the fleet. This was achievable, but would be much easier if the deck was clear for the fighters. It was also necessary to keep a flight of Swordfish in the air to keep any inquisitive U-boats firmly underwater.

In the end it was decided by the fact that Warspite was already closing with the damaged battlecruiser; the ships had been 'cutting the corner' in their interception, and would be in range in under an hour. As a result, it was decided to plan another strike, but not launch it until the result of the Warspite's action was known, or if the damaged ship managed to regain enough speed to get away from the pursuing force.

1530, the North Sea, HMS Warspite and Gneisenau.

The decision for the German Admiral, while logical, was still cruelly difficult to make. It was already clear that the Gneisenau was badly damaged, reduced to half the speed of her consort. If they stayed together, it was quite probably that both would be sunk. The harsh decision had to be made to leave her, and hope she could evade the British fleet until nightfall. Urgent and demanding messages had been sent, requesting the maximum air cover and also an airstrike on the British fleet, but as yet there were no signs of friendly aircraft. The last time the

Scharnhorst saw her sister ship was the sight of her, still burning, disappearing over the horizon to the north as they made their way south at maximum speed. This was reported back to the British fleet. The orbiting SeaLance was ordered to follow the Scharnhorst south as soon as the Warspite was in visual range of the burning battlecruiser.

The hits had initially slowed the Gneisenau down to 15 knots, but after an hour of desperate work, her engineers had got her speed up to 19 knots on her remaining undamaged shaft. It was hoped that this would allow them to get far enough south that the threat of the Luftwaffe would keep them safe until dark. However the attack and the damage had lost her a lot of time, and when they sighted smoke to the north, it was clear that this time had run out. Nemesis, in the form of HMS Warspite and her escorts, had arrived.

The time was 1530. Since it was rational that the Luftwaffe would, if possible, try and stop the Warspite by an air attack, a CAP of six Goshawks was accompanying the force. Another eight were circling the fleet, just in case. It was already becoming clear that the carriers needed more fighters, especially if the Luftwaffe started to take a serious interest in them.

At first the Gneisenau crew hoped that they could outrun the battleship, but although the engineers, by dint of a supreme effort, got her speed up to 20 knots the Warspite was closing (if slowly), opening fire at 26,000 yards. A final hope that they would be under the cover of night, or at least the Luftwaffe, soon was dashed as the British ship, at a range of no less that 25,000yards, scored a direct hit on the Gneisenau. The heavy 15" shell drove down through the ship's deck armour easily, finally detonating just aft of the engine room, and as a result casing serious flooding aft. While no immediately disabling damage was done, this cost the ship a good three knots, the last thing the captain wanted at this time.

There was no sign of any Luftwaffe presence, and under the circumstances they were obviously not going to escape. Instead, the Gneisenau turned to present all six of her 11" rifles to the approaching Warspite (A turret was immovable after the bomb damage, and could not be brought into action), and to allow at least some of her secondary armament to engage the accompanying cruisers. The battleship continued to close to 15,000 yards, apparently confident its thick armour would defeat the German shells. While one hit was obtained on the Warspite, it seemed to cause no critical damage, and she finally turned to expose her rear gun arcs. This doubled her rate of fire, and though the Gneisenau was armoured more like a battleship than the battlecruiser she was designated, it was not sufficient to stop the shells, weighing nearly a ton each, both destroying her superstructure and penetrating her armour belt. The Warspite's fire remained accurate - terrifyingly accurate to the Germans, and in 30 minutes had reduced the ship to a burning, listing wreck, aided by a considerable number of hits by the cruisers 6" guns. The final coup de grace was given by one of the escorting British destroyers, HMS Acasta, which as the Gneisenau fire slowly ground to a halt amid the shattered steel and flames of her deck, fired three 21" torpedoes into her port side. This was the end, and the crew abandoned ship into the cold waters of the North Sea, their ship sliding downwards as the icy water poured into her, until 10 minutes later she slid under the surface of the North Sea.

1630, the North Sea, HMS Warspite

While the engagement had been most satisfactory for the British ships, it had not been a completely one-sided battle. The Warspite had been struck by a total of five 11" shells during the engagement, although she had only received one hit before she closed to decisive range, which as early damage to the Gneisenau fire control systems had meant her guns were being fired under local control, was not a bad result. Two of the shells had hit on the Warspite's armoured belt, and this was thick enough to defeat the shells and thus taking only minor damage. Three more had hit her on her superstructure; one had wrecked her aircraft and hanger, causing a fuel fire that took some time to put out, while the second had destroyed two of her casemented 6" guns. The fifth shall had embedded itself between two of her 4" AA turrets, the fuse having failed.

HMS Sheffield had taken two hits from the battlecruisers secondary 6" armament; one had temporarily knocked out X turret, the other had hit her right forward and passed right through, destroying her cable locker and leaving an rather impressive exit hole.

The destroyers were busy picking up survivors when, belatedly, the Luftwaffe arrived. This sadly caused the destroyers to break off rescue operations in order to reform around Warspite and take evasive action. There was only limited warning of the attack as the Sheffield's radar had been temporarily damaged by blast and shock action during the surface engagement. This was to be the Royal Navy's introduction to the Ju87R

The observers on the ship were in fact rather surprised; they recognised the Ju87 - its distinctive shape could hardly be mistaken for anything else - but they had thought they were well out of range. In fact, the raid hadn't been intended for them at all. The Ju87's were carrying their long range drop tanks, and had intended to attack the main fleet. However due to the increasingly desperate pleas for help by the Gneisenau, they had diverted slightly in the hope of supporting her. But as a result of the distance to the fleet, they were only carrying 250kg GP bombs; this had been considered sufficient to damage or destroy the carriers which had been their intended target, but were going to be far less useful against the Warspite.

The attack consisted of 12 Ju87's escorted by six Me110's (while Me109's were now established in southern Norway, the fleet was at the moment out of their range to escort a strike). The force was still being covered by six Goshawks, but with the limited warning time they were barely able to close the raid before it arrived. As it was, they were intercepted by the escorting Me110's, allowing the divebombers to attack unmolested by fighters. The Goshawks had been concentrating on the Stukas, and as a result two were shot down in the initial attack by the heavy forward armament of the Me110's. The fighters then turned into the Me110's to attack, then end result of which was three Me110 shot down for the loss of two more Goshawks.

While the fighters were dog-fighting, the Stuka's calmly made their approach before settling into the dives. While the fleets HA AA was as enthusiastic as ever, only one Stuka was hit, forcing it to attempt a landing in the sea. The other 11 split up, seven attacking the battleship while the remaining four went for HMS Sheffield. The pilots knew their bombs were not heavy enough to cause serious damage to a battleship, but they hoped to damage her severely enough that a new raid or U-boat attack might finish her off.

The observers on the ships watched with a professional detachment as the Stukas peeled off one by one to attack them, noting the extreme angle of their dives - even steeper it seemed than the FAA's Cormorants managed. Meanwhile the Warspite's captain tried his best to emulate a destroyer's agility, not the easiest of tasks with 34,000 tons of WW1 battleship.

Of the seven planes bombing, two achieved hits - a worrying high percentage which the ships hoped was not typical for the Stuka crews. The Warspite's deck armour was too heavy for the 250 kg bombs to penetrate, but they did do considerable damage. One hit directly on top of Y turret; while the heavy armour on the turret roof defeated the bomb, the concussion put the turret out of action. The second bomb hit close to the already destroyed hanger - the Captain was starting to wonder if ships aircraft arrangements were exhibiting some sort of perverse attraction for attacking planes, destroying one 4" AA turret and killing and injuring a number of men. Despite a hail of fire from the ships close AA guns, only one of the attacking planes was shot down.

The four planes attacking the Sheffield found that a cruiser was a more difficult target than a battleship, and indeed Sheffield managed to dodge all four bombs, although one fell close enough to cause some underwater leakage and splinter damage that riddled the port side of the ship. All the attacking Stukas escaped damage from the cruisers AA.

1600, North Sea, Home Fleet and Scharnhorst

While the satisfying news was coming in of the Warspite's demolition of the Gneisenau, work was going on preparing a new strike for the Scharnhorst. This was complicated by the worry about the possibility of air attack; a carrier with a hanger deck full of loaded planes was very vulnerable indeed.

Pre-war FAA doctrine had been to keep the hangar deck as non-inflammable as possible. Aircraft were unfuelled, unarmed, and there was no fuel in the refuelling system. This fitted in with the concept that a bomb, if it hit, would explode in the hangar deck, and if a major fire was avoided (a minor one was thought unavoidable), the hangar could be quickly repaired and no additional damage to the ship would ensue.

The problem was that this doctrine clashed with the ability to launch continual strikes (an ability which had been miss-estimated before Norway). So there was, in this case, a compromise. Illustrious continued to control the CAP while Formidable ranged a torpedo strike. To minimise the danger in case of attack, the planes were armed and fuelled in small groups, which added to the time needed to assemble the strike, but meant that as long as there was radar warning, the loaded planes could be brought on deck and the hangar closed (a loaded plane on deck was of course still a vulnerability, but less so that in the hangar).

By 1600, Formidable had ranged 15 torpedo bombers, which took off heading for the Scharnhorst, accompanied by six Goshawks.

The planes sighted the fleeing battlecruiser at 1655; by which time she was well south of the fleet and, although not realised at the time, inside the cover of Me109 fighters (while the Luftwaffe was still not terribly enthusiastic about donating aircraft to protect the Kriegsmarine, the obvious disaster happening to the German fleet off Norway had wrung some of the fighters they had only just based close to Bergen free for use). However they still did not have any land-based warning, and as the Me109 didn't have a long range, they were held ready until the ships radar detected a raid and asked for cover.

Indeed, the Scharnhorst's radar had detected the incoming flight at 1640 (at this point in time, the Royal Navy was still very uncertain if the Kriegsmarine had radar - the prevailing opinion was that they did not, so the incoming flight was at 10,000 feet to acquire the target, and easy target for the ships radar). An immediate call had gone out for fighter protection, and the fighters had started to take off two minutes later. It wasn't clear which would arrive first, the torpedo planes or the fighter cover.

In fact, the torpedo planes arrived first. They circled around to attack the target in two groups, while their protecting fighters stayed at 10,000 feet to cover them if needed. As usual the planes were attacking in flights of three, and the first six (attacking from both sides) were at low level and had started their attack runs before the Me109's had arrived. As a result they were the most successful. The Scharnhorst managed to evade five of the torpedoes, but she took a hit forward from one. The torpedo did not do any serious damage, but it did cause hundreds of tons of icy water to flood into the ship close to B turret, and although the guns themselves were not damaged, the flooding forced the magazine to have to be evacuated.

Before the next planes could attack, the Me109's finally arrived - 12 of them. They split up into two formations, six attacking the defending fighters, the other six going for the torpedo planes. This was the first time the Goshawk pilots had encountered the Me109, and it proved a far more difficult opponent than the Me110 they were getting used to. The Me109 was not much faster, but it was more manoeuvrable, and the Luftwaffe pilots highly skilled. As a result, the attackers shot down four Goshawks for the loss of two of their own planes (one of the Goshawk pilots managed to ditch close to a rather surprised Norwegian fishing boat - to end up being delivered to Narvik a week later, safe but smelling rather strongly of fish).

The other six Me109's had dived on the torpedo planes. They weren't quite as easy a target as they first assumed - the SeaLance was fast for a torpedo plane, and a plane jinking and swerving a few feet above the waves was an awkward target, however an evading torpedo plane wasn't a very accurate delivery system. Of the first three planes attacked, two were shot down before they could release, the only one that got in a shot missing the battlecruiser.

The remaining two flights fared little better. Three more planes were shot down, with no torpedo hits on the ship. One Me109 did hit the water as it tried to close with one of the planes, its pilot obviously not used to flying so low over water, but the result of the action was very unfavourable to the FAA.

The Me109's didn't chase the planes as they headed off to the North, at full speed and just above the waves; the action had already left them low on fuel, and as soon as the attackers left they were heading back to their base.

The carrier planes made it back at 1815; after hearing the radio reports of the attack, it had been decided that the Scharnhorst was now too far under fighter cover to attack without proper preparation. It was hoped that the torpedo damage might be serious enough to make her take cover in Bergen, where a full strength attack with fighter cover could be made tomorrow, but in fact the ship kept on going (her speed had only been reduced to 25 knots), obviously reluctant to stay anywhere near the British carriers for any longer than absolutely necessary.

Chapter 17

11th April, Midnight, North of Denmark.

The pocket battleship Lutzow (nee Deutschland), was on her way home from Oslo after taking part in the invasion. The last heavy German warship involved in the Norwegian invasion found that while the water between Norway and Germanys was free of British carrier aircraft, it wasn't free of their submarines.

The Lutzow had already had the bad luck to be badly damaged by the Norwegian shore batteries during the invasion, and her luck wasn't getting any better. Despite sailing at full speed to avoid submarines, HMS Spearfish put two 21" torpedoes into her stern, blowing off her propellers and so damaging her stern that she was lucky to get back to Germany. Later photographs by an RAF reconnaissance plane showed her stern under water as far as X turret, and the Admiralty estimated it would take 6-12 months to repair the damage.

11th - 12th April, night, at Narvik.

Four cruisers carrying 1,600 troops between them arrive in Narvik fjord. The ships had made the run at high speed, and it is hoped that they were not spotted by U-boats. The allies had 400 men (sailors drafted in from the battlecruisers and destroyers), plus 200 Norwegian reservists west of the port. They were in contact with the German force, (but under orders not to attack, but to keep them occupied). Two of the cruisers landed their men under supervision of local fishermen to join them. While the country outside the town was still under thick snow, the help of the locals, and the fact they only had to cover a few miles, made the job practical if chilly.

The other two cruisers carried on up the fjord to meet with one of the British destroyers. She had been maintaining contact with a small force of Norwegians, about 150 strong, who were part of a force blocking the railway line to Sweden at Bjørnefjell. The men were again brought to shore by small boats, and with local help started to move the 5 miles or so to the eastern outskirts of the town. The locals also reported that a train containing 'some hundreds' of German troops has come through from Sweden, and 100 men were detached to prevent a repetition of this by damaging parts of the line.

The local forces also reported that there had been two actions between the Norwegian 6th Division and the Germans at Gratangen. The first attack, by the Germans, routed an unprepared battalion of Norwegian troops, but they report that a counter-attack had driven the Germans back. The German commander was now surrounded, and outnumbered, with 1,400 men west of the town, nearly 1,000 east, and a Norwegian force estimated at some 4,000 20km to his north and approaching the port. He had some 1,700 men, but only 1,400 are trained infantry, and some have had to be used to secure the town and the prisoners taken when the local commander surrendered. His situation was not good, and due to the speed with which the allies have reacted, there was little chance of any help from the forces from central Norway for some days at best. In view of this, he started making contingency plans for a withdrawal up the railway line into Sweden.

12th - 15th April, actions at Narvik and Trondheim

13th April.

The RAF withdrew the only two bomber squadrons serving with coastal command. The Admiralty is not impressed. Neither is Churchill, who demands to know why the RAF seems to be the only part of the armed forces not actively engaging the enemy. The RAF reply, that they are saving their strength for the decisive blow against German cities, does nothing to satisfy the critics.

The light carrier HMS Venerable arrives to join the battlecruiser force off Narvik. She had been recalled from convoy escort, and was now carrying 12 fighters and 12 TBR, which in addition to HMS Colossus's airgroup gave the force 21 fighters.

14th April.

British forces (the 146th Infantry Brigade) under General Carton de Wiart, one of the more colourful Generals in the British Army, landed at Namsos north of Trondheim. This was intended to be part of a coordinated attack on the German forces around Trondheim.

In order to block allied landings, a Fallschirmjager company made a combat drop at the Dombas railway junction. This successfully blocked the road and rail network (the local geography was very restrictive, especially in the snow), and the force survived until finally being forced to surrender to the Norwegian army on the 19th.

Forces under Major General Pierse Mackesy, the 24th Guards Brigade as well as French and Polish units under the French Brigadier Bethouart land at Harstad. Again the ships were not combat loaded, but as the landing was unopposed this was not a fatal flaw. The intention was for this force to join up with the Norwegians north of the port and assault the town, while the two lighter forces to the east and west moved in to force the defenders to defend the entire perimeter.

As it turns out, this was not to be necessary. On the evening of the 13th, the local British commander had been in negotiations with the German commander (at the time he refused to talk to the Norwegians directly), pointing out he was surrounded, with no hope of reinforcements, and severely outnumbered (the British glossed over the fact that the Harstad landing would only take place that night and that it would be some days before the troops could arrive at Narvik, hoping that the rapid, though improvised, actions so far would deceive him as to the speed with which the British could actually mount a serious attack). It was suggested he should surrender to prevent unnecessary loss of life in the town.

On the morning of the 14th, the British reinforced the negotiations by the arrival of the Renown in the fjord, who lay off the town with her 15" guns trained on the port, along with a number of destroyers and cruisers, including an AA cruiser. The German commander reported this, and insisted on an air attack 'to show the British they cannot use the fjord'. The response to this was a raid by 20 He111 bombers at 1400.

The British had been wary of some sort of Luftwaffe attack on Narvik - it was, after all, the only likely way of supporting the occupying force. As a result there were four Goshawk fighters from HMS Venerable circling the town (the battlecruiser and carrier force was about 50 miles offshore). Although the AA cruiser was equipped with radar, the confines of the fjord made detection difficult, and the raid was not spotted until it was 10 miles away. As arranged, the carriers CAP was sent to help, while they launched a new CAP in case a new raid targeted them).

The Heinkels first ran into the four fighters defending the town. Since they hadn't been informed that there were any fighters in the vicinity (the German commander understood the local airfield to be non-operational at the moment, due to the snow, and no-one had passed on the possibility of British carriers in the area to the squadron), two aircraft were destroyed by the Goshawks cannon before they realized what was happening. However four fighters were not enough to stop the attack, although they managed to shoot down two more before having to break off. The bombers then commenced an attack on the British ships lying in the fjord.

They were met with a very heavy AA barrage, which shot down one bomber and forced the rest to break up their formation and bomb individually. While quite a few near misses were obtained, the only hit was on the destroyer HMS Mohawk by a 250kg bomb. The bomb damaged the destroyer severely, knocking out X turret and her rear engine room. However the damage was not fatal (this time the protection of the fjord and the calmer waters worked to help the British), and she would later make it back home for repairs. Two bombers were damaged during the attack (one later crash-landing, killing her crew). The additional fighters were too late to stop the attack, although their appearance did cause the Heinkels to flee south as fast as possible, two being destroyed as they fled. Sadly, the attack itself also hit the town, a number of houses being destroyed and causing 11 civilian fatalities.

The defeat with little success seemed to be what made up the mind of the German commander (it might also have been influenced by the sight of one of the bombers which had actually crashed not too far from his improvised headquarters). As a result, a compromise was made. The Germans would surrender the town on the condition they were allowed to retreat to Sweden and be interred, rather than captured. After some short discussions, this was agreed by the British and Norwegians - the German force was small, and possession of the town was far more important than the destruction of its garrison. Accordingly on the morning of the 15th the German force was allowed to make its way east under guard (but retaining their weapons), up the damaged rail line and then into Sweden

12th - 15th April, North Sea

As the allied forces started to land at Namsos, the Home fleet units at sea moved north to support them. There was concern over the shortage of fighters - with losses, damaged planes that needed repair and a couple of accidents, they were down to around half their initial complement. The situation was solved by HMS Victorious; she had unloaded her Malta-bound planes and reloaded her airgroup. In addition, she carried additional fighters for HMS Formidable which would be flown on to bring both carriers up to full strength. HMS Illustrious, and a number of cruisers and destroyers which needed refuelling and resupply, would head back to Scapa where Illustrious's airgroup would be brought up to full strength again. As there was now little likelihood of any major German surface forces interfering off Norway, the intention was to keep two carriers on station with the fleet, rotating one back home to refuel and replace lost planes as necessary. As more escorted raids were expected as the Luftwaffe settled in to southern Norway, consideration was being given to finding additional fighters and pilots. The RAF was also asked when it was actually going to be putting some planes on the ground (or at least getting them ready now that it looked liked air bases around Narvik would be available soon).

A British vanguard force arrived at Andalsnes on the 12th; a force built around the 148th Infantry Brigade was being prepared for deployment there to attempt to cut off and take Trondheim.

On the 14th the submarine HMS Tarpon was sunk off southern Norway (the allied submarine force was very active in this area trying to slow the reinforcement and resupply ships from Germany). The allies were having better luck against the U-boats still infesting the North Sea; two destroyers escorting the troop convoy to Harstad sank the U-49, and the U-1 sank off Stavanger after hitting a mine (probably a British one, although no-one was quiet sure). The most benefit was obtained by documents captured from the U-49 before she sank giving information on U-boat deployments in the area.

While the Luftwaffe was still only considered a threat in Southern Norway, it was decided not to attack Bergen with a mixed force of cruisers and destroyers (as had been suggested). The attack on Warspite had shown that the likely threat would be on withdrawal, and that it would require a heavy fighter escort over the ships. More efficient was an attack by dive bombers on the shipping thought to be using the port; while this wouldn't do as much damage, it would be less likely to incur losses, and had the advantage of forcing the Germans to assume that FAA planes could arrive at any time over any coastal area, forcing them to increase their defences (and hopefully as a result taking pressure of the Norwegians, who, with little effective AA capability, were suffering heavily from air attack)

According on the 14th, a strike of 24 Cormorants escorted by 9 Goshawks was made from the Formidable and the Victorious. No fighter cover was encountered over the target, but the accuracy of the dive bombing was affected by the low cloud ceiling (under 5,000 feet), and as a result only two merchant ships were hit - both sinking from the damage caused by the 1,000lb bombs. Some light German naval craft were also strafed by the Goshawks as the Cormorants withdrew, causing some damage to them. No aircraft were lost.

Some consideration had also been given to direct strikes against Bergen from the UK, which is in range of the Cormorants if they reduce their load to a 500lb bomb. While considered an possible option, the only two squadrons available are those working up for the new carriers, and so this idea is kept in reserve in case the fleet is forced to withdraw north (in which case another attack may well confuse the Germans as to its location).

Some activity is finally visible from the RAF; Coastal command planes conduct reconnaissance over the coastal areas of southern Norway. In the afternoon, six Hudsons bomb Stavanger airfield; Me110's are encountered and one is claimed as shot down. Barbed comments are made by the FAA in the wardrooms that night that 'it's just as well they used patrol planes, if they'd used RAF bombers they'd probably have missed Norway!'.

The RAF does try to attack some of the German shipping passing between Germany and Norway that night, but the force of Blenheims is unable to find anything in poor weather. Hampdens do lay mines in the area.

On the 14th, under increasing pressure from the War Cabinet and Churchill in particular, the RAF again raids Stavanger - a massive raid by three Wellingtons. A few He111's are damaged.

The FAA again pays Bergen a visit - in addition to damaging the shipping there, the hope is to make the Germans consider it untenable for the moment, hopefully reducing pressure on the Norwegian defence which is being slowly driven North. The raid is again by 24 Cormorants escorted by 9 fighters. They find considerable shipping in the harbour, and two U-boats. The dive bombers concentrate on the U-boats (easy targets, tied up at the dock - rather surprising the FAA, who thought the Germans would have learned from yesterday), and 12 bombs later both boats (the U-60 and the U-7) are still at the docks, but this time under water. Two merchant ships are also sunk. This time one Cormorant is lost, shot down by the AA defences.

That night, the RAF sends 24 aircraft to lay mines in the Great and Little Belt areas. Only 9 succeed due to bad weather. The FAA are even more scathing - 'only the RAF could miss the bloody OCEAN!' The Navy, and the FAA in particular, are fast losing what faith they had in RAF Bomber command, and after their own successes off Norway aren't shy about making the point to the First Lord.

Despite his success in Norway and Denmark, General Jodl noted that the Fuhrer is suffering a 'nervous crisis' and 'terrible excitement', after he receives news of the naval losses off Norway.

The Danes (who are, technically, not defeated by Germany) bring 90% of Danish shipping into allied and friendly ports, a welcome addition to the allies merchant shipping.

On the 15th, the RAF redoubles its efforts to attack Stavanger airfield. This time six aircraft bomb the airfield, with little effect.

A single Hudson, flying off the Norwegian coast, is attacked by two Me110's. One of the fighters crashed into a mountain while trying to attack the Hudson. An Admiral is heard to remark, perhaps only half-jokingly, that the Hudson should be re-specified as a fighter.

After the losses due to allied air attacks, in particular those from the FAA, the Luftwaffe increases its commitment in Norway, establishing Luftlotte 5's HQ in Hamburg under Milch to oversee operations.

16th April.

It is considered fortunate that the German commander was persuaded to abandon Narvik earlier, as only part of the British force has arrived there before heavy snowstorms strand the rest of the force north of the town. The commander, General Macksey, has already been criticised for his caution, and this new delay doesn't help that reputation. The British and Norwegian force start preparations for heading south on the railway line to attack Trondheim.

The submarine HMS Porpoise makes an attack on the U-3 southwest of Stavanger, without success.

The RAF this time raids four airfields with small forces of bombers, again without any noticeable results.

A reconnaissance is made of Bergen by a flight of Goshawks; the navy suspects that after the last two raids it isn't in use, so send some fighters to check (they reason that if they were in command there would be fighters there now, so don't want to risk strike planes unless there are targets). The Goshawks spot a submarine making its way unconcernedly up the fjord on the surface (the U-58); accordingly, a strike of 12 Swordfish escorted by 9 fighters is authorised which takes off 40 minutes later. When they arrive at the fjord, they are happily surprised to see the submarine still on the surface - apparently it hadn't seen the earlier Goshawks, or maybe it had misidentified the fighters as German planes.

The Swordfish glide bomb the submarine with the new shallow depth charge bombs (these have now replaced the old, ineffectual RAF 100lb antisubmarine bombs). The results are satisfying; the submarine is left sinking as her crew abandon her. All the planes return without loss. One other result of the raid is that the Germans stop using the fjord (at least in daylight) for the time being.

As a result of the actions of Germany, Iceland declares its independence and the Icelandic government appeals to the USA for recognition and aid.

The news of the Narvik garrisons retreat finally reaches Germany. Hitler has a fit of hysteria, demanding that Goering evacuate the troops by air. It is pointed out that this cant now be done (in any case, there isn't anywhere for Ju52's to land), but is assured that they will be repatriated speedily from Sweden. Jodl noted in his diary 'Every piece of bad news leads to the worst fears'.

While the rest of the British force north of Narvik slogs its way there through the snow, the two battalions that arrived on the cruisers (now having received their full equipment and supplies from the UK, and an equal force of Norwegian infantry head down the railway line south towards Trondheim. Their mission is to make sure the Germans don't advance past Trondheim, and to aid the British forces about to land outside the port. As soon as the rest of the British force at Narvik has reorganised itself, it will follow with more Norwegian forces. The sailors landed from the battlecruisers and destroyers have been re-embarked, as Narvik is now fully occupied by the Allies.

17th April

British troops land at Aandalsnes and Namsos. These locations are not close to Trondheim (100m and 80m respectively), and the need to transfer troops to destroyers at Namsos (the fjord being too winding and narrow for the troop transports) leads to delay and confusion. The force has no transport, and will have to get closer to Trondheim by rail. The force commander, General de Wiart, is not happy about what he considers the lethargic speed of the force coming down from Narvik, and insists his own troops should press on as fast as possible, before Trondheim can be reinforced.

Royal Navy destroyers, operating off Trondheim, have intercepted a couple of small ships over the last couple of days, apparently trying to run supplies to Trondheim. However since the raids on Bergen, the Kriegsmarine seems to have given up on using any surface forces north of Stavanger, due to lack of air cover. In order to keep the pressure on Bergen, a raid is staged from the UK using Cormorants. At this distance, they can only carry 500lb bombs, but in the event they find no shipping in the harbour.

In order to try and reduce the German air presence, the Admiralty decide to use the heavy cruiser Suffolk to bombard the airfield at Stavanger. While more dangerous than an air raid, the intention is to give the Germans another threat to worry about. It is planned to cover the ship with a flight of six Goshawks, which will be sent as soon as requested (it is hoped that the Suffolk's arrival will be a surprise, so the intent is to ask for cover once the bombardment starts).

While the bombardment goes off reasonably well (although it does not close the airfield), the cover finds the ship under heavy attack from the Luftwaffe, and when they try to intervene they are intercepted by fighters, making it very difficult to protect the ship from the dive-bombing. They do shoot down two Me109's and a Ju88, but for the loss of three Goshawks. The Suffolk continues to make her escape, but due to her distance from the carriers it is not practical to keep more than six fighters available (the fleet has to keep a reserve in case it too is spotted). The Suffolk is hit by one bomb right aft, after 88 misses. The bomb destroyed her rudder and left her very low in the water aft. Fortunately, by this time she was out of range of cover from the short ranged Me109's, and when the next attackers met the covering fighters, the attacks were broken off. The ship arrived at Scapa half sinking, her stern nearly under water. It drove home the lesson that ships were in grave danger if in range of enemy air attack and without fighter cover, as the ships AA had only shot down one plane. The FAA fighters had shot down another four, as well as driving off a number of attackers. However it was noted that it had taken considerable effort by the Luftwaffe to damage her, and that it wasn't impossible to use lighter warships in these situations, just dangerous.

Most of the heavy home fleet units returned to Scapa to refuel, except for the carriers. It is intended to use three carriers to keep two permanently on station, supported by at least one battleship or battlecruiser.

That night, news is received that the Scharnhorst, making her way back to Kiel to repair her torpedo damage, has been torpedoed by a Polish submarine, who hit her aft with one 21" torpedo. The Scharnhorst will be in dock for some time.

18th April

Bomber command again darkens the skies over Norwegian airfields. Three planes to Kjeller and three to Fornebu, followed by three more split between the two airfields. None of the planes bomb due to poor weather.

The British 148th Brigade and the French 5th Chesseurs Alpines are landed at Narvik. The original plan had been to land them at Andalsnes and Namsos, but the paucity of port facilities and the possession of the rail lines south has changed their destination, As their supplies are still being loaded rather randomly, they will not be able to move south for at least a day, although advance parties go south to talk with the command. The current allied plan is to move on Trondheim from the east, with the forces landed to the west and north blocking their escape.

The Norwegian defence in the south is slowly being defeated and driven north. General Ruges plan is to try and take back Bergen and hold as far south as possible; if this fails, he intends to withdraw north to a position south of Trondheim, which he hopes will have been recaptured.

HMS Colossus has been refuelling at Tromso. While transiting the Grotsund fjord she is surprised in poor weather by a single Fw-200 plane, which drops two 250kg bombs, neither of which hits. The British are becoming concerned at the way the fjords diminish the effectiveness of radar, which the carriers have been depending on. It is the Royal Navy's first encounter with the big four-engined Fw200.

Four days after sinking the gunnery training ship Brummer, submarine HMS Sterlet is presumed lost in the Skagerrak to A/S trawlers. Allied troops occupy the Faeroe Islands north of Scotland.

19th April

HMS Colossus had to return to sea without having fully fuelled due to air attacks on Tromso. While effective, it is becoming clear that radar has limits, sometimes severe limits, over land, especially when attacking planes have high mountains to use in their approach. It is decided to refuel at Scapa where possible; the number of carriers available makes this practical, though it is a concern that it reduces the available air cover by 1/3. Pressure is again put on the RAF to deploy some modern fighters in defence of the army and the ports. The result of this seems to be a reconnaissance of Hamburg, which leaves both the Army and Navy puzzled as to how this is supposed to help them.

An attack on Trondheim has to be postponed due to the urgent need to reinforce the Norwegians southwards; unless this is done it is feared they will collapse, which would render the capture of the port pointless. Accordingly the 148th Brigade is ordered south to Lillehammer, taking up positions to the south of the city.The 146th Brigade, which has encountered the German forces based at Trondheim at the town of Steinker, is forced to retreat back towards Namsos.

It is hoped to start an attack on Trondheim from the east in the next day or so, weather permitting.

20th April

RAF Bomber command finally mount a sizeable raid - 35 Wellingtons attack Stavanger airfield, reporting heavy damage to parked aircraft and to the runways.

The Luftwaffe mounted large scale raids against Namsos. The wooden houses were set alight and the jetty damaged. Aandalsnes was bombed three times.

Steinkjaer is reduced to ruins.

Using 150 bombers (He-111's and Ju88's) and 60 Ju87's, Fliegerkorps X mounted an attack on the Allied landings that was so intense that it prevented supplies from being landed to reinforce the troops already on Norwegian soil. The FAA were unable to intercept due to bad weather. Renewed demands are put on the RAF for land-based fighter support, and the RAF finally agreed to deploy two squadrons of Hurricanes and Gladiators.

The German air attacks ignore Narvik, possibly because of the proximity of the carriers (the main fleet carrier force is actually to the west of Trondheim rather than to the north, the planes seen over Narvik belonging to the Venerable and Colossus.

On his 51st birthday, Hitler ordered a new SS regiment to be set up containing Norwegians and Danes as well as Germans.

21st April

The troops hurriedly rushed to Lillehammer are pushed out of the town by a German attack. Meanwhile a German column of mountain troops moved overland from Trondheim by road and rail to attack the British troops at Steinker. This was probably a mistake, as the attack by the British and Norwegian units east of Trondheim begins. While not as well organised as the defenders, they number the best part of a division and steadily pushed the Germans back towards the town. As a result of this increased pressure, the attack towards Steinker was called off; the troops will be needed at Trondheim.

The weather was better, and possibly as a result there was no major raid mounted by the Luftwaffe, although the RAF visits Aalborg and Stavanger airfields again.

22nd April

Allied forces continue to press on Trondheim, aided by Royal Navy destroyers and a cruiser giving heavy gunfire support from the fjord. The better weather allows the carriers to maintain a CAP of 9 Goshawks over the area, and as a result there was no Luftwaffe activity. Reconnaissance reveals a number of German planes on a frozen lake - Ju-52's Ju-87's and He-111's. They did not appear to be in use, but a raid was mounted anyway, 24 SeaLance glide bombing with 250lb bombs. The frozen lake surface was broken up and a number of aircraft destroyed.

The German forces in Trondheim were now running very low of ammunition and supplies; due to the control of the air and sea around the port, no supplies have reached them by ship, as was the original plan. Some limited supplies have arrived by air, but nothing near enough. By the end of the day, the allied forces are close to the east of the town.

The British troops at Lillehammer were forced to fall back along the east bank of the Lagen River to a bridge at the village of Trettin. The bridge had to be held until the Norwegians and British west of the river could retreat across it. Little support was available from the exhausted Norwegian forces

HMS Formidable, who has been refuelling and replacing planes at Scapa, takes on deck 24 Hurricane fighters and 18 Gladiators; these will fly from Norwegian airfields to reduce the load on the FAA. She leaves 18 of her SeaLance behind to accommodate some of the planes; these will be flown on later from the UK once the RAF planes have been flown off.

23rd April

RAF Bomber command visit Norway again. This time 14 aircraft are used. A single aircraft was sent to bomb shipping in Oslofjord, but does not return. The Navy is scathing at the ideas of the RAF with regard to sinking shipping. Unfortunately Oslo is too far inside German air cover to strike from the carriers without exposing the fleet to a serious bombing attack. In view of the number of aircraft used on the 20th, this was considered too dangerous with regard to any benefits obtained.

The 148th Brigade was attacked for the first time by tanks, which cut off a considerable part of the force. As a result the Brigade was forced to retire north towards Andalsnes. The 15th Brigade was landed at Andalsnes to reinforce and cover them.

The attack pressed on Trondheim, and during the night the resistance faded away. While the defenders have proved more efficient and better soldiers than their attackers, they have basically run out of ammunition. A small rearguard is left to cover as the bulk of the German mountain troops scatter into the countryside to hopefully retire to their advancing formations - in fact, the bulk of these highly trained men will make it. Before they leave, they also demolish much of the ports facilities, so the bulk of supplies will have to be brought down from Narvik.

HMS Formidable left for Norway with the RAF fighters on board. The Gladiators will be flown off onto a frozen lake near Trondheim to give local cover; the Hurricanes are expected to use either Bodo or Narvik, which locals have been clearing of snow.

24th April

As a result of Trondheim finally being recaptured, and the presence and breakthrough of panzers further south, General Ruges decided to slowly withdraw north while the troops around Trondheim prepare a defensive line for them to retire behind. It has become obvious that with the steadily increasing strength of the Germans in the air and on the ground, that southern Norway cannot be held with the allied forces currently available, and this option gave him the best chance of preserving his army.

The army landings at Andalsnes had been covered by the AA cruiser HMS Curacoa, as the army is extremely short of its own AA weapons. Her guns had been supplemented by fighter patrols when weather permits. She was caught in a heavy air raid while the fighter cover was absent and badly damaged by bombs. The fighter cover arrived in time to shoot down two Ju87's, but after temporary repairs the ship has to be escorted back to the UK for repairs.

The fleet carrier group joins HMS Formidable to cover her while she launches off the RAF planes; Six Cormorants from the Illustrious will escort the two groups to ensure their safe arrival (the FAA is somewhat dubious about the navigation skills of the RAF pilots). They intend to conduct fighter operations over Trondheim and the surrounding area to give the RAF squadrons time to get organised. As a result, they do find a formation of He-111 bombers, shooting down two and damaging a third.

25th April

The RAF raids the Norwegian airfields again, this time with eight aircraft. Meanwhile Blenheim bombers search some of the southern fjords, finding and sinking a medium sized merchant ship and destroying a couple of flying boats.

The British 15th Brigade and Norwegian units gave fierce resistance in the Gudbrondsdal but fell back slowly as planned. The 15th is a regular army brigade, with antitank guns, and is a much tougher proposition than the 148th Brigade. The defence is not helped by constant German air attacks; it is hoped that on the following day the RAF fighters can provide more cover. The Navy promises (weather permitting) some air operations which it is hoped will divert the Germans and ease the pressure on the Army

26th April

The RAF bombs Stavanger airfield and fjord, and oil tanks and a refinery at Vallo and Grisbeu.

As the RAF fighters are now operational, the fleet carriers mount an attack on Aalsund - 24 SeaLance acting as bombers, 18 Cormorant dive-bombers and 16 Goshawks as escort. Very considerable damage is done to the airfield, a number of aircraft being destroyed or damaged on the ground. The fighters encounter a force of He-111, shooting down five. One SeaLance is shot down by AA fire; the airfield will not be in operation for some days. Aided by some subtle propaganda (and helped by the Army) it is noted in London that one raid by the carriers seems to have done more damage than a week or so of raids by RAF bombers (not quite true, but close enough)

Goshawks patrolling Andalsnes encounter a flight of three He-111, shooting down two and damaging one which gets away. As a result, the Luftwaffe becomes much more reluctant to send small raids north of the fighting as they are seen as far too vulnerable.

The British and Norwegian forces continue a fighting retreat north to Kjorem. The slowing of the German advance allows the faster withdrawal of some of the more exhausted Norwegian units behind friendly lines where they can rest and recover.

27th April

British and Norwegian forces continue their withdrawal north, where the troops around Trondheim were busily construction defensive positions. It is hoped to halt the German advance here where the terrain naturally bottlenecks them into a narrow front.

A combat patrol of six Goshawks encounters a large formation of German planes about to attack a convoy heading for Trondheim. Three Ju88's are shot down. They are joined by a flight of six Hurricanes on their first air patrols (which causes some confusion as they find their radio systems won't actually talk to each other), and find themselves encountering a formation of 15 Heinkels of KGr100. Between them the FAA and RAF planes shoot down 10 of the Heinkels and damage two more. These are the older Hurricanes, with 8x0.303 guns (the newer model with 2 20mm cannon are being held in the UK), and it is interesting to the pilots to note how much more effective the cannon are at bringing down the bombers.

That evening, Germany officially declares war on Norway.

28th - 30th April.

The Allied forces finally retreat to the defensive line south of Trondheim. This is now occupied by around two divisions of troops from three countries, and as a result the Germans decide to pause to reorganise and resupply.

On the 29th HMS Glasgow evacuates King Haakon and the Norwegian government from Molde. They will arrive at Tromso on the 1st May. General Ruge is on a British destroyer. The Norwegian gold reserves are also on the cruiser.

A force of RAF Blenheim bombers reports over 150 aircraft on Stavanger airfield on the 30th. As attacks by the RAF have proved too small to be effective, the Navy is asked if they can raid the airfield. This caused some problems as to availability of carriers. HMS Victorious is currently refuelling in the UK, and Formidable and Illustrious are fully committed with running patrols over the convoys and fleet. As Venerable and Colossus are available, it is decided to send them south, escorted by HMS Renown and destroyers, close enough to conduct a strike. They currently carry 9TBR, 9DB and 9 Fighters each. The raid is planned to be 18TBR (in bomber mode), 18 DB escorted by 6 fighters (the others being retained for CAP). While this raid is seen as risky, it is hoped to catch the defenders by surprise and then steam north as soon as the strike is recovered.

Believing that the Scandinavian campaign is over, Hitler orders his generals to make their final preparations for an attack in the west. He informs General Jodl and other military commanders to be prepared to launch operations on 5 May or within 24 hours of any later day.

1st May - 5th May

It had been hoped to coordinate the carrier strike with the RAF, and the RAF promises to bomb the airfield again in the afternoon. Six aircraft would bomb Stavanger in the late afternoon.

The strike from Venerable and Colossus goes in just after dawn, as it was hoped this will catch the maximum number of planes on the ground. Since the two light carriers are uncomfortably far south of the main force, and have limited fighters, two flights of Goshawks are kept back on HMS Illustrious in case they need support.

The air strike is effective. There are indeed many aircraft on the field, and the combination of 250lb, 500lb and 20lb bombs dropped by the 39 attacking planes is thought to have destroyed at least 20 aircraft as well as doing much damage to the facilities. Only two Me109 fighters rise to defend the base, both are shot down. One Goshawk is lost to the fighters, while a Cormorant and a SeaLance are lost to AA fire.

There is a problem, however. Shortly after the strike goes in, the main fleet finds themselves the centre of unwelcome Luftwaffe attention. A mixed force of Ju88 and Ju87 bombers makes a number of attacks in small groups, only some of which are properly intercepted by the defenders. No bombs actually come close to the ships, and two Ju88 and a Ju87 are shot down, but it does occupy the attention of the carriers. As a result, it is not possible to add to the defences of the two light carriers further south.

Stung by the success of the carrier raid on Stavanger, the Luftwaffe is quick to respond. The two light carriers headed north as soon as they had landed on the strike force; due to an oversight, no-one had informed them that the main fleet was also under attack, and so they only kept six fighters up as air cover. At 1300 a heavy raid in two groups is detected from the east and south. The CAP is vectored onto the closest formation, and the ready planes got ready for launch. They are sent up in time to intercept the second raid, but both groups are much larger than first anticipated.

The first formation is 24 He-111 and 12 Ju88's. The fighters concentrate on the Ju88 as its dive bombing capability is seen as more dangerous. Four of the bombers are brought down, and two more driven off. The He-111's encounter the fleets AA defence, however this time they try and hold their formation. Even so, the evasive action taken by the ships is almost successful; one 250kg bomb hits HMS Renown, destroying two of her 4.5" AA mounts. The JU88's attack HMS Colossus, but although the ships AA fire is weak compared to a fleet carrier, the handling of the ship is superb and all the bombs miss. Two more of the JU-88's are destroyed as they leave the scene.

The second wave of attackers is more dangerous. This time 16 He-111 bombers accompany 24 Ju87 dive bombers. The new CAP is not yet at altitude, so attack the Ju-87's as they ascend. The Ju87 is an easy target under normal circumstances, but there is no time for a proper interception before most of them are too close to attack. The defenders shoot down or drive off five of them, but 19 of them are able to start their dives before interception.

The Ju87's are operating at a long range for them (these are not the extended range variant), and are only carrying 250kg bombs. Unfortunately, while the fleet carriers are armoured against these, the light carriers only have protection above their magazines. Despite the presence of the fighters, the Stukas take their time in order to carry out a textbook attack on HMS Venerable. Despite the weaving of the Venerable, she is hit by a total of five bombs.

One bomb hits forward, destroying her forward elevator and causing a fire in the lift shaft. A second hits well aft, penetrating the flight deck and exploding just above her hanger deck, destroying a number of planes and causing a severe fire. The third and fourth bombs hit close to the centre of the ship, causing more damage as they pass through the hangar where one of them explodes, causing another fire, but the other bomb penetrates deeper, and the forward engineering space is rendered inoperable. It is the final bomb which does the most serious damage; although it doesn't quite hit the ship, it explodes very close to the stern in the water, damaging the propellers. The resultant vibration forces the ship to slow to no more than 5 knots. The vengeful Goshawks shoot down four Ju87's as they flee the scene, but this is little consolation.

The Venerable is burning heavily; although RN policy is for no armed or fuelled planes in the hangers, and fuel lines are always drained when not in use, there is still, inevitably, plenty of flammable material. The hits deep in the ship have affected the fire-fighting ability of the crew, and although the main Avgas tanks are not in any danger, the hanger fires are at first only contained, not brought under control. As Colossus is undamaged, all the airborne fighters land on her, although this does mean leaving some on deck as there isn't room in her hangers now for the planes she has on board.

The fleet commander is now faced with the decision of what to do with the Venerable. She can't make more than 5 knots, is on fire, and they are well in range of more air attacks. The fleet carriers cannot send more than six fighters due to the distance and their own problems, and there is plenty of daylight left. As an interim measure, he orders the ship to evacuate her FAA personnel while he decides what to do.

The Captain of the Venerable informs him, as the evacuation is taking place, that he hopes to have the fires under control in an hour or so (without fuel or explosives, there is a limited amount of inflammable material in the hanger), but that it seems unlikely the ship will be able to make more than 6 knots without the propellers dropping off.

The final decision is taken out of the Admirals hands by the arrival of a new raid (fortunately for the small fleet, the last of that day). This time it is a force of He-115 torpedo planes. After the retrieval of the earlier CAP, Colossus has only been able to put up another four planes - due to the unexpected arrival of the Venerable's fighters, they do not have the usual replacement CAP spotted), and there are 18 planes in the raid.

The fighters do their best - the floatplanes are easy targets, and the pilots are a lot more experienced than they were at the start of the Norwegian affair, but even so only manage to intercept a third of them. Two more are shot down by the desperate fire of the fleet AA guns, but the remaining ten head straight for the burning HMS Venerable. Hardly able to manoeuvre, the ship is an easy target, although one of her 40mm guns does destroy one of the torpedo planes before it releases, Nine torpedoes are launched. Four of them hit as the planes bore in with impressive dedication - indeed, two are shot down or crash after they release.

Three of the torpedoes hit her on the port side, one on the starboard. To the amazement of the officers watching from HMS Renown, although she takes on a list, she isn't obviously sinking (although certainly lower in the water), as her anti-torpedo measure prove most efficient. Sadly that doesn't matter, as one of the torpedoes has already doomed her, hitting next to her aft machinery space and cutting off the remaining power (while the ship does have a diesel generator, this was destroyed in the earlier bombing). As a result, there is no way to stop the inexorable flooding, or to allow the fires in the ship to be brought under control.

The captain orders the crew to abandon ship, and two destroyers close to pick them up; the ships scuttling charges are set (given her protection against torpedoes, charges against the hull were intended for use if possible as the usual way of sinking a damaged ship by torpedo would prove difficult). Fifteen minutes after the last survivors are rescued, the ship shudders, heels over, and sinks quickly, taking 245 of her crew with her.

Chapter 18

May 1940, Norway and France.

After the retreat to Trondheim, the Norwegian campaign stabilised for a time. The allies were still reinforcing with British and French forces, and the Norwegians are regrouping what troops have made it to the north, while the German forces are consolidating their grip on the south of the country and making local probing attacks to keep the allies on their toes. There is a noticeable drop in Luftwaffe activity, and as a result the forward naval force is reduced to a battlecruiser and a single fleet carrier plus supporting ships, while the convoys to Narvik are escorted by the light carriers (two more are now available from Atlantic convoys, so the loss of HMS Venerable does not affect operations).

HMS Glorious has finished her refit, and is loaded with fighters; 16 Goshawk Mk IA, and 16 Gladiators, headed for Malta. She will act as escort for the convoy also delivering arms, supplies and troops and RAF personnel to the island.

British troops occupy Iceland; this is viewed with mixed feelings by the inhabitants, and the British forces start a campaign of winning them over to the allied cause.

The most important event happens on the 7th May, when a debate in the House of Commons on 'the conduct of the war'. Prime Minister Chamberlain is castigated for the poor preparation and performance of the forces 'which have only been saved by the professionalism of the Royal Navy', as it is put by Leo Avery. He follows this with pointing at Chamberlain and quoting Oliver Cromwell 'You have sat too long for any good you have been doing. Depart, I say, and let us have done with you. In the name of God, go!'

There were startling moments before that. Admiral of the Fleet Sir Roger Keyes, a Tory MP and hero of the last war, arrived in the House in full uniform with six rows of medal ribbons on his chest. He denounced the Prime Minister and volunteered personally to lead another naval assault on the enemy in Norway. The First Lord, Winston Churchill, takes responsibility for the performance of all the forces involved, RAF and Army as well as the Royal Navy. While the gesture of him trying to protect the government is recognised, he is one of the few people to come out of the Norway operation with any credibility.

In the vote at the end of the debate, the governments majority is reduced from over 200 to 81, many Tory MP's abstaining. It is a devastating blow to Chamberlain. As a result, on the 9th may Chamberlain asked the Labour party to join him in a coalition government. They refused to do so as long as he was Prime Minister. The next day he was chairing a meeting of the War Cabinet when he was handed a note informing him that the Labour party will only accept Winston Churchill as Prime Minister of a coalition government. His situation was made worse by the news of Germany's attack in the west; he broadcast to the nation that evening announcing his resignation.

German forces continued to advance through Holland and Belgium. The Royal Navy's participation is mainly to aid in helping Dutch and Belgian shipping to be recovered to the UK, and to evacuate items such as gold and diamonds. The Italian propaganda machine, growing increasingly pro-German, announces that Britain's Royal Navy is largely obsolete and no match for their impressive array of battleships which are taking part in well-publicised exercises in the Adriatic. The FAA finds this somewhat amusing, as the Italian fleet does not have any carriers.

While the armies are moving west, the RAF (and also the French Air Force) attempted to intervene to destroy bridges and generally aid the army. The operations are ineffectual, and merely result in the loss of trained and brave airmen.

The FAA had been mounting small raids to harass the Germans in Norway; there has been little Luftwaffe activity, and it is assumed that all but a small force has been withdrawn to take part in the operations in France and the Low Countries. On the 12th, an interesting raid was mounted from HMS Sparrowhawk (RNAS Hatston). Twelve SeaLance, carrying 500lb bombs, were sent to attack a ship carrying supplies and AA artillery off Bergen. They were escorted by six Goshawks which join them from HMS Illustrious. What makes this raid different is that it is the first one to be based on information gained by ULTRA intercepts. They catch the target, escorted by two torpedo boats, as it is about to enter the fjord, just before noon, and by 1230 the ship is sinking into the waters of the fjord. The accompanying fighters finished by strafing the torpedo boats.

On May 13th the government of the Netherlands and Queen Wilhemina are evacuated to the UK by British destroyers.

On 14th the new coalition government is formed. Also formed is a new Ministry of Aircraft Production under Lord Beaverbrook.

On May 15th a number of Dutch and British warships are sunk off Holland by the Luftwaffe; the Royal Navy loses the destroyers HMS Valentine (had to be beached and abandoned) and HMS Winchester (seriously damaged). The Navy demands (politely, so far) to know why the RAF is not covering its ships, and asks if maybe the RAF would like the FAA to help them. The answer is stony silence.

May 16th

The government authorises another four squadrons of Hurricane fighters to go to France, leaving Fighter Command with only 22 squadrons of the 52 considered necessary for defence. Meanwhile the British and French armies in the north of France and Belgium are retreating towards the coast.

May 18th

Belgium surrenders. The BEF and the French Army fall back onto the coast of Belgium, as they now have to cover the gap left by the Belgian surrender. While this is happening Bomber command was attacking strategic targets in Germany, with little success or impact on the attacking German Army.

May 19th

The destroyer HMS Whitley is bombed two miles off Neiuport on the Belgian coast. After taking severe bomb damage, she has to be beached and sunk by gunfire from another destroyer. After their last inquiry as to air support of their ships, the Admiralty decide to try a different approach and talk directly to Air Marshall Dowding, head of fighter command. They are shocked when they find how few fighters he has to protect the country. As a result of this meeting, they offer two squadrons of Goshawks (these are the two they maintain in Scotland as a replacement reserve for the carriers operating out of the UK) to help cover the ships and coast. Dowding asks the Air Ministry to allow this, but the request vanishes into the maze of the Air Ministry bureaucracy.

May 22nd

German panzers reach Calais and Boulogne. The BEF is now cut off from retreat to the south. By the 24th the BEF and French army were falling back on the port of Dunkirk.

May 26th

After the way in which the situation on land has been deteriorating, the Navy has been making plans for an evacuation of as much of the BEF as is possible. The operation will be controlled by Admiral Ramsey at Dover, and it was hoped

157

that as many as 45,000 men could be lifted off before the rest of the force is forced to surrender. With the situation now so critical, the Navy again brought up the issue of loaning two squadrons of fighters directly to the Prime Minister, as they point out that their earlier offer seems to have been lost by the RAF. The PM is shocked, and on being informed that Dowding was already in favour (but awaiting permission from the Air Ministry), tells them to expedite it immediately. The 'or else' is left implied. Arrangements were made to fly the squadrons down to East Anglia the following day

May 27th - June 4th France.

Over this period the Royal Navy, aided by merchant ships, the French navy, and numerous allied ships evacuated 340,000 men; the entire BEF plus many French troops. The total number evacuated is almost ten times what was originally thought possible. The operation was given limited air cover; due to the distance from the UK, only the Goshawks had the range to effectively cover the operation, and strong Luftwaffe formations meant RAF fighters could only be committed in small numbers. The Goshawks have mainly been used to cover the sea areas against the Luftwaffe as their endurance and familiarity in operating over the sea has made them the logical choice, allowing the RAF fighter squadrons to concentrate over the beaches and the BEF.

The operation has not been without naval loss; the RN has lost four destroyers and numerous other craft. Fighter command has lost nearly 100 aircraft, and the FAA squadrons 12. However between them they have cost the Luftwaffe the best part of 200 planes.

It had already been decided when the BEF was retreating towards the coast that it would be impossible to continue any major support of the forces in Norway. Accordingly plans were made for an evacuation. The Norwegian government was not informed until the 1st June, when the Dunkirk operation made it obvious no forces could be spared for Norway. While the campaign had gone reasonably for the allies, the German occupation of the southern part of the country meant that it would be far easier for Germany to supply and reinforce its forces than it would be for the allies, and that there was no reasonable likelihood of being able to force the Germans out.

The meetings to inform the Norwegians of this were emotional, especially after all that had been done to retain the northern part of the country. However the logic was clear; the Germans could resupply via a short sea route to Oslo that would be almost impossible for the Allies to interdict, while allied forces had to go a long distance to Narvik. While the Royal Navy had sufficient forces to do this, the real problem was that after Dunkirk there were simply no land or air forces or supplies available. The meeting was finally concluded when the Norwegian King informed his staff and the British that he agreed there was no choice; he, his family and the Norwegian government would evacuate to the UK to continue the war. He stated he was not prepared for the allies to risk all to try and hold Northern Norway in view of the circumstances. When the text of his statements was later sent to Churchill, he replied with a personal message that' Britain would not cease to wage war against Germany until Norway was again free'. It also made a deep impression on the commander of the French forces in Norway, which would have later consequences when they were withdrawn to Britain.

The evacuation, both men and equipment, would take around two weeks; first from Narvik, leaving only the Norwegian forces in control, then the allied forces around Trondheim were taken off by sea, again with as much of their equipment as possible. The operations and convoys were covered by the Royal navy and its carriers. There was only fitful effort from the Luftwaffe (the bulk of which was heavily engaged in France), and while the army units did mount some attacks, these were held off by the Norwegian army.

Due to the heavy escort provided, there were no losses to aircraft during the evacuation. However there was damage to one of the carriers due to a U-boat attack. Although the carriers were flying a constant A/S cover of four swordfish (in all weathers), U-46 must have been waiting undetected as the last convoy left from Narvik. She fired 4 torpedoes at HMS Formidable; one struck. The carriers TDS did about as well as expected, however the heavy torpedo hit her amidships, quickly flooding the forward port boiler room and some adjacent spaces. Flooding was limited, and although the carrier quickly took on a 10 degree list, this was brought under control by counter-flooding and shifting fuel, leaving her listing only by 5 degrees, the situation she returned to Britain in.

The unfortunate consequence to the submarine of attacking a well-escorted convoy was to be heavily depth-charged by the escorting destroyers; after some 20 minutes of this, the submarine was seen to surface. While a destroyer turned to race towards her, she was strafed by a Goshawk as her crew attempted to get up on deck, at which point a white flag was hurriedly waved from the conning tower. Deciding not to ram, the destroyers instead pulled alongside and took the submarines surrender; she would be taken back to Britain for evaluation.

The damage to Formidable, though serious, was not considered dangerous; she would be operational again in two to three months (in fact it would take until September due to the heavy dockyard workload on small craft and destroyers after Dunkirk). Considering the number of U-boats operating off Norway, the Admiralty was quite pleased that this is the only damage to a large ship by submarine in the campaign (it was not realised at the time that a number of ships had been spared by the poor performance of the German torpedoes magnetic exploders).

It is suggested that the Kriegsmarine could sortie Bismarck to intercept the Norway-British convoys. This is rejected by the analysts as (a) she is working up, and (b) on her own she is a sitting target for the FAA, and she is then going to face 3-4 battleships of the Home Fleet, with inevitable results.

9th June

The King of Norway and the Norwegian government arrived back in Britain on the heavy cruiser HMS Devonshire. The exiled government had not surrendered, and will carry on the fight from Britain.

The last Hurricanes in Norway follow a SeaLance guide out to HMS Illustrious at sea. It had been intended to destroy the planes in Norway, as they did not have the range to make it back to Britain, but fighters are in short supply, and three pilots have volunteered to attempt to land them on the carrier. The carrier heads into the wind at full power, making 32 knots, to make the landing as easy as possible. All three of the planes land successfully, and arrangements are made to fly out the rest of the planes on the following day. This will be the final convoy to leave Norway.

10th June

The remaining ten Hurricanes and nine Gladiators are led to Illustrious. As on the previous day, the landings are made with no incidents other than to increase the number of grey hairs on the RAF pilots. The planes on the deck make it difficult for Illustrious to fly off cover, so the air duties are being handled by HMS Colossus and HMS Mars. The last of 30,000 allied troops, and over 6,000 Norwegian volunteers (who will form the core of the Free Norwegian forces) are evacuated. The Norwegian forces left in the country have orders to surrender as soon as the King and parliament have reached safety.

The convoy is spotted by the Luftwaffe, and six He-111's attack it later that day. In a final end to the Norwegian conflict, the FAA enacts some revenge by shooting down five of the bombers for no loss.

The final naval tally for the Norwegian operation is:

Royal Navy

One light fleet carrier, two destroyers, a number of submarines and other light vessels such as A/S trawlers

A battleship, fleet carrier, three cruisers and a number of other ships have been damaged.

Kriegsmarine

One Battlecruiser, one Pocket battleship, two heavy cruisers, two light cruisers, nine destroyers as well as at least six submarines plus other light vessels

The Royal navy is quietly happy at this result. The Kriegsmarine has been rendered almost non-operational for relatively minor losses. Although a number of warships have been damaged (some quite severely) by the Luftwaffe, the presence or intervention of the FAA has saved more damage. Indeed, if allowed to press their attacks without fighter opposition, it is considered very likely that some of the damaged ships would have been sunk. Apart from the Graf Zeppelin and the Bismarck, both of which have only started to work up, the only operational ships in the Kriegsmarine are nine destroyers.

The situation for the Navy got worse, however, as Mussolini finally declared war on the allies. Fortunately HMS Glorious had safely delivered her fighters and convoy to Malta so the exposed island fortress, so close to Italy, had at least some fighter protection. The ending of the Norwegian campaign means there are heavy ships available, although due to damage and losses during Dunkirk, and the need to keep forces in home waters, there is a shortage of light ships such as destroyers. Ships are also needed to cover the evacuation of British troops from France.

11th June

In the Mediterranean, the Italian air force raided Malta. One Gladiator is lost on the ground. SM79 bombers escorted by Mc200 fighters attack Grand Harbour and two of the airfields. The Italian fighters are small planes with some resemblance to the Goshawk, manoeuvrable but slower and far less heavily armed. The defenders shot down three Mc200 fighters and three of the SM79 bombers for the loss of one Goshawk shot down and one forced to land. On Gladiator was also damaged.

13th June.

The US Congress votes $1.8B for the Army and $1.3B for naval construction. The first shipment of arms requested by Britain leave the US; they have been sold as scrap to a steel company then bought by the UK.

14th June

The German Army enters Paris, which has been declared an open city. The swastika now flies from the Eiffel tower.

After a long and sometimes heated conversation with Churchill, Brooke (who is in France to organise the remaining British formations) convinces the Prime Minister that there is little hope of any further French resistance, and that all remaining British troops are to be evacuated to the UK.

A single Italian aircraft, missed by the defences, dropped bombs on Malta, damaging a few buildings before escaping. The current joke among the naval personnel on the island is that they 'must have learned about mass attacks from the RAF'.

15th June.

The Royal navy commences Operation Aerial, the evacuation of all remaining British forces in France

The Red Army marches into Lithuania, aided by hordes of NKVD agents. The Lithuanians are resigned to their occupation; there is little that can be done with the major European powers busy in the West.

In the USA, President Roosevelt signs a Congressional Act authorising the USN to have strength of not less than 10,000 aircraft and 16,000 aircrew. These numbers are not really taken seriously in Germany, although the President is indeed deadly serious.

16th June.

The UK government offers to form a Union with France to continue the war. France declines, and instead asks to be released from its obligation not to make a separate peace with Germany.

18th June

General Charles de Gaulle, who became under-secretary for national defence in the last days of the Reynaud government, flies to England and broadcasts this appeal:

"Speaking in full knowledge of the facts," he said, "I ask you to believe me when I say that the cause of France is not lost." He called on French officers and men, including civilians, to get in touch with him. "Whatever happens," declared the general, "the flames of French resistance must not and shall not die."

The U.S. Secretary of State Cordell Hull directs the Deputy U.S. Ambassador to France to advise the French government that if the French fleet falls into German hands, France would "permanently lose the friendship and goodwill of the Government of the U.S." The French reiterate their statement that the French fleet "would not be surrendered to the Germans."

20th June

The French government asks Italy for armistice terms.

In Libya, Italo Balbo writes to Marshall Badoglio,

"Our light tanks, already old and armed only with machineguns, are completely outclassed. The machineguns of the British armoured cars pepper them with bullets which pierce their armour easily. We have no armoured cars. Our antitank defences are largely a matter of make-do: our modern weapons lack adequate ammunition. Thus the conflict has taken on the character of steel against flesh..." The British, badly outnumbered but highly mechanized, had surprisingly seized the initiative from the start, mainly via their armoured car patrols, which raided on the Italian side of the frontier with impunity. Balbo wrote of "infernal armoured cars, which run over all types of ground at fifty kilometres per hour"

Balbo is given a provisional go-ahead for his project to invade Egypt.

Japan takes advantage of the fall of France by warning the French administration in Indochina that it must stop helping the Chinese Nationalist government in Chungking immediately.

The protest was delivered by Japan's foreign minister, Mr. Tani, to the French ambassador. He was warned that France's governor in Indochina must stop the transit of war materials across the Chinese border or face severe repercussions. At the same time Japan has formally asked Germany and Italy to preserve the status quo in Indo-china.

Reports that Japanese forces are massing on Hainan island have increased fears that Japan is about to invade the French colony. French and British ships have been told not to call at Indochinese ports.

21st June

Churchill orders a body of 5,000 men to be 'trained in parachuting'. The British Army has been impressed by the use of German airborne troops in Norway and in the West.

Evidence about "Knickebein", a German radio navigation aid, is given to a British cabinet level committee, by R.V. Jones. The actions taken after this meeting result in progress and play a large part in lessening the effects of the German Blitz. The eminent scientist Henry Tizard, who argued that the beams did not exist, is persuaded not to resign due to giving misleading advice; the original evidence had, after all, not been conclusive.

The French received the terms for Armistice by the Germans in a railroad carriage at Compiègne, France. There will be no discussion of the terms allowed by the Germans. This is the same location and the same railroad carriage used to present the Allied terms to the Germans in 1918.

22nd June

France agrees and signed the terms of a harsh armistice with Germany. The remnant of the Polish army sails for England on the liner Batory

In Japan, a new Japanese cabinet is formed by Prince Konoye Fumiaro, with General Tojo Hideki as Minister of War and Matsuoka Yosuke as Minister of Foreign Affairs

Force H is formed at Gibraltar under Sir James Somerville. The force is joined by the new fleet carrier Implacable on her first operational duties.

Over the last week actions have been taking place off the coast of Africa between Italian submarines and British destroyers, sloops and light forces. Consideration is giving to basing a force of Swordfish at Aden to help them; these are available at Alexandria, but there is a shortage of aircrew after the losses off Norway.

24th June

Japan formally requests Britain to close the Burma Road, stop the flow of war materials through Hong Kong and withdraw its garrison at Shanghai. The British government agrees to consider this. While under normal circumstances they would refuse, in view of the current emergency they cannot afford to antagonise the Japanese Empire.

The commander of the French force withdrawn from Norway, Général de Brigade Bethouart and General DeGaulle, speak with their troops, asking them to remain and fight as Free French, despite the 'abject surrender' of the French government. General de Bethouart, who had been particularly moved by the words and actions of King Haakon during the decisions to leave Norway, gives a particularly effective speech. Many of the men, who consider that they didn't lose the battle, but had to withdraw due to failure elsewhere, and which include such elite units as the French Foreign Legion, decide to stay. Although most of the French troops recovered at Dunkirk and later decide to return to France, a total of some 15,000 men form what will become the First Free French Division, which will serve with such distinction in North Africa and the Mediterranean later in the war.

The Polish troops who were evacuated from Norway, the Polish Independent Highland Brigade, volunteer as a man to stay and fight.

25th June

Despite a call by the Petain government in Bordeaux to cease hostilities, French colonies show no sign of giving up the battle against Germany. At least one commander, General Nogues in North Africa, has refused orders from Petain to return to France. French generals in Somaliland have cabled their support for the Allies; calls have come from Syria and Lebanon for France to continue the fight, and the French governor-general in Indochina has refused to lower the tricouleur. The general overall situation in the French colonies is confusing.

Operation Aerial ends; the Royal Navy had evacuated over 215,000 servicemen and civilians from France.

Chapter 19

HMS King George V (always referred to in the fleet as KGV) is commissioned. Displacing over 35,000 tons and with 9x15" guns, she is the first of the new battleships to be completed after the building holidays of the Washington and London naval treaties. She immediately starts an intensive workup to be operational as soon as possible.

As a result of the surrender of France, a study had been made of the possibility of aerial attack on the United Kingdom, possibly followed by a seaborne invasion. Since it is clear from the activity of the Luftwaffe that their Air Fleets are reorganising and building up strength in Northern France, it is taken as given that some sort of bombing campaign will ensue. RAF Fighter Command has already been planning for this, as have the AA defences, but there are problems due to the insufficient number of fighters available.

The Navy is already well advanced with its preparations to repel any seaborne invasion, but in the meantime they offer the help of the FAA to defend the country. While the FAA aircraft can communicate with the RAF stations (common frequencies and equipment has been worked on since the FAA took over defence of Scapa Flow and had to coordinate with the RAF), operational procedures are different.

The FAA can offer 36 Goshawks (these are the operation reserve held in the UK for the carriers, plus a further 18 aircraft from HMS Formidable (currently undergoing repairs for her torpedo damage). In order to simplify the integration of the forces, it is suggested that the FAA take over responsibility for the North. This will allow Fighter Command to allocate 3 squadrons of replaced fighters into the south. In view of the Goshawks range and training in working over water, this area is thought particularly appropriate for them to defend. The FAA say that while more planes will be available soon (as in the Spitfire and Hurricane factories, the Goshawk has been given priority and production will soon be at nearly 50 planes a month), they have a shortage of pilots.

The FAA had been building up its pilot roster from the RNVR and new pilot trainees, as they knew they had five carriers finishing this year. As a result, they have not had the chance to build up a pool of replacements (this was scheduled for after the new carriers airgroups had been filled out), and they have had to replace their losses over Norway. If they were to provide more pilots for the air defence of the UK, then the fleet carriers would be underprotected, and Norway has already shown how dangerous this is. As a compromise, some of the pilots serving on the light carriers escorting convoys were marked as emergency replacements.

Looking at the planes they have in reserve, the FAA can probably supply another couple of squadrons if it can find the manpower - this would be useful, as five squadrons of the longer-ranged Goshawk can probably cover the North of England. Then someone wrestling with the problem wondered what happened to the RAF pilots who used to fly with the FAA up till late 1939, when they finally had enough pilots to manage on their own?

3rd July - the French Navy

The old French battleships Courbet and Paris and several destroyers and submarines, including the giant Surcouf, are in British ports. They were boarded and seized by the Royal Navy, but not before there are casualties on both sides; three British personnel and a French seaman die in scuffles on board the submarine Surcouf; In total 59 French warships are seized; they will all be commissioned into the Royal Navy, where most of them will end up being manned by the Free French forces.

In Alexandria, Admiral Cunningham is able to reach agreement, after considerable discussion, with the French Admiral Godfrey on the demilitarisation of battleship Lorraine, four cruisers and a number of smaller ships. There is, however, a considerably more serious problem with the French ships at Mers-el-Kebir near Oran. The French force here is much more powerful (the old battleships Provence and Bretagne, the modern battleships Dunkerque and Strasbourg, the Seaplane carrier Commondante Teste, and 6 destroyers), under the command of Admiral Gensoul.

The British force, commanded by Admiral Somerville, consisted of the battleships Hood, Resolution and Valiant, the aircraft carriers Ark Royal, Glorious, and Implacable, and supporting cruisers and destroyers. Somerville is under strict orders from Churchill to make sure the French ships do not fall into German hands, even if that means sinking them himself. Somerville is not himself enthusiastic about the order, but he has received a message from Frazer telling him that he will back his attempts to negotiate with the French, but that the ships must not get away to France.

Accordingly, Somerville starts by letting the French see his force, before the carriers pull out to sea and he sends Captain Holland, the Ark Royal commander, to negotiate. Before he leaves, Holland informs him that the French Admiral is very conscious of protocol, and asks if Somerville will negotiate in person (with him to translate) if it would seem to offer better results. Somerville has no objection; he is quite confident that with three fleet carriers available the French ships cannot escape without being damaged and then brought down by his battleships.

Holland, who knows some of the French officers personally, finds that indeed Gensoul would be offended by talking terms with him. He signals this to Somerville, who joins him ashore. The terms from the British are simple:

(1) Sail with us and continue the fight until victory against the Germans.

(2) Sail with reduced crews under our control to a British port. The reduced crews would be repatriated at the earliest moment.

If of these courses is adopted by you we will either restore your ships to France at the conclusion of the war or pay full compensation if they are damaged meanwhile.

(3) Alternatively if you feel bound to stipulate that your ships should not be used against the Germans unless they break the armistice, then sail them with us with reduced crews to some French port in the West Indies - Martinique for example - where they can be demilitarised to our satisfaction, or perhaps be entrusted to the USA and remain safe until the end of the war, the crews being repatriated.

(4) If you refuse these fair offers, I must with profound regret, require you to sink your ships within 6 hours.

(5)Finally, failing the above, I have the orders from His Majesty's Government to use whatever force may be necessary to prevent your ships from falling into German hands.

Gensoul is unhappy with all of these options, but having been told of the force Somerville has outside the harbour, he felt there was little or no chance of his ships escaping to France unless they could escape under cover of night, or maybe with the aid of submarines. He has already sent a signal asking for submarine support.

The British are happy to negotiate for any of the first three options. They do point out (having a reasonable idea of what options Gensoul has to break out) that the area off the coast is being patrolled by their planes, and in view of the risk from Axis submarines, any submarine sighted that attempts to submerge will of course have to be sunk 'as a precaution'. Gensoul hadn't told Admiral Darlan of all the options he has been given, and tries to stall the negotiations until dark.

Oddly the British don't seem too concerned at this, and the reason why is shown as twilight deepens; Gensoul has ordered his ships to be at 30 minutes notice, and these preparations are shown in clear detail by the flares dropped by the first of what will be a continual stream of Swordfish (who seem to be stuffed full of flares) that circle the harbour all night. The British point out blandly that this is just 'to make sure no unfortunate incidents happen that might be confused by darkness'. He has already been informed that the British carriers haven't gone away, they are just out of sight; that evening, French Curtiss H-75 fighters flew over the British battleships in a show of force; one answered by a full squadron of Goshawks, who obligingly tailed and escorted them over the fleet and home again.

By the morning, Gensoul realised he had run out of options. Somerville has pointed out he MUST have a decision that day, and asks if it would help if he signalled Admiral Darlan himself? Gensoul knew that if this happens his mendacity will be exposed, and that Darlan will probably be unhappy. His decision was helped by the news that Admiral Godfrey at Alexandria has agreed to demilitarise his ships. He will now not be the first French Admiral to allow his ships to be rendered impotent.

According he agreed, very grudgingly, to sail to Martinique under US escort and be interred there. The USA will handle the arrangements, which means that the French ships will not appear to have been taken there by the Royal Navy. He didn't see he has any option; the results of the Royal navy's carriers and surface ships off Norway made him think he had no chance of reaching France with a breakout.

For his part, Somerville is satisfied; he had no desire to have to sink the French ships, and he knew they would have been easy targets (unknown to Gensoul some 60 bombers have been spotted on the carriers, armed and fuelled, to fly off if any French ships were seen to attempt to leave the harbour). He has been politely ignoring constant signals from Churchill to hurry up, aided by Fraser who has been pointing out that with the carriers and battleships there they is little chance, short of divine intervention by the weather, of the French ships making an escape. While Churchill was adamant that the French ships must not end up in German hands, the performance of the Royal Navy and the FAA off Norway made the decision to allow Somerville more time acceptable to him.

5th July - the Mediterranean Sea

Twelve Cormorant dive bombers of 813 Squadron, nominally assigned to HMS Courageous (they were actually the reserve force at Alexandria), had been forwarded to an advanced airbase near Sidi Barrani, giving them the range to hit shipping in and around Tobruk, 110 nm away. Besides sinking the destroyer Zeffiro and the destroyer Euro, one merchant ship was sunk and one damaged.

The actions of the Royal Navy in impounding the French ships in British ports were condemned by the Vichy government, who broke off diplomatic relations.

The actions in North Africa to peacefully resolve the situations was announced by London as a major diplomatic success, and a special effort was made to point this out to any and all French colonies, many of which were still wavering over supporting Vichy.

HMS Warspite arrived at Gibraltar. She was intended to join the East Mediterranean fleet at Alexandria and allow one of the ships there to go home for a short refit - she had received an updated radar while her damage from the Gneisenau battle was being repaired.

6th July

The Sudan Defence Force at the frontier post is attacked by a greatly superior Italian force, but fought a successful delaying action and inflicted heavy losses on the enemy.

7th - 8th July - Dakar, off Africa

The Royal Navy carrier HMS Colossus and the heavy cruisers HMS Dorsetshire and HMAS Australia, with accompanying destroyers, laid off Dakar Harbour. Their mission was to obtain a surrender from the French garrison, but the French blocked the port to prevent it being delivered. Colossus was carrying a full deck park for the first time, as there wasn't another carrier immediately available to support her (42 planes have been squeezed onto the light carrier, her deck officer praying daily they don't encounter bad weather).

The British sent a small boat to deliver the ultimatum anyway. After it docked, 12 Swordfish and 12 Cormorants flew over the port in a show of force. After recent events, it's a rather unsubtle reminder of what the Royal Navy can do to ships in port. Despite this the Vichy French authorities sent the British messenger back, ultimatum unopened. As a result, the British make a dummy run over the Richelieu, to make it clear what they are going to do. AA fire is desultory and ineffective.

The next wave of aircraft drop torpedoes. Immobilised in the harbour, the Richelieu is a helpless target, and was hit by 3 torpedoes. She took on an immediate list. The FAA break off their attack - there are no heavy repair facilities at Dakar, and the ship is now effectively immobilised. It is an unsatisfactory ending for the allies, but they have no troops with them and while they could sink all the ships in the harbour, it seems that this would be unlikely to force the commander to surrender.

On the 6th of July an Italian convoy left Naples, destination Benghazi. It was escorted by three groups of ships; a close escort of eight destroyers and four torpedo boats, six heavy cruisers and four destroyers 35 miles to the east, and the main force consisting of the battleships Cesare and Cavour, eight light cruisers and 16 destroyers.

At the same time the Royal Navy was involved in its own convoy run, this time from Alexandria to Malta. Two convoys were actually involved, a fast convoy at 13kt and a slow one at 9kt. Protecting them were three groups of ships; Force A, with five cruisers and a destroyer, Force B with the battleship Malaya and five destroyers, and Force C with the battleships Ramilles and Royal Sovereign, the carrier Courageous and 11 destroyers.

At 0800 on the 8th, Admiral Cunningham received a report from the submarine HMS Phoenix that at 0515 she had sighted two Italian battleships and four destroyers some 200m east of Malta, steering south. Malta was instructed to search the area with flying boats, and Cunningham altered course to the NW.

While this search was going on, Cunningham's force received unwelcome visits from the RA. First, the fleet was located by two Cant Z.506 reconnaissance seaplanes from Tobruk. While they radioed the location back to Admiral Campioni, the two slow seaplanes very soon learnt that attempting to shadow a fleet covered by Goshawks is a very dangerous undertaking. One was shot down; the second was damaged but managed to make its escape by hiding in the clouds. Admiral Campioni ordered his fleet to defend the convoy by turning eastward and preparing for action. The Italian Supreme Command, however, was reluctant to risk its warships in a night time encounter, and they ordered the fleet to avoid contact. During the initial positioning the Italians suffered technical problems on three destroyers and two light cruisers, so these ships, with several additional destroyers, were detached to refuel in Sicily.

An hour later, the British warships were visited by the first of 72 bombers. These were making high level attacks from about 12,000ft. The bombers were not escorted (presumably the carrier had not been spotted by the seaplanes before they had been driven off). The Goshawks thus found them fairly easy to intercept once a raid had been detected, however the constant stream of raids made the managing of the CAP very difficult. In order to avoid having fuelled and armed planes on the hangar deck (a dangerous situation which the British wanted to avoid, especially when under air attack), the replacement fighters had to be rearmed and refuelled on deck. This was a slower operation than doing it in the hangar. As a result the fighters only managed to shoot down nine of the bombers, although a number were damaged (the fleet AA shot down one more bomber).The cruiser HMS Gloucester was hit by one bomb on the bridge, which caused serious damage. Although many other ships (including HMS Malaya, Cunningham's flagship) received close misses, no other ships were damaged.

9th July

At dawn the Courageous flew off a search of three Swordfish. During the morning these planes, and the seaplanes still searching from Malta, confirmed an Italian fleet of at least two battleships, 12 cruisers and 'many' destroyers was some 50 miles off Cape Spartivento, some 100 miles to the west of the British fleet. Admiral Cunningham, although hampered by the slow speed of his old unmodernised battleships, altered course to engage. The Courageous, which had been alerted as soon as the first sighting report came in, had already spotted a full strike of 15 Swordfish and 12 Cormorants ,with four Goshawks as escort (this was the maximum she could spot for a single strike, and it was hoped to catch the Italians by surprise)

At 1200 the strike saw the Italian ships moving south, in good weather. First to attack were the Swordfish, their target the battleships Cesare and Cavour. Attacking in flights of three, the planes managed two torpedo hits on Cesare and one on the Cavour, in the face of fierce AA fire - two Swordfish were shot down. Sadly none of these were decisive hits (the Courageous had not yet received the newer, heavier torpedoes as she was still operating Swordfish), although both ships were slowed. However even with torpedo damage, they could still make 21 knots, which was faster than Admiral Cunningham's old battleships could do.

The Cormorant attack was more successful. As they were using 1,000lb bombs, they had not targeted the battleships, as it was felt they would not be able to penetrate their deck armour, so they had targeted two of the heavy cruisers. Diving down as the torpedo attacks were still going in against the battleships, the first six planes benefitted from the distraction, and indeed the first three released their bombs before any defensive fire was aimed in their direction. As a result they made a textbook attack, three of their six bombs hitting the cruiser, which slewed to a halt, belching flames and obviously in serious trouble. Seeing this, the second six planes attacked a different ship, but by now the defences were fully alerted and although none of the planes were shot down, only one bomb hit.

The strike recovered to the carrier, now well behind the battleships, and landed on around 1330. Meanwhile Cunningham's cruiser screen had met the Italian cruisers, and exchanged fire. The Italian reaction was somewhat confused, possibly due to lack of orders from the damaged flagship, and although the Italian ships outnumbered the British, the exchange of fire did little damage. The battleships finally got into range at 1500, and started to exchange fire with the two Italian battleships, Although the Italian ships outranged the old British battleships, they stayed close to a cruiser in obvious difficulty (this was the one hit by the single bomb in the earlier raid; the first cruiser, hit by three 1,000lb bombs, had sunk some time earlier.

The Italian gunnery was not the most effective, and eventually the Malaya landed a hit on one of the battleships (the Cesare). This proved the final straw for the Italian admiral, who then withdrew using his superior speed to the north, abandoning his damaged cruiser. Even slowed by torpedo damage, they had no difficulty disengaging from the British fleet. A second strike was ordered from the Courageous, this time 12 Swordfish (some planes had been damaged in the previous attack) and eight Cormorants, escorted by six Goshawks. Due to increasing cloud, the planes had some difficulty finding the fleeing Italians, and as a result rather hurried the attack. A heavy cruiser was miss-identified as a battleship, and as a result all 12 Swordfish attacked it; more agile than a battleship, the cruiser managed to dodge all 12 torpedoes by some superlative shiphandling. The dive bombers had a little more success; one heavy cruiser was hit, incapacitating her two forward turrets, and the final two Cormorants, who had gotten separated from the other planes, made a speculative attack on a destroyer, which took a 1,000lb bomb near the stern, and was obviously sinking as the planes left.

By the time the planes had been recovered, there was no time for any further attacks, and the Italian fleet was able to make its escape from the British force.

10th July.

HMS Ark Royal, escorted by four destroyers, left Gibraltar, her destination Alexandria via the Cape.

Believing the Italian Fleet has returned to Augusta, nine Swordfish from HMS Courageous delivered a torpedo attack on the Augusta roads. The destroyer Leone Pancaldo was hit and sunk in shallow water (it was later salvaged) and a motor ship was damaged.

In the English Channel, the newly-relocated Luftwaffe began its attacks on the convoys using the Straights of Dover. 20 Dive bombers attack a convoy off Dover

The Royal Navy report on the possibility of invasion is handed to the War Cabinet. It makes interesting reading. The report considers three types of possibilities for invasion.

(1) Some sort of fast, improvised attack on the East Coast. This has been mooted by a number of people. The Navy's considered opinion is that these are the stuff of poor fiction rather than anything believable. A successful invasion requires far more that just landing unsupported troops with no resupply on beaches or even ports. They point out Norway as an example of what an invasion actually requires. While such a landing MIGHT be possible, it would first require absolute air superiority (the attack by surprise used in Norway is obviously out of the question), and also no possibility of local counter-strikes. The Admiralty rule these options out unless RAF Fighter Command is completely destroyed.

(2) A long distance invasion by steamer from Germany or, more likely, the Low Countries, aimed at East Anglia. This is considered possible. However in order to achieve it there are a number of prerequisites for Germany to fulfil. A sufficient force of ships, for both the initial invasion plus its supply, must be mustered in ports in Northern Germany and the Low Countries. The ships will require escorts, and since the Kriegsmarine is basically non-existent at the moment, this means again complete control of the air sufficient to prevent the Royal Navy from destroying the convoys.

The Navy suggests a number of responses to minimise this threat, and to give adequate warning if it is attempted. First, reconnaissance is needed of the northern German ports, the Low Countries ports, and ideally as far west as western Poland. This will enable any build-up of ships (and possibly troops) to be detected and plans amended accordingly. Assuming such a build-up is seen, sufficient forces need to be in place to sink the invasion convoys before they reach the coast.

The first need is for some means of conducting reliable reconnaissance so far east. Currently the RAF is trying to use the Blenheim bomber as a long range recon plane, a task for which it is not suited, delivers poor results and causes high loss rates. The FAA has therefore been talking to some of the aeroplane companies to see if there are any other alternatives. There is indeed one. The Westland Company has been manufacturing for some time the Mk2 version of its Whirlwind twin engined fighter. The Mk1 used the Rolls-Royce Peregrine engine, but some time ago it was clear that this engine would have a low priority, and as a result they modified the plane (making it somewhat larger) to take two R-R Merlin engines and more fuel (the original smaller design wasn't a long ranged plane; the new one carried more fuel). This had flown in the spring of 1939, and a contract had been placed for a limited number of them. The first ones were ready, and it had been expected to form a squadron later this year.

After listening to the RN requirements, the company had suggested modifying (on an urgent basis) some of the first batch as a reconnaissance plane. A large drop tank would extend the range, and taking out the guns and cleaning up the plane would increase its speed. The original design had achieved around 380mph with the Merlin XII, and one of the trial aircraft had managed over 400mph with the new Merlin XX. They promised at least 425mph with a reconnaissance version. This would enable it to basically fly away from any current Luftwaffe fighter, thus making successful reconnaissance flights over defended targets practical. Only a small number of the aircraft were currently available, but only a few were required for reconnaissance.

In addition to this, the FAA has suggested putting a temporary fuel tank in a few SeaLance TBR planes, ones already fitted with the AS MkII radar. This was by no means perfect yet, but they now had considerable operational experience. With the aid of a team from the manufacturer, and some tlc (tender loving care) by specially selected maintenance crews, they could put planes out along the enemy coast, at night, for a considerable distance. This would make it much more difficult for the Germans to sneak convoys out under cover of night, and give the RN more warning time. It was considered that with these two methods of reconnaissance, ample warning would be available for Home Fleet and local units, as well as FAA aircraft, to devastate any attempted invasion convoy. There was a strike squadron of TBR planes and one of dive-bombers available as their carrier was currently under repair. These could be moved to East Anglian bases; if the invasion occurred these would be supplemented either by more planes flying from airfields, or the Home Fleet carriers.

(3) A short invasion route across the channel. This was in fact considered the most likely, however it still required certain prerequisites. Air superiority was needed. In view of the fact that there were few suitable ports on the channel (and the ones that existed were defended and prepared for demolition), the most like form of invasion would be by small craft, probably assisted by small steamers. This meant that this type of invasion was possible without full control of the air, as a mass of smaller landing craft could accept a percentage of losses more easily (and the numbers would require more effort to destroy an equal number of troops to larger shipping)

Such an invasion force would require the small craft and shipping to be built up in France. As this type of craft was relatively slow, it would probably be based in the French Channel ports, and maybe also in the Low Countries. These were all well in range of surveillance, and so any build-up would be impossible without detection.

The Royal navy intended to saturate the channel at night with light craft to give warning. This type of invasion would be best countered at sea by destroyers (who, while not invulnerable, had shown at Dunkirk that they were difficult to sink from the air). These would be held ready at a suitable distance. The heavy units of the Home Fleet would be kept ready in case Kriegsmarine heavy units were encountered (the Navy was not certain that some of the heavy units attacked off Norway were easily repairable or not), but if not it was felt unnecessary to risk them. The night-capable SeaLance planes would also be used (if this type of attack was seen to be in preparation); although the radar performance was not good against smaller ships, the numbers needed for a successful invasion should be clearly seen.

This type of invasion was also limited by weather. The Channel is a rough piece of sea, and it was considered unlikely this type of invasion would be practical after October due to the unpredictable winter storms

The net result of the report was that the Royal Navy considered an invasion possible, but that if prudent measures (as given in the report) were taken, no surprise invasion was possible. An invasion must defeat the RAF to have any chance of success, so as long as Fighter Command was in being any invasion would either have to be postponed or would fail. In addition to the direct means discussed, it was also assumed all possible intelligence sources would be used to help clarify the situation.

While it was realised that the German Army had a massive superiority over the forces available, they pointed out that what the Germans could invade with was severely limited by shipping, something the Germans did not have ample supplies of. Defeat the shipping, and the German Army was helpless on the Continent.

While there was of course considerable discussion over this report, the general theme was accepted. Anti-invasion preparations continued at full speed, of course, and Lord Beaverbrook tasked with getting the maximum number of fighters available, as this was clearly the best means of rendering an invasion impossible. The confidence of the Royal Navy to stop the invasion, with the help of the RAF and the precautions mentioned, did help to reduce the incipient panic in some departments at the thought of invasion.

11th July

Force H, which had put to sea on receiving reports of the Italian fleet, was now returning to Gibraltar, when screening destroyer HMS Escort was attacked by the Italian submarine Marconi north of Algiers. The Escort sank around an hour later after all her crew had been transferred to HMS Forester. There were no casualties.

The Regia Aeronautica delivered a series of raids on the Mediterranean fleet in the Ionian Sea. There were 126 sorties, broken into four raids. It was noticed by the defenders that the Italians seem to have picked up very quickly the understanding that small raids against a fighter defence are costly and usually ineffective, while larger raids tend to swamp the fighter defence. HMS Courageous Goshawks shoot down six S-79's and disrupt the attacks of many more. As a result, the fleet suffered no casualties, although HMS Gloucester was damaged by splinters from a near miss.

13th July

Hitler issues Directive No 15 which orders the Luftwaffe to destroy the RAF in preparation for Operation Sealion. Hitler politely declines Mussolini's offer of Italian forces to aid in the invasion.

The first Free Polish squadron of the RAF, No 302 squadron, is formed.

The first six Westland Whirlwind Mk 2's produced go back to the factory for modification. This involves plumbing for drop tanks, removal of the armament and polishing the aircraft for maximum speed. It was hoped that with the workforce working flat out the first plane would be available for use in a week.

14th July

Luftwaffe attacks on the Straights convoys continue. 45 Ju87's, escorted by fighters, attacked a convoy and were intercepted by RAF fighters. Fighter Command claim seven aircraft destroyed.

15th July

Britain's latest commando raid has ended in farce. A team of untrained men designated as Special Forces of No. 3 Commando attempts to raid Guernsey airport. Compass failure sent it in error to the tiny island of Sark. Other men hit undefended points on Guernsey to no purpose. As they withdrew, their commanding officer slipped and fired his revolver, alerting the enemy. Three men said that they could not swim to the pick-up boat.

In the English Channel, a force of 15 Do17's attempts to bomb a convoy but are driven off by RAF Hurricanes

Plebiscites held yesterday in Estonia, Lithuania and Latvia are said to show unanimous support for union with the USSR. In a triumph of local democracy, some regions registered more than 100% support.

FAA squadrons were established on some of the RAF northern bases as agreed; initially three squadrons were involved; it is hoped to add more as planes and pilots permit. The RAF squadrons were allocated to 11 Groups reserve. The transition isn't as smooth as had been hoped. While the FAA are broadly familiar with the system of RAF control (they based their own system on it), there are differences. The FAA squadrons will spend the next few weeks in training on how the RAF system operates. There is also a certain amount of friction between the base (RAF) staff and the (Naval) pilots. The FAA is used to operating ashore from its own establishments, but these are not set up as fighter stations and so are unsuitable for use in the short time period available.

The FAA has more spare planes than pilots at the moment. It takes longer to train a naval pilot, and the training program was never intended to cope with the sorts of extra number suddenly needed. The RN agreed to train two squadrons of Norwegian naval pilots (evacuated from Norway), but integrating them is expected to take some months. Fortunately the language problem isn't as acute as it has been for some of the other foreign squadrons. The FAA also started a search for some of the Goshawk RAF pilots who are now on other duties. It is hoped that some of these are on non-essential jobs and can be used to form another squadron.

16th July

Hitler issues directive no 16, "On the Preparation of a Landing Operation against England (Sealion)". He talks of invading England with 20 divisions, to be put ashore on the south coast between Ramsgate and Lyme Regis. Hitler states that the aim is to "eliminate the English mother country as a base from which the war against Germany can be continued."

General Alfred Jodl says that the invasion should be seen as a river crossing on a broad front, and in place of bridging operations the navy would keep the sea lanes secure against British attacks. The Luftwaffe would knock out the RAF, allowing them to help the navy to control the Channel. Operation Sealion will be ready in nine weeks.

But the admirals in the Kriegsmarine are unhappy. In the absence of purpose-built landing craft, they say that they cannot guarantee to protect hundreds of river barges being towed slowly across the Channel. They also ask how they are expected to get the thousands of horses needed by the Army across the Channel while under fire

The unpleasantness in the Mediterranean continued at a lower intensity. Italian planes raid Haifa; RN and RAN ships bombard the Libyan port of Bardia.

18th July

Two FAA squadrons, one of Cormorant dive bombers and one of SeaLance TBR planes arrived in East Anglia. They are intended for use in anti-invasion duties, but their first task was to integrate with Coastal Command. They also started to prepare supplies for use by more aircraft; in the case of an invasion warning, it is expected to add more squadrons if they are available - this would be faster and safer than bringing the Fleet carriers that far south.

In an attempt to reduce tension in the Far East, Britain acceded to Japanese demands to close the Burma Road for a period of three months. As it is the monsoon period, this closure has little practical impact.

In the USA, The Democratic Party's national convention in Chicago, Illinois, nominates President Franklin D. Roosevelt for their candidate for president. If he wins, it will be an unprecedented third term in office.

19th July

General Alan Brooke was appointed C-in-C Home Forces, replacing Field Marshal Sir Edmund Ironside who retired, promoted to Field Marshal.

The first prototype cavity magnetron was delivered to TRE -- the British radar research centre -- near Swanage, on the south-west coast.

Hitler issued a "Last Appeal to Reason", urging Britain to make peace; he also promoted 12 generals to field marshal, including von Brauchitsch, Keitel, von Rundstedt and Kesselring. Field Marshal Goering was given the new and unique title of Reichsmarschall.

A naval action occurred off Cape Spada (the northwest extremity of Crete) between an allied squadron patrolling the Aegean and two Italian light cruisers transferring between Tripoli and Leros. The allied force consisted of the cruiser HMAS Sydney and five destroyers. In the running battle that ensued, the Bartolomeo Colleoni was first hit by shells from HMAS Sydney and then sunk by three torpedoes from her accompanying destroyers. The Bande Nere was hit twice, but the Sydney was forced to break off due to lack of ammunition. The

British destroyers were bombed by Italian aircraft in the aftermath, resulting in damage to HMS Havock, whose # 2 boiler room was flooded.

In Washington, the US Congress passed the bill asked for by the President to pay for a "two-ocean" navy. The House of Representatives approved a bill appropriating an additional $4 billion to build enough warships to enable the US to confront the danger of war with Germany and its allies in the Atlantic, and simultaneously with the Japanese in the Pacific. There will be an additional 1,325,000 tons of warships and 15,000 naval aircraft. The US fleet will then number 35 battleships, 20 aircraft carriers and 88 cruisers. Previous opposition to these levels of military spending have been swept away by the disaster in France.

20th July

While escorting a channel convoy, the destroyer HMS Brazen was attacked by a large formation of German planes near Dover. Damaged and taken under tow, she later sank. Three planes were reported shot down.

The FAA squadron sunning themselves at Sidi Barrani aerodrome launched an evening raid on Tobruk harbour using torpedoes. In the face of heavy anti-aircraft fire they succeeded in torpedoing and sinking the destroyers Nembo and Ostro

The MAP (Ministry of Aircraft Production) laid out rules designed to maximise the air defences of the country during the current invasion crises. Their initial ideas are met with screams of horror from the RAF, the Navy, and just about everyone else. Indeed, their idea to shut down naval air for at least 3 months to concentrate on RAF planes causes the First and Fifth Sea Lords to have a personal meeting with Churchill. They aren't the only ones, and as a result the MAP's ideas were looked at again, as it had been pointed out that panicking over the possible invasion isn't the best way to win the war. In addition, the RN made some changes to maximise the availability of destroyers.

It was finally decided that the vital planes are the fighters. Spitfire and Hurricane production get top priority over everything else. Next come the FAA and the RAF's beloved bombers; production continues at full speed on the Wellington, Blenheim, and Goshawk. Other combat planes would continue to be built where they don't draw resources from the first two groups. Aircraft development would continue where again it doesn't steal any resources (in general, the needs of these programs are so small in comparison with the main manufacturing lines that they don't make very much difference).

The Navy accepted that the Army currently had priority for guns, and agreed to give them priority for all guns and mounts except where these don't intrude on Army production. This included all single 40mm guns going to the army for the next three months. Dockyard and shipbuilding priority will be given to repairs of destroyers and other light units. Other building will continue where it doesn't impact on this. This is considered a sensible arrangement; distorting and stopping so much other work to get a very small number of extra fighters is seen as unproductive, as the other planes, ships and so on are also helpful in case of invasion. It is agreed to review the priority system in three months, by which time if an invasion hasn't happened it will be unlikely until the spring due to bad weather.

During the second half of July raids on convoys and shipping intensified. The RAF took an increasing toll of the bombers, but their losses also mounted. Coastal shipping was very vulnerable to these attacks as it was impossible to provide constant escorts and it was often not possible to scramble fighters in time.

On the 27th, the RN lost two destroyers; one escorting minesweepers off Sussex, the other in the port of Dover. The increasing intensity of the raids, and the information that the Germans are emplacing heavy guns across the channel, caused the Admiralty to move the small destroyer force from Dover to the Nore.

A night attack on the 27th showed that at the moment the RAF have little hope of stopping night attacks. Work on AI radar is already a top priority, and tests are ongoing using Blenheims; unfortunately when carrying a radar set these planes are barely able to catch a German bomber. Dowding asks that work on a faster night fighter be speeded up; the best prospect is the two-man version of the Reaper, but even with priority it isn't expected until the end of the year at best. The other plane that could be used, the Beaufighter, starts arriving with the squadrons in July; all the planes available will be tasked for night fighters once the squadrons are up to speed, which will take some time as they not only have to get used to the new plane but also to the use of the AI system. In the longer term, the Reaper will take over and the Beaufighters and Blenheims will be phased out.

The next day (the 28th) the Luftwaffe launched raids against the north of England as well as against the channel. Only one of the northern raids was intercepted, by an RAF squadron. It is clear that the FAA squadrons need to become more familiar with the RAF control system in order to be efficient, and the training and integration program intensifies.

The FAA had managed to find quite a few RAF pilots with recent FAA experience flying mahogany bombers (desks). While some of these are in obviously important jobs, many are not. To a man, the RAF pilots approached were eager to help, but the Air Ministry refuses to release them, even when a letter from Dowding asks for them. More than a dozen pilots turned up at FAA bases anyway, a fact to which the RN turns a Nelsonianly blind eye; soon there were enough pilots to form another squadron of Goshawks. The FAA had also released another squadrons worth of pilots from their training program by allocating them to a land-based squadron before they have finished the additional naval pilot training. This gives the FAA five squadrons in the North, with two more manned by Norwegians training. This had freed five Hurricane and Spitfire squadrons, which were allocated to 10 and 12 Groups so they can carry on training and be a ready reserve for 11 Group.

In the Mediterranean, the Royal Navy continued to escort convoys between Alexandria and Aegean ports. As well as a close escort, they are covered by the Mediterranean fleet, including HMS Malaya and HMS Royal Sovereign. During these convoys the RA press home a number of attacks, during which Goshawks from HMS Courageous shoot down some five planes, and the AA accounts for another one. Only one Goshawk was lost (forced to ditch), and the attacks were broken up and disrupted. As a result no ships receive more than splinter damage

By the end of the month HMS Warspite and HMS Implacable have finally arrived via the Cape, and will strengthen the force. It had originally been intended to relieve Courageous and allow her to return home for a refit, but she was considered far too useful where she is now.

Churchill continues to press Wavell for action against the Italians in Ethiopia, using the recently arrives South African Brigade. Wavell's reply states:

"...South African Brigade is only partially trained at present and requires further training before being employed offensively. They must also become acclimatised and learn anti-malaria precautions, etc.

Conditions in East Africa necessitate crossing of 200 miles of almost roadless and waterless bush desert before offensive against Italian East Africa can be made. African native troops who have smaller requirements and are more accustomed to bush conditions are more suitable than white troops for forward role...As to use elsewhere, I understood when the brigade was offered that Smuts had given pledge in Union that South Africans would not be used north of the Equator...I am sure you will keep considerations of geography, climate, deserts, distances etc., constantly in the minds of Middle East Committee. It all looks so simple to them and others on a small-scale map."

Chapter 20

Operation Hurry (Mediterranean)

On the first of August the first opposed mission to fly off fighters to Malta began. This involved both Force H (doing the actual delivery), and the Mediterranean Fleet from Alexandria as a decoy.

Cunningham sought to divert the Italians by a sortie west of Crete with Warspite, Malaya and Implacable, while cruisers and destroyers feinted westwards through the Kithera Channel; at the same time other ships simulated an attack on the island of Kastellorizo in the Dodecanese. This dummy seemed to be sold so successfully that the Italian navy remained in port, apparently unwilling to venture out into such an unknown situation.

Force H launched its own diversion on the 2nd August, when HMS Ark Royal (escorted by HMS Hood) launched an air strike on Cagliari. Just after dawn 15 SeaLance and 12 Cormorants caused severe damage to hangars, aircraft, and other facilities, started fires and laid mines in the outer harbour. One Cormorant was shot down by a defending fighter; due to an error in information, it had been thought there were no fighters based at the airfield. Meanwhile the light carrier HMS Glory (sent out from the UK with 15 Goshawk fighters on deck) had flown off her planes, accompanied by two Cormorants as navigators (the Goshawks were RAF-crewed planes).

The Regia Aeronautica attacks Force H after the planes have been flown off, and the S-79's run into the combined CAP of the Ark Royal and the Glory, with unpleasant results for the Italians. All the attacks are broken up, and five S.79's are shot down, some others being damaged. Force H returned to Gibraltar on the 4th (HMS Glory would return with the next convoy and resume her role as an escort carrier for the time being)

It had originally been considered to send Hurricanes, but this had been changed to the Goshawk for two reasons; with the current air battle over the UK, Hurricanes were in shorter supply than Goshawks, and it was felt that the longer range of the naval fighter would be particularly useful in Malta in helping to protect the inbound convoys, which were already starting to attract the interest of the Regia Aeronautica. The naval aircraft were also better equipped to manage over water. It was also helpful in that the greater range of the Goshawk allowed an earlier flying off of aircraft, minimizing the risk to Force H.

On the 1st, Hitler set the date for the invasion of Britain at 15 September, and issued his directive no.17 ordering intensification of the air war from 5 August.

OKW issued Fuhrer Directive #17: In order to establish the necessary conditions for the conquest of England, air and sea warfare will be intensified against the English homeland.

(i) The Luftwaffe is to overpower the RAF with all the forces at its command. The attacks are to be directed primarily against flying units, their ground installations, and their supply organizations. The aircraft industry (including anti-aircraft production) should also be targeted.

(ii) After local air superiority is won, the air war will continue against ports and stores of food and provisions. Damage to ports on the south coast must be minimized in view of our future operations.

(iii) Attacks on enemy warships and shipping may be reduced in order to concentrate on above mentioned operations. Operations should be carried out such that air support can be called upon for urgent naval activity, or an invasion, at any time.

(iv) The Führer reserves the right to order terror attacks as measures of reprisal.

(v) Intensified air and sea operations should begin on or after 5th August, weather permitting.

On the 3rd August General de Simone crossed the Ethiopian frontier into British Somaliland with 12 Eritrean battalions and four Blackshirt battalions. He has six battalions in reserve. The British force of five battalions and a camel corps cannot hold out for ever - something of an understatement considering Somaliland's defence budget of just GBP 900.

The Somali town of Hargeisa fell to the Italian army on the 5th, after being assaulted by infantry and tanks after a three-hour bombardment. It was defended by two battalions of Indian and East African troops plus some of the Somali Camel Corps - most of who got away.
Any serious defence of Somaliland failed when the pro-Allied governor of neighbouring French Somaliland, General Legentilhomme resigned today and was replaced by General Germain, who was under heavy Vichy pressure to obey the terms of the Franco-Italian armistice.
Elsewhere, on the borders of Ethiopia, Italy's 300,000 man army seemed reluctant to act aggressively, content with the symbolic occupation of a few border towns, such as Moyale in Kenya and Kassala in the Sudan, and in harassing the British in northern Kenya with some remarkably effective guerrilla columns. It is so short of petrol that it can do nothing else.

Attacks have continued by the Luftwaffe on the channel convoys, as well as other targets all over the UK. On the 8th August a convoy of 20 ships was attacked heavily; six ships were badly damage, four were sunk and only four reached their destination. The RAF lost 19 fighters and shot down 31 German aircraft. After this the Admiralty cancelled the channel convoys and moved the cargoes by rail instead.

2nd August.

The funeral is held for Major Werner Molders. One of the most experienced fighter pilots in the Luftwaffe, Molders had been part of the heavy fighter escort for a bombing raid on Dover on the 28th July. He had encountered the leader of the RAF fighter squadron, 'Sailor' Malan, and in a brief but deadly dogfight his Me109 had been severely damaged by the Spitfires 20mm cannon. He had been seen to fall into the Channel with his stricken aircraft.

12th August- 23rd August, Adlerangriff

During this period the Luftwaffe made determined attacks on the coastal airfields, the fighter squadrons using them, and the Radar system. In addition attacks were carried out during both day and night all over the UK.

The attacks on the Radar system, while serious, were not followed up and the system remained operation and functioning, to the detriment of the Luftwaffe. Although repeated raids were made on the Radar chain, it proved resilient to bombing attacks. The Luftwaffe seemed unaware that a station put out of action could be quickly repaired.

The raids suffered heavy casualties due to the defending RAF fighters. The cannon-armed Hurricanes and Spitfires were proving the medium Luftwaffe bombers insufficiently protected, and as a result more and more fighters were allocated to defence of the bomber formations. The losses suffered by the slow Ju87 were so heavy it was withdrawn from the attack (a point which was immediately noted by the navy, as this was the plane that most worried them from the point of view of air attack on their ships).

With the exception of the rather random attacks across the country, the bombing was concentrated in the South East, meaning that the FAA formations in the north had little to do. The exception came on the 15th, when Luftflotte 5 (operating from Norway) made two separate large scale attacks. It was not clear if this was because they thought all RAF fighters were in the South, or simply to find out if this was the case. One attack, by 50 unescorted Ju88's was made on RAF Great Driffield. This was intercepted by a Hurricane squadron. The squadron was inexperienced (it was in the area to complete the training of many of its new pilots), and the Ju88 was a slippery opponent, but even so they shot down six of them, one Hurricane being damaged. The disruption to the attacks meant little damage was done to targets

The attack on the North East was made by 65 He111's escorted by 34 Me110's. In order to get greater range, the Me110's were using drop tanks and has left their gunners behind. The raid was intercepted by 27 Goshawks (one squadron which had been scrambled, and a further flight of 9 planes which had been already in the air, training, and were close enough (thanks to the Goshawks range) to be vectored onto the raid. The result was a disaster for the Luftwaffe. 10 of the Me110's were shot down (indeed, a couple exploded when the notoriously unreliable drop tanks failed to detach, the petrol vapours exploding when hit by shells). 19 of the He111's were seen to fall (and a further 5 failed to make it home due to damage). Three Goshawks were damaged, but none were lost. The total loss to the Luftwaffe was 40 planes for no losses to the defenders. No further heavy raids against the mainland were made by Luftflotte 5.

On the 12th August the first Bristol Beaufighters are delivered to the Fighter Interception Unit at Tangmere, They are equipped with A.I. MkIV (airborne interception) radar.

An experimental British radar, using the cavity magnetron which was developed only six months earlier, tracks an aircraft for the first time.

The following day, the same cavity magnetron experimental radar, tracks a man on a bicycle for the first time - though his radar cross-section is enhanced somewhat by the tin lid from a box of biscuits.

For some time the British and US government representatives have been negotiating for some sort of deal over the exchange of the base rights for the USA that have been ongoing for some years for military supplies. Prime Minister Churchill has been suggesting that some old US destroyers could be part of a deal, but this has attracted significant resistance from the navy who view them as old, obsolete and worn out. They would far prefer modern ships in exchange for the base rights.

At the beginning of July, a secret mission was undertaken by Cdr Wright, a Canadian engineering officer in the RN, and two civilian engineers. Masquerading as a USN officer (with the aid and connivance of the USA, in order not to reveal anything to the powerful isolationist lobby in the US), he spent 2 weeks examining a number of the destroyers held in reserve. His report was not promising.

Basically the destroyers were in poor condition, especially their machinery which was suffering from severe defects. His estimate was that it would take 4-8 months of dockyard work to put them into a condition suitable for deployment in a North Atlantic winter. As a result, the Admiralty made some suggestions, and these and the engineering report were discussed with Churchill.

On the 16th August the famous 'escorts for bases' deal between the USA and the UK was announced. This would exchange base rights for the USA in a number of strategic areas (which would significantly aid the USA's security) in exchange for 30 Corvettes and 30 of the new 'frigates' (currently in their final design stage), which would be built in US yards. The corvettes would take around 7-8 months to build, the frigates would commence in October (when the design would be complete and plans supplied to the US shipbuilders), and take an estimated 10 months to build.

Knowing he had to push this past the isolationist lobby, President Roosevelt announced this both as a measure to enhance US security in the face of a dangerous world situation (a phrasing that made it more difficult for the isolationists to object to), and that these ships would be used to defend the lives of the civilian victims of the U-boats.

While there would be a delay before the ships would be available, they would come into service not very long after the old destroyers would have done, and the Admiralty considered them much more useful as A/S escorts. While damage to destroyers had been heavy during the Dunkirk evacuation and also in the Battle of Britain so far, the number of ships sunk was far smaller, and the yards expected to have all but a few ships ready for action within a few months.

In the Mediterranean, the fleet bombarded Italian positions at Bardia and Fort Capuzzo. The ships had air cover provided from HMS Implacable, in addition to RAF Gladiators. 10 Regia Aeronautica planes were shot down, three by the fleet air arm, and as a result of the disruption to the attackers no successful attacks were made on the fleet.

With the Empire's recent gains in Libya, the Royal Navy begins laying plans to send several of HMS Courageous's Swordfish aircraft to the Bardia area to operate against Italian supply lanes in the Gulf of Bomba.

On the 21st, the FAA demonstrates that it can hurt the Italian navy even when its carriers are not in the area. Having been informed of an Italian "depot ship" at An-el-Gazala, three Swordfish of HMS Courageous's 824 Squadron, FAA, temporarily based at Ma'aten Bagush, are transferred to Sidi Barrani, equipped with auxiliary fuel tanks and torpedoes. In the late-afternoon, the three headed out on the 180 mile flight to the Gulf of Bomba, routing 30 miles out to sea so as to approach the target from seaward.

Approaching the target, they sighted the Italian Submarine Iride (the mother ship for Italian human torpedoes arriving to attack Alexandria) approaching on the surface. Heading straight for her, the flight leader Captain Patch RM released his torpedo, which struck Iride amidships, sinking her.

Having had no opportunity to attack themselves, the other two continued on the mission assigned. As they approached, they discovered the depot ship Monte Gargano with a submarine and a destroyer tied up alongside. Both torpedoes ran true into the ships, the resulting explosions "sinking whole bloody lot". Initially treated with a certain amount of scepticism when they reported sinking four ships with three torpedoes, the crews were quite exuberant when recon photos the next morning verified that all three in harbour had, in fact, sank, though apparently the destroyer and the submarine were only beached.

26th August

Chad declared its allegiance to Free France and General de Gaulle. French Equatorial Africa is the latest French colony to support General de Gaulle's Free French. Governor Eboue of Chad, France's first black governor in Africa, said today that he refused to accept capitulation. The other Equatorial territories make similar statements in the following days. Elsewhere in French Africa, recent weeks have seen the replacement of pro-Allied officials with Vichy supporters, although the Ivory Coast rallied to de Gaulle on 26 July. The first colony to back de Gaulle was the New Hebrides in the Pacific on 22 July.

30th August

The Vichy French government signed the Matsuoka-Henry Pact and yielded to Japanese. It also acceded to the following demands from the Japanese

(1) An end to shipments of war material to the Chinese nationalists via the Hanoi - Kunming railway

(2) Granting Japanese forces transit rights and access to military facilities in Indochina

(3) The right to station troops in Tokinchina.

In return, Japan agreed to recognize continued French sovereignty over Indochina. Vichy reciprocated with formal recognition of Japan's "pre-eminent" role in the Greater East Asia Co-prosperity Sphere.

This action is of considerable worry to the British government, as Japanese troops in FIC pose a threat to the Imperial forces in Malaya; until now, it has been considered that the sheer distance of the nearest Japanese bases has afforded the British possessions in SE Asia protection.

31st August

Much of French Equatorial Africa has joined the Free French cause, but the Vichy government is using its base at Dakar to intervene and pressurise French governors whenever possible. In order to improve this situation it is intended to launch an operation to capture Dakar and hopefully persuade much more of the French African colonies to join the Free French cause. Accordingly an Anglo-Free French task force under Admiral Cunningham and General DeGaulle departs Liverpool for Dakar, French West Africa. Originally intended as a small force, with hopes that Dakar will surrender, the actions of Dakar so far have made the invasion force more formidable.

In July, Charles de Gaulle had asked Captain Jacques Philippe, Vicomte de Hautecloque (alias Philippe LeClerc) to rally Free French forces in Equatorial Africa. He has been attempting to do so, but is concerned at the resistance he feels will be encountered at Dakar. He has also pointed out a secondary reason for capturing Dakar that is important enough to increase the forces sent there.

In Berlin, Hitler had dismissed the misgivings of his generals and admirals, and had given orders for Operation SeaLion to go ahead. Goering had promised to destroy the fighter defences in the south of England in four days, and the RAF in two to three weeks. The Fuhrer states he will decide on the invasion date during the next fortnight.

For the last week the Luftwaffe has been staging very heavy raids against the airfields and infrastructure of the RAF in the south east. Heavy losses have been incurred by both the RAF and the Luftwaffe, but the action, while damaging to the RAF, is not rendering their bases inoperable. The biggest issue for the RAF is the availability of fighter pilots; the FAA has added two more squadrons in the north, allowing all the RAF fighter squadrons there to be allocated to the critical area, and the RAF is also using pilots from some of the Fairy Battle squadrons (the Battle having been shown to be an ineffective aeroplane). Foreign squadrons are also now part of the RAF's defence.

While the attrition is worrying for the RAF, it is slowly becoming critical for the Luftwaffe. They are losing crews at the rate of 5:1 (bombers carry more men, and many of the RAF pilots who bail out survive to fight again), and it is fast becoming obvious that the light machine gun armament of the light bombers is outmatched by the heavy cannon mounted by the RAF fighters. The armament contest is a bit more even for the fighters, but here the losses are also becoming critical.

The transfer of shipping to the Channel ports is beginning, and plans for a feint attack against the east coast of Britain have been made. But Hitler has still not resolved a bitter dispute between the army and navy over the deployment of the invasion   force.
The army had planned a landing on a 200-mile front from Ramsgate to Lyme Regis, throwing into action 1,722 barges, 1,161 motor boats, 470 tugs and 155 transports. Grand Admiral Erich Raeder says that it is quite impossible for his navy to protect such a vast and widely dispersed force

Raeder, who was made a Grand Admiral by Hitler on 1 April 1939, says that the army should concentrate on a narrow front between Folkestone and Eastbourne, "Complete suicide," General Halder, the chief of staff, responded furiously. The British would hit them with overwhelming force. "I might just as well put the troops through a sausage machine."

The RAF and the FAA are continuing their reconnaissance of the Northern ports and likely staging areas. At the moment, there is no sign of any significant activity involving larger ships to the East, but a stream of barges, tugs, and other small vessels has been noted heading for the Low Countries and the French channel ports. Currently the opinion is that the Germans will go for the cross-channel option, and plans are being made to bomb barge concentrations as soon as they get large enough to make this worthwhile. The RAF, which is currently using its heavier bombers to make small raids into Germany, is being pressured by the Navy (and the Army) to use these as well as other available planes to seed the northern ports and the coastal routes with mines. This is being resisted by the RAF, but the pressure to help defeat the invasion finally makes them change the bombers targets accordingly (the fact that the FAA had already agreed to use its available TBR aircraft in this role may have had something to do with their change in policy)

Long range Focke Wulf Condors started operating from a base near Bordeux in France. The initial encounters show that they are intended to be used to both bomb convoys and vector U-boats onto the convoy or an intercepting position. The Royal Navy currently has four light carriers plus its new escort carrier available to escort convoys; these ships and their escort groups are allocated to what are felt to be the most vulnerable locations.

Operation Hats - 30th Aug, Mediterranean Sea

Hats was a very complex operation carried out by the Mediterranean fleet and Force H, with a number of objectives:

To reinforce the eastern fleet with two antiaircraft cruisers, Coventry and Calcutta, the modernised battleship Valiant and the fleet carrier Indefatigable.

To run a supply convoy to Malta

To attack a number of Italian targets in passing, including Rhodes and Cagliari.

Force H left Gibraltar under Admiral Somerville on the 30th August, including the carriers Ark Royal and Indefatigable, and the capital ships Valiant and Hood and with 17 destroyers. On the 31st the squadron encountered two Italian floatplanes, both of which were shot down by the forces CAP. Later that day two destroyers were detached to head north in an attempt to deceive the Italians that Force H was heading for Genoa. The fleet then turned southeast, heading for Cagliari.

At 0325 on the 1st September 18 SeaLance planes armed with bombs and escorted by six Goshawks attacked the airfield at Cagliari with high explosive bombs and incendiaries. Significant damage was done to the installations, many of which were set on fire, and a number of planes destroyed on the ground. All the planes returned to the carrier without loss. It was expected that the Regia Aeronautica would respond to this attack, but in fact the rest of that day passed without incident. At 2200, the reinforcements for the eastern fleet headed southeast while the remainder of Force H headed north.

Force H again attacked Cagliari on the night of the 1st, but haze and low cloud obscured the target and little damage was done. At 0800 on the 2nd Somerville headed west towards Gibraltar, expecting again to be attacked, but again there was no sign of the Regia Aeronautica, which rather disappointed Somerville who had been looking forward to giving them a warm reception.

While this was going on Admiral Cunningham had left Alexandria on the 30th August with Warspite, Malaya, Implacable, two cruisers and nine destroyers. At 1430 the fleet was sighted by an Italian aircraft, which was shot down a short while later by one of the Goshawks on CAP. Late in the afternoon another shadower was detected, but it managed to evade interception in cloud.

At noon on the 31st the fleet rendezvoused with the 3rd Cruiser squadron (Kent, Gloucester and Liverpool) south west of Cape Matapan, and a convoy of two stores ships and a tanker which would be escorted to Malta. On the afternoon of the 30th the merchant ships had been attacked by the Regia Aeronautica, but the attackers had been driven off by a flight of Goshawks kept close to them for exactly this purpose, although they failed to shoot down any of the attackers.

At 1600 the fleet altered course to the south to try and make the Italians believe they were immediately returning to Alexandria. However at 1613 one of HMS Implacable's search planes reported an Italian surface force of two battleships, seven cruisers and some destroyers 180miles west of the force. Cunningham's dilemma was that if he moved to engage at night, it would be easy for the enemy to evade and attack the Malta-bound convoy. A night attack on the battleships was considered, but decided against as the intentions of the enemy were unclear, and by the time a strike could be mounted they could have moved uncomfortably close to the convoy; the last thing Cunningham wanted to do was to torpedo his own merchant ships at night!

The fleet therefore closed the merchant ships to stay with them overnight, hoping to arrange a morning strike on the battleships. Disappointingly though, a RAF flying boat out of Malta spotted the force at the entrance of the Gulf of Taranto and heading home, too far away now for an air strike. The fleet continued west, and at 0900 on the 2nd met the Indefatigable and Valiant. While the fleet cruised some 35 miles south of Malta, the Valiant and the two cruisers entered harbour to offload personnel and equipment. The Regia Aeronautica made two light raids while the ships were unloading, but both times were driven off by Goshawks from the carriers.

On the voyage back to Alexandria, Cunningham intended to use his two fleet carriers to strike the airfields of Maritza and Callato on Rhodes. 12 SeaLance carrying bombs and 12 Cormorants hit each of the targets at 0600, 40 minutes before dawn. Considerable destruction was done to the airfields and their infrastructure. At the same time HMAS Sydney bombarded Scarpanto airfield, her escorting destroyers sinking two torpedo boats. The fleet sailed into Alexandria without further incident on the 3rd.

Churchill was pleased with the success of the mission and the damage done to the Italians, and wanted Cunningham to continue to strike at the Italians during the autumn. Cunningham pointed out that in order to do this successfully, reconnaissance by land based RAF aircraft was needed, of which at present there was a lack; he requested that when they could be released from the UK, a squadron or part squadron of the long range Whirlwinds would be most useful if based at Malta, as well as shorter ranged planes to fly from North Africa. He also pointed out that the already-proposed Operation Judgment depended on reconnaissance. He was promised 'at least 3' aircraft by the end of September.

3rd September

Heavy air attacks on Fighter Command's southern airfields continued. While the targeted airfields were damaged, the damage is not serious enough to put them out of action, and the Luftwaffe continued to miss many of the dispersal fields used by the squadrons. Losses of RAF fighters were heavy, but the Luftwaffe losses are considerably worse, and it starting to look as if they will be unable to achieve any sort of air superiority during September, especially as the carcasses of downed Luftwaffe aircraft are now a common sight in the south east of England. More worrying to the RAF was the steady losses of fighter pilots

Worry as to the success of the air campaign seems to be felt in Germany as well; Hitler postponed the invasion of Britain, scheduled for 15 September, to 21 September, but issued Operational orders covering it.

The German navy continued to build up its forces of light craft and barges in the Channel ports. These were now the subject of regular night bombing by the RAF's light bombers; the individual attacks are not terribly effective, but the combined total was steadily reducing the number of barges available.

In the Far East, The Japanese army and navy agreed on a southern advance strategy. The army needs considerable time to prepare itself for the Southward Advance even after mobilization was approved formally. When the admirals procrastinated, Tanaka Shin'ichi, head of the Army General Staff's Operations Division, scathingly asked if the navy was up to its old game of using the name of war preparations to secure additional allocations of funds and materials. But he also agreed to a simultaneous attack on Malaya and the Philippines using ten, not six, divisions. This concession got the navy off the hook and, by September 3, it agreed to join the army in pressing for a definitive peace-or-war decision by early October at the latest, as the generals had desired.

In an unrelated move, the US government warns the Japanese government against making aggressive moves in Indochina. The Japanese government is unimpressed by the warning.

7th September

An unexpected change in Luftwaffe tactics is immediately obvious as over 300 bombers escorted by as many fighters raid London Docks. The attack caused huge fires, which spread during the evening to cause serious damage to the dock area. Opinion is divided as to whether this change is the final prelude to an invasion, or a last gasp by a failing attacker. There was no sign of any of the barges moving, and signals intelligence as well as Bletchley Park report nothing unusual; there was some cautious optimism that the Luftwaffe has shot its bolt.

Over the next few days, the pattern of a number of small attacks and one large one on the London area was repeated. Belief in Britain is now that either the invasion will occur within the week, or it will be called off. Bomber Command has now destroyed over 15% of the massed barges, and nightly raids continue. The fleet has been put on alert and all boiler-cleaning stopped; the heavy Home Fleet units are at 2 hours notice for steam at Scapa. The Royal navy continued to saturate the channel with small craft. In order not to make them feel forgotten, the FAA squadrons based in East Anglia mount a dawn strike on two German destroyers in Calais; one is sunk by dive bombing, and the Cormorants strafe barges as they head back home just above the sea. The French channel ports are now so well lit up at night by burning barges and anti-aircraft fire that the RAF is referring to them as the 'Blackpool front'.

On the 10th September what was later seen as the final daylight effort of the Luftwaffe was made. Two massive and heavily escorted raids were made, in what was seen as an attempt to find if 11 Group remains in being. Reinforced over the last few days by fresh pilots and squadrons from 10 and 12 Groups, it most certainly is, over 80 German aircraft being shot down for the loss of 30 fighters. This would be the last large daytime offensive for the Luftwaffe; rather than defeating RAF fighter command is steady, high losses have instead gutted the German bomber and fighter force. Small daylight raids would continue, but shortly the heavy attacks would resume at night where the British defences are at the moment less effective.

13th September

An Italian offensive started at Sollum, on the border of Libya and Egypt. After months of prodding by Mussolini, Marshal Graziani's reluctant army makes a ponderous advance in North Africa and finally crossed the barbed-wire fence that marks the Egyptian border with Libya. Bells are rung in Rome to celebrate the capture of Sollum, a tiny settlement of mud huts. Graziani has insisted on "digging in" at frequent points along the coastal road, harassed continually by British defenders.

The attack on British forces in Egypt was originally to coincide with Operation Sealion (the invasion of England by Germany). When it became apparent to Mussolini that "Sealion" was postponed indefinitely, he ordered Marshal Graziani, Governor-General of Libya and Commander in Chief North Africa, to launch an attack into Egypt by the seven divisions of his 10th Army. British tanks and armoured cars made bold attacks into Libya in response, forcing the Italians to transfer troops from the 5th Army to the 10th and acquiring 2,500 motor vehicles and gaining the delivery of 70 M-11 medium tanks from Italy. The British retreated to buy time and receive reinforcements. After four days and a 60 mile (97 kilometer) advance into Egypt, Graziani halts his attack due to logistics. Graziani was now 80 miles (129 kilometres) west of the British defences in Mersa Matruh; to risk going any farther, Graziani said, would risk being defeated until supplies were available. Mussolini, angered over the sudden stop of the 10th Army, urges Graziani to continue 300 miles (483 kilometres) into the port of Alexandria. Graziani is appalled. Eventually Field Marshal Pietro Badoglio, Chief of the Supreme General Staff, promises 1,000 tanks to Graziani but this promise is never kept. The recent military operations in Ethiopia and Spain have drained Italy of many needed supplies and equipment and Graziani is forced to change his attack plan and he cannot (or will not) penetrate further than Sidi Barrani.

16th September

The effects of the war in Europe were making changes in the United States. On the 16th, the US Congress passed the Burke-Wadsworth Bill (the Selective Training and Service Act) by wide margins in both the Senate and the House of Representatives. This bill provided for the first peacetime draft (conscription) in the history of the United States but also provided that not more than 900,000 men are to be in training at any one time and it limits military service to 12 months. It also provided for the establishment of the Selective Service System as an independent Federal agency. President Roosevelt immediately signs the bill into law. The first draftees will be selected next month

The first call up of National Guard units also occurs. Called into Federal service are four divisions, 12 brigades, 50 regiments and four observation squadrons from 26 states. The divisions are New Jersey's 44th, Oklahoma's 45th, Oregon's 41st, and South Carolina's 30th. Eighteen of the 50 regiments are coast artillery regiments.

The keel of the Iowa-class battleship New Jersey (BB-62) is laid at the Philadelphia Naval Shipyard, Pennsylvania.

The news of the postponement of the invasion came in an Enigma decoding of a message from the German General Staff to the officer responsible for loading the transport aircraft earmarked for invasion. The message ordered him to dismantle his air-loading equipment; without that equipment there can be no invasion.

17th September

Night raiders used the 1000-kg blast bombs on Britain for the first time. Adapted from sea mines these cylindrical objects were about eight feet long and two feet in diameter. Each descends suspended from a 27-foot diameter silk parachute.

Thin case and large charge combine to produce a colossal hollow bang, tremendous shock waves and extensive blast damage over a quarter mile radius. While the damage is of course deplorable, interest is taken at the effectiveness compared to the current designs of RAF bombs.

In warmer climes, units of the Mediterranean Fleet including HMS Valiant sail with HMS Indefatigable for a raid on Benghazi. SeaLance planes from the carrier torpedo the destroyer Borea, and mines laid by them off the port sink another, the Aquilone. On the return to Alexandria, the heavy cruiser HMS Kent was detached to bombard Bardia. She is torpedoed and badly damaged by Italian aircraft. While she was escorted by fighters, poor control of them from the ship allowed some of the torpedo bombers to get through without interception. It is clear that more work needs to be done on directing fighters, and on equipping all major warships with better radar.

18th September

In North Africa, Italian forces came to a halt and started fortifying their position. The Italian 10th Army halted, officially because of supply difficulties. They began building fortified camps and do not stay in contact with British forces. British intelligence describes the Italians as 'unenthusiastic'. The British troops themselves are rather more blunt.

In order to strengthen the RAF force in North Africa, a regular air-bridge has been opened across Central Africa by the RAF, over which short-range aircraft can be transported to strengthen the units in Egypt. A base has been set up in Takoradi, the Gold Coast, where aircraft arriving from England by ship can be equipped and then moved to Cairo via a 4,350 mile route across Nigeria, French Equatorial Africa and the Sudan. The aircraft are mainly Hurricanes , which can be easily re-assembled after unloading, although a small number of Goshawks are also shipped (these cannot be so easily assembled, so have to be carried as deck cargo). The flights are accompanied by a twin engine plane to help the fighters navigate.

Having suffered 20% losses, the barge concentrations started to disperse back to Germany. More will be lost during this withdrawal to the mines the RAF have been persuaded to sow along the coastal shipping routes and harbours.

20th September

A British delegation, sent to the USA some weeks earlier to discuss technology exchanges between the two nations, showed the US scientists one of the cavity magnetrons they have brought with them. The USA has had no idea that such a breakthrough had been made in the transmitting power of microwave radar, and indeed had some difficulty believing the British figures.

The delegation had covered a number of areas where the British think that exchange or cooperation will be in the interest of both countries, while trying not to look as if they are desperate; the magnetron was the crown jewel they had to show, and it made a significant impression, especially when the American scientists involved explained exactly how critically useful centimetric radar could be. As a result of the British information, a number of decisions were made on the transfer of data, and on joint research projects.

For techniques and information where both sides had made progress, but differed in their technique and results, each country would share this with the other for a nominal fee. This basically covered technology of use in the war effort of both countries, but which was not critical. If research programs were ongoing in these areas, they would be coordinated to avoid too much duplication of effort.

For technology such as radar, where both countries had invested heavily, it was realised that this was a critical invention to the British war effort and the development of American armaments. It was agreed a joint program of research would be set up, with both countries sharing in the information. In order to help the USA, the British would license the cavity magnetron for the nominal fee of $1 per unit built, and give full information on them. It was agreed that a number of other projects would be set up to develop specific products, such as the radar proximity fuse.

A number of British projects such a jet engines were discussed, but these were not considered advanced enough as yet for any joint work, it was agreed that the two countries would supply each other with developmental information as research progressed.

The one item the British were not offered was the Norden bombsight; the acquisition of this had been pushed by the RAF, who were happy to give away just about anything in order to get it. However before the delegation had left it had been pointed out that this was hardly a critical invention; the Navy at least had no difficulty hitting precision targets in daytime, and since the RAF had decided to go to night bombing, where the bombsight would be of relatively little use, it was not by any means a critical item. Indeed, some of the British technical people were rather of the opinion that its performance had been exaggerated, since they had not seen any demonstration of it under a typical European combat condition.

Chapter 21

Operation Menace

On the 23rd September, allied forces commenced Operation Menace, the occupation of the French port of Dakar in French West Africa. The port was far superior to the only allied port in the area (Freetown), but so far had been a staunch supporter of Vichy France. Only a few days ago a French force of three cruisers and three destroyers from Toulon had passed through the Straits of Gibraltar on their way to reinforce the Dakar naval forces, which now consisted of the still-damaged battleship Richelieu, two cruisers, three destroyers, three submarines and shore batteries.

The allied force was based around Force H plus the escorts that had attended the convoy from Britain - the aircraft carriers Ark Royal and Glorious, the battleships Barham and Resolution, three heavy and two light cruisers and 10 destroyers. They were also accompanied by two of the Free French destroyers which had been captured in the UK and which were now crewed by the Free French. The original plan had included some 8,000 troops, mainly Royal Marine commandoes. However a few weeks before the troopships were to sail, the commander of the Free French army in the UK, General Bethouart (who had been in command of the French army in Norway), had pointed out two facts; first, that despite the enthusiasm among the Free French leadership (especially DeGaulle) that Dakar would defect to the allies, this had not happened when an earlier visit had been made to the port. And secondly, there was a very important resource to be captured at Dakar, which made its capture much more important to the Free French cause. At his suggestion, additional Free French forces were assigned (mainly the French Foreign Legion troops he had commanded in Norway, bring the invasion force up to 12,000 men.

Initially an emissary was sent to the port on a Free French ship under a truce. It was still hoped that the display of force would encourage the authorities there to surrender, or at least agree to honourable terms such as had been agreed at Mers-el-Kebir earlier in the year. However the commander refused to even see the emissaries. Accordingly a message was left stating that unless the commander agreed to negotiate surrender terms (including selecting one of the naval options, similar to those offered the French ships in North Africa), the allies would neutralise the French ships in the harbour (a polite way of pointing out that the Royal Navy would sink them) by 1600 that day the allies would have no choice but to take military action. It was also stated that any attempt by the French ships to leave harbour would be taken as a hostile act and responded to accordingly.

In advance, reconnaissance had already been made by the FAA of possible landing sites outside the town which would allow it to be surrounded and attacked; it was felt that if there was serious resistance the shore batteries might make a direct attack impracticable. The FAA had also dropped propaganda leaflets over the town, as it was felt that many Frenchmen there were not in support of the local commanders. In the meantime, two Free French aircraft were flown off Ark Royal to land at the airport (it was hoped that perhaps the airport commander was not a Vichy supporter), but the crews were arrested and taken prisoner. In the meantime the British carriers kept an A/S patrol of eight planes in the air, as if the French submarines tried to sortie it was best to damage or sink them immediately; the French surface ships were considered a lesser threat.

In view of the refusal of the French commanders at Dakar to negotiate, preparations were made for landing troops. The original idea, backed by DeGaulle, had been to land at Dakar itself, or failing that to land at Rufisque, some distance from Dakar. These plans had not impressed General Bethouart, and in view of the resistance at Dakar he suggested instead two landings, one close to the small town of Guédiawaye, and one close to Thiaroye. Neither of these two towns (villages, really) had much in the way of infrastructure, but since the bulk of the invasion force have no specialized landing craft (a few are available, but most of the force was expected to land from ships boats) there were no plans to land heavy equipment anyway. Landing at these two points might well give the advantage of surprise, and the landings would only be some 6 miles apart; joining the two would cut off Dakar completely, and Thiaroye would allow easy cutting of the railway line to the port.

At 1500, two of the French submarines were seen to be moving out of the harbour. This was in defiance of the instructions given by the allies (and also dropped on leaflets over the port by the FAA). As a result four Swordfish closed the port, escorted by four Goshawks. They arrived as the submarines were just clearing the harbour, and attacked as soon as they were clear of the entrance. No enemy fighters attempted to intercept, but there was ineffectual AA fire. The first Swordfish dropped its anti-submarine bombs close to the submarine (going in very low indeed), and as they exploded the submarine was seen to be in immediate difficulties. A second pair of Swordfish attacked the other submarine; this time the result was not quite as effective, but the submarine turned and headed back to the harbour trailing oil (it was not certain if it had in fact been seriously damaged or if the crew had decided against a breakout). The first submarine, well down by the stern, drove herself aground just outside of the harbour to avoid sinking, her crew successfully evacuating.

The order was given to land the troops; although there was some local opposition from infantry, the landings seemed to surprise the garrison (it was later ascertained that poor security by the Free French in London had informed them of the original plans, and that the defenders had deployed their forces to contain these. General Bethouart's changes had caught them by surprise), and despite the shortage of proper landing craft soon had sufficient men ashore to secure the two beachheads. While this was going on, further leaflets were dropped over Dakar informing them that the allies did not want to destroy them or the French ships, but that they could not allow them to continue to support the aims of Germany. Appeals were made to their honour, and offering terms that allowed them to withdraw with their arms if they wished, pointing out that so far the allies had been as restrained as possible due to their consideration for the French defenders.

This seemed to at least cause confusion among the defenders (it was found later that there were serious disagreements between the pro-Vichy leaders and many of the subordinate commanders, and that at least three of the ships in harbour had refused to sail against the Free French). Although the landings had made contact with some French troops, there were only a few desultory exchanges of fire, and the allied troops used the night to bring in the rest of their force and basic supplies over the beaches.

On the following day the landing troops pressed forward to meet and cut off the port (it had already been effectively isolated since the landing, as the French Foreign Legion troops had cut the railway link). Some of the defenders exchanged fire with the Royal Marines on the northern landing, but retreated when pressed. There were a number of local discussions between the defenders and the Free French troops under flags of truce, as a result of which the defenders moved back to the port.

The naval force meanwhile tried again to send a small boat under a white flag. This time it was allowed into the harbour, but the envoys were not allowed ashore. They were allowed to hand over a document containing terms, which also pointed out that the port was surrounded, allied aircraft controlled the air and allied battleships were, if necessary, prepared to destroy both the harbour and town. The garrison made them wait some hours, possibly while they checked to see if they were in fact cut off, and considerable radio traffic was detected between them and France.

While this was going on, more air action was taking place, not near Dakar but at Gibraltar. It was inevitable, after the British operation in Dakar, that the Vichy government would have to make some reprisal. Six bomber groups of the former Armee de l'Air and four escadrilles of the French naval air arm took part. The bombers were all stationed at the bases of Oran and Tafaroui in Algeria and Merknes, Mediouna and Port Lyautey in Morocco. The operation was approved by the German and Italian cease-fire commissions, and directed by Air Force Brigadier General Tarnier, commander of the French Air Force in Morocco. Just after 12:20 pm the first Leo 45 bomber groups (I/23 and II/23) took off from Merknes airfield and headed for Gibraltar. They reached their target at 1:00pm and bombed from 19,500 feet. There was no fighter cover (at this time Gibraltar depended on Force H for air cover). Between 1:30 and 2:15 pm a number of French fighter planes were deployed over Gibraltar to provide protection for the bombers. They included 12 Dewoitine 520s of GC II/3 based on Mediouna, 12 Curtiss Hawks of GC II/5 based on Casablanca and 12 Hawks of GC I/5 based on Rabat. Two escadrilles (2B and 3B) of Glenn Martin bombers from Port Lyautey concluded operations at 4:15 pm. The 64-bomber raid should have wrecked the port, 41 metric tons of bombs being dropped, but a considerable number of the French pilots appear to have deliberately dropped their loads into the sea, and a larger number of the fuses of the bombs that did land had apparently been tampered with so that they would not explode.

After receiving news of the attack on Gibraltar, the allies gave the Dakar authorities a final ultimatum. The troops outside the town were slowly moving on the port, and had already sabotaged the rail link in case reinforcements tried to use it. A message from Generals Bethouart and DeGaulle, aimed at the troops rather than their leaders was again dropped by air, and it was noticed that there seemed to be considerable disturbances in the town. The attack on Gibraltar meant that the allies could not wait much longer. If no discussions were started by tonight, an attack would commence in the morning, the battleships and bombers starting by reducing the ports fortifications and then supporting the land attack as necessary

Fortunately this was not in the end needed. The Vichy commanders agreed to meet with the envoys already in the harbour at 1630, and discussions took place over conditions for surrender of the port. It was clear to the envoys that the locals were by no means uniform in their support of Vichy. It was agreed that all those who wished to leave could do so with their arms and with honour. All those who wished to stay could either join the Free French cause or be interned for the duration of the war. The same offer was made to the ships as had been made in Mers-el-Kebir; interestingly the ships made individual decisions, one cruiser and one destroyer joining the exiles in the West Indies, the others (including the damaged battleship Richelieu) agreeing to joining the Free French.

The port was formally surrendered at 0800 on the 25th, and secured by the troops outside the town. The Vichy supporters were allowed to leave as soon as the rail link had been restored. The port would be occupied by Free French forces (that no British troops would be in the occupation had been a demand by the defenders), and the French and Polish gold reserves, which had been held in Dakar since the fall of France, were loaded onto the battleship Resolution to be shipped to South Africa under the supervision of representatives of the two governments in exile.

The allies were surprised to find after the surrender of Dakar just how oppressive the Vichy regime had been to the locals. It had been pro-Allied street demonstrations and an unsuccessful naval mutiny that persuaded the Allies earlier in the year that Senegal was fertile ground for the Free French. However the Vichy authorities had responded by appointing a Vichy governor and purging the Free French supporters, many of whom were released from jail after the allies took control of the town. The port had also been reinforced by loyal Vichy troops, but the need to confront the allied landings had stretched these too thin to also allow them to fully control the town, and the growing discontent, and in many cases outright rioting and local mutinies had forced the governor to admit that it was not going to be possible to drive off the allies. Part of the reason that Vichy had been so keen to hold on the port was the fact that the considerable French gold reserves (as well as some of those held by the French for allied powers such as Poland) had been sent to Dakar for safe-keeping. These would now be in the hands of the Free French, and the equipment this gold could buy would aid considerably the development of the Free French armies.

25th September

Although the Luftwaffe had been restricting daylight raids to small 'nuisance' attacks by small, heavily escorted formations, today they tried again with a large attack on the British Aeroplane works at Filton in Bristol. While the two week respite had allowed the Luftwaffe formations to recover from their low point, it had also allowed Fighter command to fully recover its front line squadrons, and the raid was heavily handled, 12 bombers being shot down by the fighters and AA. The losses seemed to convince the Luftwaffe that large daylight raids are not worth the losses in trained bomber crews (who have taken heavy casualties over the last couple of months), and that night bombing is a better use of their resources. It is clear that the old tactics of close escort of bombers by fighters was simply too costly; 12 bombers and five fighters conceded for the loss of seven RAF fighters.

27th September

Today, in the Berlin chancellery, the Japanese ambassador, Saburo Kurusu put his signature to a tri-partite pact which extends the Rome-Berlin Axis to the Far

East. In a move clearly directed at the United States, the three countries pledge themselves to aid one another with "all political, economic and military means" should one of them be attacked by "a power not involved in the European war."

Japan accepts the hegemony of Germany and Italy in Europe, and they in turn recognise Japan's right to organise "the Greater East-Asia Co-prosperity Sphere". The pact contained a clause promising to preserve the status quo in relations with the Soviet Union. Following the signing of this pact, Hitler secretly ordered war production to be geared towards the invasion of Russia.

In Washington, a navy department spokesman said that the pact would not mean any change of policy. The navy, he said, would continue to be based at Pearl Harbour.

29th September

Britain informs Japan that it intended to re-open the Burma Road to China when the current three-month agreement expires on 17 October. The move, announced by Churchill, was the first direct result of the Japan-Axis pact. He told the House of Commons that Britain had originally agreed to ban the transit of war materials from Burma to China while the two sides tried to reach a settlement. Japan had not taken the opportunity and had signed a ten-year pact with the Axis. To cheers from the House, the Prime Minister said that in the circumstances Britain could not see its way to renewing the agreement.

30th September

The Italian submarine 'Gondar' approaches Alexandria with human torpedoes for an attack on the base. She is located by an RAF Sunderland of No 230 Squadron and sunk by the destroyer HMAS Stuart.

Early in the month the first wolf-pack attacks were directed by Admiral Donitz against the convoy SC2. Five of the 53 ships are sunk. A similar operation is mounted two weeks later against the 40 ships of HX72. The U-boats present include those commanded by the aces Kretschmer, Prien and Schepke. Eleven ships are lost, seven to Schepke's U-100, in one night. The German B-Service is instrumental in directing U-boats to many convoys, where they hold the advantage as they manoeuvre on the surface between the merchantmen and escorts.

This new tactic was of considerable worry to the Royal Navy. While losses in the Atlantic have been high over the last few months, this has been accepted as a necessary short term price to pay for the invasion defence (many of the destroyers and escorts normally employed in the Atlantic have been held back in

Britain in case of invasion). Now that the invasion has obviously been called off (at least until the spring), pressure was being applied to allocate the light carriers and many of the escorts back into the Atlantic to reinforce the very minimal current escorts

10th October.

Although mass attacks were now only being attempted by the Luftwaffe at night, there was a constant stream of small, high speed daytime attacks, by Me110 fighter-bombers and Ju88 bombers. These were difficult to intercept due to the high speed and the varied choice or targets (it is noted with some irony by the RAF that the Luftwaffe finally seem to be targeting the British aero industry). Even so, these daytime attacks were losing the Luftwaffe planes at the rate of more than 2:1 (and a far worse ratio of pilots) for little damage. As by now Britain is heavily out-producing the Luftwaffe in planes, the RAF is steadily increasing its strength relative to the Luftwaffe, which only makes the losses steadily improve in the defenders favour.

12th October

Earlier in the month a resupply convoy had been mounted from Alexandria. This had been escorted by the Implacable and Indefatigable, and the battleships Warspite and Valiant, as well as six cruisers and 16 destroyers; there was also a close escort force of two AA cruisers and four destroyers. Twelve Goshawks were successfully flown off on the 10th, and the convoy of four merchant ships arrived on the 11th. The Italian fleet had been prevented from intervening by poor weather. However on the 11th an Italian patrol aircraft spotted the ships returning from Malta. While this was happening, the cruiser HMS Ajax had been detached for a scouting mission (the poor weather was also affecting British air reconnaissance)

The Italian commander ordered a force of four destroyers to Cape Bon, in the chance the British ships were heading for Gibraltar (he judged that if they were in fact retiring to Alexandria that it would not be possible to intercept them). At the same time, a force of four destroyers and three large torpedo boats were on patrol in the same area as Ajax.

At 0137 on the 12th Ajax was sighted by the three torpedo craft. They turned to engage (Ajax not having noticed them), and launched an attack with torpedoes and guns from a range of 1,900 yards. Ajax was hit three times, twice on the bridge and once below the waterline by 3.9" shells. The cruiser returned fire, hitting the Ariel (which would sink some 20 minutes later), and the Airone, left burning (she would sink some 2 hours later). The third craft, the Alcione, broke off contact.

Ajax resumed her course to the east, and at 0215 her radar detected two Italian destroyers. Aviere was hit by a surprise broadside, and forced to retire southwards. Artigliere managed to fire torpedoes and a number of salvoes before being hit by the cruiser and crippled. Ajax then engaged another destroyer, the Camicia Nera, but one of the hits from the Artigliere had disabled her radar, and at 0330 she broke off the action, short of ammunition.

The disabled Artigliere was taken in tow by the Camicia Nera, while the Aviere managed to withdraw under her own power. However although the damaged Ajax made her way back to the main body (she would require a month in dock to repair her damage), a strike was ordered from Implacable. Eight SeaLance and 16 Cormorant armed with 1,000lb bombs set off before dawn to intercept the fleeing Italian destroyers. The first ships spotted were the Camica Nera, still towing the Aviere, at 0730. Although the destroyers slipped her tow to try and evade the dive bombers, she was hit by two 1,000 pound bombs and sank within 15 minutes. The helpless Aviere sank after a single bomb hit. Four of the Cormorants still had bombs, and the planes then carried on to search for the other damaged destroyer. She was sighted at 0815, and received the attentions of all eight SeaLance and the remaining four Cormorants. Although she managed to avoid the dive bombing attack, in doing so she was hit by a torpedo, and left disabled and sinking (she sank some hours later after her crew had been taken off by another destroyer). No planes were lost to the destroyer's AA fire.

While the daytime sinkings were not unexpected, the Italian Navy was very concerned at the efficiency the Royal Navy had shown in the night action; the use of starshells, searchlights and incendiary shells, plus the suspected use of radar, had completely outclassed the Italian night fighting skills.

14th October

The fleet returning to Alexandria was the subject of a number of attacks by the RA. These are driven off and disrupted by the carriers CAP; after months of experience the carriers and steadily increasing in their efficiency of managing and directing their fighters, although it appreciated there are still many improvements to be made. No ships are sunk or damaged, although the cruiser HMS Liverpool gets a nasty shock when a torpedo passes only yards from the ship; the torpedo plane had been attacked by a Goshawk and had launched just a little too soon before it was shot down.

18th October

The Japanese and authorities in the Dutch East Indies have discussions regarding oil supplies. It is agreed to supply 40% of production to the Japanese for the next six months. Attempts are made by the British to block this agreement, but the Dutch government does not wish to antagonise the Japanese Empire too greatly.

In China, the first lorries to bring war supplies along the re-opened Burma Road - closed three months ago by agreement between Japan and Britain - arrived from Lashio. Drivers reported an uneventful journey free from the air attacks threatened by Japan against the Chinese section of the road. Sixty lorries arrived in the first convoy and another 2,000 - given a banquet send off in Burma - are expected tomorrow. Waiting at Rangoon are another 500,000 tons of war supplies, including planes and munitions. On the return leg the lorries will carry tungsten, wood, tin, oil and pig bristles for export to the US.

19th October

In the Mediterranean theatre, four Italian aircraft make an audacious long-range attack on the British oil refinery at Bahrein, in the Persian Gulf. The SM82 bombers were in the air for more than 15 hours, flying 3,000 miles from Rhodes in the Mediterranean to Massawa, in Eritrea, on a triangular route whose most easterly point was Bahrein Island. Each aircraft dropped 66 30-pound bombs on the complex. The pilots claimed significant damage with huge fires visible for 'hundreds of miles'. The refinery engineers had in fact turned up the refinery safety flares to simulate uncontrolled fires.

 In the Atlantic the Royal navy was evaluating the new German U-boat tactic of the wolf pack, consisting of up to a dozen U-boats. A heavy attack had taken place on the slow convoy SC-7. This convoy, escorted only by two sloops and a corvette, had been spotted by U-48. After reporting the sighting, the captain attacked himself without waiting for the rest of the pack, sinking two merchant ships. He was then chased off by a sloop and a Sunderland flying boat, but these were unable to force him out of contact with the convoy. After dark he was joined by another five U-boats, and with them sank 15 merchant ships in six hours. The escorts were unable to provide any effective defence.

U-48 and two of the other U-boats headed for home having used up all their torpedoes. The rest stayed to pick off any stragglers and search for another convoy to attack. They detected the fast convoy HX-79 (49 ships), however when they attempted to close they were repeatedly forced to submerge by patrolling Swordfish A/S aircraft from the light carrier HMS Glory. The frustrated U-boats tried to get into an attacking position; however their slow underwater speed made this almost impossible.

The pack was joined by three more U-boats, by which time the convoy escort was now two destroyers, four corvettes and three A/S trawlers as well as the light carrier. The carrier was keeping a steady standing patrol in the air around the convoy, and as a result only one U-boat was able to get into an attacking position. Unfortunately for the convoy this was the boat of Gunther Prien, and despite the difficult conditions, he sank two ships before having to withdraw under attack by two of the escorts. The air cover had forced the other boats too far away from the convoy to make a successful night attack. However the following day the remainder of the pack found the outbound convoy HX-79A (with no air cover), and attacked as a group sinking a further seven ships.

The new tactics were obviously very dangerous, and the effect of continual air cover quite obvious; unfortunately for the Admiralty they did not have unlimited carriers to deploy, although a number of escort carriers and merchant conversions would be available soon. Until then all that could be done was to try and give the maximum cover from Coastal Command aircraft and to use their available carriers on the most important convoys.

20th October

That night the Italians sent four small destroyers on a sortie to intercept a British Red Sea convoy, which was protected by a light cruiser, a destroyer, and five smaller escorts. Contact was briefly made, and there was a short and ineffective exchange of fire, mainly between the Italian destroyer Nullo and the British destroyer HMS Kimberly. Shortly after beginning this indecisive affair, the Nullo developed a severe mechanical problem with its steering, and was forced to break off and head as best it could back toward its base.

As part of their regular reviews of the possible threats posed by other powers, the Admiralty considers the October report on their countries naval aviation during 1940. While the USA is now considered a friendly power, its capabilities have also been evaluated to allow for the case of the USA becoming a co-belligerent.

USA

The USN had been observing the use of air power by the Royal Navy with considerable interest (aided by the 'Canadian' observers on ships) and the full reports they have been given. The main building plans include huge increases in the number of planes, and the building of the large Essex class carriers, however the first of these is not scheduled to be at sea before early 1943. Although the possibility of speeding them up is being looked at, the proposed build times are already very short and the design is not yet complete.

In the meantime, the USA has ordered the construction of a fourth Yorktown-class fleet carrier, the USS Ticonderoga. The ship was laid down in March 1940 and given priority; it was expected to commission her in May 1942. After the fall of France and the corresponding increase in planned USN construction, the ship is given a maximum priority - it is now hoped to have her complete by February 1942. The designers also hope to incorporate a heavier AA armament; they have noted that the Yorktown class carry only 16 27mm cannon and 25 0.5" mg, compared to the British Formidable class carry 64 40mm and around 30 20mm cannon. The designers are told that the excellence of the USN's AA control makes the fitted guns far more effective than those fitted to Royal Navy ships, but this statement is controversial. When asked, the RN simply says 'the more guns the better'. As a compromise, 2 additional quad 27mm will be fitted.

The production of the Wildcat (F4F) fighter has been speeded up, although at the moment many of the planes being produced are scheduled to be sold to the British and French. The USN is rather concerned that its frontline fighter, by no means in full operation in the fleet, is already outclassed in power and armament by the Goshawk (and the Goshawk engine is still being developed further). A new and much more powerful aircraft, the Vought F4U Corsair, has flown for the first time in March 1940 (its development has been brought forward as much as was possible). The plane undergoes acceptance trials for the USN in late November of 1940.

Japan

Japan has also been following the success of the FAA with great interest, as it indicates to them that their intention of making naval aviation of major importance in the IJN is correct. Indeed, the aviation enthusiasts claim that this shows that all future resources should be aimed at carriers rather than battleships, a claim that is refuted completely by the battleships traditionalists in the IJN. In any case, the current building program is full, with six fleet carriers expected to be available by late 1941.

However it is possible to increase the 'shadow carrier' program; these are large liners designed to be quickly converted into carriers as war nears. Two of these, the Hiyo and the Junyu were laid down in 1939 with completion expected in 1942. Two additional ships are laid down in March 1940, and it is hoped to have these complete by 1942. While not as fast as fleet carriers, they do carry over 50 planes. A small expansion of the naval aviator training program is made to allow for the extra 100 pilots these carriers will need, although due to the extreme difficulty and length of the IJN training programs this target will in fact not be met.

Germany

The Graf Zeppelin completed her basic working up in October. Although the ship is classed as operational, her flight operations are still the subject of much experimentation (although some advice has been obtained from the Japanese). An air group has been assigned, and the carrier is continuing training in the Baltic, safe from the Royal Navy, along with the Bismarck (who has also completed basic workup and is undergoing gunnery training while working with the Graf Zeppelin)

As a result of the success of the Royal Navy in naval air operations, the specialised anti-ship unit Fliegerkorps X has been given more resources. Founded in 1939, the formation has been in poor repute with the Kriegsmarine after the disastrous Operation Wikinger incident where the aircraft had sunk a German destroyer and caused a second one to be sunk in a minefield. However the obvious need to use aircraft to attack the Royal Navy has led to its rehabilitation after a more successful campaign in Norway. The unit will be transferred from Norway once it has been decided if it is best to deploy it in the North Sea or the Mediterranean - the current advice from the Kriegsmarine is in the Mediterranean. There is also a need to transfer additional planes; the unit currently consists mainly of Ju87 and Me109, and longer ranged aircraft are seen as necessary to attack the Royal Navy at sea. Priority is given for additional Ju87R, and Me110 (although this means reducing the daylight raids on England, this is actually seen as a bonus by the Luftwaffe due to the losses they are sustaining). He111 bombers are also being allocated. The support structure for the force is being moved to Sicily, and it is expected to be operational by the end of the year

Italy

While the Italian navy is very slowly building an aircraft carrier, it is obvious that one carrier will simply be a fat target for the Royal Navy. Resources are therefore being given to building up the land-based attack capability, and looking at ways of arranging more and longer ranged fighter escort - the fighters defending the RN forces have showed that it is very difficult to arrange a good attack unless they can be suppressed or distracted, as even a few unopposed fighters can ruin an attack. The problem is the relatively backwardness of the Italian aviation industry. There is some pressure to license German engines, but the Germans want to charge licensing fees and there is considerable resistance to the idea itself inside Italy.

Appendix One

This describes some of the aircraft in use by the Royal Navy and other air forces during the period covered by this book (1932 - 1940). Only naval aircraft or aircraft encountered in actions in the book have been included.

Aircraft in use by the Royal Navy

Gloster Goshawk (fighter)

The Goshawk is a single-engine fighter powered by the Bristol Hercules engine. Performance is similar to that of the historic Hurricane and Spitfire, coming in between the two. As was the usual practice with carrier aircraft of the period, performance was optimised for under 20,000 feet (since bombing above this altitude was too inaccurate for success against ships). The early versions were armed with 0.5" guns, but by 1940 the armament had increased to 2x20mm cannon and 4 0.5" guns, and the guns would be replaced by an additional 2 cannon as they became available. As with most naval planes, the Goshawk had rather longer range than its land-based equivalents, at the cost of a heavier aircraft (compensated for by the more powerful Hercules engine)

Fairy Swordfish (TBR - Torpedo, Bomber, Reconnaissance)

Developed in the early 1930's as a private venture, the 'Stringbag' as it was known would be used throughout the war in many different roles. As the war started it was the operation torpedo and bombing plane of the FAA, although it would soon be replaced by more capable aircraft. However due to its versatility and its ability to operate off of very small carriers in all sorts of weather, it would carry on as the anti-submarine plane on escort carriers and conversions throughout the war.

Martin-Baker Cormorant (Divebomber)

Developed in the 1930's, the Hercules-powered Cormorant was the Royal Navies first dedicated dive bomber. Initial versions carried either a 500lb HE bomb (on longer missions) or a 1,000lb against larger targets. With a later-version Hercules (with more power), it could also carry the 1,600lb AP bomb designed for use against battleships and similarly armoured targets

Boulton-Paul SeaLance (TBR - Torpedo, Bomber, Reconnaissance)

The replacement for the Swordfish, the SeaLance was an interim deign using the Griffon engine. Faster than the Swordfish, it was much more survivable against defended targets. With its increased performance, the Royal Navy carried on development of its aerial torpedoes to allow them to be dropped at a higher speed and from a greater height, also giving the crews more chance of surviving the attack.

Aircraft in use by the RAF

Hudson (anti-submarine)

The Hudson was a twin-engine light bomber in use by RAF Coastal Command as a reconnaissance and anti-submarine plane. The aircraft was bought from the USA, where it had originally been designed as a civilian aircraft, modified by the RAF to carry bombs and armed with a quadruple 0.303 gun turret.

Hawker Hurricane (fighter)

The Hurricane was a single-engines fighter powered by the Rolls-Royce Merlin. The first modern monoplane fighter in service in the RAF, its performance was similar to the Goshawk. Initially armed with 8x0.303" guns, by 1940 production aircraft were being armed with 2x20mm cannon and 4x0.303" guns, giving them more destructive power against German bombers. The plane would be one of the two mainstays of fighter command in 1940, before being phased out. The design did not benefit from a more powerful engine, and it was replaced in 1941 by the de-navalised version of the Goshawk, the Sparrowhawk.

Supermarine Spitfire (fighter)

The Spitfire was one of the great fighter aircraft of WW2. Developed before the war, it only entered service shortly before the conflict started. By 1940, it was already equal in performance to the best German fighters, and by the Battle of Britain was steadily replacing the Hurricane as the RAF frontline fighter. The airframe was far more capable of increasing performance when fitted with more powerful engines, and its development would continue throughout the war. Like the Hurricane, it was initially armed with 8x0.303" guns, but it was also upgraded to cannon by the time the Battle of Britain started.

Short Sunderland (anti-submarine)

The Sunderland was a long range, heavily armed flying boat, used for anti-submarine patrols. The heavy defensive armament led to it being used in areas like the Bay of Biscay where enemy fighters were encountered, and it was also capable of rescue.

Bristol Beaufighter (fighter, bomber, torpedo, attack)

The Beaufighter was the first true 'multi-role' plane in service in Britain. A powerful and heavy plane powered by two Hercules engines, it was capable of defending itself against all but the latest enemy fighters. Heavily armed, it was also used as a naval strike plane against light targets, and when carrying a torpedo, against larger ships. Its long range meant it was also used as a reconnaissance aircraft

Aircraft in use by the Luftwaffe

Heinkel He115 (torpedo)

Developed shortly before the start of the war, the He115 was a fast, twin engine floatplane designed to carry torpedoes and mines. Intended to fly from coastal bases, it was fast for the time and had a long range. However it was never manufactured in large quantities and its weak defensive armament made it vulnerable to fighters

Messerschmitt Me109 (fighter)

This single-engine fighter was the Luftwaffe's frontline fighter during the first part of the war. Agile and fast, it was the equal of the Spitfire (and in some respects its superior) at this time. Its main disadvantage was its short range and the delicate landing gear - although a version was produced for use on the German carriers, development shows a disheartening number of landing accidents.

Junkers Ju87 (Stuka) (dive bomber)

This aircraft was the iconic dive bomber of the war. A simple aircraft, its ability to dive extremely steeply made it very accurate. The early versions were limited in bomb load, but later versions with a more powerful engine had both a longer range and the ability to deliver a 500kg bomb at effective ranges. Fortunately for the Royal Navy the Luftwaffe neglected the anti-shipping role before the war, and so early attacks by the Stuka were often ineffective.

Junkers Ju88 (bomber)

Probably the best light/medium bomber of the early part of the war, this twin engine plane was fast and could carry a useful bomb load. Its performance was affected by the requirement that it be able to dive-bomb, a task it was never suited for (the Stuka being far more effective).

Heinkel He111 (bomber)

The standard Luftwaffe medium bomber of the early War years, this twin-engined level bomber was ineffective against ships at sea.

Messerschmitt Me110 (escort fighter)

A heavy twin-engine fighter, in some respects it resembled the Beaufighter. However its role was quite different. Intended as a long-range fighter to protect bombers, it was found incapable f protecting itself against the modern RAF and FAA single-engine fighters. It was also employed as a light fast bomber carrying one or two 250kg bombs.

Aircraft in use by the Italian Air Force

Savoia-Marchetti SM.79 Sparviero (bomber)

This was a three-engined bomber designed in the 1930's. It had a good performance for the time, and was the main Italian bomber of the war. One feature found useful by the crews in its naval use was that the wooden framework allowed the aircraft to often remain afloat for some 30 minutes. By 1940 its limited defensive armament was ineffective against the modern FAA fighters, making it very vulnerable.

Macchi C.200 Saetta (Mc200) (fighter)

The front-line fighter for Italy at the start of the war, this plane had excellent manoeuvrability but was slower than the equivalent RAF and FAA fighters, and poorly armed - 2x0.5" guns were not adequate, especially against the robust naval fighters it was to encounter. It also suffered from the common land-based fighter problem of limited range.

Appendix Two

Aircraft Carriers in service

Royal Navy

HMS Eagle

26,000t displacement, speed 22.5 kt ; 5x4" guns, approx 10x20mm

Normal aircraft complement 21

HMS Hermes

13,000t displacement, 25kt ; 4x4" guns, approx 10x20mm

Normal aircraft complement 20

HMS Argus

14,500t displacement, 20kt ; 6x4" guns, approx 12 20mm

HMS Furious

23,000t displacement, 31kt ; 12x20mm

Normal aircraft complement 36

HMS Courageous, HMS Glorious

27,500t displacement, 30kt ; 8x40mm, approx 8x20mm

Normal aircraft complement 48

HMS Ark Royal, HMS Illustrious

24,000t displacement, speed 31.5kt ; 16x4.5" guns, 64x40mm, approx 20x20mm

Normal aircraft complement 65

HMS Formidable, HMS Victorious, HMS Indefatigable, HMS Implacable

24,500t displacement, speed 32kt ; 16x4.5" guns, 64x40mm, approx 20x20mm

Normal aircraft complement 68

HMS Colossus, HMS Mars, HMS Vengeance, HMS Glory, HMS Ocean, HMS Theseus, HMAS Melbourne

13,000t displacement, speed 27kt ; 16x40mm guns, approx 16x20mm

Normal aircraft complement 24 (40 maximum with deck park)

United States Navy

USS Saratoga, USS Lexington

39,000t displacement, 34kt ; 12x5" guns

Normal aircraft complement (pre-war) 90

USS Ranger

17,500t, speed 29kt ; 8x5" guns, 40x0.5" mg

Normal aircraft complement (pre-war) 75 planes

USS Yorktown, USS Enterprise USS Hornet, USS Ticonderoga

22,000t displacement, 32.5kt ; 8x5" guns, 16x1.1"mg, 24 0.5"mg

Normal aircraft complement (pre-war) 90

USS Wasp

16,000t displacement, 29kt ; 8x5" guns, 16 1.1"mg, 24x0.5"mg

Normal aircraft complement (pre-war) 80

Germany Kriegsmarine

Graf Zeppelin

28,000t displacement, 35kt ; 8x5.9"guns, 16x4.1" guns, 22x37mm c, 28x20mm

Normal aircraft complement 40

French Navy

MNS Bearne

28,000t displacement, 21kt ; 8x6.1" guns, 6x3" guns, 8x37mm, 16mg

Normal aircraft complement 40

Notes :

(1) The displacement is given as a 'normal' displacement. The displacement of a ship varies as it uses fuel and stores, and even the 'normal' displacement is somewhat variable, especially when reported to keep inside treaty limits

(2) The aircraft capacity of a carrier can be quite variable. In addition to the 'complete' aircraft carried, most fleet carriers would also carry a number of replacements, broken down into parts in the hangar which could be used to cover normal operational losses. The US carriers carried the most planes as they used a full deck park - aircraft were held on deck. The RN carriers and the Japanese carriers normally kept all their planes in the hangar, although they could increase the number available by using a deck park if they wished.

Irrespective of the number of planes actually carried, carriers were also limited to how many planes they could launch in a single 'strike' due to deck space. During this period in time it was about 30-35 planes, after which planes would have to be brought on deck, armed, fuelled and placed ready for a second strike, a process which usually took around an hour or so (depending on the skill of the carrier crews).

(3) Armament, especially of the light 20mm cannon which tended to be fitted on wherever they could fit, also varied through the War. The numbers given are those deigned in; where major changes were made these are listed with date

(4) Speed. This assumes the ship is in good mechanical condition and with a clean bottom. During wartime service the actual speed was often lower due to the inability to refit the machinery and dock the ship for bottom-cleaning.

Glossary

AA - Anti Aircraft (guns).

AI - Airborne Intercept (radar). A small light radar set capable of being carried on a plane to allow it to intercept another aircraft at night.

ASDIC - what later became known as SONAR, a high-frequency sound system designed to detect a submerged submarine. At this time, rarely usable above 1,500 - 2000 metres.

A/S - Antisubmarine

ASV - Air to Surface radar, a small airborne set designed to spot ships and, later, smaller objects such as submarines.

Avgas - Aviation Gasoline (fuel), very volatile and very dangerous.

CAP - Combat Air Patrol, the act of keeping a number of fighters in the air above the carrier or fleet ready to intercept enemy aircraft.

DB - Dive Bomber, an aircraft designed to deliver a single bomb in a very steep (normally over 70°) dive.

FAA - Fleet Air Arm, the aeroplanes flown and controlled by the Royal Navy

HA - also known as HA(AA), the guns capable of attacking a high-altitude enemy plane. Normally used against high altitude level bombing. While not terribly accurate at this time, the aim was to disrupt the formation of the attackers, making them miss, rather than to shoot them down. Level bombers depended on the 'shotgun' principle of bombing during this period.

Hammer-and-Anvil attack - a type of attack by torpedo planes. Two groups of planes will attack 90° apart, one the 'hammer', the other the 'anvil'. Dodging the torpedoes of one group will put the ship broadside on to the other group. The ideal torpedo attack against a moving ship.

HMS - His Majesties Ship (British); also HMAS - His Majesties Australian Ship, HMCS - His Majesties Canadian Ship, HMNZS - His Majesties New Zealand Ship.

HIMJS - His Imperial Japanese Majesties Ship (Japan)

Kriegsmarine - the German Navy

LA - Low angle guns, normally those unable to elevate above about 40 degrees, so unable to fire on a plane over the ship. In fact, these guns can be used as anti-aircraft guns, but only on aircraft some distance away (the angle of the aircraft increases as it closes the ship). Usually even less accurate than HA fire, as this type of gun was not usually matched with the control system designed to engage aircraft.

Luftwaffe - the German Air Force

MN - Marine Nationale, the French navy

Pom-pom - the name given in the RN to a fast-firing light AA weapon. Originally firing a 2-pdr shell, then the 40mm shell, given its name due to the sound the multi-barrel version made

RA - Regia Aeronautica, the Italian Air Force (Italy did not have a separate naval air force)

RAF - the British Air force

RDF - Radio Direction Finding, an early (British) name for Radar (so named to try and mislead what it actually did)

RN - Royal Navy, the British naval forces. Also the RAN (Australian), RCN (Canadian), and RNZN (New Zealand).

Round down - the aft part of a carrier's flight deck. This was 'rounded down' in a downward curve, which improved the airflow and made it easier for a plane to land. It also reduced the available deck parking area, and so was reduced on British carriers as larger strikes became more common.

SAP - Semi Armour Piercing (bomb or shell)

Shadow factory - A set of factories built in the mid-30's in Britain ready to be used as aircraft factories in war. In fact the need for aircraft due to the expansion of the Luftwaffe meant they were brought into use before the war, and more built. The term 'shadow program' came to be used for anything built in advance of wartime needs, such as the Japanese programme of 'Shadow Carriers', merchant ships built ready for easy conversion into light carriers.

TBR - Torpedo, Bomber, Reconnaissance. A class of plane used by most navies in these three roles. Bombing was normally level bombing with light bombs, although some aircraft like the Swordfish could dive bomb at shallow dive angles.

Twins - or the twins, the two German Battlecruisers Scharnhorst and Gneisenau.

USS - United States Ship (USA)

Information on the next book in this series (The Whale Has Wings Vol 2, Taranto to Singapore) may be found at

http://www.AstroDragon.co.uk/Books/TheWhaleHasWings.htm

Made in the USA
Lexington, KY
26 February 2014